Selected praise for the novels of Janice Maynard

"Maynard delivers in spades."   —LifetimeTV.com

"[Janice Maynard is] sensual, sassy and emotionally riveting!"   —Thoughts of a Blonde

"A Must Read... I wasn't ready for this one to end."
                      —Romance Junkies on Hot Mail

"With its well-crafted story line and characters, this is a delightful read."   —RT Book Reviews on Hot Mail

"[Maynard] never disappoints." —Romance, Jane and Louis

"Witty and provocative."   —Affaire de Coeur on Perfect Ten

Also by Janice Maynard

Return of the Rancher
The Comeback Heir
Staking a Claim

Look for Janice Maynard's next Blossom Branch novel
The Summer Heiress of Sweetgrass Spring
available soon from Canary Street Press.

For additional books by Janice Maynard,
visit her website, www.janicemaynard.com.

THE
Runaway Bride
OF
BLOSSOM BRANCH

JANICE MAYNARD

CANARY STREET PRESS

CANARY
STREET
PRESS™

ISBN-13: 978-1-335-52303-7

The Runaway Bride of Blossom Branch

Copyright © 2023 by Harlequin Enterprises ULC

The Runaway Bride of Blossom Branch
Copyright © 2023 by Janice Maynard

Act Like You Love Me
Copyright © 2023 by Janice Maynard

For questions and comments about the quality of this book, please contact us at CustomerService@Harlequin.com.

Canary Street Press
22 Adelaide St. West, 41st Floor
Toronto, Ontario M5H 4E3, Canada
CanaryStPress.com

Printed in U.S.A.

CONTENTS

THE RUNAWAY BRIDE OF BLOSSOM BRANCH   7

ACT LIKE YOU LOVE ME   327

THE RUNAWAY BRIDE
OF BLOSSOM BRANCH

For Charles—

I married you—my best friend—
when I was nineteen and you were twenty.
I'm not sure at that age I even understood the concept of *soulmate*,
but you have been that and so much more.

There is no one I would rather travel with, laugh with, mourn with,
celebrate with... Even a quiet evening at home is a sweet gift.
I love the family we have created and the life we share.
Thank you for always making my dreams your own.

Love always,

Janice

One

Once upon a time, Cate Penland had predicted she would have it all. Now, with this huge, perfect wedding at an Atlanta cathedral in front of twelve hundred guests, her dreams were coming true. A great marriage, and soon to be an interesting career.

Serious words interrupted her private jubilation.

"Jason, wilt thou have Cate to be thy wedded wife, to live together in the covenant of marriage..."

She zoned out momentarily. A no-expense-spared, traditional event wasn't how she used to imagine her special day. At thirteen or fourteen, she had dreamed of a low-key, romantic wedding.

But to be fair, she had fully participated in planning this enormous, glitzy social affair.

She was pinning her hopes on family and home.

She and Jason were good together. Their life would be as perfect as Cate could make it.

Once they were settled in a place of their own, the plan to open a trendy art gallery and gift shop would meld their individual talents and interests—his photography and Cate's artistic bent.

Cate *needed* to know that life wouldn't knock her down again, not like it had when she was twelve. Today, she was insulating herself against pain.

She was going to be gloriously happy.

The old priest's sonorous words wafted over her head and disappeared into the shadows of the soaring vaulted ceiling. A benediction of light filtered through ornate stained glass windows, painting the wedding party in a soft rainbow palette.

The first Saturday in June was the ideal and most highly sought-after wedding date at St. Matthew's Episcopal Cathedral on West Paces Ferry Road in the ritzy Buckhead neighborhood of Atlanta. Half a dozen brides had wanted the venue. Cate's father had written a six-figure check to the building fund, and the deed was done.

The female attendants included her sister and four of Cate's dearest friends. Two of the four, shy Leah and reserved Gabby, had known Cate since they were childhood classmates at Blossom Branch Elementary School. Their lives had zigged and zagged because of financial circumstances and other realities, but they had reconnected as freshmen at the University of Georgia, and their friendship had deepened exponentially. The other two bridesmaids, Lara and Ivy, were also college relationships, shorter in nature, but no less important. All four of the women had been fellow sorority sisters with Cate. Zeta Zeta Pi.

Cate had dragged Leah and Gabby into Greek life knowing they needed her support. Leah's extreme shyness and Gabby's money woes had made entering college challenging. Cate had tried to smooth the rough edges for her friends.

Despite her mother's vehement objections to the non-traditional, Cate had elected to outfit her bridesmaids all in white, with only narrow black sashes for accent. Cate loved the crisp, modern look. In this golden moment, she knew she had made the right decision.

Behind her, a gratifying crowd sat shoulder to shoulder in the honey-colored wooden pews polished by decades of worshippers. The air-conditioning in the lovely, decades-old stone building labored to keep up. Cate's forehead and hands were damp. She gripped her bouquet of white roses and eucalyptus and tried to breathe. The wedding party carried calla lilies and freesias. The combined scent of the flowers in the close quarters at the altar smelled a little too *funeral home* for Cate's comfort.

Her old hometown of Blossom Branch would have been so much more suited to Cate's love of simplicity than this big Atlanta event. But her parents had insisted they had too many friends and business associates to have their elder daughter tie the knot in a tiny, semi-rural community, no matter how charming.

Why was she so nervous? Today was the culmination of her life plan. If she had made a few concessions, it was only natural. That's what grown-ups did. Unlike her parents, who fought frequently, Cate had chosen to marry her very best friend. Jason would give her security. Everything else would flow from there.

Her stomach curled as the mixed floral scents intensified. She shifted from one foot to the other, desperately glad she had opted to wear ballet slippers instead of heels. Swallowing hard, she tried to focus.

Then she realized something was awry. The priest had repeated a line from the script.

"Jason, wilt thou have Cate to be thy wedded wife, to live together in the covenant of marriage…" The familiar words continued.

Oh, God. Had she spaced out so long she'd missed her cue? Had they backed up to give her another chance?

Confused, she stared at the priest. His wrinkled face reflected mild alarm and consternation. The silence grew.

The priest had asked a question, and the groom was hesitating.

Cate looked up at Jason. Dear, handsome Jason. They had known each other since kindergarten. He was the gentlest, most dependable, compassionate man she had ever known.

His brilliant blue eyes filled with tears. She had never seen him cry. Not once. Not ever.

"I'm sorry, Cate," he said. He shot the priest an apologetic glance. "Give us a minute."

Jason took her hand and tugged until she had no choice but to follow him. It was a good thing she had decided a train was too fussy for her personal style. Even so, the skirt was voluminous. Somehow, they dodged the giant tiers of candles and the cascading ferns and found a tiny pocket of floor space.

It was hardly private.

In the distance, a murmur swept over the gathered throng like the portent of a storm.

Jason cupped her face in his hands. His body was rigid, his expression distraught.

A hole opened up in her chest.

He kissed her softly. In apology. Not passion. "I'm so sorry, Cate. This is wrong. I've known it for a while, but I couldn't seem to stop the momentum. You know it, too, I think. We both let ourselves get caught up in the excitement and the way our families were so delighted for us, but we've made a mistake."

The hole grew bigger, sucking all the oxygen out of her body. Little yellow spots danced in front of her eyes. "Don't do this to me," she pleaded. "I'm begging you, Jason. Don't do this. You can't. I'll never forgive you."

He released her, his face dead white.

They were speaking in whispers, but any one of the wedding party could easily pick up the essence of the drama. In the enormous sanctuary, no one moved. No one coughed. No one made a sound. The candles and the flowers were a paltry hiding place.

He wiped his damp face with the back of his hand and cursed in soft agony. "We love each other, Cate, but we're not *in* love."

Those ten words were a knife to the heart. Severing her last hope. This day was supposed to be a beginning. She had given up so much—Blossom Branch, her dream wedding. She had convinced herself that marriage was what she desperately needed and wanted. The *only* thing she wanted. And Jason, of course.

If she didn't have this, who was she? What was left?

Everything inside her shut down. Her body went into survival mode. For eighteen months she had done little more than to think and plan and orchestrate this day. It was the social event of the season. In a century when newspapers all over the country were disappearing, not one but two society-page journalists sat in the audience.

Garden & Gun magazine, arguably the arbiter of all things hip and classy in the modern South, had sent several reporters and photographers to document the day for a future spread on quintessential Georgia weddings.

Terror filled her veins. She couldn't cope with this. It was too terrible to contemplate.

Panic like the rushing force of a tsunami galvanized her. Pushing past her startled groom-to-be, she fled.

It wasn't easy. Her dress hampered her movements. Adrenaline fueled her desperation.

She had been a member of this church since she was twelve years old. Her parents had each served terms on the vestry. Cate had been an acolyte and had sung in the choir. She knew every narrow hallway and musty closet and crooked passage.

Which meant that in no time at all, she found herself outside.

The cobblestone driveway was oddly silent. Despite the tightly packed cars, everyone was inside. Cate was completely alone.

The sun beat down on her head. The silver comb of her pearl-studded tiara dug into her scalp.

She had no purse, no money, and no means of transportation. Hysteria threatened, but she shoved it away. No one was bleeding. This wasn't a hurricane or an earthquake or any other natural disaster. She wasn't going to die.

Was she?

A large, warm hand came down on her shoulder. "Steady, Catie-girl. It's going to be okay."

Without sunglasses, the afternoon light was punishing. She shaded her eyes with her free hand and blinked up at the large, tuxedo-clad man. "Harry?"

Everything inside her shriveled into a tiny ball of misery and embarrassment. On the long list of people she would rather *not* have witnessed the absolute debacle that was her wedding day, Prescott Harrington III, better known in their social circle as *Harry*, was at the top.

"None other," he said mildly. "You seem surprised. I *did* RSVP."

"But without a plus one."

"No. Just me." He slid an arm around her waist. "Are you sentimentally attached to those flowers, honey?"

She glanced down dumbly at her beautiful bouquet. "No."

He was forced to peel her chilled fingers loose one at a time because she couldn't seem to uncurl her hand on her own. When the task was accomplished, he tossed the poor undeserving roses on the hood of an ice-blue Lamborghini and steered Cate toward his own car, a sleek black roadster that was quietly sophisticated rather than flashy, much like Harry himself.

Opening the passenger door without fanfare, he tucked her in and fastened her seat belt, careful not to damage the acres of tulle and satin. Then he slammed the door, ran around to the driver's side and hopped behind the wheel.

The car smelled amazing. Because it had been sitting in the hot sun, the butter-soft leather was warm and scented with the owner's subtle aftershave.

Cate leaned back and rested her head. She was conscious the vehicle was moving, but little else impinged on her trance of utter disbelief and pain.

Harry drove as he did most things, with quiet confidence. At one point, he reached into the back seat and handed her a bottle of water. "You need to drink this. It was hot as hell in that church."

She uncapped the bottle and downed half the water, wondering if her crushing headache was the product of dehydration or shattered dreams.

They zipped along Peachtree Street amidst lushly flowering landscapes and eye-catching glass skyscrapers. Buckhead on a lazy summer afternoon was Atlanta at her finest. This upscale neighborhood had been Cate's stomping grounds since her father relocated the family from Blossom Branch to Atlanta more than a decade ago.

"Where are you taking me?" she asked dully, not really caring, but feeling the need to fill the awkward silence.

He shot her a brief sideways glance. "My place."

Cate nodded. Made sense. The destination wasn't far, and it had the added bonus of building security, which meant no one could get to her.

Harry, a decade her senior, had been a wunderkind architect who graduated from business school a few years after the financial crisis of '08. Thanks to his genius and a driving urge to succeed, he had waded into the midst of the recovery. He'd begun by building houses. Now his preference was commercial real estate. Already, two iconic structures bearing his stamp graced the Atlanta skyline.

Though his architectural firm had fancy offices downtown, Harry preferred working in the privacy of his home study offsite. He was a distant part of her social circle in Atlanta because he was from Blossom Branch, also. There was something about that small, wonderful town that drew its expats together—like alumni who bonded over shared memories.

Because Harry was older, though, if he and Jason hadn't been cousins, she probably would barely know him. Cate had been to one dinner party with Jason at Harry's place, but that was three years ago, and she hadn't been back since.

They drove into the underground parking garage and slid into a numbered spot. Harry came around and helped her out. A nearby couple goggled at them, but Harry shielded Cate with his large frame. "Come on, kiddo. Let's get you upstairs."

The elevator ride was swift and silent. Harry's penthouse apartment occupied half of the top floor. The luxurious home boasted floor-to-ceiling windows in the public spaces and breathtaking views of the Atlanta skyline. Far in the distance, the unmistakable, monolithic, dome-shaped Stone Mountain marked the other horizon.

Cate sank into a chair, her legs literally unable to support her any longer.

Harry crouched at her side and wrapped a small, fuzzy blanket around her shoulders.

She clutched it tightly. Somewhere on the ride over, she had started shaking and couldn't seem to stop. "Why are you being nice to me?" she asked. His usual MO was to tease her unmercifully and snipe at her clothes and her friends and her social life. In his presence, she always felt like a stupid, gawky kid.

Harry's lopsided smile held so much sympathy her throat ached. He smoothed a stray hair from her forehead. "You've had a rough day, Cate. I've decided to cut you a break." He put the back of his hand to her cheek and frowned. "You're in shock, I think. I'm going to call my doctor and see what to do."

"Okay…"

His words didn't really make any sense. Her whole body ached with exhaustion. Pulling the warm cover all the way around herself, she drew her knees to her chest and rested her head against the arm of the chair.

It might have been minutes or hours later when Harry returned. "Open your mouth," he said. "This is a mild sedative. The doc said it will help. Wash it down with this milk."

She wrinkled her nose. "I don't like milk."

"Doesn't matter. Open up."

Protesting was too much work. She swallowed the pill along with the cold liquid and made a face. "You're a bully."

He chuckled. Scooping her up in his arms, he took the handful of steps to the sofa and laid her down as if she were unable to walk on her own. Without asking permission, he carefully removed her veil and headpiece and all the hairpins that were holding it in place. "I think you should sleep for a little while. We'll talk when you wake up."

That sounded ominous. "You won't leave me?" She clutched

the edge of the coverlet, hating the feelings of vulnerability and utter despair that stripped her raw and made her fearful.

His expression softened to something resembling gentleness, though *gentle* was the last word anyone would use to describe Harry. If Jason was her dear Ashley Wilkes, then Prescott Harrington III, was definitely the dangerous rogue Rhett Butler. One never knew what he was thinking...

Grabbing a second blanket from a stash under the coffee table, he smoothed it over her lower half until not a single swathe of tulle or bare ankle was showing. Then he stood and looked down at her with his arms folded over his chest. "Sleep, Cate."

His expression was inscrutable. She was nothing more to him than an experiment, a slide under a microscope. Suddenly, she blinked. "Why were there sedatives in your medicine cabinet?"

He shrugged. "I had to have a complicated dental procedure several months ago. They told me to take the drug the night before and the morning of so I would be calm."

"And did you do it? Was this pill you gave me a leftover?"

His grin was an unexpected flash of white. "Nah. I didn't see the point."

Of course he didn't. The man was impervious to typical human weaknesses. "Sometimes I hate you, you know."

He blinked. "Oh, really?"

"All the rest of us mortals struggle day to day, and yet whatever you touch turns to gold. Everything you've ever wanted in life has dropped into your lap."

Something flashed in his eyes. Something dark and dangerous and frightening. His jaw tightened. "I'm going to let that one slide. Go to sleep, Cate. I'll be in my office if you need anything."

Two

It was six in the evening when she woke up. She knew the time because Harry's fancy mantel clock chimed the hour. *Oh, God.* The memories came rushing back. It hadn't been a dream...or a terrible nightmare...

Jason had walked out on their wedding.

Instead of being a joyous newlywed, Cate was that most pitiful of stock characters, the jilted bride. She pulled her hand from beneath the covers and stared at her engagement ring. She and Jason had selected it together. He had studied the four Cs of diamonds, and Cate had scoured Pinterest for settings she liked.

In the end, they had gone with a modest center stone and two smaller sapphires on the sides, all set in platinum. Yesterday she had adored her ring. Now she hated it.

Her fingers were slightly swollen from the summer heat and humidity. It took several minutes, but she wrenched and pulled until she finally got the ring off. Reaching over toward the coffee table, she dropped what had been her prized piece of jewelry into a shallow pewter dish. Then she pressed her forehead against the back of the sofa and sobbed.

When someone turned on a lamp, she froze, not wanting Harry to see her tearstained face. But fate was not on her side.

He sat down on the coffee table and sighed. "Jason wants to come up and make sure you're all right," he said quietly.

She sat up in shock, no longer caring that her cheeks were splotchy, and her makeup was a mess. "How did he know I was here?"

Harry cocked his head, frowning. "I sent him and your parents a text as soon as we got home. I didn't want them to worry."

"Oh." In her utter desolation, she had been unable to think about anything but fleeing the church. What did it say about her that she hadn't considered the ramifications of disappearing? She had always been a *good girl*. Never a misstep. Never rocking the boat. Always keeping up appearances. But she was done with that. "I don't want to see him." Panic fluttered in her chest.

"I figured you would say that. I told him you were napping and that I was going to feed you. I said he could try again in a couple of hours. You might as well get it over with, Catie-girl. The confrontation will only get worse the longer you put it off."

She bit down hard on her bottom lip to keep it from trembling. "What makes you such an authority on interpersonal relationships?"

His smile was wry. "Can I tempt you with carryout? The restaurant downstairs has Angus burgers and shoestring fries that would make a grandma weep, they're so good. Or I could order you a salad if you don't feel like tackling a big meal yet."

Cate's stomach growled on cue. "I've been eating kale smoothies, yogurt and lettuce salads for three months, so I could fit into my dress. A burger sounds amazing." Suddenly, she was ravenous. A person could only sustain a nervous breakdown for so long before needing caloric sustenance.

Harry pulled out his cell phone and placed the order. Then he disappeared for five minutes and returned carrying a long-sleeved button-up shirt in pale blue. "I'm half a foot taller than you are," he said. "This should come down to your knees. I don't have any bottoms or shoes that will come close to fitting you, but I adjusted the AC, so you won't get too cold."

She took the shirt. "Thank you."

"Bathroom is down the hall in the guest room. First door on the left."

"Um…" The hole in her chest opened up again. Maybe this was going to be a permanent fixture of her new persona.

Harry frowned. "What's wrong?"

Her face flamed. "I need help getting out of the dress."

For a split second, he actually seemed disconcerted. But the moment passed, and she was certain she was wrong.

He grinned at her and waggled his eyebrows. "Lucky for you I have plenty of experience in that area."

"Hilarious," she said, glaring at him. "I'm not in the mood to hear about all your sexual conquests. Jason says Apple had to get you a special iPhone with extra gigs just to hold all the contacts in your little black book."

"Now who's the smart-ass? Turn around, Cate. Let's get this over with."

It was a very bad moment to regret her choice of wedding dress. The strapless, classic gown fastened in back with no less than sixty-two cloth-covered buttons. Cate held her breath for the first dozen.

She had imagined Jason helping her out of this dress in their fancy room at the Ritz-Carlton where they were planning to stay overnight before leaving on their honeymoon. Instead, big, ornery Harry Harrington attacked the back of her gown as if every little button was an affront to his male pride.

He made it to just below her waist before giving up and ripping the two sides apart, sending buttons flying everywhere.

"Hey," Cate said indignantly, grabbing the bodice close to her breasts to protect her modesty. "I could have sold this on eBay if you hadn't destroyed it."

"Sorry," he muttered. "I'll pay you for the dress if it's that important. Besides, I doubt anyone wants a wedding gown with bad mojo."

She gaped at him. The brutally honest comment surprised her after he had been so caring earlier. Maybe pretending to be a decent human being had taxed his acting abilities.

"Excuse me," she said, her voice barely a whisper. It was all she could do not to cry again. She wouldn't give him the satisfaction.

In the bathroom she stared into the mirror and hit rock bottom. She looked like hell. Her eyes were puffy and red. Even worse was the raccoon-ish mask forged of smudged mascara and salty tears. With her hair half up and half down, she looked like someone who had been on an all-night bender.

Suddenly, she had a desperate urge to be clean. Fortunately, Harry's guest bathroom was fully stocked. She wrapped a big fluffy towel around her hair to keep it dry and hopped in the shower. The hot water felt like heaven. She washed her face and then everything else.

Since she had been wearing nothing but a thong under her dress, she washed the undies as well. When she got out, she felt a hundred times better. At least until she put on Harry's shirt and glanced in the mirror again. She was pretty sure anyone who looked carefully could see her nipples.

Using the hairdryer, she dried her undies and put them back on. They were next to nothing, but she needed all the armor she could muster. After that, the only thing left was to take down the rest of her hair and shake it loose as best she could without a brush or a comb.

The hair salon had used half a can of spray on her up-do this morning. It would take a ton of hair products to get herself back to normal.

Thinking about tomorrow brought back the hole in her chest. She had no clue what the next day would bring, no idea what she would do. Instead, she concentrated on getting through the next half hour. And then the next half hour after that. When she heard the doorbell ring, she found the courage to leave the bathroom.

She arrived in time to see the young delivery boy smiling broadly as Harry tipped him. "Thank you, sir."

Harry closed the door and held up the bag. "Do you want to eat in here or in the kitchen?"

"Here is fine."

They sat down on opposite sides of the coffee table. With her knees pressed together and the shirt pulled down over them, she still felt the need to drape the small blanket across her lap.

Harry didn't waste time with small talk. Instead, he opened the bag and handed her a share of the bounty. He'd not been lying about the hamburgers and fries. Cate gobbled down half of hers, barely pausing to breathe.

While she had been in the shower, Harry had opened a bottle of pinot. She drank recklessly, hoping to blunt the feeling of desperation that made her ill. It was all well and good to pretend she could hide out in Prescott Harrington's glamorous apartment indefinitely, but her reprieve would likely be measured in hours.

"Thank you for the food," she said.

He wiped his mouth on a napkin and nodded. "At least it

put some color in your cheeks." He gathered the remnants of their meal, stuffed it all in the large white paper sack and crushed it between his two big hands. "Jason is waiting outside the door."

Cate shot to her feet. "No. I don't want to see him." Her newly manicured fingernails dug into her palms. "I won't."

"You owe him that much, Cate. The man is a mess. Let him speak his piece."

Her jaw dropped. "*I* owe *him*? Are you insane? *He* betrayed *me*."

Harry shot her a steely-eyed stare. "We both know that Jason is one of the finest men who ever walked this earth. He had a good reason. I don't know what it is, but the two of you both live in Buckhead. You move in the same circles. This has to be settled. One way or another."

"It must be nice to be God."

"Settle down. It's like ripping off a Band-Aid. Do it fast and let the healing begin."

She loathed him in that moment. Actually, she loathed the entire male sex. Every damn one of them thought they had all the answers. "Fine. Bring him in. Why not end this wretched day with more pain and sadness? I won't break." I won't break."

It was a brave speech. Unfortunately, the underpinnings were like cotton candy in the rain. As soon as Jason walked into the room, her chin wobbled, and a painful lump filled her throat.

Just inside the door, he set down her trio of matching suitcases and her purse. The lightweight trendy luggage had been a gift from her parents at her first wedding shower.

Harry was right. Jason looked dreadful. His eyes were sunken, his posture defeated. He shoved his hands in his pockets. "Hello, Cate."

"I'll leave you two to talk." Harry picked up the food sack and started to walk away.

Cate panicked. "No. I want you in the room. I don't want to be alone with him."

If it were possible, the misery in Jason's expression deepened.

Cate sat down again and pulled the lap blankets around her, using them as shields. With the two men on either side of the room, she felt small and anxious and utterly defeated.

Harry waved a hand. "Have a seat, Jason."

The younger man shook his head. "I'll stand if you don't mind." He shifted his focus to Cate. "I am so desperately sorry, Cate. I was an idiot and a coward to wait so late to call it off. You can't possibly hate me more right now than I hate myself."

Her limbs began to tremble again. Maybe some tiny part of her hoped he had come begging for a reconciliation. He *was* apologizing. But only for his timing. Not for anything else.

"Did I do something wrong?" The question tumbled forth, uncensored. It had festered in her brain since the moment her groom-to-be had backed out of their wedding.

"Oh, God. *No.* Of course not." At last, Jason moved. He took the armchair nearest the sofa and sat. With his fists clenched on his thighs, he grimaced. "We screwed up, Cate. And it goes back a very long time, I think."

She swallowed. "I don't understand."

"Be honest, Cate. You chose me in the beginning because I was *safe.* You knew the two of us would never argue like your parents do. I would never have an affair. I would be faithful."

It hurt to hear him say those things aloud. She had been twelve when her father arbitrarily decided to move the family to Atlanta. He'd been offered a huge promotion, and he took it, family be damned. Cate's mother was furious. Cate and her sister had been devastated. They loved Blossom Branch.

It was home. Atlanta was fine for shopping trips and concerts, but it hadn't felt like home, not then. Cate had been forced to adjust. To suppress her needs and wants.

Her whole world had changed overnight.

Years later, she had chosen Jason because she was positive he would never inflict such turmoil on her life.

"I suppose there might be an element of truth to that," she said. "But I love you, Jason."

For the first time, a small smile lit his handsome face. "I know you do. And I love you, too. We've been part of each other's lives forever."

"But…"

He rubbed his forehead with the heel of his hand. "Do you remember when you proposed to me?"

Every ounce of her self-esteem winnowed away. Harry, one arm propped on the mantel, had made a sound. A quickly muffled sound, but a sound nevertheless. This was a heck of a time to rethink her insistence on having him in the room.

She nodded glumly. "I remember." Now that she thought back on it, Jason had hesitated that day, too. Just as he had when the priest asked a question the skittish groom couldn't answer. "So why did you say yes?"

"If you'll recall, we were in bed at the time. You were so cute and excited, and I thought, *what the hell*. Surely you and I could make it work. We have everything in common. I wanted to get married someday. My own parents are miserably wed. If I had any shot at long-term happiness, I figured it would be with you."

"But something changed."

He reached for her hand. She jerked it back. She couldn't bear to have him touch her, not with Harry watching their every move.

Jason winced. "Actually, nothing changed, not really. We

spent a year and a half playing the part of the happily engaged couple in front of our friends. We made plans, we basked in the glow of our families' approval. It became this giant, lumbering freight train that couldn't be stopped. Not even when I realized we were both doing this for the wrong reasons."

"And those were?"

"Convenience. Fear of the unknown. Friendship."

"I see." If she could have argued, she would have, but the longer he talked, the more she realized what an idiot she had been. "So that's it?" She hurt so badly, she wanted to throw up.

"Here's the thing, Cate. When you finished your master's degree and your parents paid for you to study in Paris and Rome for a year, I was pumped to spend part of that time with you. We had a blast. Then you came home, we got engaged and suddenly you threw yourself into planning a wedding. You didn't even try to get a job."

She blinked backed tears of humiliation. "Daddy told me not to rush. What's wrong with that?"

"Nothing…not a thing. But neither of us has spent much time deciding what we want out of life. It's all been fun and games and not much of the nuts and bolts of being an adult. I don't know exactly when it happened, but I started to get scared, scared that we both still have a lot of growing up to do. The one thing I know for sure is that I never want to lose you from my life, but I can't be your husband."

"I see." She was a parrot. A clueless, pitiful parrot unable to speak more than the same two syllables.

"If you're honest, and once you've had a few days to recover, I truly believe you'll agree with everything I've said. I know this is damn hard. You were in an impossible situation. Your parents had spent a crap load of money on the social event of the season. It was unreasonable to expect *you* to pull the plug. I had to be the one to do it, but I didn't have the nerve. So I waited too damn long, and I hurt the woman I love dearly, and for that, I am deeply sorry. I'm going to repay your parents every cent of the money as soon as I can."

For the first time, Harry spoke up. "I'll take care of the money. I have an embarrassing abundance of it and no one to spend it on but me. Let me do this, Jason."

The men were cousins. And more than that, friends. Cate shook her head vehemently. "That's not necessary."

Harry frowned. "This is between Jason and me."

Cate sputtered and felt her face heat with frustration.

Jason shot him a glare. "Why do you go out of your way to rile her up?"

"Because she rises to the bait so beautifully."

"Enough." Cate stood on wobbly legs and wrapped her arms around her waist. Jason was blond and blue-eyed and so very dear. Harry was broad through the shoulders and dark-headed, a dangerous, overtly masculine beast with barely softened edges. "Thank you for coming, Jason," she said quietly. "I'd like you to do one thing for me."

"Anything," he vowed. He stood as well, his body rigid.

Did he expect her to punish him somehow?

She swallowed her pride and her hurt feelings and did the only thing that made sense. "Get on that plane in the morning, Jason. Take a friend or fly alone. But go to Machu Picchu. Four weeks in Peru was your bucket list item. The wedding was mine. I don't want you to miss it. And to be honest, I'd rather not have to worry about running into you for the next month. I need a breather from *us*. Some time to know it's over and to start again."

He was so pale she thought he might collapse. The skin on his face was drawn tight. "If that's what you want."

"It is."

"I'm sorry, Cate."

She swallowed the urge to scream and throw a tantrum. Instead, she managed a weak smile. "Me, too. Go, Jason. Go find the life you deserve."

He nodded curtly, strode across the room, walked out of the apartment and out of her life.

When the door slammed behind him, she choked out a sob and collapsed on the sofa, no longer caring that Harry watched. He had witnessed the most horrific moments of her life, and all in one day. He must think her an utter fool.

There was nothing she could do to stem the flow of tears. They came and they came and they came. Hot, wrenching and raw.

Harry picked her up and sat her in his lap, tucking her head against his hard shoulder and stroking her hair. "This is the worst, Cate. You survived. I'm proud of you."

The unexpected words from her nemesis made her weep all the harder. But she made no move to escape his tight hold. His strong arms were the only thing keeping her from shattering into a million broken pieces. Her world had fallen apart around her. Harry, for better or for worse, and at least for the moment, was helping her survive.

She had no idea how long she sat in his embrace. The apartment was quiet. Part of her stood at a distance, wincing in embarrassment for the pitiful woman wallowing in her own misery.

Eventually, the tears dried up—though not before soaking the expensive fabric of Harry's dress shirt. He had worn a bespoke suit to the wedding. After returning to the apartment, she'd watched him shed his jacket and kick off his shoes, but other than that, he was still dressed.

Now that she was numb and no longer crying, she realized her cheek was pressed right over his heart, unconsciously recording the steady *ka-thud* of each beat. She could feel the warmth of his skin through his shirt. The hard wall of his chest smelled faintly of what she assumed was his shower gel.

For the first time, his comfort made her uncomfortable. Odd, but true.

She forced herself to get up. "I'm fine," she lied. "But I think I'd like to go to my room now." Even if it *was* early.

Harry stood as well, his narrow-eyed gaze cataloging her mental and physical state. "I'm sorry, Cate." In his words, she heard genuine sympathy and concern.

"It is what it is," she said, the words dull.

"I'll carry your bags," he said, putting his offer into practice. "Is there anything else you need?"

She followed him down the hall. *A do-over? A time machine? Some kind of patch for the scary hole in my chest?*

When he came back out into the hall after arranging her luggage at the foot of her bed, she managed a smile. "Not a thing. I appreciate all you've done for me today."

Harry didn't smile in return. If anything, a frown shadowed his gaze. "My place is huge," he said. "You can stay as long as you like. I won't even notice you're here."

That statement should have reassured her. After all, the situation was anything but normal. Still, his words made her feel even more alone.

Her throat was tight, but she managed a reply. "Thank you," she said. She eased past him, entered her borrowed bedroom and closed the door.

Three

Cate huddled under the covers and blindly watched HGTV until her eyes crossed. At 2:00 a.m., she finally slept. The few times she woke up, she went to the bathroom, splashed water on her face, and went right back to sleep.

In one of her college classes, she had learned about the stages of grief. Depending upon whom you studied, there were five or seven or even twelve. God help her, she hoped it was only five.

Already, she had skated past denial. That was Harry's doing. He had made her confront the impossible by inviting Jason into his home. Now there was no way for Cate to pretend she might be able to turn this situation around.

Neither was bargaining a choice. If God heard her prayers, He or She was probably disappointed in Cate. After all, she had inconvenienced hundreds of people.

Now her dreams were in ruins. She had never been *less* safe and secure. The last time she remembered feeling so lost and helpless was when her father closed the door of the station wagon as they prepared to leave Blossom Branch, and he impatiently told twelve-year-old Cate to stop crying.

She couldn't blame herself for that awful day in the past. She was only a child. But this new disaster was different. She'd been so intent on protecting herself and her emotions, she'd been blind to reality. She was not the woman Jason wanted and needed in a wife. Even worse, she was letting a man she barely knew give her shelter.

Well, maybe that last one wasn't entirely true. She knew Harry plenty well...from a distance. Something about him had always seemed intimidating, so she had kept a healthy no-man's-land between them whenever their paths happened to cross.

Cate knew that Jason thought the world of Harry. Maybe it was why she had been willing to accept Harry's sanctuary.

Or maybe Harry had been the only person who jumped in to help when her wedding imploded.

After a long, dream-ridden night, Cate woke up Sunday morning and—for a moment—forgot that her perfect life had derailed. When all the terrible details came rushing back, nausea churned in her gut.

The room-darkening drapes were drawn. The guest suite was gloomy. That suited her just fine. When she returned from the bathroom, she spotted a small white piece of paper that had been pushed under her door. The missive was covered in Harry's dark, forceful scrawl...

The fridge is stocked. Help yourself to anything you want. I'll be upstairs in my office if you need me...

She was hungry. But no way did she want to encounter her host. After listening at the door, she eased it open. When she convinced herself that Harry must indeed be upstairs, she scuttled into the kitchen.

Like a timid mouse trying to avoid a large, hungry cat, Cate quickly foraged for enough supplies to last her through the day. Gourmet cheese, fancy crackers, bananas and nuts and grapes. And an assortment of flavored waters and teas. Her arms were full, but she made it back to her room undetected.

The guest suite had a small refrigerator. That was handy.

Because she really did feel hungry, she tried to eat a few cashews and half a banana. Soon, the food swirled unpleasantly in her stomach.

Without warning, the tears started again.

She climbed into bed, pulled the covers over her head and went back to sleep.

That pattern carried her into the week. She wanted to feel anger, wanted to know she was healing. Then again, maybe it was naive and immature to think she could *will* herself through the grieving process.

She would be the first to say that her life while growing up had been golden. Other than losing a pet or two—and having to move from Blossom Branch—she had never really faced heartbreak. Fate must have decided it was time to catch up on several back payments.

Monday morning brought a second note with a cell number.

I have to go into the office. Will be there most of the day. Several colleagues flying in from out of town. Text me anytime.

Though Cate had made a point of avoiding her host, hearing that he was gone gave her a hollow feeling. Knowing he had been close by in the past forty-eight hours had given her a sense of security.

Even so, she took advantage of his absence to snoop.

The luxurious apartment was enormous and beautifully furnished with exquisite, modern flair. The main floor where she was staying encompassed the kitchen along with a large, open living room/den space for entertaining, and Harry's suite. Upstairs was one additional guest room, Harry's big office, and a rooftop terrace with a built-in grill, lap pool, and pots of hibiscus and other flowering plants.

She examined his work space with interest, expecting to see all sorts of techy gadgets. Instead, Harry's sanctum was almost monastic in its lack of clutter. A long, cherry table—obviously made for the space—nestled just under the sill of a huge bank of windows.

She saw a paper desk pad covered with neat doodles, a wireless printer and a single laptop. On one wall, built-in bookcases held a wide range of volumes, mostly architecture-themed. A small refrigerator—like the one in her room—held nothing but glass bottles of water. On the wall opposite the desk, a rowing machine gave evidence of one way Harry nurtured his impressive physique.

He wasn't really her type. She preferred men who resembled Jason—with the tall, rangy build of a baseball player. Harry was more like a bodyguard. Solid. Dangerous. Still tall, but very different.

Since she didn't want to think of *either* man, she stood at the window and wondered what it must be like to work in this bright, airy space day after day. Harry would be able to see violent summer storms sweep across the sky. Or watch a gentle, rare Atlanta snowfall.

In a sudden, panicked moment, it occurred to her she had no place to live. She had given up her apartment. The plan had been for her and Jason to rent a modest home somewhere when they returned from Peru and then later to pick out plans and a lot on which to build their dream house.

There it was again. Evidence of her naiveté. Who in their midtwenties built a dream house? Had she and Jason been planning a life together or writing the script for a romantic comedy? They had laughed together a lot. It was one thing she loved about him.

Her heart clenched with a stabbing pain. Jason said he loved her, but he wasn't *in love* with her. If the deep affection she had for him wasn't the real thing, how would she ever find that? How would she even recognize it?

Because she didn't know how long Harry would be gone, she abandoned his office and walked downstairs to his bedroom. Here, her stomach got queasy again, but not from grief.

Some other strange emotion held her in thrall as she examined Harry's most private space. He hadn't made up his bed. It was large and comfy, the sheets and covers rumpled as if he had endured a restless night. She could see that at a glance. Did he entertain sexual partners here, or was he the kind of man who liked to make love to a woman at *her* place so he could walk away later?

She stood just inside the door, unwilling to go any farther. There was a book on his bedside table, but she couldn't read the title from where she was. Did he read every night? There was no visible TV, though one might be hiding in the rough-oak armoire.

Suddenly, she was struck by an unanswerable question. Why had Harry left the church and intercepted her in the driveway? Anyone else could have, but no one did. Or maybe they might have thought about it but hadn't had the presence of mind to move as quickly as Harry.

Why had he rescued her and swept her away to safety?

Perhaps it was something as simple as compassion. But more likely, he had done it out of his affection for Jason. The two men were very close.

For the past half hour, her pain and her grief had receded. Exploring Harry's beautiful home had been a welcome distraction.

Now her mood tumbled again. Was this the trajectory of grief? One step forward and two steps back?

She was tired of crying, tired of being a pitiful jilted bride.

But even as she told herself she needed to buck up and move on, the heavy weight of depression and loss dragged at her heels.

And then there was the risk of being caught. She assumed Harry would be gone for hours, but what if he came back unexpectedly?

She made her way back to the comfort and safety of the guest room and buried herself in the covers again.

Tuesday morning brought another note...

I'm trying to give you your space, but you're not eating enough.

She was surprised he had noticed. Maybe he was keeping track of the kitchen inventory.

That day she rewatched all six seasons of *Downton Abbey*, cried, and slept in between.

Wednesday morning's note was shorter but more personal...

Your life is not over...

She grimaced, smoothing the note between her fingers. What did Harry know about her life? He had power and influence and a career that made full use of his talents. Cate was stuck. And not even in second gear. Probably only first. Or perhaps she had stripped *all* her gears. The analogy was too clunky for her befuddled brain.

That day she didn't watch TV at all. She chewed her fingernail and stared at the ceiling, trying to make even one tiny decision. The effort was exhausting. So far, she had avoided social media. Occasionally, she picked up her phone, tempted to check Instagram for any notes of sympathy. But she was afraid she would see the opposite.

What did her friends think? Her mother had sent a few texts. Cate had assured her she was fine but needed time to regroup. What rumors were circulating?

The possibilities were too awful to contemplate.

At dinnertime, Harry knocked and called out to her. "Pizza's here. I put two slices outside your door."

She waited until she heard his footsteps recede on the hardwood floor. Then she opened the door a few inches, snatched the plate and went back into hiding, moaning with appreciation as she wolfed down the hot, gooey treat.

If pizza still tasted this good, maybe all was not lost.

Thursday morning all hell broke loose.

Not a note. Something far more in-your-face. Apparently, she had taxed Prescott Harrington's ability to be empathetic and supportive.

At roughly 9:30 a.m., the bedroom door burst open, and her host stomped into the room, practically snarling. When he turned on the overhead light, she grimaced and threw an arm over her face. "Go away," she pleaded.

Harry ignored her petulant whine. Instead, he grabbed the covers, threw them to the foot of the bed and stared at her with apparent disgust. "Enough is enough, Cate. Get the hell out of this bed." He leaned down and took a theatrical sniff. "I'm pretty sure you stink."

"You can't boss me around," she said. "Besides, you're supposed to be nice to me. I've been abandoned at the altar. Haven't you heard?"

His hair was tousled as if he hadn't had time to comb it yet. How long had he been planning this? The fire in his eyes and the slashes of color across his cheekbones said his mood was volatile.

He put his hands on his hips. "You've had plenty of opportunity to wallow in misery, Cate. Now it's time to show what you're made of."

She glared at him. "That's bad grammar."

"I don't give a crap. Get up. Take a shower. Get dressed. And be in the kitchen in twenty minutes."

"Why?" she wailed, trying to reach the quilt and failing. She felt monstrously exposed. What kind of man could be so cruel?

His glare softened. "It's like falling off a horse, honey. You've got to get back out there. The world is sailing along without you."

Her bottom lip trembled. "And what if I don't care?"

"You're hurt. You're scared. But hiding out in this bedroom indefinitely isn't an option." His smile was oddly sweet given his recent actions. "The Cate Penland I know isn't a coward."

"I beg to differ," she muttered. But she scooted to the side of the bed and stood up. She was still wearing the same high-end shirt Harry had given her Saturday night when the two of them pried her out of her wedding dress.

Harry winced when he saw the assorted stains on the fabric. "I could have given you another shirt," he said. "You're a mess."

"Thanks for the vote of confidence." The Cate from a few days ago might have started crying again, but the moderately more composed Cate was made of sterner stuff. "I'll have it cleaned," she said. "Or buy you a new one."

"I don't care about the damn shirt," he said, glaring at her with his arms folded over his chest. "But if you're not in the kitchen when the eggs are ready, you won't like what happens next."

He turned on his heel and stomped out, leaving Cate to wander into the bathroom and gasp when she saw her reflection. The days had run together. When *had* she last bathed?

Because she absolutely believed Harry's dire threat, she jumped in the shower and grabbed the shampoo. Although his timetable was strict, she couldn't skip washing her hair. When she was done in the bathroom, she had no choice but to open her luggage. There, neatly packed, were all the beautiful outfits she had bought for her trip with Jason.

A few of her bras and matching undies still had the tags attached. On Saturday morning, she had thought she would be taking the first steps of a brand-new life. Instead, she was facing the whole phoenix-rising-from-the-ashes thing.

The process sounded difficult and painful.

Tears stung her eyes, but she didn't let them fall. The lump in her chest threatened to crush her spirit and steal her breath, but she thrust out her jaw and rummaged in the larger of her two suitcases to find a pair of cream linen pants and a matching ecru lace tunic.

If Harry expected her to venture back out into the world, she was going to do it in style. There was no time to dry her hair, so she combed it out and left it to brush her shoulders.

Fortunately, she made it to the kitchen with thirty seconds to spare. Harry stood at the range nursing an iron skillet of fluffy eggs. On the back of the stove a plate of biscuits kept warm. The delicious smell in the air was perfectly crisped bacon waiting to be served.

He shot her an unreadable glance over his shoulder. When he first saw her, she thought his jaw dropped, but he turned his back so quickly she couldn't be sure. "Is there anything I can do to help?" she asked.

"Nope. We can sit at the counter if that's okay with you."

She would have preferred a solid table between them, but she hopped up on a stool. "I've never seen you cook."

He served two plates from the stove and turned to face her. "I like to eat," he said, setting her meal in front of her. "Coffee? Juice?"

"Orange juice would be nice."

He reached in the fridge and pulled out a carafe of fresh-squeezed. "That explains it," he said.

"Explains what?" She frowned, not following his meaning.

"Well," he said with a droll smile, "I brewed coffee every morning thinking the caffeine would coax you out of hiding. But it never worked."

She felt her face flush. "I'm sorry if I was a poor house-guest." He sat down beside her, smelling as yummy as the home-cooked breakfast. She eased her stool a few inches to the right and took a bite of bacon. "This is very good," she said.

They ate in silence. Surprisingly, Cate discovered it was nice to feel normal, even if for only a few moments. Her mood mellowed considerably, but Harry unexpectedly dented her moment of peace.

"Your family is expecting you for lunch," he said. "I told them you'd be there no later than eleven thirty."

She turned and gaped at him, her face flushing with aggravation. "Who made you king of my schedule?" she snapped.

One large male shoulder lifted and fell. His expression was hard to read. "Somebody had to. You weren't doing it."

"You're the most arrogant man I've ever met," she said, wondering why she was still sitting in his kitchen when he made her so frustrated. His dark hair, an intriguing mix of raven black with the occasional lighter strand, was still ruffled.

His gaze was guarded. Like everything about him, Harry's eyes were oddly unsettling. The beautiful irises were steel gray with a tiny line of silver around the pupils.

He stood abruptly and carried his plate to the sink. "When you're ready, I'll take you downstairs and show you the car. It's electric. You can use it as long as you need to. I'll give you those keys and ones for this place."

Panic set in. "I don't want to go home right now," she said.

"You have to…your parents and your sister are worried about you."

His implacable certainty triggered the tears again. "Don't you get it?" she cried. "I've suffered a major life disappointment. I'm not ready to move on. This hurts, damn it."

Harry leaned against the counter, his hands propped behind him. The pose made his shirt draw taut over his abs. Not that she noticed.

He sighed audibly. "Tragedy and heartache happen to all of us at one time or another. And you're right. It hurts. But moving forward is the only option." He paused, for a moment seeming unsure of himself.

"What?" she asked. "What is it? What aren't you saying?"

"I've talked to Jason a couple of times. He made it safely to his hotel in Peru. I thought you would want to know."

She trembled, glad she wasn't standing. Her fists clenched in her lap. Thinking about Jason was agonizing. That was why she had done her best not to. What did Harry expect from her?

"Super," she said, infusing the two syllables with snark.

"Do you want to talk about it?" he asked quietly.

On the huge list of things she absolutely did *not* want to do, discussing her ex-fiancé with Harry was number one. "No thank you."

He stared at her, his intense regard making the trembling worse. "I'm not the enemy, Cate. You're not a prisoner. No one is keeping you here. You're welcome to pack up your things and go."

She closed her eyes briefly, trying to stop the tears. One escaped. Then another. Swallowing hard, she lifted her chin and found the courage to speak. "I don't want to go," she said, her throat tight. "I appreciate you letting me stay here. I'm sorry if I seem ungrateful."

Harry's eyes flashed. He straightened. "Oh, for God's sake. This isn't a soap opera. All I did was offer you a bedroom and a chance to catch your breath. It's no big deal. And this isn't some kind of quid pro quo. I love Jason like a brother. I'm doing this for him mostly."

"I see." For some reason, that hurt even more. Of *course* it was Jason he cared about. Not Cate. He might feel sorry for her, but she was little more than an inconvenient acquaintance to him. She had hoped that wasn't the case, but now she knew.

"Leave the dishes," he said abruptly. "My housekeeper will be in today. I'll meet you at the elevator in five."

Four

The atmosphere was strained during the elevator ride from the penthouse apartment down to the underground parking garage. As it turned out, Harry owned *three cars*—the expensive sedan Cate had ridden in on her wedding day, a tricked-out Jeep for off-roading in the north Georgia mountains and a small, all-electric vehicle that was cherry red.

He handed her the keys to the last one. "It's fully charged. As long as you don't try to run away and cross state lines, you should be fine."

"That's a joke, right?" Sometimes she wasn't entirely sure.

"It is," he said solemnly, but his eyes danced with humor. "The only thing you have to remember is to turn off the car when you get where you're going. Because it's so quiet."

"Got it."

"The apartment keys are on the same ring. And the attendant knows to let you through when you get back."

"Thanks."

Harry rotated his head on his neck as if this stilted conversation was a struggle. "I could order dinner in tonight. How do you feel about Thai food?" he asked, studying her face.

"Massaman curry?" she said hopefully.

"Sounds good."

When she got settled in the driver's seat, he closed her door. Suddenly, she flashed back to those big, masculine hands gently tucking her wedding dress beneath her as she was escaping the church.

"Thank you, Harry," she said, looking up at him.

His expression was almost grim. "I don't want your gratitude, Cate. I just want you to get back on your feet, so Jason won't destroy his life with guilt."

"Do you think that's what he's doing?"

"Right now, yes. But I'm hoping this phase is temporary. Both of you have to recover from what happened."

"You make it sound so easy," she muttered, still resentful of the way he supported Jason.

"Nothing worth having comes easy. At least not in my experience. You'll get over this, Cate. And so will Jason. You're both good people. But that doesn't mean it won't be hard as hell in the short term."

She nodded, suddenly desperate to get away. As she started the engine and shifted into Reverse, Harry stepped back. In the rearview mirror, she saw him watch her as she maneuvered. It would be the final straw if she scraped one of the concrete pillars and crumpled the bumper of his car.

By the time she made it out onto the street, her fingers hurt from gripping the steering wheel. Even with her sunglasses on, the world seemed too bright. She knew this city as well as she knew her own name, but for a split second, she was disoriented.

Taking a deep breath, she exhaled, telling herself everything was okay.

For a moment, she flashed back to a time when she was sixteen. She'd suffered a ruptured appendix and had been rushed into surgery. It was scary and traumatic and painful.

After five or six days in the hospital, hooked up to IV antibiotics and feeling weak and vulnerable, she'd finally been released. The world had seemed as it did right now. Too loud, too bustling, too everything.

She deliberately took the long way to her house. To be honest, she had no idea what she was walking into. Were her parents and her sister pissed that she had gone into hiding with Harry?

When she parked in the circular driveway of the home where she had lived for many years, she tried to study it as a stranger would. The sprawling Tudor-style structure with its steeply pitched slate rooflines and gently aging copper guttering was architecturally stunning.

This home had signaled to friends and family and the community at large that Cate's father had "made it"—whatever that meant. His advertising business was exploding back then. No matter that the three women in his life were grieving the loss of their life in Blossom Branch, Cate's father, Reggie, was determined to enjoy the fruits of his labor.

Cate locked the car and slung her purse over her shoulder. Though she could, of course, have walked right in, it felt weird to do so. Instead, she rang the bell.

Her sister, Becca, answered. When the door swung wide, Becca grimaced. "Oh, it's you," she said.

"I've missed you, too," Cate quipped. She immediately regretted her sarcasm. Her relationship with her younger sister had been strained for a long time. At some point over the years, Becca had heard a reference to her mother's *accidental* pregnancy and had immediately adopted the narrative that she was unwanted.

It wasn't true. Cate's parents loved Becca dearly. Unfortunately, she had always felt eclipsed by her older sister. When she graduated from high school a month ago, there had been plenty of family parties and celebrations. But she kept insisting that Cate's wedding had *overshadowed* her own big moment.

Well, Becca could certainly have all the attention now. Cate wanted to fade into the woodwork. Though she had always wanted to be closer to her sister, the six and a half years between them sometimes seemed like an unbridgeable gap.

As Cate and Becca hovered awkwardly in the foyer, Gillian Penland appeared through a doorway. "Oh, Catie," she said, holding out her arms.

The warm, tight hug took Cate by surprise. Her mother was not usually a physically demonstrative person. That she chose to be so now made Cate's throat constrict with emotion.

After a moment, her mother released her, patting Cate's shoulder. "Don't you look beautiful, sweetheart. Come on, you two. We're eating in the kitchen nook. Daddy's waiting."

Cate's eyes widened. "He's not at work?"

Her mother frowned. "Of course not. When we heard you were coming by, we all wanted to be here for you."

Cate couldn't help shooting a look at her sister. Becca rolled her eyes.

Reggie Penland stood as his three *girls* entered the room. "There you are," he said. "How are you doing, sweetheart?" He hugged her, too.

Had Cate slipped into some adjacent dimension where her family was warm and fuzzy instead of complaining and confrontational? One look at Becca dispelled that idea. The girl sat down with a grumpy expression on her face. "Let's eat," she said. "I'm starving."

The Penlands employed a longtime housekeeper. But she was nowhere in sight. The food—barbecue and a trio of sides—had been set out on the table already, along with a pitcher of iced tea.

Perhaps Gillian read her daughter's unspoken question. "I gave Amelia the day off. She's gone to the zoo with her daughter and grandkids. I love her to death, but you know how she gossips."

Cate heard the subtext loud and clear. This lunch might include moments of embarrassing conversation best kept between family. "I'm sorry I missed her," she said, taking her usual seat and pretending she was hungry.

Her father pinned her with a curious gaze. "How are you doing, Cate? There's been a lot of talk, of course."

Becca snickered. "Not to mention a few hilarious Cate-and-Jason memes on the internet."

Cate kept her expression calm with an effort. "I've been better. But I'm making it. The hard part is deciding what to do next."

Her mother passed a bowl of potato salad. "I'm sure you'll find your way." She paused. "Have you spoken to Jason?"

"Yes. Briefly. On Saturday night," Cate said. "I told him to go on to Peru. No point in wasting the trip."

Her father frowned. "Did he go alone?"

"I have no idea, Daddy. Why does it matter?"

An uncomfortable silence fell over the table.

Gillian shot her husband a warning glance. For once, Becca was silent.

Cate looked at each one of them, confused. "Am I missing something?"

Becca huffed an exasperated breath. "They want to know about the other woman. The one he left you for."

All the blood drained from Cate's face. She felt it go and saw the room swirl drunkenly. "Oh, my gosh," she whispered. "There is no other woman. Jason's not like that."

Her mother blanched. "Is he gay? And you just found out?"

Cate wanted to laugh hysterically. Her parents stared at her with identical looks of consternation. Becca kept right on eating.

This was a disaster. Damn Harry and his meddling. Cate sucked in a much-needed breath. "Jason realized that he loved me, but he wasn't *in love* with me. That's it. No big secret. Are you happy? Now you all know as much as I do."

Reggie muttered something under his breath but filled his plate. Gillian still looked distressed. "Did *you* do something unforgiveable, Cate? Did you cheat on him? Maybe with his cousin, the one you're staying with?"

The question hurt. A lot. Cate stared open-mouthed at her mother. "Of course not. How could you ever imagine that?"

Her father joined the fray. "Well, everyone we know thinks Jason hung the moon. Our friends were all jealous that we were getting the perfect son-in-law. So it's kind of hard to imagine him leaving you at the altar unless he had a damn good reason."

In an instant, Cate knew that her life-changing crisis was far from being over. If her own parents thought she might have sabotaged her relationship with Jason, what was everyone else in her social circle thinking?

The pain was intense. She wanted badly to stand up and walk out. Harry had thought she needed to come home because her family was worried about her. This wasn't exactly what Cate had expected.

But family was family, and she couldn't afford to pitch a big hissy fit or burn any bridges. She didn't want to... So she swallowed her hurt pride and her heartache. "May we change the subject?" she asked politely.

Her mother nodded. "Of course, dear. But before we abandon the wedding entirely, I should tell you that Prescott

Harrington sent your father a huge check that covers all our financial losses."

"It wasn't necessary," her father said, smiling. "But it was much appreciated. I gather that Jason is just about the only family he has."

"The two men are close," she said. "But no one actually calls him Prescott. He goes by Harry."

Becca snickered. "And tell us again why you're shacking up with some old, rich dude?"

"He's not old," Cate snapped. "And he's been very nice to me."

It was one of the more uncomfortable meals of Cate's life. And that included the ones with Harry.

Finally, everyone was done.

Cate laid her napkin on the table. "Well, as you can see, I'm fine. I'll let you know my plans when I figure out something. For now, I'll be staying at Harry's place. He works all the time, so I have privacy and time to think." She stood up. "I'll drop by again in a couple of weeks."

Becca shot to her feet also. "Not so fast. Mom and I have worked our butts off packing and returning wedding gifts ever since Saturday. It's time for you to pitch in."

"Gifts?" Cate put her hands to her face. "Oh, damn. I didn't even think about that."

Gillian's expression was wry. "We've done about half of them. A few dozen people called and suggested we donate their gifts to charity or simply keep them. It's a difficult task, but Becca and I are happy to help, aren't we?"

Becca gave a sullen nod. "Oh, sure. The golden girl is suffering. So we have to carry the load."

Cate stared at her sister. "I'm really sorry, Becca. Thank you for everything you've been helping with. And you, too,

Mama. Can we go look at what's left? I'll work on it for several hours while you relax. You've done enough."

"Nonsense," her mother said. "Besides, Becca and I have worked out a system. I pack the boxes and write the name on the front. She seals and addresses them. Then we load up the Suburban and make a trek to the UPS store."

Cate was mortified. While she had been sleeping and moping, her family had been cleaning up the carnage. For the first time, she wondered what had happened in that church. But she didn't really want to know.

Gillian had always been good at reading minds. "Once you ran out, Jason said something sweet to the guests. Everyone got up and left. We had already hired a cleaning service for the sanctuary. Your father called ahead to the country club and instructed them to take all the reception goodies to a local food bank. Not the booze, of course. We got a credit for that. So really, the gifts were the only hurdle. Some of my friends told me not to worry about it, but your grandmother was horrified at the idea. Of course, we had to do the right thing."

"Of course." Cate parroted her response, incredulous that she hadn't given a thought to what had happened in her absence. "I'm so sorry. I wasn't thinking straight."

For once, Becca gave her a genuine smile. "It's really okay. I'm just giving you a hard time. You got dumped in front of twelve hundred people. No one expected you to be rational."

"Gee, thanks," Cate muttered.

Reggie finished his tea, stood, and kissed his older daughter on the forehead. "I'm sorry this happened to you, Cate. But what doesn't kill you makes you stronger, or so I've heard." His pedantic advice might have been funny in other circumstances. "If you ladies are going to deal with gifts, I think I'll head back to the office."

In his absence, Cate followed her mother and sister down

the hall to the den. Half a dozen card tables and one entire sofa were covered with boxes and tissue paper and everything from blenders and Instant Pots and bed linens to china and silver. Cate hadn't wanted to register for those last two. She and Jason preferred casual entertaining. But her mother had insisted.

Now this abundance of gifts seemed like an obscene reminder of the life that was never going to be.

Cate opened the flaps of one very large box, refusing to give in to the emotion clogging her throat. "What the heck is this thing?" It was so ugly it was almost beautiful.

Becca snitched the tag from the corner of the carton and read aloud in a singsong voice. "A hand-hammered stainless-steel ice tub anchored by two pewter elk heads. Retail price, eight hundred bucks."

"It does *not* have the price on there, does it?" Cate said, aghast.

Her sister grinned. "Of course not, but I looked it up online."

Their mother frowned. "Talking about prices is in very poor taste."

Cate shook her head slowly. "Well, I like ice and Jason likes elk, but I can't imagine we'd have used that very often. It will cost a fortune to ship it back to the donor."

"Not to worry," Gillian said. "It came from someone in the neighborhood. I'll just drop it on the porch."

Becca lost interest. "If the two of you have this under control, I'm going to meet some friends for coffee." She hugged her sister. "Hang in there, Cate. Somebody will have an affair or run off to South America with his nanny. You'll be old news soon."

"Thanks, I think."

When it was just the two of them, Cate looked at her mother. "I really am sorry, Mama."

"About what, dear?" Her mother's smile was kind. "You didn't do anything wrong."

"Maybe I did. Maybe Jason was right. He thinks we got carried away with the whole idea of a wedding and marriage, and the situation got away from us. He said I might have some growing up to do." Her jaw wobbled.

"Oh, Catie. Come with me. Let's go out to the lanai where we can relax. There's no place here to sit down."

On the screened-in porch, Cate curled up in her favorite chair with the view of the goldfish pond. The day was hot, but with the ceiling fan overhead and a slight breeze, the veranda was comfortable. Her mother had always called it a lanai, perhaps because the word was more exotic.

After a few moments of silence, Gillian grimaced. "I will admit, I had a few reservations when I heard you and Jason were engaged."

"But why? I thought you loved him."

"I did and I do. But when I watched the two of you together, you sometimes acted more like brother and sister."

Cate cringed. "I wouldn't sleep with my brother."

"Fair enough. Maybe I explained that wrong. You seemed..." She hesitated, looking for the right word. "Comfortable."

"I don't understand. Shouldn't a married couple be comfortable?"

"Oh, Cate. Not at first. Comfortable is the last thing you should be. More like passionate...horny."

"Mama!" Cate's blush scalded her cheeks.

"My goodness, Cate. You're a grown woman. I think we should be able to talk about these things."

Cate wanted desperately to invent a reason to disappear, but her mother looked at her expectantly. "I thought Jason and I were happy," Cate said, feeling those stupid tears well up again. "Everything was perfect."

"But it wasn't," her mother replied, "or dear Jason wouldn't have called things off. I'll admit, he should have spoken up far sooner, but I imagine it was a very hard thing to do."

"I have nightmares," Cate admitted quietly. "About that moment. I don't know if I'll ever be able to forget it."

"Probably not. But the memory will lose its sting eventually." Gillian cocked her head and smiled. "One last personal question. How many men did you sleep with before Jason?"

Five

Oh, my God.

"Does it matter?" Cate's mortification was complete.

"Humor me."

"Only Jason," Cate muttered.

Her mother sighed. "Your father and I were very protective of you. Even during college, you came home three out of four weekends. I'm sorry, Cate. Maybe I should have pushed you out of the nest more firmly, but I loved having you around. You've always been my golden child, the easy one, the girl who made everyone smile."

"I don't feel very golden right now." It was true. Cate felt like a failure, but worse than that, she felt stupid and clueless. Like a caricature of herself.

"Tell me why you chose Jason in the beginning," her mother said. "What drew you to a man you had known almost your entire life? We should have had this conversation a long time ago, but you and I haven't been ones to discuss intimate topics. Our family prefers yelling to talking things out, don't we?"

Not me, Cate thought wistfully. Now it was her turn to hesitate. "I don't want to hurt your feelings, Mama," she said.

Gillian's eyes widened. "This is a safe space. Isn't that what they say?" Her attempt at humor gave Cate the courage she needed for a hard conversation.

"I didn't want a marriage like you and Daddy had. All the arguing, fighting, yelling. I hated it as a child, and I looked for the exact opposite as an adult. Jason is an even-keel kind of man. I knew he would always take my wishes into account, and he would never cheat on me."

"So you picked him because he was safe."

"Yes. And I won't apologize for that."

Gillian sighed. "Children don't always see the heart of the matter. Your father and I are very different people, hence the fireworks. I'm sorry we weren't better at keeping our conflicts away from you girls."

"Did you ever consider divorcing him?"

"No. Not seriously. The truth is, Cate, as angry as I was at your father for dragging us away from Blossom Branch, it was ultimately good for our marriage. As long as we were in that small town, people would always have judged him for his past, the poverty, you know. And I was a mama's girl, always running to your Grammy whenever I didn't get my way. Coming to Atlanta gave us a fresh start. Your father and I are very much in love, Cate. And to be clear, good sex is a big part of our relationship."

Cate stuck her fingers in her ears. "Ew, stop," she said, laughing in spite of herself.

"You and I *should* be able to talk about hard things, Cate. I wish I had told you that sooner. We weren't sure about you marrying so young, but you seemed very happy, so we didn't intervene. Now you've had a terrible trauma, but you'll come out the other side stronger and more resilient."

Cate's throat tightened. She hated this feeling of never having control. Grief overwhelmed her at the oddest moments, and without warning. How long would that last?

"It sucks," she said, rubbing her sternum where the lump of pain grew. "I thought Jason was the one person in my life who would never, ever hurt me. But in the end, he did the most awful thing to me..."

"Have you thought about how he's feeling, Cate? He does love you, which is the reason he finally found the courage to make the hard choice. He knew he couldn't be the husband you deserved."

"Everybody keeps defending him."

"And that makes you angry..."

"Yes," Cate said, feeling petty and mean but also righteously indignant. "It does."

Gillian laughed. "So now you see there's a downside to almost marrying a great guy. Everyone else loves him, too."

Cate was willing to talk, but not about Jason. "I should go work on the presents," she said.

"Forget the gifts," Gillian said. "I have all the time in the world to deal with those. You concentrate on picking yourself up and finding some peace."

"I did have an idea about that," Cate said. Truthfully, the thought had only gelled in the last few hours. "I wonder if Grammy and Grandpa would let me come stay a few weeks." While Cate was growing up, she had spent lots of time at her grandparents' house. Even when she turned twelve and her father dragged them all to a new life in Atlanta, Cate had continued to spend her summers in Blossom Branch. Becca joined her occasionally, but Cate was the one who never wanted to leave.

Her mother beamed. "I think that's a wonderful idea. It would do you good to get out of the city."

"Was Becca planning to be there any time?"

"No. One of her friends has invited her to go on a two-week cruise with the girlfriend's family. Besides, Becca was never as attached to Blossom Branch as you were. It makes sense, I guess. She was only five when we moved."

"Just me, then. Will you call her and ask?"

Gillian frowned. "You can't call your own grandmother?"

"I'm embarrassed," Cate admitted. "I hate disappointing her."

"I'll call," her mother said, "but you're worrying about nothing."

"Thanks. I hope you're right." Cate wandered back into the house and went to her bedroom. Until recently, she and Jason had been living together in his modest apartment. But a month before the wedding, they both decided she should move back home to make their special day even more special. The last time she walked out of this space, she had been on her way to the church. The room was disheveled, as if the previous occupant had left in a hurry.

There was no hurry now.

Cate grabbed another suitcase from her closet and began filling it with shirts and shorts and sundresses, along with shoes and everything else she would need for a long visit with her grandparents.

Her room still held her trophies and scrapbooks and her collection of Barbie dolls. Perhaps sometime soon she should give away most of it and pack up the mementos she wanted to keep.

This house was no longer her home. To be accurate, she didn't have a home at all. Harry had taken her in at first. Now she was planning to descend on her grandparents. Sooner or later, Cate was going to have to make some decisions about the future.

But every time she tried to imagine the future, all she wanted to do was pull the covers over her head and hide.

Harry would no longer tolerate that behavior. And it was a sure bet her grandmother wouldn't. So Cate would be forced out into the world of reality whether she was ready or not.

She said her goodbyes and left soon after. With her father and Becca out of the house, she knew her mother would want to leave also. This was one of the days she went to the gym for spin class.

Cate stowed her suitcase in the back seat and got into Harry's little electric car. It was hot from sitting in the sun, so she rolled down the windows to give the AC a chance to catch up.

As she exited her parents' beautifully landscaped property, she was struck by the fact that *today* was the beginning of her new life. She had thought Saturday was, but she had been painfully wrong.

It was too early to go back to Harry's. There was nothing for her to do there anyway except watch TV and eat and sleep.

She drove aimlessly, seeing her neighborhood through new eyes. Jason's parents' home was on her route. She managed to pass it without flinching. His mom had thrown them a beautiful wedding shower back in the winter. His parents still maintained a lavish lake house near Blossom Branch, but they had chosen city life long ago.

What was Cate supposed to do now? The gnawing uncertainty was almost more painful than the raw grief of the first twenty-four hours.

She had known Jason in elementary school, but both families relocated and she lost touch with the blue-eyed, blond-haired boy. When he ran into her again—this time at UGA—they were drawn together almost immediately by their mutual connections to Blossom Branch. They made plans together, dreamed dreams together. So maybe they hadn't jumped each

other's bones every single night, but they had been happy.
Hadn't they?

Everything that was supposed to happen in the next two
years was *couple* stuff. All of that was worthless now.

Without meaning to, or at least not consciously, she ended
up on West Paces Ferry Road heading toward the church.
Something drew her there. Perhaps like gawkers who flock
to the scene of an accident, Cate wanted to see for herself if
anything had changed.

She still had a key to the church. The associate minister had
signed it out to Cate with the understanding that she would
return it after she had changed into her reception gown post-
wedding. Only, Cate had fled. The key had been hiding all
this time in the bottom of her leather bag...the purse Jason
had dropped off Saturday night. Had anyone missed the key?
Or been afraid to ask for it under the circumstances?

Everything at the church was locked on a weekday. Cate
dug for the key and used it to access the two beautiful doors
that opened directly into the sanctuary. These were the steps
where she and Jason would have paused in the sunshine, taking a moment to realize they were husband and wife. She had
pictured that moment time and again and had asked the pho-
tographer to make sure and capture the two of them in the
very first minutes of their marriage.

Shaking off the unpleasant fantasy, she went inside. The
large room was silent, of course. Sunlight coursed through
the stained glass.

She walked right up to the altar, paced off in her head the
spots where the bridesmaids and groomsmen had been standing. Then she took her place right in front, center stage. Shivers ran down her spine. Goose bumps erupted on her arms.
She felt dizzy and sick and faint. Surely the past six days were
nothing but a nightmare.

But then she saw it. A tiny piece of eucalyptus the cleaners had missed. It was stuck in the altar rail, down near the floor. No one would have noticed it during Sunday services.

She retrieved the bruised greenery and stroked a tiny leaf. When she held it up to her nose, it still retained a whiff of fragrance.

This was the spot where her life changed irrevocably.

Turning around, she gazed out at the empty pews, trying to imagine what it had been like at the end. Whispers and shock and consternation. Most people would have been kind. A few might have enjoyed the juicy drama of the aborted wedding.

As she stood there, frozen with the painful memories, the old parish rector ambled in. "Ah, it's you," he said. "Hello, Catherine."

"Hello, Father." No one ever called her by her full name. The rector had been here before Cate and her family came. He was long past retirement age, but the congregation loved him.

"I see you've returned to the scene of the crime," he said.

His apparent levity startled her, but she saw compassion in his eyes. He had been taller once. In recent years, his body had *settled*. His thinning white hair and bushy eyebrows gave him a gnomelike appearance. A benevolent one, though. The kind who was supposed to bring good luck.

"I didn't plan to come," she said. "The car just brought me here."

"Or your subconscious, hmm?" He stood beside her, choosing to stare out over the empty room as she was. "The view is different up here. Did you notice that on Saturday?"

"I can't say that I did," she admitted. "I was pretty nervous."

"It takes courage to stand up in front of twelve hundred people and declare your love for someone."

She shot the old man a sideways look. "Were you shocked when Jason pulled me aside?"

The priest scrunched up his nose and scratched his head. "Ah, Catherine. I've lived a long time. So I suppose I've seen more than most. Your Jason is a fine man. It takes guts to follow your convictions."

Which wasn't really an answer. And there it was again. Another person taking Jason's side. Wasn't there anyone she could find to curse him and call him names?

She finally formulated the thought that had been nagging at her all week. "I suppose he knew this was a holy place. And he couldn't bring himself to speak vows that weren't true."

"Perhaps."

Cate twisted her hands together. "Was it my fault? Did I somehow disrespect the covenant of marriage?"

"Don't be daft, child. You acted in good faith. And so did your young man. Certain things happen in our lives that pull a thread from one tapestry and begin to weave another."

She frowned, irritated. "Is this where you tell me that everything happens for a reason?"

He straightened an inch and glowered as much as a benevolent gnome can. "Not even for a moment, Catherine. God isn't some manipulative puppeteer who throws disaster our way to teach us things."

Something inside her chest loosened…a stifled breath she hadn't even known she had been holding since Saturday. "Can you be absolutely certain about that, Father?"

He patted her shoulder but reached up to do so. Cate had a good six inches on him. "I may not have all the answers, young Cate," he said firmly. "But I do know that."

"So you're saying when we screw up our lives it's all on us?"

His grin was oddly youthful. "Sometimes yes. And sometimes, it's pure bad luck."

"Then what's the point of church and all the bells and whistles?"

"Ah, now that's easy. It keeps us from being alone on the journey."

Before she could absorb that bit of homegrown theology, the old man ambled away, leaving Cate alone again in the echoing room.

She pondered the priest's last statement as she walked back down the aisle. The symbolism wasn't lost on her. The original plan had been for her to exit the sanctuary on her husband's arm. Yet here she was. Walking alone.

But when she opened those heavy double doors, the sunshine outside was still as warm and the day still as bright. For the first time, she felt a flicker of hope. Not that Jason would change his mind. That was done. She had no illusions about her ex-fiancé and their relationship.

No, the hope was for *her*. She was going to start over. No matter that Saturday had been the worst day of her life. No matter that she had lost her best friend. She was not going to let life stomp her into the ground.

There were plenty of people in the world with *real* problems. Hunger. Homelessness. All kinds of terrible challenges.

Cate was lucky. She had a stable family, dear friends who loved her. Good health. Financial freedom. And then there was Harry. Harry, who had gone out of his way to look after her when she was at her lowest point. Harry, who had given her space and privacy, but hadn't been afraid to employ tough love when she spent too much time feeling sorry for herself. Thinking of him gave her the oddest feeling.

She had to resist the urge to cling to her benefactor like a port in a storm. Taking advantage of his kindness would be cowardly.

By now, it was late afternoon. Atlanta at rush hour was a challenge on the best of days. She steered the little car in the direction of home… Harry's home. The place that had been her sanctuary in recent days.

At a stoplight, when her phone dinged, she risked a glance. It was a text asking when to have dinner ready. Since the light was still red, she tapped out a reply. On my way now. Starving. ☺ Harry responded with a thumbs-up emoji.

As Harry had promised, the garage attendant waved her through when she arrived. Cate parked, retrieved her purse and suitcase, and made her way upstairs. At Harry's door, she dithered. He had given her a key. There was no reason she couldn't walk right in. But it felt weird. On the other hand, if she knocked, he would probably want to know why.

Either way, she felt awkward.

In the end, she put the key in the lock, knocked quietly and let herself in.

Harry met her in the foyer with a bemused look on his face. "You're free to come and go, Cate." He glanced at the suitcase. "Although if you're planning to stay till Christmas, we may have to talk."

His gentle teasing flustered her. She dropped the purse and bag. "I needed more stuff. I'm going to Blossom Branch sometime soon to visit my grandparents."

"Ah." He rubbed a hand across the back of his neck, his gaze hard to read. "I had another note from Jason. He suggested you might want to get the last of your things out of his place while he's gone. I've always had a key for emergencies. I'll be glad to help."

"Well…" Another unpleasant reality she had blanked out of her mind. Being jilted was complicated. Her heart sank, and she felt a blush warm her cheeks. "There's not much, mostly books and winter clothes. I had already brought a lot of my stuff to Mom and Dad's a month ago because Jason and I decided I should stay with them until the wedding."

"Because?" His gaze narrowed.

She was pretty sure he understood what she was saying, but she spelled out for him. "Because we wanted our wedding night to be special," she said defiantly, daring him to make fun of her.

Harry's mood suddenly seemed volatile, so much so that she backed up half a step without meaning to.

His jaw firmed, and his eyes flashed heat. "That's the stupidest dumbass thing I've ever heard."

Six

Cate stood frozen, afraid to move. Her innocent comment had provoked a reaction she never expected. "What do you mean?"

He glowered. "If I had a prospective bride living with me, I'd sure as hell keep her close until the ink was dry on the marriage license, and I had my ring on her finger." He scraped his hands over his face. His shoulders slumped. "Sorry," he muttered. "It was a crap day at the office."

"Oh? How so?" She wasn't entirely sure the storm had passed, so she stayed where she was.

He sighed. "We have a new hire, a brilliant architect. But he's been on staff a total of twenty-nine days, and he's already asking for time off—two weeks—to go to Cozumel with his girlfriend."

"Is it the destination you object to or the woman?" Cate dared to tease him. The more she learned of Harry, the more she realized she needed to stand up to him or risk letting him bulldoze her into *his* way of doing things.

"Very funny." He shook his head, staring at her with an

intensity that was mildly disturbing. "Whatever happened to having a work ethic?"

"People are different. Some employees are motivated by a paycheck, others not so much. What happened in the end?"

"HR granted his request. So he'll be in the hole regarding vacation time. It's not how I would have handled the situation, but I've learned not to micromanage...mostly."

"Why do I find that hard to believe?" His discomfiture entertained her. To see the unflappable Prescott Harrington disgruntled had the effect of diverting her attentions from her own woes.

Harry lifted his chin. Shoved his hands in his pockets. Gave her a look that made her shiver. "You're not at all scared of me, are you?"

"Should I be?"

"Most people tread softly in my presence."

Cate shrugged. "You seem like a cuddly old teddy bear to me." It was the biggest lie she had ever told. But she was trying her best to get, or keep, the upper hand.

His lips twitched. "I'm grumpy when I'm calorie deprived."

"*Hangry?*" She grinned at him. "In that case, let's eat."

"By all means."

Harry insisted on carrying her suitcase to the bedroom. In the short time he was missing, Cate saw that they were going to eat by one of the tall plate glass windows with a view of the city. Two places had been set. Not at either end, not side by side, but adjacent to a corner. Very cozy.

Harry's pale maple dining table was large enough to seat a dozen. The matching chairs looked handmade. His dinnerware was thin china, white-on-white with a Greek design around the rim. The silver was sleek and modern.

When he walked back into the room, she smiled at him. "This is beautiful. You have very good taste."

"Thank you," he said. He held up the bottle of wine. "Does this suit you? I have others if you'd prefer."

"I'm not picky. That will be perfect."

He poured her glass, then his. "Have a seat," he said.

They opened the cartons of food together. Cate's stomach growled audibly as the wonderful spicy aromas filled the air. In addition to the main course, Harry had ordered appetizers—lettuce wraps, spring rolls with peanut sauce and coconut shrimp with lemongrass guacamole.

She raised an eyebrow. "We're supposed to eat all this?"

"It won't hurt you," he said firmly, scooping out a serving of the entrée onto her plate. "You've hardly eaten a thing since you've been here."

"That's not true," she muttered. But she didn't waste any time digging in. The food was amazing.

They chatted about random subjects in the beginning. Then, after a few moments of silence, Harry quizzed her "How was today?" he asked.

She grimaced. "Not terrible, but not great. I didn't think about everything that had to be dealt with after the wedding."

"Not surprising."

"My mother and my sister have gradually been returning all the gifts. So many gifts..."

"Was that the problem?"

"Not really. Becca gave me a hard time about not helping, but I think she was mostly kidding. Mom swears she doesn't mind dealing with the presents. I guess I believe her. She's always been a bit of an organization freak, so she has the process down to a fine science."

"I still haven't heard any real friction."

"It was my parents," she blurted out. "They asked me if I had cheated on Jason, and he discovered the truth." Even now, the accusation bothered her. "Everybody assumes the problem is *me*, because he's *such a great guy.*"

Harry poured more wine for each of them. "Are you angry, Cate? Nice Southern girls are taught *not* to be angry, but you're entitled. So I'll ask you again. Are you angry?"

She had to bite down hard when her bottom lip trembled. "Yes," she whispered.

"Louder," he said, watching her carefully.

Harsh breaths sawed in and out of her lungs. "Yes."

"One more time. Make me believe it. Are. You. Angry?"

Her pulse raced. Her forehead dampened. Tears trickled from her eyes. Every emotion she had tamped down in the last six days came roaring to the surface. "Yes," she yelled. "I'm angry. I'm furious that Jason dumped me on our wedding day. There. Are you happy now?"

Harry reached out and squeezed her hand. "Good. That's what I wanted to hear. And I have an idea."

"For what?" she asked, confused.

"Finish your meal, and I'll tell you."

Strangely, her outburst hadn't upset her. If anything, she felt calmer than she had all day.

Harry asked more questions about how she spent the hours they had been apart. She told him additional details about the visit with her family—omitting the embarrassing sex and marriage talk with her mother—and then she admitted stopping by the church.

His hand stilled in midair, a bite of chicken halfway to his mouth. "How was that?" he asked studying her face.

"Okay, I guess. Or no, I suppose it was good. I think it helped me to stand where I stood and to go through it all one more time. A shrink would say I needed closure, right?"

"Maybe."

"The old rector came in while I was there. We chatted briefly. Even *he* wouldn't take Jason's name in vain."

"Poor Cate," Harry said with a smile.

"Don't patronize me," she huffed. "You think he's wonderful, too."

"I do," Harry said slowly, as if he were choosing his words. "But that doesn't mean I take any pleasure at all in the pain he caused you. You didn't deserve what happened to you, Cate."

There was no answer for that, so she finished her meal in silence.

When they were done, Harry glanced at his watch. "Do you have exercise clothes with you?"

"Yes." She frowned. "Why?"

"I want to take you downstairs and show you the gym on the seventh floor. I think you'll like it."

They gathered up the meal debris, and Harry stuffed it all in the metal trash can in the kitchen. "Meet me in the foyer in fifteen minutes," he said. And then he disappeared.

Cate had to scramble. Because she possessed at least as much vanity as the next woman, she chose the brand-new black spandex pants with the turquoise-and-black cropped top she had packed for her honeymoon. The bottoms hit her just below the knee. The tank top accentuated her modest boobs.

She added lightweight sneakers that matched. Because she didn't know how serious Harry was about this exercise/gym thing, she pulled her hair back in a ponytail.

It was the tiniest of victories to realize she beat him to the foyer. He showed up sixty seconds later, stealing all the oxygen from the room. To be honest, she had mostly only seen Prescott Harrington in suits and dress clothes in the past. In fact, she couldn't think of a single time he had appeared in casual wear.

Now she had to hide her shock. She knew he was young

and fit. Still, she'd had no notion how ripped he was. His black athletic pants accentuated his long legs. He wore sneakers with no socks. The heather-gray Emory University T-shirt strained across an impressive chest.

When he saw her, something in his eyes flickered. A spark of reaction? Her clothes were modest by any standard.

Since she had been watching her calories and working out for weeks ahead of the wedding, she knew she looked her best. Not that she wanted to impress Harry. Not at all. But if that really *was* admiration she saw in his quickly shuttered gaze, it was a balm to her bruised pride.

"Let's go," he said.

When they exited the elevator on the seventh floor, neat brass placards pointed the way to the workout room. Harry's building was top-notch all the way. She knew these huge apartments were not rentals. The residents owned their fancy digs, much like the occupants of upscale residential buildings in the heart of Manhattan.

The after-dinner hour was probably not peak time for working out. Harry and Cate had the gym to themselves. It wasn't as large as a commercial facility, but it wasn't small either.

"What are we doing here?" Cate asked. She saw ellipticals, treadmills, free weights and a wide assortment of fancy machines that targeted specific areas of the body.

Harry pointed to the far corner. "I'm gonna show you how to box with a punching bag."

"Um…" Cate wrinkled her nose. "This might be a good time to tell you I'm not particularly coordinated. Back in high school, they let me be a cheerleader, but not a rifle girl. And don't even mention marching band."

"*Let* you be a cheerleader? Come on, Cate. You were born

for the job. You're gorgeous and outgoing, and you fit the profile."

She frowned. "Why do I feel like I've just been insulted?"

"Not at all," he insisted. "Jason has told me a lot about you over the years...like the fact that you spent all your summers in Blossom Branch and were Miss Georgia Peach Blossom four years running."

"All I had to do for that title was sit on the back of a convertible and wave. Easy peasy. Now, you're talking about me punching a target that moves. This won't end well."

His grin was remarkably cheerful. "Trust me," he said. "Some people say I'm tightly wound. The punching bag helps me loosen up and relax. And as it happens, it's good for dealing with anger, too."

She watched as he walked to a low cabinet, studied something inside and pulled out a pair of boxing gloves— black with pink trim.

"Oh, goody," she said, laying the sarcasm on thick. "Why does everyone think women need to wear pink?"

"Forget about the color. You're getting ready to beat the crap out of this bag."

"If you say so." She was dubious at best.

Harry stood in front of her. "Hold up your hands, palms toward you."

When Cate did as he asked, Harry slid the first glove on her left hand and laced it up. Then he repeated the procedure with her right hand.

"I feel ridiculous," she complained.

"You won't soon. I think you'll like this."

"And are you going to *suit up*?"

"Nope. It's all about you today."

His bent head was close to hers as he pulled and tightened

the laces. All his attention was focused on his task. Cate wasn't sure he even noticed her. But the reverse was not true.

It was hard to ignore a man like Harry. When she was twenty-one, the years between them would have seemed like an impossible divide. But now that she was twenty-five, Harry definitely felt like her contemporary. Almost. At least when he wasn't poking fun at her and making her feel young and dumb.

"All set," he said.

She sucked in a breath, startled by the teasing warmth in his gray-eyed gaze. "Is that it? End of lesson?"

"Nope." He took her by the arm and pulled her toward the bag. "There are a variety of punches. We'll start with the two easiest. Here, look at my hand."

"Okay."

He pointed to the area between his first and second row of knuckles. "This is the part that's supposed to hit the bag dead on. Otherwise, you run the danger of spraining your wrist."

"Where do I stand?"

He put his hands on her shoulders briefly and squared her up in relation to the bag. "For this first one, the straight punch, you want to be at arm's length. Then you simply punch straight. The name says it all. And hit with the part I showed you."

Cate felt ridiculous. "What is this supposed to accomplish?"

"You can pretend the bag is Jason."

She sighed. "I've never hit anyone in my life. That won't work."

Harry seemed stymied. Then he nodded. "Fair enough. Let's go at it another way. Tell me the things you're angry about."

"Do I have to?"

He shrugged. "No. But it might help. This isn't a game. I'm serious."

She inhaled and let out the breath slowly. "I'm angry at all those people who saw me get dumped."

"Why them? What did they do?"

"They were *there*. I never said all my anger was rational."

"Then imagine the crowd. See their faces on the bag. Hit them."

She tried, she really did. Carefully, she pulled back her elbow and punched wildly. On the plus side, she made contact. The bad news was, it hurt. All the way down to her gut.

"Ouch, Harry. I thought this was supposed to help."

"It will. Hit them again."

For a moment, she closed her eyes and remembered. All those people watching her. The embarrassment. The shame. *Wham.*

"Better," Harry said. "What else?"

"I'm angry with Jason."

"For dumping you?"

She thought about that for a full thirty seconds. If he did what he did for reasons that were clear to him, she couldn't fault that. "I'm angry that he waited until the last damn minute," she cried. Then she put all her weight into the next swing and slugged the bag hard.

The shock reverberated up her arm all the way to her shoulder.

But it felt good.

She swung again. And again. By the fourth punch she was sweating. "Teach me another one," she panted.

Harry nodded. His gaze was hooded, his face wiped clean of all expression. "This next one is a hook. You want to get right up against the bag. In fact, you can rest your cheek against the side you're not punching." He wasn't wearing gloves, but he demonstrated. *Bam. Bam. Bam-bam.* "Remember, don't bend your wrist. But you're coming from the side this time."

Cate felt winded, even though the physical effort she had expended thus far was minimal. It was scary to let all her emotions rise to the surface.

Maybe Harry understood a little of what she was feeling. He brushed the back of his hand across her cheek, his smile encouraging. "Don't be afraid. A little anger never hurt anyone, not in this setting."

She nodded, suddenly at the mercy of those damn tears. The fact that she couldn't control them brought the anger back. Resting her forehead against the bag, she swung her right fist in for a hard punch.

But it felt so weak. She didn't want to be weak. So what if a thousand-plus friends and family and strangers witnessed her abject humiliation? She was strong enough to get past it.

Umph. She slugged as hard as she could. A right hook, then a left, then a right again. Her moves felt like slow motion. That made her angry, too.

Rage welled up inside her, burning away the sick feelings of hurt and failure. This had happened to her. No changing that. But it wasn't the end. Her eyes burned, and her throat hurt. She swung and punched. Again. And again. The anger was terrifying and liberating.

Umph. Umph. Umph.

Her hands hurt. Her whole body hurt. There was a loud roaring in her ears. She felt like she was in a tunnel with no way out.

At last, she realized something was happening. Harry's hands were on her shoulders, pulling her backward. She fought him momentarily. "I'm not done," she said, the words barely audible.

He turned her around and pulled her close to his chest. "Yes, Catie-girl, you are."

She broke down then. If she thought she had cried before,

it was nothing compared to this. The sobs were raw and wild, and they hurt like a thousand hammers.

Harry stroked her back, her hair. His big frame was all that stood between her and the abyss.

Seven

In the midst of the storm, a tiny rational part of her psyche hovered above the scene and wondered if she was hysterical or merely grief-stricken. Was there a difference?

It was impossible to gauge how long the hurricane of emotions lasted. In the end, she simply ran out of steam. Limp and exhausted, she leaned into him, her cheek against his collarbone.

He smelled nice, and he felt solid. Comforting. Unchangeable.

She barely noticed when he scooped her up and carried her over to a weight bench. He sat down with her in his arms. Her head rested against his shoulder. Harry struggled briefly, tugged his T-shirt to his armpits, and used it to dry her face. "Maybe I went too far," he said quietly. "The punching bag has great power. Not to be used lightly."

"You're teasing me now."

"Yep."

She managed a smile. "Did I look like a maniac?"

"Not at all," he said solemnly. "You're one of the few

women I know who can get all sweaty and gross and still be beautiful."

"That's a backhanded compliment if I ever heard one."

He moved a damp strand of her hair from her temple and tucked it behind her ear. "I'm pretty sure you've been getting compliments about your looks since you were a toddler. But there's something you need to understand."

Cate tensed involuntarily, braced for criticism about being the clichéd blonde, rudderless beauty queen. "Oh?"

A big sigh lifted his chest and let it fall. "You are so much more than your beauty, Cate. You're smart and funny and kind. From what I've seen and things Jason has told me over the years, your most impressive gift is your ability to bring people together and make them feel special."

She literally didn't know how to respond to that.

Harry ignored her stunned silence and went on. "Case in point, your two friends Gabby and Leah. Leah was terribly shy, and Gabby barely skated by on cobbled-together scholarships. Without the way you took them under your wing, their college experiences at UGA would have been very different. You had every reason to be the stereotypical mean girl, but you weren't."

"Um..."

Harry went on. "You have a good heart, Cate. Whatever you decide to do next, wherever you go, you're going to be fine. More than fine."

Tears threatened again, but this time, they were born of positive emotion. "Thank you," she said, scrambling to her feet and blinking away the evidence of how much his words had rocked her. "I appreciate the vote of confidence."

Harry stood and pulled his shirt down, but not before she glimpsed his flat stomach and sculpted abs. The sight gobsmacked her. She'd often thought of him as a cerebral businessman. Clearly, she hadn't appreciated the whole package. Not that she meant *package* in the masculine sense. *Oh, Lord.*

He eyed her with a smile. "Are we done punching things?"

"Oh, yes. It was therapeutic, but I can already tell I'll be sore tomorrow. Worth it, though. Definitely worth it."

In the elevator, she felt remarkably awkward. Yet at the same time, her gratitude toward Harry overwhelmed her.

As he unlocked the door and they entered the apartment, she turned to him impulsively. "Would you like to watch a movie? I saw microwave popcorn in your kitchen."

Harry hesitated. In much the same way Jason had at their wedding. That tiny physical·"tell" crushed her.

His face was oddly blank. "Unfortunately, I still have work to do," he said, jingling his keys in his hand. "I've gotten a little behind this week."

Because I've been busy rescuing your pitiful, sorry ass.

He didn't say those words aloud, but he might as well have.

Once again, the gap between them grew. Harry the confident, successful architect, and Cate, who—from his perspective— was too young, too immature, too everything.

She swallowed the pain and smiled cheerily, though her facial movements felt wooden. "No worries. I think I'll have a girls' night. Redo my manicure, watch *The Bachelor.*"

Cate was desperate to escape, but Harry stood between her and the hallway.

He frowned. "One last thing. I need you to know that you can stay here as long as you want. Going back to your parents' house doesn't sound like a good option. Nor is Jason's place, obviously. But until you have a plan, it doesn't make sense to rent an apartment or buy a house. My place is huge. I work all the time. I'll barely notice you're here."

I'll barely notice you're here. There it was again.

Cate winced inwardly. Harry hadn't intended his words to be hurtful. He was only trying to help.

But the inference was clear. She wasn't really on his radar.

Why that pained her...why that mattered, she wasn't exactly sure.

"Thank you," she said. Easing past him, she headed for her temporary quarters. "Good night, Harry."

The next morning Cate made two phone calls she had been dreading. Actually, she chickened out and texted.

Any chance you're both free for lunch today?

Leah answered first.

Yes! Just tell me where and when!

Gabby's reply came a couple of minutes later.

I'm slammed but I could do The Creperie at one.

Cate was unsettled to realize she'd been hoping they would both say no. Why? They were her dearest friends.

Unfortunately, she still felt raw. Like a fresh wound exposed to the elements, her emotional state was tender. Her friends would want explanations. She had no idea what to say.

Nevertheless, she had to do this.

Works for me, she said.

Leah sealed the deal. Me too.

Cate showed up at the restaurant early. She wanted to get a somewhat private table, and she wanted to steel herself against any renegade emotions that might sabotage her.

Ten minutes after she was seated, Gabby and Leah walked

in together. Had they planned that? Were they intending to *handle* an awkward situation?

Cate stood and smiled. "Hi, you two."

Her friends' tight hugs threatened her composure.

Leah sat down and hung her purse on the back of the chair. "We've been worried about you," she said bluntly. "We've gone back and forth between giving you your space and wanting to stage an intervention."

Cate frowned. "Intervention?"

Gabby didn't have a purse. Her figure-hugging black pants had pockets where she stuffed her keys. She laid her phone on the table. "There's a rumor that Prescott Harrington kidnapped you."

Cate's cheeks reddened. "That's ridiculous. He was outside the church, gave me a ride, and he's been letting me crash at his place."

A flash of hurt crossed Leah's expressive face. "You know I would have been glad to have you."

"I get that," Cate said. "And I appreciate it. But Harry's place is huge. And he left me alone to grieve. The fact that he didn't have any kind of relationship with me made things easier. I didn't have to put on a show."

Gabby's eyes narrowed. "A show?"

"I'm sorry. That came out wrong. It's just that if I had stayed with either of you, I would have tried to be *okay*—so I wouldn't upset or worry you. With Harry, I didn't have to pretend."

Her two friends stared at her with almost identical expressions of bafflement.

Leah pursed her lips. "You didn't think we knew how to deal with a friend in crisis?"

Gabby piled on. "You didn't trust us to offer you the support you needed?"

Cate was exasperated. "*This* is what I'm talking about. I've been a total mess. Too much to consider your feelings. I'm not sure Harry even *has* tender feelings, so I stayed there. End of story."

"Fine," Leah said grumpily. "Let's order. I need to eat."

The conversation advanced in jerks and starts. Occasionally, somebody made a joke. The other two laughed. But sitting in the middle of the table was the huge, impossible-to-forget elephant that was Cate's aborted wedding.

Leah introduced the first real moment of fun. "Tell me you've heard the big news out of Blossom Branch."

Cate shook her head. "I've been kind of busy," she said wryly.

"My mother hasn't mentioned anything." Gabby frowned. "What is it?"

"Britain Sheffield was back in town earlier this spring. Incognito."

Britain was one of Blossom Branch's most famous sons. A wildly successful actor.

"What for?" Cate asked.

"You remember the drama teacher at the high school? The one who helped Britain get his start? The guy died, and Brit came back for the funeral. While he was home, he reconnected with his high school sweetheart, and now she's flown off to the other side of the world with him while he's making movies."

"Wow," Gabby said, her expression mildly envious. "I'm not much of a romantic, but even I admit that's a fairy tale."

Leah sighed. "I know. It's the perfect romance."

"Lucky them." Cate hoped her comment didn't sound sarcastic. It was hard to hear a story like that and not compare it to her own tale of woe.

Her friends changed the subject quickly as if belatedly aware that Cate didn't want to hear any more.

They had all three ordered chicken and mushroom crepes with a green salad. Cate thought it was a good sign that she was starving. She cleared her plate down to the last crumb.

No one tried to initiate a serious conversation while they were eating. But finally, Gabby looked at her watch. "I have twenty more minutes. Tell us what you want to say, Cate. Obviously, it was a terrible day."

Something seemed *off* with Gabby, but maybe Cate was imagining things. "Well," she said. "I don't know how much you could hear..."

"Not enough," Leah said, aggrieved. "We've been in the dark all week. No one can reach Jason."

"That's because he's in Peru." Cate took a deep breath. "Jason said he loves me, but he's not *in love* with me. That's it. End of story." Inwardly, she felt enormous relief. This time she managed the explanation without falling apart. Surely that was progress.

Leah's face always reflected every emotion. At the moment, she appeared torn between indignation and sorrow. "Is there another woman?"

Cate counted to ten. That question was really starting to annoy her. "No," she said flatly. "Jason and I made a mistake, that's all."

Gabby pushed her plate aside and crossed her arms over her chest. "Or maybe another man for you?"

Leah glanced at Gabby. "Oh, surely not."

"Thank you, Leah," Cate said wryly. "And no. Not another guy."

"But you've known each other since you were practically babies," Leah said. "How could this happen?"

Cate took the question seriously, even though it might have been rhetorical. "I think maybe that was the problem. We were too comfortable with each other, and we let the wedding plans turn into an out-of-control snowball. Or Indiana Jones's boulder. Jason must have had doubts for weeks or months but couldn't bring himself to break things off."

Gabby glared. "Well, he picked a hell of a time to grow some balls."

"Gabby!" Leah was shocked. Her cheeks reddened. "That's a terrible thing to say."

"To be fair," Cate pointed out, "he didn't want to hurt me. Or disappoint our friends and family. I think he probably agonized over it for a very long time." Chagrin overwhelmed her as she realized that she, too, was defending Jason. Partly because she now saw that she was at least partly to blame for what happened. She hadn't been paying enough attention to the man she thought she wanted to marry. Not enough to see that he had doubts.

What a mess.

Gabby looked at her watch and stood abruptly. "I'm sorry I can't stay longer. But I have to get back to work." She tossed a twenty on the table. "Call me, Cate, and we'll talk again soon."

And then she was gone...

Cate stared at her tall, beautiful friend walking away. There was impatience in every step. "Is it just me, or is something weird going on with her?"

Leah shrugged. "I don't know. I think she has a lot of stress at work."

"Maybe." Cate wasn't convinced. She'd gotten a definite antagonistic vibe from Gabby. It was hard to see how Gabby could be angry with Cate, but what other explanation was there? Except that maybe she resented shelling out money for a bridesmaid dress at a doomed wedding. Gabby had grown up with nothing. She didn't believe in waste.

This time, it was Leah who stood. "I'm so sorry, Cate," she

said, "but I have a dentist appointment in twenty minutes. I've postponed it twice, so I really need to show up this time. But come over to my place for a girls' night soon. Promise?"

"Of course," Cate said. "I would love that. You go on. I'm getting the check. Thanks so much for meeting me on short notice." She stood and hugged her friend, and then suddenly, she was alone again.

Somehow, even though her life had ground to a halt last Saturday, the rest of the world kept on turning.

She didn't want to go back to Harry's apartment and spend hours doing nothing. She needed a plan, a purpose. But it wouldn't jell.

As she realized she was near one of her favorite parks, she went there and found a bench in the shade. When she called her mother, Gillian answered, out of breath.

"Hey, Cate. Everything okay?"

The question struck Cate as odd. Did everyone think she was going to suddenly be back to normal? Maybe she was supposed to. Maybe getting left at the altar was a blip on the radar. Though to be scrupulously accurate, she had left Jason standing there and not the other way around.

But what choice did she have? When he said he didn't want to get married, she had panicked. What would she have done if Harry hadn't been there?

"I'm fine, Mama," she said. "I was just wondering if you'd talked to Grammy."

"Well, sort of," she said. "We've been texting. I had forgotten that Mom and Dad were heading off on a cruise after the wedding. Four weeks in the Mediterranean with a couple of their longtime friends. They won't be back until after the Fourth. But they said for you to use the hidden key to come and go as you please. They're happy to have you stay at the house as long as you like."

"Ah. That's nice." Her stomach curled. She had been look-ing forward to hugging her grandmother and believing that Grammy could make everything okay. And if not her, then surely Grandpa.

But they were gone when she needed them most.

That was hardly a fair description. Her grandparents had been around for all the important moments of Cate's existence, up to and including the infamous wedding. They couldn't be expected to put their lives on hold with the off-chance their granddaughter might show up unexpectedly.

"Well, thanks anyway, Mom," Cate said. "I appreciate you talking to her."

"Of course, darling. And your grandmother was serious about her offer. But I've got to run. We'll talk later."

Everyone was willing to talk later. But what about today?

Cate stared at her phone screen, bemused. According to her little green icon, she had 198 contacts stored, any one of whom she could dial right now.

The trouble was, she couldn't think of a single person who might understand her situation and want to help.

Suddenly, her phone dinged. Her heart jumped when she saw it was a text from Harry.

It's the weekend. Despite all evidence to the contrary, I'm not a workaholic. Let's do something fun. What time are you coming back?

She smiled, even with the ongoing ache in her chest. This time last week she had been getting ready for her rehearsal dinner.

I'll be there in thirty minutes… She decided *not* to include a smiley face.

As she drove to Harry's, she gave herself a stern lecture. It wasn't his job to entertain her. He was only being nice.

On the other hand, if this was an olive branch after last night, she didn't want to be rude.

When she made it upstairs, Harry had already changed out of his suit and was wearing faded jeans and an ultrasoft cotton shirt, pale green, with the sleeves rolled to his elbows. His bare feet were tanned.

"Hey," he said, when she walked into the kitchen and found him. He was studying a menu app on his phone.

"Hi. You're home early." It was only four thirty.

He shrugged. "What good is it to be the boss if you can't goof off on a hot summer evening?" His smile took her off guard. It was natural and mischievous, and it unsettled her.

"What did you have in mind?"

"Well, you mentioned a movie last night. We could get Chinese delivered and do that."

Cate gnawed her bottom lip, pondering her options. Maybe it was time to go big or go home, as they say.

"Would you consider driving me to Blossom Branch?" she asked. Harry's apartment was luxurious and safe. But as long as she stayed here, the temptation would be to avoid any kind of decisions. That probably wasn't wise.

He raised an eyebrow. "Just for the evening?"

"No. I was thinking I might stay there a few weeks. My grandparents are out of town. They've offered me their house."

"I see."

"Don't be offended," she said quickly. "It has nothing to do with my not being comfortable here. I appreciate everything you've done for me."

He crossed his arms over his chest. "But?"

She shrugged. "Blossom Branch is home. I always feel grounded there. As if life itself is easier and more real. That's a fantasy, I suppose. But many of the happiest times of my life were spent in that house, that town."

"You don't have to sell me on the merits of Blossom Branch," he said, his voice dry. "But I have a counterproposal. Isn't your grandparents' house pretty large?"

"Yes. Five bedrooms. Why?"

"What if I go with you for a few days? I'll take my laptop. Sometimes a change of scenery is good for creativity."

She cocked her head and studied him. It stood to reason that he would be delighted to have her out from underfoot, his bachelor solitude undisturbed. "Oh. My. Gosh," she said, disgusted. "Jason made you promise to keep an eye on me, didn't he?"

Harry's cheekbones flushed, but he didn't say a word. He just stared at her.

Cate sighed. "I give you full dispensation. I won't go into a decline or take a bottle of sleeping pills, I swear."

Harry shot to attention, his posture rigid and angry. "Don't joke about it, Cate. If I thought that was even a remote possibility, I'd never let you out of this house."

"Sorry," she muttered. "My bad. But seriously, you don't have to babysit me. Why would you want to go to Blossom Branch?"

"I could see my mother," he said, his voice mild now.

She gaped. "You have a mother?"

"Everyone has a mother, Cate, even me."

Eight

They ended up leaving town in the worst of Friday afternoon traffic.

"I'm sorry," Cate said when they slowed to a halt on the 285 connector for the third time in forty-five minutes. "I guess we should have gone tomorrow."

Harry rubbed the back of his neck. "I know better. But we were both eager to get on the road."

It was true. They had each packed a suitcase in record time and tumbled into Harry's elegant luxury sedan. For a split second, the memories of riding in this car on her wedding day intruded, but Cate pushed them away, determined to enjoy the trip.

Harry shot her a sideways glance. "Will your grandparents be okay with me sharing the house with you?"

Cate frowned. "I don't see why not. Years ago, Blossom Branch was a hotbed of gossip, but lots of new people have moved to the area. Except for the immediate neighbors, I doubt anyone will notice we're in town."

The trip passed mostly in silence. Cate couldn't decide if

that was because the radio was on and they were enjoying the music, or whether Harry had purposely turned on the music to avoid awkward silences.

There was no getting around the fact that except for Jason, the two of them had little in common.

Even so, Cate found herself feeling happy. The emotion was such an anomaly given the past week that she had to poke and prod at it to see if it was real.

If she let herself think about Jason and the wedding, her warm feeling of contentment faded quickly.

She missed him.

But was she heartbroken? She couldn't tell.

Hurt? Yes. Humiliated? Yes. Humbled by the depth and width of her mistakes? Yes.

But heartbroken?

It was hard to say. And because the not knowing made her uneasy, she avoided the topic.

Blossom Branch was eighty miles northeast of Atlanta give or take. The longer they drove, the odder it seemed to be sharing this relatively short trip with Harry. Something about inhabiting the confines of a car with another person was intimate. You were breathing the same air. Sitting close.

Eventually, she picked up her phone out of habit and checked Instagram. Her mood plummeted a few minutes later when she scrolled past a post that made her gasp. Quickly, she dropped her phone into her purse on the floor of the car and wrapped her arms around her waist. As she stared out the side window, her chest ached with familiar despair. Is this who she was now? The poor little rich girl who got what she deserved for daring to have a splashy wedding?

Harry was not as disengaged as she thought. Even though she believed she was covering her emotions, he barked out a question. "What's wrong?"

She swallowed hard. "Nothing."

"Cate." His tone said he wouldn't tolerate evasion.

Her bottom lip trembled. Here it was again. The seesawing emotions. The whiplash from *I'm really okay* to *How do I ever get past this?* Just when she dared to enjoy a quiet afternoon car trip, karma decided Cate needed reminding of her true situation.

"It's nothing, really," she muttered.

Harry smiled, though his gaze stayed on the road. "Then tell me nothing."

"I saw an Instagram account," she said. "It's called #Atlanta-Fails."

"And?"

"They posted pictures from my wedding. You can see the bridesmaids and groomsmen. Jason and I are half-hidden in the back corner of the picture. The comments are brutal."

Harry suddenly turned the wheel and zipped off the road into a rest stop. He parked, left the engine running and half turned in his seat. "Let me see."

"It's not important," she said. She could feel the miserable blush that spread from her collarbone to her hairline. Harry had *been* at her wedding. This was no surprise. But revisiting her humiliation with him was somehow worse.

He held out his hand, his expression brooking no opposition. "Pull up the post and give me your phone."

She could have said no. Instead, she obeyed, her motions jerky as she handed over her cell.

Harry eyed the photo and slowly scrolled down the page. A dark flush appeared on his cheekbones. His big hand looked as if it could crush her phone into tiny, sharp pieces.

He shot her a look. "Fuck the haters," he said in a low, furious voice.

"Harry!" The profanity took her by surprise.

"I'm sorry, Catie-girl. You know it as well as I do. Social media gives people a license to be cruel without repercussions. Can you let this one go?"

"I don't know. Maybe. But the worst part is, someone Jason and I invited to our wedding either *did this* or *let it happen*. That makes me feel violated," she said quietly.

"Probably somebody's plus-one," he said, his face grim.

"Could be. You want to know the worst, heartbreaking part? About this whole situation?"

"Aside from you severing your relationship with Jason?"

She winced. "Yeah. Aside from that." His wry comment stung. "The worst part is I didn't even want to have a big wedding. Ever since I was a little girl, I always assumed I would get married in the small country church in Blossom Branch where Grammy and Grandpa had their ceremony. That church doesn't even have stained glass windows. Just clear panes where you can look outside and see blue skies and peach orchards."

"So why didn't you?"

She sighed. "Jason's parents and mine ruled that out. Once we put all their *must invites* on the list, it was already too big. Then Jason and I added our friends. And all the fringe relatives who had to be included. Plus, various business contacts. It went on and on."

Harry tossed her phone in the back seat. "Did it ever occur to *you* to put a stop to the wedding insanity? Be honest, Cate."

She thought back over the last year and a half. Lots of what she and Jason had done was fun. The planning. Visiting venues. Tasting cakes and other food. Choosing color schemes.

But if she was honest, there had been a few moments of panic.

"Yes," she said, staring out the windshield at a harried dad trying to stuff a toddler into his car seat. "After Christmas this past year, Jason and I had a fight. Over something stupid,

I can't even remember. I suddenly realized we were both really stressed out."

"So what happened?"

"I suggested a long weekend getaway. We went to Key West. It was cold and bleak in Atlanta. The trip south was great. But…"

"But what?"

"Jason seemed distracted the whole time."

"Did you talk to him?"

"No. Not really. I wanted to ask him if he had changed his mind about getting married, but I didn't have the nerve."

"You were subconsciously picking up on cues."

"Probably."

"Did *you* ever think about changing your mind?"

Her throat hurt. "Yes. Once or twice." She had never admitted that, even to herself. "But honestly, it seemed like an impossible proposition. We were so far down the road I couldn't see a way back. I told myself everything was fine… that I was letting my anxiety run away with me."

Harry shook his head slowly. "I suppose there's plenty of blame to go around. Your parents should have given you more guidance. And I had let myself get too busy with work to spend much time talking to Jason."

Cate turned and stared at Harry, her chin up. "Go ahead and say it. I was young and immature, and I let an unforgivable disaster unfold. *I* was the bride-to-be. *I'm* the one to blame."

She practically shouted that last bit.

Harry's face went still, the lines and planes wiped clean of emotion. She hated it when that happened. She had no clue what he was thinking.

Was he judging her again? Or inwardly shaking his head at her stupidity?

Why had she let him come with her to Blossom Branch?

The one person who knew for a fact she was a screw-up. Was she a glutton for punishment? Or was she simply afraid to be alone?

Without warning, Harry leaned forward, put his hands on her shoulders and placed a kiss on her forehead. Then he released her to slide back into his seat. "Don't make a bad situation worse, Cate."

The tension in the car—and that kiss—made her feel all wobbly. "How do you mean?"

He drummed his fingers on the steering wheel. "You've reached a point where it's time to move forward. Looking back might give you answers and closure, but your future is on the line now. You can't change what happened. I know it will be a long time before you forget. But you don't want to ruin your new life by..."

"By what?" she demanded. Harry was so seldom at a loss for words, she was startled.

His crooked smile flashed briefly. "By wallowing in the mud."

They got back on the road after that. In twenty minutes, they reached the outskirts of town. Cate pondered Harry's words of advice even as they passed subdivisions that hadn't existed five or six years ago.

Thankfully, the central core of Blossom Branch remained the same. "Let's drive around and look at things," Cate said. "Before we go to my grandparents' house."

"Aren't you hungry?" Harry said.

"Getting there."

"Is the Peach Dog still in business?" he asked.

"Not during the winter, but maybe now that it's summer. Let's find out."

They were in luck. The old-timey hot dog stand was little more than a wooden shed painted pale orange and white. The sign on top boasted the business's mascot—a basset hound wearing a crown of peach blossoms. In addition to the usual toppings of chili and onions and condiments, the Peach Dog offered mouthwatering peach salsa, the ingredients of which were a well-kept secret.

Harry didn't strike Cate as the type of guy to eat in his car. Fortunately, there were two rickety picnic tables nearby. Cate grabbed bottles of water out of the trunk while Harry paid for their dinner.

When she sat down across from him and took her first bite, she groaned. "This is the taste of my childhood," she said.

"Mine, too," he said, carefully stuffing one end of the hot dog into his mouth. "Though it's been far too long since I've indulged. How old is that guy, anyway?"

"At least a hundred. And tell me why the health department hasn't shut him down a long time ago. That setup can't meet code."

Harry chuckled, wiping ketchup from his chin. "I'd say the health inspector would get run out of town if he or she tried to close this particular establishment. It's an institution."

The heat of the day had abated. A breeze from the nearby river carried the scents of honeysuckle and newly mown grass. Cate loved the city, but the pace of life in Blossom Branch was undeniably sweet.

When they were done, they tossed their trash in the large can by the vendor stall and walked back to the car. "Now what?" Harry asked, resting his arm on top of the car and looking at her with a quizzical glance.

"Let's drive beside the park."

Long ago, the town had been established around a beautiful green space two blocks long, similar to a university quad. In the very center of the park stood a charming gazebo.

On every side of the grassy rectangle, Blossom Branch's businesses thrived, most of them with a peach theme. Some were old and well established. Others came and went.

At the moment, Blossom Branch was in the midst of summer tourist season. People arrived in large numbers to buy fresh peaches and to shop in the charming town. And sometimes— to spend the night. Later, July and August would be marked by parades and artisan showcases. Cate and Harry had just missed the Peach Festival at the first of the month.

She lowered her window as Harry cruised the narrow streets. "I don't know why I don't come more often," she said. "I love it here."

"Me, too."

The truth was, Cate's grandparents came to Atlanta frequently, so she saw them on a regular basis. But for Cate, making time to visit Blossom Branch hadn't been a top priority since college. She regretted that now.

When they had satisfied Cate's curiosity, Harry turned at a stop sign and headed toward the address where Cate's grandparents had lived for five decades. Though only three streets from the center of town, the distance was enough to create a quiet lane where tricycles and basketball goals filled driveways.

Harry pulled into the carport and shut off the engine. "I assume you have a key," he said.

"About to…" Cate jumped out and stepped behind the house. In a tiny chink between bricks in the foundation, she found a familiar key chain. "Got it," she said, returning to the car.

Harry grabbed the two bags and followed Cate inside. "This is nice," he said.

Cate smiled. "Grammy and Grandpa updated over the years without sacrificing charm. Back when they bought this property, it was one of only a few occupied lots on the street. They built a big house, assuming they would have several children. But my mom ended up being an only."

"Where are we sleeping?" Harry asked.

"I don't think either of us would feel comfortable taking the main bedroom on this floor."

"Um, no." Harry shook his head.

"Well, upstairs there are two sets of bedrooms with Jack and Jill baths in between. If we each take one end of the house, we won't have to share."

"And I won't hear you snore," he said, deadpan.

"Be nice," she chided.

Harry just laughed.

After Cate adjusted the AC and turned on all the ceiling fans downstairs, they went up to make the second floor comfortable. The air was a little stale, but soon began to cool down.

Suddenly, out of nowhere, Cate felt awkward. What was she doing sharing a house with Prescott Harrington? This was weird, right? Shouldn't she be here with Gabby? Or Leah? Why was Harry feeling more and more important to her?

He put her bag in one of the bedrooms and turned to walk away.

"Wait," she said. "It's not late. Do you want to go for a walk? We spent a lot of time in the car."

He shook his head, his expression impossible to read. "I think I'll catch up on email. Do they even have internet?" he asked.

Cate stifled her disappointment. "Of course. My grandparents always keep up with the latest tech. They usually leave the password in the bedside table drawers. If you can't find it, let me know."

She and Harry were going to be sleeping far closer here than in his huge Atlanta apartment. But at the moment, the distance between them seemed impossibly wide.

"Good night," he said.

She fought the urge to ask him again about the walk. "We didn't make any breakfast plans."

Harry shrugged. "Let's be spontaneous. I'll see you in the morning."

When he was gone, Cate sighed and sat down on the bed. This had been "her" bedroom growing up. Becca's was the one on the other side of the bathroom. Sleeping in this cozy spot with the thick quilt and down pillows had produced a feeling of safety and contentment that hadn't been replicated before or since.

Not that she wanted to be a kid again. She didn't. But sometimes it would be nice to go back in time, even if only for a few days.

She unpacked her things, listening all the while for sounds of Harry's presence down the hall. Whatever he was doing, he was doing it quietly.

Because she was too unsettled to sleep, she changed into shorts and a sports bra, twisted her hair on top of her head, and slipped downstairs. At the last moment, she remembered she had left the key on top of her dresser.

It didn't matter. She wasn't going far. Leaving the door unlocked was no biggie.

Outside, the air felt fresh and sweet. It was dark now, but in the west, a hint of pink lingered, leftover from sunset. She started out walking, but soon, she felt the urge for speed. Maybe she was trying to run away from her problems or even her uncomfortable thoughts.

Either way, it felt good to push herself. Instead of venturing far afield, she simply circled a three-block section of the neighborhood. Occasionally she waved when she saw people enjoying the evening on their porches.

This idyllic existence had been her world for the first twelve years of her life. Even now, the memories stirred a restless longing in her heart. Not that she wanted to live here. Did she? Atlanta was home now, right? The fact that she wasn't sure made her antsy.

But this was what marrying Jason had represented to her. A chance to put down roots, to build a family, to carve out a place and build traditions of their own. He'd moved away at a young age also, but since his family had the lake house to come back to, he was equally in tune with Blossom Branch.

She realized suddenly that her thoughts of Jason hadn't curled her stomach in a painful knot. Despite what he had done, she still loved him. Maybe her mother was right. Maybe she and Jason had been more like friends with benefits than passionate lovers.

To be fair, Cate wasn't sure the passionate love found in books and movies existed. And if she were being excruciatingly honest, who wanted that? It seemed dangerous at best.

Look at her. Losing Jason was the most painful experience of her life.

If she had been madly, desperately in love with him, this whole wedding fiasco would have been even more devastating.

Nine

At last, sweaty and exhausted, she headed for the house.

Only when she tried to open the door did she remember that it sometimes locked automatically. That was why her grandparents had hidden the key in the first place. The tiny mechanism on the knob was finicky.

No problem. She dialed Harry's number. This was embarrassing, but hardly at the top of the list.

He didn't answer. Not even when she tried a second time and a third.

Several possibilities presented themselves. He could be asleep already or in the shower. Worst of all, he might have silenced his phone for the night.

And he had no clue Cate was outside.

Damn.

She debated her options. None were ideal. Though she hadn't set the alarm when she left, she knew all the downstairs windows were locked tight. Grandpa would have done that before leaving on vacation.

And then she remembered. When she and Harry had first

gone upstairs tonight, Cate had raised both windows at the ends of the hallway to get air flowing while they waited for the AC to lower the temperature.

She remembered pulling both windows back down later, but she didn't remember turning the locks. Oh, please. Let that be true. She might have secured them automatically without thinking about it.

On the end of the house where she was sleeping, there wasn't so much as a bush to aid a burglar. But near Harry's bedroom, a sturdy trellis supported her Grammy's prized American Beauty climbing roses.

When she was ten, Cate had scrambled halfway up that trellis on a dare from a friend in the neighborhood. Young Cate had chickened out and scuttled back down. Current Cate was fifteen years older and a lot heavier.

She glanced at her watch. It was almost eleven. As her daddy would say, it was time to fish or cut bait.

Carefully, she put one sneaker-clad foot on the bottom rung of the wooden trellis. It seemed solid enough. The crossbars were spaced twelve inches apart. Cate reached up with her right hand and moved her left foot to the next perch, all the while trying to avoid large thorns.

It was an impossible task. Not the climbing. That was going reasonably well. But her attempt not to crush her grandmother's rose blossoms and at the same time protect her fingers and arms and lower legs was hopeless.

Doggedly, she moved higher. One thorn caught the top of her knuckle and dug in painfully. "Ouch, damn it," she muttered, clinging with one hand while she sucked the deep gouge.

Quickly, she had to put both hands back on the trellis or risk falling. This wasn't as easy as tackling the climbing wall at the gym.

She was trying to be quiet. Waking the neighbors was not the way to keep a low profile. Even worse would be having someone call the police.

At last, she reached the window on the second floor. Not for a thousand dollars would she risk looking down. Though she wasn't particularly afraid of heights, no point in courting danger.

The muscles in her arms trembled and ached. Supporting her own weight was no easy task. She was tired and out of breath. So much for thinking she was in great shape.

She clung to the trellis, giving her heartbeat a chance to slow down. When she thought she could handle the one-arm thing again, she reached up and shoved at the base of the window.

Amazingly, it budged. Not a lot. But enough to let her know it wasn't locked. Hallelujah.

Unfortunately, this was going to be a slow process. She clung to the trellis yet again to catch her breath. After a few moments, she tried to get her fingertips under the bottom edge of the window frame.

The house was old. The windows were old. The tracks weren't smooth. Cate panted now. The window moved upward maybe half an inch.

She needed to be able to push harder, but from her precarious position, she didn't have enough leverage.

All the pain and the disappointment of the last week came crashing down over her. Just as she felt a twinge of *why me* self-pity, another part of her pushed back. *She could do this.*

But everything changed in an instant when a loud scraping noise startled her so badly, she nearly lost her balance and tumbled to the ground.

Harry opened the window and stuck his head out, his expression incredulous. "What in the hell are you doing?"

Busted. Cate's first instinct was to laugh hysterically. But she wasn't out of danger yet.

"I locked myself out of the house," she said.

"And you didn't think to call me?" His annoyingly superior tone questioned her intelligence.

"I did call. *Three* times. I assumed you were either asleep or in the shower. But since you seem to be fully dressed and wide-awake, I guess you were screening your calls?"

He winced at her sarcasm, and his expression changed. "Had my headphones on with 'do not disturb,'" he said gruffly. "I was listening to a podcast. How long have you been hanging out here? Give me your hand."

It was a bad time for Cate to discover a fear of falling. "I don't know if I can," she said, still breathless. The combination of adrenaline and exertion left her feeling woozy. Her knuckles ached from gripping the trellis so tightly.

Harry smiled down at her. "Trust me, Catie-girl. I've picked up heavier things than you."

"I don't want to tear my rotator cuff. Or dislocate my shoulder."

He chuckled. "Obviously you've been out here awhile if you're analyzing all the possible outcomes. What if we do a slow and gentle up and over?"

Cate blinked the sweat out of her eyes. Why did his words sound like a description of sex? She must be losing it.

"Okay," she grumbled. "I'll try. But swear you won't drop me."

"I swear."

She let go with her right hand and changed her mind at the last minute. That was backward. Clearly, she needed to give Harry her *left* hand and use her stronger arm to hang on.

With both hands clutching the trellis, she gave herself a

pep talk. If she could do this, she could take a shower and go to bed.

"Here goes," she mumbled.

"Wait," Harry said urgently. "Can you climb up one more rung? That would make what we're about to do easier."

Her legs were wobbly. She was pretty sure she was bleeding in at least a dozen different places. "I'll try."

Though nothing in her body wanted to move, she made herself bend a knee, lift a leg, find a foothold and heft herself upward. Now at least her head was above the windowsill.

Harry leaned down, his face practically touching hers. "Good girl."

They were so close, Cate could have kissed him easily. Not that she wanted to. Of course, she didn't. This was cross, bossy, arrogant Harry. Not Jason.

She offered him her fingers. He reached down and gripped her forearm in two big hands.

"Don't *you* fall out of the window," she cried, suddenly panicked.

"I've got my feet braced. Nobody is going to fall. But you've got to let go of the trellis completely."

"I can't," she whispered.

At this point, she probably had splinters in her palm. The fingers of her right hand were permanently curled. Even with Harry holding one of her arms, she was scared, so scared. It was a heck of a long way to the ground.

When he spoke, his breath brushed her ear. "Take your right arm and curl it behind my neck. I'll do the rest."

Letting go of her grandmother's trellis was the second hardest thing Cate had faced in the last seven days. Slowly, she told her right hand to relax and release. For a split second, she wobbled in midair. Then, with all her might, she flung her arm skyward and wrapped it around Harry's warm, solid neck.

Now only her feet were on the trellis.

Harry grunted as he started to drag her inside.

It wasn't comfortable for either of them.

The deadweight pull must have been agony on his back. Cate wasn't exactly having a good time either as her belly scraped over the windowsill and both knees knocked against the side of the house.

After what seemed like forever, but must have been only minutes, Harry fell backward, taking Cate with him. They landed in a heap, battered and bruised, and—in Cate's case— bleeding.

Harry's chest rose and fell with his labored breathing. He put his hands on her cheeks. The hall light was on, so she could see every expression in his silvery steel eyes.

"Don't you ever," he said, struggling to breathe. "Don't you ever scare me like that again."

"Duly noted."

She was plastered against his body in a very inappropriate fashion. But she was so exhausted and sore, she couldn't find the energy to move.

Harry didn't seem in a hurry either.

His face was flushed, but that was probably from exertion. "Do you enjoy rescuing people?" she asked.

His classically sculpted, masculine lips twitched. "Not particularly. But for you I seem to make an exception."

And then something bizarre and stunning and inexplicable happened. *Another* part of Harry's body twitched. And grew.

Cate froze, mortified. Nothing personal, right? It was a mechanical response. Something that happened to guys.

She swallowed hard. "I should get up, I think."

Every trace of humor fled Harry's face. Those pewter eyes were blank, though a muscle in his jaw moved. "Probably."

"No problem." She gave the blithe assurance, totally ignoring the state of her aching body. Carefully, she moved onto her hands and knees and scooted backward.

When she was standing, Harry looked up at her and cursed. "What the hell happened to you?" He rolled to his feet and took both of her hands in his, extending her arms.

"Grammy's roses challenged me to a duel. I lost." Now that Cate was safely inside the house, all her various cuts began to sting and burn.

"I'd say so. Come to the bathroom," he said. "We've got to get you cleaned up. Those could get infected."

Cate was perfectly capable of washing up. But the last forty-five minutes had been stressful. She closed the lid on the toilet and sat down in a kind of trance as Harry found a bottle of hydrogen peroxide under the sink.

When he began to clean her battle wounds one at a time, she flinched and protested. But Harry was a determined medic.

Her arms and hands had taken the worst of it.

Harry frowned. "You don't want Band-Aids, do you? There are so many places, you'll look like a mummy."

"No. I'll be fine."

What was making her feel faint was having Harry so close as he bent his head and tended to her cuts. He smelled like the leather in his car. Masculine and expensive. He wore that same Emory T-shirt, only this time, with thin navy sleep pants. His feet were bare.

"We'll do your legs over the tub," he said.

Dutifully, she swung around and propped her legs across the side of the tub. Harry used half a bottle of liquid as he poured the peroxide over each and every scrape.

At last, it was over. He dried her arms and legs with a clean towel.

Cate yawned as she stood. "Thanks, Harry. Don't wait on me for breakfast. I have a feeling I'll sleep in. There's always coffee in the freezer and probably some homemade cinnamon rolls. Grammy would tell you to help yourself."

She was babbling because she was nervous. As she tried to sidle past him out of the bathroom, Harry touched her shoulder. "Hold on. One more."

He pointed at her bare midriff. Her cropped spandex top ended a good nine inches above her low waistband. Right in the center of her abdomen, a particularly vicious thorn had gouged a path above her navel…like a drunken comet traversing the uncharted sky that was her belly.

Harry picked up the peroxide again. "Oh, no," Cate said quickly. Something about the thought of his fingers brushing her stomach sucked all the air out of the room. "Leave it," she said firmly. "I'll wash it when I take my shower."

He shrugged. "Sure."

She paused in the doorway. "Thank you. I always seem to be saying that to you."

He scowled. "I don't need thanks. But maybe I should have a key, too?"

"Of course. You should find an extra in the drawer under the coffeepot. I'll keep the one that was hidden out back." She hesitated. Something about the intimacy she and Harry shared made her want to bring her ex-fiancé back into the equation. "Have you heard any more from Jason?"

Harry's face changed. Cate couldn't explain how, but she saw it. He nodded slowly, his lips pressed together. "Yes. He's having a great trip. Spectacular weather. Exciting photographs."

Cate nodded slowly. "I'm glad." She gnawed her bottom lip. "Did he use my ticket or is he alone?"

"Alone. As far as I know." Harry's jaw tightened. "Why does it matter? He wouldn't have taken another woman."

"I know that," Cate said impatiently. "I guess I was hoping he'd have invited a friend. So he wouldn't be by himself."

"Some people enjoy solitude."

Those four words sounded like a warning. "People like you?" She stared at Harry, trying to see past that wall of silvery gray. How could one man's eyes be so opaque, even in such close quarters?

"Yes. People like me."

Her temper, usually dormant, bubbled over. "You don't have to babysit me, Harry. Go back to Atlanta in the morning. I'm not going to have a nervous breakdown, and I'm perfectly capable of staying alone for however long it takes me to figure out what comes next."

He tapped one of her injuries with a careless flick of his finger. "Your recent exploits would say otherwise."

Her gaze narrowed. Anger fizzed in her veins and pounded in her temples. "On my wedding day I wasn't entirely coherent, but didn't I say something about hating you?"

Harry's smile was insolent. Mocking. "You might have mentioned it."

"Well, now I remember why. You have a god complex. It's very annoying. I can get along fine without you now. You're free to go."

"Do I bother you by being here?"

Did he bother her? What kind of question was that? Her breath caught in her throat. She sensed danger in the air, though she couldn't say why. "I don't care either way," she said, lying to his face. "But I'm not your responsibility. I'm a competent, capable, fully grown woman."

Harry's gaze dropped for a split second to her breasts and then returned to her face. He took a step closer. "Competent adults don't climb rickety trellises in the middle of the night," he said. The words came at her like tiny bullets, puncturing her self-esteem.

She took a step closer, too. "It's not rickety," she yelled. "My grandpa is a very good carpenter."

Suddenly, she and Harry were in touching distance again. Some part of her marveled at how long his eyelashes were. In one split second of self-awareness, she realized with horrified insight that she either wanted to punch him or kiss him. What kind of monster was she?

Was he staring at her mouth? Was that yearning she saw on his face? Maybe she really had hit her head on the way up. That was the only explanation for this insanity.

"Harry," she whispered.

"Cate." The single word was gravelly. It sent a frisson of *something* down her spine.

The hour was late. There had been a lot of adrenaline and feelings flying around. No way in hell was she going to do something stupid so soon after her aborted wedding. Harry would use her flightiness to mock her or point out that she was a *kid* who didn't know her own mind.

Part of her wanted to stay and see what happened. Wanted it rather desperately, in fact. But it was the very depth of her fascination with Harry's tense, volatile posture that convinced her to take a step back. And another.

"Good night," she said. And she fled.

Ten

She was going to have to buy Grammy a new set of sheets.

When Cate woke up and saw all the little traces of blood on the bed linens, she felt like one of the walking dead. Even worse was the way her arm muscles screamed at her when she tried to use them.

Last night she had showered and changed into a soft T-shirt and a clean pair of undies. Then she had taken a couple of ibuprofen and crawled into bed. Falling asleep hadn't been a problem. But she had tossed and turned during the night. Her dreams were bizarre.

Because her bedroom faced east and she hadn't closed the drapes, the morning sun woke her far too early. She pulled the pillow over her head and tried to go back to sleep, but it was no use—especially with the smell of coffee permeating the house.

She might not be a coffee drinker, but she loved the way it smelled.

Once she was up and dressed in jeans and a cute top, she

grabbed her phone and did a search for local masseuses. There were two. Maybe she could grab an early appointment.

She got lucky on her second try.

Last night still felt weird, so she wasn't eager to run into Harry. She waited until she heard his footsteps coming to the second floor and his bedroom door opening and closing.

Then she sneaked down the staircase, avoiding all the creaky spots, and left the house. She didn't need Harry's car. It was a gorgeous day for a walk, and not nearly as hot as it would be later in the afternoon.

Once she reached the town square, she felt guilty, so she sent him a text. Running errands. Be back after lunch. That was vague enough. It said loud and clear that she was out and about doing her own thing.

No need to be rude. But she also wanted to send the message that he needed to back off and let her take care of herself. He'd brought all his fancy work-computer stuff. The aggravating man had plenty to keep him busy, even if it *was* the weekend.

Her masseuse turned out to be a gentle giant who was a shade older than Harry. Cate had seen male therapists before, so it didn't bother her. "I'll do Swedish today, not deep tissue," she said.

He chuckled as he hit Play on a boom box and introduced the sounds of a mountain stream mixed with wind chimes. "Too much ambition at the gym?" he asked.

"Something like that."

When he saw the scratches on her arms and legs, he raised an eyebrow. "Cats?"

"Nope. Rosebushes."

It didn't take long for the familiar routines of the massage to relax her body *and* her psyche. She let her brain idle, choosing instead to listen to the music and feel her muscles unkink a bit at a time. By the time it was over an hour later, she felt like a new woman.

Since she had skipped breakfast, her stomach was growling by eleven. She wandered the streets, getting acquainted with newer businesses. A familiar mom-and-pop lunch place caught her eye. Locals were already starting to pour in, always a good sign.

She opened the door, waited to be seated in a scarred wooden booth and perused the menu. The restaurant was named for its signature dessert, the peach crumble.

Lots of companies in Blossom Branch did that, used peaches in their offerings or gave their businesses peach-themed names. Sometimes both. Tourists loved it. Staying on brand kept the small town alive and flourishing.

A female employee delivered food to a nearby table and then crossed the room with a notepad in her hand. The fifty-ish waitress looked familiar. "Shirley?" Cate beamed. "I can't believe you're still here." Cate remembered the server from summer visits with her grandparents.

The other woman pulled a pencil from behind her ear and laughed. "Where else would I go? Some things in this town may change, but not the Peach Crumble. They'll probably take me out of here feet first." She cocked her head. "What brings you in today? I heard your grandparents are out of town."

"Just a nostalgic visit," Cate said lightly.

Shirley's expression sobered. "Me and my big mouth. I heard about the wedding, darlin'. I'm so very sorry. But don't you worry. Lots of fish in the sea and all that."

"Thanks. I'm going to be okay. Blossom Branch is good for me."

"Damn skippy. If the world was more like Blossom Branch, I wouldn't be afraid to watch the evening news. You take care of yourself, Cate. And enjoy your visit."

Once Cate's BLT and Diet Coke were in front of her, she felt a teensy bit bad for avoiding Harry. He hadn't done anything wrong. It was Cate's weird reactions the night before that had caused the kerfuffle.

She wasn't exactly ghosting him. She had sent a text.

But she still felt guilty. For so many reasons that went far beyond Harry. She had let the wedding get out of control. She had suppressed her doubts about marrying Jason. And now that her original dreams were crushed, she felt guilty for being unable to find a new path.

During lunch, she studied her fellow diners. The old-timers were easy to spot. Farmers in overalls. Gray-haired women who knew the restaurant workers by name.

Then there were the more upscale residents of Blossom Branch. Many of them had bought vacation homes here. Weekend getaways from Atlanta. The women were fit and tanned. The men were glued to their phones, dealing with business calls.

And then, of course, there were the children and grand-children of the longtime residents. The newer generations who worked as mechanics or bank tellers or teachers. Blossom Branch was an eclectic meld of demographics. As far as Cate could tell, the mix worked.

Though the peach crumble sounded good, she decided to save that rich dessert for a later day. She had seen an ice cream shop a few doors down. A kid-size cone was just what she wanted.

Peaches and Cream sported an eye-catching red-and-white-striped awning over the doorway. When Cate entered the bright, airy shop, she was in luck. Only one other customer stood at the counter.

The flavors were handwritten in colorful chalk on a huge blackboard on the back wall and bordered with whimsical drawings. When it was Cate's turn, she smiled. "I'll have a kid cone of mint chocolate chip."

"Coming right up." The woman behind the counter was about Cate's age. She had strawberry blond, naturally curly hair, most of it tucked under a red-and-white ball cap that matched the awning.

"Are you the proprietor?" Cate asked. The woman's name tag said *Ginny Black*. Something about her confidence suggested she might be the owner, rather than an hourly employee.

Ginny handed over the cone. "I sure am."

Cate took a lick and sighed. "This is great."

"Thanks. Are you new in town? Just visiting?"

"Neither really. I lived here until I was twelve. But I haven't been back in some time. I'd forgotten how much I love Blossom Branch."

"This little town is a peach," Ginny said, grinning.

"Very funny." Cate rolled her eyes. "So what's it like to own a business here?"

Ginny wiped her hands on a clean towel. "Honestly? Good and bad. We're dead from the first of January until the end of March. April is so-so. Things start picking up in May. Right now, I'm busier than ever and will be through the October fall boost, but November is dismal. Then December shoppers come."

"So what you're saying is that you love it, but it's a struggle."

"How do you know I love it?" Ginny asked, her head cocked.

"Just a hunch. Did you do the chalkboards?"

"Yep. That's what happens to an art major who didn't get certified to teach." She laughed.

"We have that in common," Cate said with a rueful smile. As far as she could see, Ginny was happy with her situation.

"I suppose the freedom to be your own boss is nice. And the down months."

"It is." Ginny gave Cate a searching look. "I get the feeling these aren't idle questions."

"Busted." Cate smiled. "Seeing your cute shop has suddenly made me wonder about starting my own store here." She swallowed, forcing a light tone. "I was supposed to open a gallery in Atlanta with a friend, but the project fell through. I have some savings. What would you think about the kind of place where someone could buy a baby gift or a graduation present? Maybe a small piece of art for a bedroom or bathroom. That kind of thing." Cate realized this idea had been percolating in her subconscious ever since she decided to come to Blossom Branch.

Ginny's face lit up. "That sounds amazing. And honestly, we don't have anything exactly like that. You should call a Realtor. There's a place across the park that just came on the market."

"Seriously?"

"Only yesterday, I think. Someone will snap it up. You'll have to move fast."

"Thanks for the tip," Cate said. A gaggle of customers entered, so Cate headed for the door.

"Keep me posted," Ginny called out as she started dipping cones.

Thirty minutes later, Cate found herself hovering impatiently in front of a vacant shop front, waiting for the listing agent. Making this appointment was probably too impulsive, too spontaneous. But hadn't fate plopped this possibility in her lap? It wouldn't hurt to test it out.

So far, she'd been able to ascertain that an older couple had operated a furniture store at this address for three decades.

Now they were both retired. No one wanted to take over the existing business, so the assets had been sold.

She looked up the tax records online and studied the price. Everything seemed in order.

When the agent arrived, he introduced himself and unlocked the double front doors. "It's a large space," he said. "The previous owners used the second floor for inventory storage. But you could easily add a wall or two and have an apartment up there."

The more Cate explored, the more her veins fizzed with excitement. She had the strongest urge to call Harry and have him come look, too. But she stopped herself. She was a grown woman. She could make decisions without her rescuer overseeing every detail.

Still, doubts threatened. What did she know about starting a business on her own? She and Jason had planned to tackle a project together. Was that another dream Cate had to give up, or could she trust her instincts? Maybe this situation was easier and less messy than relationships. Besides, she had the significant cash wedding gift from her parents. They had insisted she keep it. That was the biggest hurdle.

When the tour was complete, Cate didn't let herself dither. She had to learn to follow her instincts. "I'd like to put down earnest money," she said, "and then consider my options for forty-eight hours and come up with an offer. Would that work?"

The man nodded. "I'm sure that will be fine but let me check with my clients."

Cate stood amidst the dusty, cluttered space and tried to imagine what it *could* look like. Wasn't this what she needed? A goal? A project? A place to pour her energies and her talents?

She wasn't part of a couple anymore. She was a single woman with her whole life ahead of her. Starting over after what happened last weekend might be hard, but it would also help prove to herself that she wasn't a failure.

When the agent returned, he was smiling. "They agreed to your suggestion. But they said seventy-two hours is acceptable." Then he named a figure for the earnest money.

Cate winced. It wasn't a ridiculously huge amount, but it wasn't inconsequential either. If she was letting her imagination run away with her and this idea was a bust, she would be losing a significant sum of cash.

For a moment, she stared out the plate glass windows at the front of the store. On a busy Saturday, Blossom Branch hummed with activity. Cate tried to imagine herself in this very spot, interacting with customers, placing merchandise, tracking sales.

She'd been wrong about Jason. She'd been wrong about the wedding. But this was different. She had to learn to trust herself. This wasn't something she *thought* she should want. She *knew*. It was a place she could see herself growing and thriving.

Certainty settled into a warm glow. The knot in her stomach was excitement, not fear or concern. She *wanted* this opportunity. But she was giving herself three days to be sure.

She faced the agent and smiled. "Where do I sign?"

Cate spent another hour exploring town before she returned to her grandparents' home. Her earlier text to Harry had mentioned an indefinite amount of time called *after lunch*. It was now almost five.

Had he been expecting her sooner? Was her absence of any concern to him? Did his habit of losing himself in work mean he hadn't even noticed she still wasn't back?

After the disturbing moments in the upstairs hallway last night, she was unsure about seeing him again. The fact that she never knew what he was thinking made their situation fraught with tension.

Was he bored? Did he want to be back in Atlanta? Had a promise to Jason tied him to Cate's side?

The thought of being *anyone's* obligation frustrated her.

When she let herself into the house, two things struck her at once. Something smelled amazing. And she heard Harry singing. That couldn't be right. It was a pop song. One that had been all over the radio for weeks now.

His voice was beautiful but hearing him sing along with America's favorite superstar blonde diva suggested that Harry had a lighthearted side. It would be easier to believe alien beings had taken over his body.

She found him in the kitchen. His back was to her as he tended something on the stove.

"Harry?" she said.

It wasn't too late to rule out the alien-being idea.

He turned around and gave her an odd look. "Next time, give me a heads-up when you plan to go walkabout. I might have called in the cops to drag the river."

"I sent you a text," she said. Guilty and defensive. Not the best way to approach the man who had sort of saved her life.

Harry raised a single eyebrow. "Maybe your idea and mine of 'after lunch' are different," he said.

"Whatcha doin' there?" Cate asked, eager to change the subject.

"Making spaghetti sauce."

"I thought breakfast was the limit of your repertoire."

She was so shocked, she forgot to keep her distance. When she joined him at the stove, she could see the large pot of bubbling tomatoey goodness.

Harry shook his head and mumbled something under his

breath. "I wouldn't say I can cook," he said. "But I have a recipe or two in my back pocket. I do entertain occasionally."

"Is this what you serve your lady friends when you have them over?"

His eyes narrowed. "If you mean lovers, no. This is much too heavy a meal to have sex afterward."

Cate was so shocked, she forgot to breathe. She felt her face turn hot and red. Embarrassment choked her.

Harry burst out laughing. "You are far too easy to tease, Catie-girl. Are you hungry?"

She managed to clear the knot in her throat. "I could eat." There were two places already set at the kitchen table.

"Go do whatever you need to do upstairs. I'll put the pasta on to cook shortly. The bread will be ready in twenty minutes. I was only waiting to hear from you before I got them started."

Guilt swamped her again. "Thank you, Harry." The man had cooked for her. It wasn't necessary. Any one of a half dozen restaurants in Blossom Branch had great takeout. But he had cooked. For her.

In her bathroom, she made time for a three-minute shower, then rifled through the clothes she had hung in the closet. The sophisticated businessman, Prescott Harrington, had been replaced by a relaxed guy in faded jeans, a navy pullover and bare feet.

It was the feet that got her. She had never thought of feet as an attractive male body part. Harry's, though, were just right.

Because she couldn't decide what to wear, she opted to mirror his vibe. Her skinny jeans weren't as faded, and her thin, cotton short-sleeve sweater was Chanel, but he probably wouldn't know that.

When she returned to the kitchen fifteen minutes later, Harry was ladling angel hair pasta onto two plates. "How much sauce do you want?" he asked, shooting her a glance over his shoulder.

Her stomach growled. The high carb meal made her mouth water. Since her reason for dieting was dead in the water, she waved a hand. "Lots."

Harry grinned. He had already prepared two small salads and put them on the table. Now he added the plates of spaghetti and went back for the bread, which he dumped into a straw basket lined with paper towels.

The presentation might have been a tad on the informal side, but the food was spectacular. They ate in silence for five whole minutes before she looked up and found him watching her.

"What?" she asked. "Do I have sauce on my chin?"

Something in his gaze made her uncomfortable. Not in a bad way. But as if her senses had been painfully heightened all at once.

He shook his head slowly. "No sauce," he said. "I was just thinking lavender is a good color on you. It makes your eyes seem even more blue."

She didn't know what to say to that. It was more of a statement than a compliment. So she deflected. "What did *you* do today?" she asked.

"Work." He shrugged. "I'm not good at relaxing."

"I've noticed. What kind of work?" It was like prying open a stubborn clamshell.

He twirled his fork in the pasta but didn't take a bite. In fact, he set down his fork. "I'm designing another building for downtown. The owner wants a three-story atrium in the center. It's challenging, but fun."

She cocked her head and smiled at him. "At the risk of inflating your ego, I have to say I'm impressed by what you do.

Artistic and practical at the same time. Your work is spectacular, Harry. It truly is."

Clearly, he hadn't been expecting her to offer praise or compliments. He blinked once, then twice, before he managed to respond. "Thanks," he said gruffly. "I enjoy it."

She left it at that, choosing to finish her meal.

Silence fell, an intimate vacuum that was equal parts comfortable and electric.

After a few moments, Harry finished his spaghetti and wine and turned the tables. "And what about you, Cate? Blossom Branch isn't all that big. How did you fill your day?"

Her instinct was to blurt out her news, but she was scared. "Oh, this and that."

He leaned his chair back on two legs and studied her face. "You seemed pretty excited when you came in."

"I did?" How could he tell?

"You bounced into the kitchen. What happened, Cate?"

Eleven

Cate took a reckless sip of Chablis. "I'd rather not talk about it."

"Another embarrassing encounter with a rosebush? Another attempt at B and E?"

"Very funny."

"The more you evade the subject, the more curious I am. What's the big deal?"

She sighed, twisting her hands in her lap. "I want to talk about it, I do. But I'm afraid you'll tell me how immature and impulsive I am and that jumping into things doesn't end well."

All the humor left his face. He frowned. "Am I such an ogre? It's not fair of you to create whole conversations in your head and make up my part from scratch. How in the hell do you know what I'll say?"

"Because you're you," she said glumly. "You always know what's best."

"I assume that's sarcasm?"

"Well, of course it is," she said, flustered. "I feel like every time you look at me, you're making a mental list of all my shortcomings."

The temperature in the room dropped ten degrees. His gaze iced over. His scowl made her shudder inwardly. "I'm trying really hard here, Cate," he said through clenched teeth. "But I fail to see how I'm the villain in this scenario. You're way the hell off base with my assumptions."

"You don't think I'm young and immature? Catie-*girl*?" She threw the words at him.

The red flush on his cheekbones deepened. "Young, yes. That's a matter of the calendar. Immature? Not that I can tell. Perhaps a little naive and sheltered. For the record, I use that name as a term of affection. Where is this coming from?"

Affection? Her heart stuttered.

Here it was. The moment of truth. It was a can of worms she probably shouldn't open, but Harry's opinion of her had stung for years. "Every time Jason and I visited you," she said quietly, "or when you came over to his house, you always sniped at me. Teasing, yes, but the kind of teasing that leaves marks. You made it very clear that you thought your sainted cousin was making a mistake in dating me…that I was flighty and not too bright. You ragged on my clothes and my friends and even my college major."

Harry stood abruptly, his demeanor guarded. "I'm sorry you felt that way, Catherine. That was never my intention. I apologize for being insensitive and unkind."

Cate stood, too. She faced him, her resolve wavering. But she pushed on. "Then why did you do it?"

His jawline firmed in grim angles. "Maybe I have a sucky sense of humor. Or maybe—"

He stopped abruptly. She saw his Adam's apple ripple in his throat. For the flash of a second the expression in his gaze wasn't guarded at all. It was something that looked a lot like pain.

"Maybe what?" she asked quietly. "Maybe what, Harry?"

He looked at her for so long and so hard, she found herself unable to breathe. The air between them sizzled. Cate felt dizzy and weak.

At first, she thought he wasn't going to answer at all. He rubbed the back of his neck, cursed softly and met her gaze straight on.

"Maybe I was jealous," he said.

Then he walked out of the room.

Cate didn't know how long she stood there. Her body was in two states at once, frozen with shock and hot with *something*.

This was a joke, right? Harry was joking. His wit leaned toward the dry side. Surely, he was mocking her.

She waited five minutes for him to return. None of the stairs to the second floor creaked. No squeak of the front door opening and closing. The man simply vanished.

Possibly, her heart had been pounding so hard she hadn't noted the audible signs of his exit.

Because she didn't know what else to do, she began cleaning up the kitchen. She knew from staying with Harry in his penthouse apartment that the man liked order.

That meant he also tidied up as he cooked. All Cate had to do was load the dishwasher and put away the leftovers. When her grandmother's kitchen was spotless again, she fought the panicky feeling in her chest.

If she had a car, she would hightail it back to Atlanta... and go somewhere, a hotel maybe. But she didn't have transportation.

Even worse, she had put a chunk of money down on a venture that now seemed irrelevant at best.

What was she supposed to do?

Should she go for another run to clear her head? But she didn't want Harry to think she was avoiding him. Part of her was angry. Where did he get off saying something like that and walking away?

Her first instinct was to talk to Jason about what just happened, and in the next breath, she realized how ironic that was. She had been ready to marry Jason Brightman, and now, she was what? Over him?

Maybe she needed professional help. Her head was in danger of exploding. She was confused and shocked and more than a little scared.

Years ago, her grandfather had built a small playhouse for Cate and Becca on the back corner of the property. Now Cate headed there instinctively, looking for a place where Harry wouldn't find her.

Not that he was looking...

The little structure had held its own. The plywood was warped and the shingles on the roof needed replacing, but the narrow front door still opened easily as if the hinges had been recently oiled.

In anyone else's backyard, Cate would have worried about spiderwebs and other creepy crawlies. But Grandpa would never let one of his creations get gross on his watch.

Cate squeezed through the doorframe and closed herself in. At one time, she and her sister had brought dolls here... and secret notes. Food, too.

Now, the eight-by-eight-by-eight room was empty. The inside walls were painted white. Near the top, Grammy had stenciled a garland of peach blossoms all the way around.

The flowers were faded. But the memories existed as strong as ever. Cate folded her legs crisscross applesauce and leaned against the wall. The little play structure boasted two real windows on the sides facing the neighbors' yards. She couldn't see Grammy and Grandpa's house.

She felt lost. All she could think about was Harry saying he had been jealous. For years she thought he didn't like her. Apparently, that wasn't true.

It was the oddest thing, but she couldn't decide how she felt about his revelation.

Was she upset? Relieved? Embarrassed?

Or deep down inside, was there some tiny part of her that was exultant and deeply touched?

It was hot in the small playhouse. And humid. The childhood version of a sauna. When she opened each window a couple of inches, she managed to get a nice cross breeze going.

Time lost all meaning. The comparative safety of her bolthole was not very comfortable. A bottle of water would have been nice.

How was she going to face Harry after this?

Eventually, she curled up on the bare floor and dozed. The ancient carpet had long since been removed.

Gradually, the room grew dark. Cate knew she was being irrational. A woman couldn't *literally* hide from her problems, no matter how tempting. When she finally roused and glanced at her watch, it was after nine.

Time to go inside and face the music.

Before she could convince herself to move, the playhouse door opened. Harry crouched and glared at her. "What in the devil are you doing out here?"

Instead of answering his question, she countered, "How did you find me?"

"Your purse and phone are inside. I searched the house. Your running shoes are still by the front door. Unless you've mastered time travel, this was my final option."

"Go away," she said. Sadly, she couldn't muster much heat to accompany her demand.

"I'm coming in," he said.

"You won't fit." Harry's shoulders were a million miles wide. But to her dismay, he kept right on coming.

She pulled her knees to her chest and wedged her body into a corner.

After Harry was all the way in, he sat down with a sigh and used his phone to shine a flashlight in her face. "I've picked up women in stranger places, but not many."

"That's not funny," she said. "Get that thing out of my eyes. You're blinding me."

Harry shut off the flashlight app and leaned back. "I shouldn't have said what I said. I didn't mean to freak you out. The truth is, I did have a crush on you a million years ago, but once I realized you and Jason were serious, that was the end of it. You don't have to sleep in the doghouse."

"It isn't a doghouse," she said indignantly. "Grandpa built this play structure for Becca and me fifteen years ago. It used to have a slide attached." She assessed Harry's words, unable to see his face. Was he telling the truth, or was this an attempt to cover his ass? "Besides," she said, "I'm not the one who ran out of the kitchen."

"I didn't run." His tone was mild. "I had some work stuff to deal with."

"Right."

She could see the house now because Harry had left the door open. The moon was up. The night had painted her grandparents' property in silvery hues. Suddenly, a flash of white in the yard caught her attention.

She froze. "Harry," she hissed. "Closed the door. Now!"

"Why? It's hot in here."

"Do it," she said. When he didn't move fast enough, she

reached across him and yanked the doorknob. Then, she turned and shut both windows.

"Are you trying to smother us?" he asked, his tone sarcastic.

Her heart slugged in her chest. "Harry, there's a skunk right outside. And this is mating season."

She sensed the moment when his big body froze. "You can't be serious," he croaked.

"Dead serious."

"And the mating season thing?"

"I grew up in the country. Believe me. I know what I'm talking about," she said. "I would think you'd know that, too. You're a son of Blossom Branch."

Harry snorted. "My mother didn't like me mucking around outside. I escaped when I could…to hang with my buddies, but mostly I had math tutors and French teachers who came to the house. Besides, we had a groundskeeper who tended to vermin."

Cate rolled her eyes, though he couldn't see her. "I keep forgetting you grew up rich."

"Don't hand me that line," he said. "Your father is loaded."

"Maybe now, but not always."

Cate gasped silently when a definite animal-like rustling materialized close by. "Don't move," she hissed. "Don't make a sound."

She heard Harry groan softly. "I feel like I'm being punked."

"That will be the least of your worries if a skunk sprays us," she muttered.

They sat in silence for five minutes. Then ten. *Something* was wandering around outside.

"How do we know when it's safe to go?" Harry whispered.

"I don't hear anything now. I could open the door really slowly."

"Be my guest."

Harry was occupying most of the space between Cate and freedom. He was a big man. She was forced to climb over him.

At the last second, she chickened out. "Let's give it another five minutes," she said, the words barely audible.

"Fine by me." He shifted his body as if his spot was uncomfortable. "My life was never a soap opera until I started hanging out with you."

"Nobody said you had to rescue me at the wedding."

"Are you implying you had a better plan?"

"You know I didn't," she said, feeling sulky.

"I'm only giving you a hard time, Catie-girl. For a workaholic like me, you're an *interesting* deviation."

"That sounds remarkably insulting."

"It was meant as a compliment."

"Maybe you should look up that word." When Harry laughed out loud, she shushed him. "We're still being quiet," she said.

"Oh, right."

Was it the dark that had relaxed the tension between them? Or had she totally imagined the awkwardness in the kitchen earlier? Maybe Harry had been telling the truth. Maybe the old crush was exactly what he described. Ancient news.

"We have to get out of here," she said. "I'm opening the door."

On her knees, she turned the knob and pushed. The moonlight lit up the backyard. Nothing seemed out of place. She scooted through the narrow entrance and stood.

Harry was close behind her. He stretched his arms toward the sky and unkinked his back. "Thank God. I thought we were going to cook in there."

"It wasn't that hot."

He touched her damp cheek and scooped up a trickle of sweat. "Hot enough."

Damn it. She couldn't read the man. One minute he was teasing her, and the next he touched her with a casual intimacy that made it hard to breathe.

If they went inside the house, it would be too late to talk to him. They would both go their separate ways. She sucked in a sharp breath. "You were right about me being excited earlier. Honestly, I could really use your help tomorrow. Do you have a couple of hours in the morning?"

If there had been no moon, she would have missed his flinch. His subtle body language was unmistakably negative. "Sorry," he said. "I have to go back to Atlanta. I was going to tell you at dinner, but we were talking about other things."

"For how long?" she asked. Why did she have the distinct feeling Harry had invented this trip on the fly?

He shrugged. "A couple of nights. Maybe three. Something came up that needs to be dealt with in person."

"I see."

"What's going on tomorrow?" he said. "Will it keep?"

"No. It won't." She gnawed her lip. She could handle her leap of faith without Harry. Of course, she could. But all else aside, she valued his opinion. "I need to show you something downtown. Could we go right now?"

"It's late," he muttered.

"Please, Harry. We don't have to walk. We can take your car, so it will be quick."

"You want to tell me where we're going?"

"I'd rather show you." She headed for the house. "I'm going to grab my phone, and then I'm ready."

"I've got my keys on me. I'll meet you at the car."

Five minutes later they were headed toward the center of town. At this time of night, the streets were empty. The famous gazebo loomed in the moonlight, its shape unmistakable.

"Where am I headed?" Harry asked.

"You can park at the curb. There on the left."

They got out. Harry locked the car door. "I'm confused," he said.

Cate's heart sank. The storefront she had been so excited about looked old and a little shabby at night. Not a single light had been left on inside, though she hadn't expected one. But it was going to be hard to whip up Harry's enthusiasm under these circumstances.

"This is it," Cate said. "It went on the market yesterday, I think. The listing agent showed me around."

Harry pulled her toward a nearby bench and sat. "Back up, Cate. You've lost me."

"You told me in so many words that I'm the only one who can decide what my future will be."

"Okay."

"Well, Jason and I were planning to open an art gallery in Buckhead. That was going to be our grand business venture. Both sets of parents gave us cash gifts as a wedding present. But we were pooling our money. Real estate would have been ferociously expensive in that zip code. I can't manage it without him."

"You're asking me for a loan?"

"Good grief, no. I'm asking you if it would be foolish for me to buy this building. It was a furniture store until recently. The couple who owned it used the upstairs for inventory storage. But the Realtor pointed out I could easily make the second floor into an apartment."

Harry was both silent and still. In fact, he might have been a statue. The bench was standard size. Only a few inches separated them. Was the man even breathing?

Despite the moonlight, this spot was shadowed by the buildings behind them. Cate had no clue what he was thinking.

Finally, he spoke. "You're going to leave Atlanta? Move to Blossom Branch?"

Twelve

Cate hadn't been thinking in those terms, though perhaps she should have. "Move? Well, no. I don't think so," she said. "Once everything is established, I'll probably hire a good manager and staff. All my friends and family are in Atlanta. But I could easily spend a night or two here every couple of weeks."

She realized she had hopelessly bobbled her pitch. It would have been so much easier if she could have given Harry the grand tour…and sketched out her ideas along the way.

He stirred, rotating his head on his neck. His sigh was not a good sign. "I hate to burst your bubble, Cate, but I'm not sure an art gallery is exactly right for this town."

After a split second of shocked silence, she had to laugh. "I've done all this backward. Not an art gallery. I'm thinking of a specialty boutique where people could buy a baby gift or a graduation present. Small household items. Seasonal decorations. And maybe a *little* bit of art. Small watercolors, stuff like that. I thought I could call the store Just Peachy."

Already, in her mind's eye, she could see the gold lettering on the front window. She bubbled with excitement thinking about it.

Harry chuckled. "Well, that's different. Sure, Cate. I don't see why it couldn't work."

"I was hoping to get your architectural input about the building. But if you're leaving in the morning..."

Could she get him to change his mind?

Harry was already shaking his head. "Sorry I can't be more help. If you get a thorough inspection, you should be fine."

"And adding a wall or two to make an apartment?"

"Not a problem. It's the knocking out walls where people get in trouble. How soon do you have to make up your mind?"

She gulped inwardly. "I put down earnest money this morning. And promised them an official offer in seventy-two hours."

"I see."

Was that disapproval she heard in those two syllables, or was she being paranoid?

He stood and peered through the glass, not that he could see much. "You must have really been impressed."

She followed him, sticking her nose to the glass. "The hardwood floors are original...and some of the light fixtures. It's dusty and cluttered, but the bones are good. My art classes trained me to see potential."

Harry turned to face her. Now a streetlight illuminated his bold features. The grim line of his mouth was what bothered her most.

He ran a hand through his hair and pinched the bridge of his nose momentarily. "What happens if you and Jason get back together?"

The question knocked the breath out of her. As if someone had literally punched her in the stomach. "It's not going to happen. You know that."

"*How* do I know it?" Harry asked, the words terse.

"You heard Jason. He's not in love with me." Although she had found a measure of peace about her situation, her fiancé's rejection still stung.

"But what about you, Cate? Aren't you going to try and win him back? Aren't you going to fight?"

How did she answer that? Could she own up to experiencing a tiny, deeply buried snippet of relief? Or was that too embarrassing for words? What did it say about her if the aborted wedding she had planned for months turned out to be a nightmare instead? What if she admitted that the dreams she had clung to so stubbornly were maybe not what she really wanted after all? And how could she be transparent enough to admit that Jason had likely done the right thing?

"No," she said, not dressing it up. "I'm not."

"I see."

She had no idea what Harry was thinking. Hardly a surprise there. No wonder she always felt unsettled around him. "We should get back to the house. You'll need to pack."

"I've traveled all over the world. Packing takes no time at all."

"But aren't you leaving early?"

"Around four thirty"

"Then let's go."

He didn't argue with her.

The trip home took less than five minutes. Inside the house, awkwardness bloomed again. Though they were standing in the living room and not the kitchen, Harry's earlier words echoed around the house, never to be forgotten.

Maybe I was jealous.

She watched as he checked doors and windows and gathered a stack of books he had been reading during their time in Blossom Branch. "I'll be in touch," he said, never quite looking at her.

"I hope you have a successful trip."

Suddenly, she couldn't bear the thought of climbing those stairs together. It was too much—far too normal, when the last thing she felt around Prescott Harrington was normal.

"You go on," she said. Her voice came out husky and croaky. "I'm going to take a walk around the block. Not sleepy."

Harry looked at her searchingly. "You want company?"

Her chest hurt. "No. I've got some thinking to do about the store. But thanks."

That moment in the living room was the last time Cate saw Harry for two weeks. He didn't come back to Blossom Branch after two nights or four or even six.

His mysterious chore in Atlanta was apparently time-consuming. Or so he would have her believe. Not that he left her completely in the dark. She received at least one text every day. Short. To the point.

Cate realized this was her chance to prove she could make decisions on her own. After much consideration, she put in an official offer on the store. The owners accepted. Because closing on their end was going to be complicated, they agreed to let Cate rent for a month.

That had been *Cate's* idea, and she was proud of it. They also agreed to let her begin cleaning up and painting. If the deal fell through, Cate had a contract that said she would be compensated for her financial outlay.

So she set to work. In the beginning, it was hard physical labor. Cate welcomed the exertion. She fell into bed every night, too tired to obsess about her non-wedding or to wonder about Harry and his odd behavior.

While having dinner one evening with Ginny from the ice cream shop, Cate found an unexpected source of help. Ginny's cousin, Zack, was a rising senior in high school, a football lineman. He rounded up several of his friends, and suddenly, Cate had a team of workers, five men strong.

Though she paid them more than fairly, she suspected they enjoyed the challenge. By the time Harry had been gone a week, the first floor of Cate's store was spotless, and the walls painted a beautiful celadon that would showcase her eventual inventory.

The upstairs was a bigger hurdle. She didn't want to make too many structural changes until her name was on the dotted line.

The second week of Harry's absence was less physical and more cerebral. Cate spent a lot of time at her grandparents' house researching vendors online. Her goal was to have a shop where all the merchandise was handmade. To that end, she contacted artisan guilds in Kentucky, North Carolina, Tennessee and, of course, Georgia.

That part was fun. She made endless lists of quilts and wooden stools and Quaker boxes and silver jewelry. It was far too soon to order yet. But she wanted to be ready to go when the time came.

In between her hours on the computer, she rambled around Blossom Branch, reacquainting herself with old haunts and discovering how much the community had grown. Fortunately, the core of town remained the same. Nuanced updating made everything feel fresh and upbeat yet at the same time preserved the notion that time might have stood still for the past hundred years.

Cate had been walking everywhere, but one afternoon she found a bicycle in the storage shed. It was cobwebby. Once she cleaned it up, it worked perfectly fine. Now she was able to range farther afield.

Out on the rural backroads, she recaptured the peace and joy of her childhood. Seeing the peach orchards, photographing red barns and wooden stiles, stopping on small rustic bridges to watch the creek run. Life at its simplest helped her make sense of all the turmoil she had faced.

The one aspect of her situation that still gave her heartburn was the huge mistake she had made with Jason. It was on a particularly beautiful afternoon that she paused beneath the shade of an enormous oak, parked her bike and sat down on the grass.

The silence was deep. Except for the distant mooing of a cow and the hum of nearby bees, Cate was able to hear nothing but her own heart. She closed her eyes and leaned back against the tree trunk.

In that private moment, she let herself accept the truth. Jason had been right to do what he did. Cate wasn't "in" love with Jason, but she loved him dearly. Somehow, she had convinced herself that the grand passion portrayed in books and movies was fake. She'd believed that kindness and companionship were sufficient to maintain a marriage.

Maybe in some situations that was true. She wouldn't presume to judge other people's relationships. But clearly, Jason had recognized the danger before Cate had—unfortunately, almost too late.

Neither of them had ever been involved in a wildly passionate, all-consuming love affair. That didn't mean such a thing didn't exist. If Jason had let the wedding ceremony progress, the two of them might have been locked in a marriage and then found that "other" person.

The resultant damage and the upheaval of divorce would

have traumatized them both. Either that, or they would have stayed together and begun living a lie.

So now what?

It might be a long time before Cate trusted herself again. She had been so wrong about such an important life choice. How would she recognize the man who was right for her when he came along? For that matter, now that she had admitted even her dreams had been flawed, how would she know what was right about any of it?

Sunday morning, Cate moped around the house feeling sorry for herself. Harry had been gone for two whole weeks. She had a hunch he wasn't coming back. Apparently, admitting to a years-old jealous crush made him too uncomfortable.

He needn't have worried. She understood better than anyone that Harry wasn't right for her. The ten-year age gap wasn't a huge hurdle, but it made for an uneven playing field. He would undoubtedly end up one day with a sophisticated, leggy brunette model. Or maybe even a gorgeous philanthropist.

If he ever married at all.

Late in the afternoon, Cate was in the living room texting back and forth with Leah and Gabby about the new store.

I can't wait for you guys to see the building, she said.

Leah jumped in. Will you tell us when we can come help? Gabby agreed.

Mom might even want to pitch in too.

Cate didn't mention Harry because she didn't know what to say. Leah and Gabby were excited for her. To be honest, there was probably an undertone of relief in their texts. As if they could quit worrying about her so much.

After Cate ended the conversation, she was surprised to hear a car pull up in the carport followed by the unmistakable sound of a door opening and closing. Before she could do more than stand and turn around, Harry walked right into the house. When he saw her there, he gave a guarded smile. "I'm back," he said.

Cate's heart jumped in an alarming fashion. "So I see. You didn't mention you were returning... in your last text. I half expected you on Friday for the weekend. Don't you have to work in the morning?"

He set down his bags and yawned. "I'm officially on vacation."

"Really? Where are you going? Cancun? Barbados? No wait, Papua New Guinea?"

Now his smile was quizzical. "Why would I go to Papua New Guinea? What's there?"

"I have no idea. I just like saying it."

He laughed. "I had no idea how boring my life was until you came long."

"Seriously," she said. "What are you doing for vacation? A road trip?"

He took off his sport coat and tie and tossed them on a chair. "I'm here to help you with the store."

Her jaw dropped. "But..."

"But what?" He tapped her chin until she closed her mouth. His eyes crinkled at the corners. His smile was genuine. "I like a project as much as the next guy. Besides, I wasn't about to let some strange contractor design your apartment. I have skills, woman."

"I know that." She swallowed hard, thrown off-balance by the casual way he dropped back into her life as if he hadn't gone missing for fourteen days. "You realize my closing isn't for another two and a half weeks. I've done the cleaning and the cosmetic stuff. I'm not sure what else there is."

"We can measure and plan. I'll incorporate your vision and

get it on paper. Once you own the building outright, we'll be ready to begin."

"That would be great, Harry. Thank you."

Then he grimaced. "There's just one other thing I need to do tomorrow before we can get started. Somebody in town recognized me and ratted me out to my mother. She's on my case about not visiting."

Cate frowned. "Well, of course she is. Why didn't you drop by when you were here before?"

His face tightened. "People don't *drop by* on my mother. She prefers plenty of notice so she can get the set just right."

The note of bitterness in his voice was unmistakable. "I don't understand," Cate said. "Honestly, Jason never told me much about your family."

"It's better that way."

His scowl didn't deter her. "But Harry—you know everything there is to know about me and my relatives. I hardly think it's fair for you to be so mysterious about yours. You and I might have lived in the same small town for years, but you were older, and your family was posh."

"No one ever said life was fair. You, Cate, should know that as well as anybody." His grim words matched the expression on his face.

She touched his arm briefly. "I didn't mean to quarrel with you right off the bat. Are you hungry? You want to grab dinner somewhere?" She sensed there were hurts buried in his past. Ones that Jason might or might not be privy to…but Cate was here, in Blossom Branch. She wanted to help Harry if it was possible. He had done a great deal for her.

They ended up at a new steak house on the outskirts of town. Apparently, not everybody was onboard with peach mania. Ye Olde Steak House didn't exactly fit the community theme, but the service and the food were excellent.

Over filet mignon with new potatoes and sautéed asparagus, Cate brought Harry up to date with everything that had happened at the store. His brief texts during the days he'd been gone hadn't lent themselves to long narratives.

"I'm impressed," he said. "Sounds like you've accomplished a lot in a short amount of time. Do you plan on staying here until closing day?"

For the first time, Cate felt a tad uncomfortable. "No. Saturday is the Fourth of July. I thought it would be fun to see the craft festival and watch the fireworks that evening. I'll head back to Atlanta Sunday midday."

"Why then?"

"Well, I know Grammy and Grandpa are returning after the holiday sometime. They'll be tired from traveling. I'm sure they'll want the house to themselves for a bit. I'll stay with them when I come back for closing. But besides…" She grimaced.

"Besides what?"

"I need to get my things out of Jason's apartment. He'll be flying home soon, too…unless he changed our tickets."

"Ah, yes." Harry's expression was inscrutable. "And how were you planning to get back to Atlanta?"

"If you hadn't returned by the weekend, I was going to rent a car. Still can if you have other plans for the holiday."

For all she knew, Harry might have a cadre of friends who expected him to participate in house parties or golf tournaments or boating adventures. The Fourth was a big holiday in the South. And since the weather was supposed to be perfect, Blossom Branch would be overrun with revelers.

Harry grabbed one last roll from the breadbasket. "No plans," he said. "Your idea sounds like fun. Count me in."

Cate tried not to let on how pleased she was to hear him say that. She had thoroughly enjoyed her time in Blossom Branch, even the two weeks alone. But being with Harry again made everything brighter. His presence filled a room. He was boldly masculine, but at the same time creative and brilliant.

She tried not to let herself think about his sex appeal. Even when she was engaged to Jason, she had felt uneasy around Harry. Aside from the fact that his constant teasing bothered her, there was something about him that literally made her feel…shivery.

Now that they had shared living arrangements in two different places, she understood that her reaction to him was elemental. He was a man. She was a woman. No matter how she tried to spin it, the truth was alarming.

She was attracted to Harry.

Recognizing and admitting that earth-shattering fact stole her breath and left her forehead damp and her legs wobbly.

Cate barely noticed when the server arrived at their table and asked about dessert.

Harry said her name, maybe for the second or third time. "Cate?" he asked. "Do you want a piece of carrot cake? Or something else?" He was looking at her with an odd expression.

She cleared her throat. "Not for me, thanks. But you go ahead."

When Harry declined as well, she felt a rush of relief. If she could only get back to the house and escape to her room, all would be well.

Cate found herself in a trance. She couldn't judge how much time passed between the paying of the check and the stroll to the car. Unlike two weeks ago, it was dark out. The full moon was long gone.

Harry unlocked the car, opened her door and waited for

her to be seated. Then he rounded the front bumper, got in and started the engine.

"What do you want to do when we get back to the house?" he asked.

Thirteen

Cate was horrified to realize she almost giggled. Like a middle school girl. At the last second, she swallowed her inappropriate response.

Fortunately, Harry had no clue about her reaction to him.

"Um," she said. "I might go for a run. That was a lot of calories." She paused. "You're welcome to join me."

It was a short trip home. When Harry pulled into the driveway a few minutes later, he said, "I think I'm up for a run. I promised my administrative assistant I'd give her a couple of things she needs for a morning meeting, but I can do that when we get back."

"Good," Cate said. "I'll meet you here in fifteen minutes."

Upstairs, she changed into the same running clothes Harry had already seen. She wasn't putting on a show. This was about exercise.

Even when she made it outside and saw Harry stretching against the bumper of his car, she kept herself in check. His shorts and T-shirt were loose fitting, but it was impossible to miss the fact that he was incredibly fit.

He stretched both arms over his head and grabbed his left elbow. "All set?"

She nodded, trying not to notice the way muscles rippled in his thighs. "Sure."

"You set the pace," he said.

"Got it."

In the days Harry had been away, Cate had worked out a familiar routine. Three blocks toward the town square. Left on Court Street. One block over and then straight east toward the open fields and orchards. After half a mile, she turned back toward Grammy and Grandpa's house.

There were plenty of streetlights closer to town, but out here, the country landscape was dark. Eventually, the sidewalk petered out. "I turn around here," she said, puffing.

She had pushed herself hard, mildly disgusted to realize that Harry was breathing normally. The man was a machine. A computerlike brain. A body that could handle any punishment. And a personality perfectly happy to be an island. An uninhabited island, at that.

They had been running side by side. Cate slowed down, remembering this section of broken concrete. Now Harry was a few steps behind her. At least it was too dark for him to see her butt.

She half turned to warn him. "Watch your step," she said. At that exact moment, her companion grunted, made a loud *aaaaagh* sound and hit the ground hard.

"Oh, my God. Harry!" She was at his side in a split second. Clearly, he hadn't struck his head. If he had, he wouldn't be capable of sitting up and cradling his right leg. Would he?

She grabbed the phone out of her pocket and illuminated the scene with her flashlight. Blood gushed from a cut below his knee. The knee itself was a nasty mishmash of dirt, grass, bits of gravel and more blood.

His palms were scraped, too.

"I'm fine," he muttered. "Caught my toe."

She crouched in front of him. "It's my fault," she fretted. "I should have warned you sooner. I've been avoiding this spot every time I run. In fact, I usually move into the street, but it was so dark, I didn't realize where we were. I'll have to call 9-1-1."

"No," he roared. "That's absurd. I'm not in any danger."

"You might be disoriented from blood loss." She was teasing him now, trying to lighten the mood, but Harry didn't appear to notice.

"Quit worrying," he said. "It's nothing."

It wasn't *nothing*. It was very clearly *something*. But men were notoriously stubborn. Maybe that was sexist. Cate had her own moments of bullheadedness. Still, she wasn't the one on the ground in pain.

"I think if we can get you on your feet, you can lean on me," she said.

"Won't work." His response was instantaneous. "I outweigh you by a good fifty pounds."

"You could at least try," she said, trying to be reasonable and supportive at the same time. "Please, Harry."

He capitulated, but he wasn't happy about it. "Don't try to help me."

A tiny dogwood sapling in the yard of the nearest homeowner served as a brace for Harry to pull himself up. The effort took far too long. And Cate was going to have to buy the neighbor a new tree.

At the last minute, Harry lost his balance and fell sideways onto his hip, uttering a string of choice words under his breath.

This time Cate knew better than to hover. "Okay," she said with faux calm. "Plan B. When I was getting a bicycle out of the storage shed the other day, I saw a pair of crutches. We're about a quarter mile from the house. I'll run as fast as I can, grab them and be right back."

A long silence ensued. Harry didn't protest this time, but he didn't seem at all happy about her idea. "You can't run if you're carrying crutches," he said, his tone snarly.

"Then I'll walk fast. We're out of options," Cate pointed out tartly.

"Be careful," he muttered.

"I will. Swear to me you won't try to get up until I'm back." She still had the flashlight shining in his direction, so she saw the look of incredulity on his face. "No problem."

It was ridiculous to worry about leaving him. In this town, no one was going to mug him. The worst thing that could happen was another skunk encounter. The random thought made her snort out a laugh. She bit down on her amusement quickly, but not before Harry scowled.

"Is my situation funny to you, Cate?"

"Not at all." She knelt again, holding his injured leg with her right hand and using the flashlight with her left. "It's swelling fast," she said, running her thumb gently over the abraded skin to loosen the largest of the gravel pieces. "Are you sure we can't call an ambulance?"

When she looked at him, they were on eye level. Even without the flashlight, she could see the way his whole body tensed. "No ambulance," he croaked.

She put the phone back in her pocket and used both hands on either side of his knee. "I think you should keep it straight while I'm gone." Then she moved her thumbs above his knee and squeezed. "Does it hurt up here, too?"

"Cate?" His voice sounded funny.

"What?" she asked, absently stroking his lower thigh.

"Please stop touching me."

She sucked in a breath, frowning. "Why?"

Harry was leaning back in the grass, supporting himself with one hand. With his free arm, he put his hand behind her neck, pulled her close and kissed her gently. "Because I can only handle one crisis at a time," he said, the words husky and low.

Cate froze. Like a deer on the highway caught in a car's headlights, she was afraid to move. And she was still holding Harry's leg.

The kiss was over so quickly, her stunned brain wondered if she had imagined it. "Oh." That single, scintillating syllable was all she could manage. "Okay."

She peeled her fingers away from his warm, lightly hair-dusted skin one at a time, as if trying not to detonate a bomb. Then she lurched to her feet, turned her back on him and ran.

Cate made it to the house and back in forty-two minutes. It wouldn't have taken that long, but the crutches had to be wiped down. And she realized Harry probably needed water.

She downed half of a bottle herself so she wouldn't have to carry two. It crossed her mind to take first aid supplies, but then decided it made more sense to get her patient back to air-conditioning and a comfortable seat before she started cleaning up his knee.

Jogging—or fast walking—whatever you wanted to call it, was not easy carrying two moderately heavy crutches and water for her patient. Her Lycra pants accommodated a phone, but not the plastic bottle.

When she made it back to where she had left Harry sitting on the ground, she was sweaty and out of breath. She found him flat on his back, a fact that caused alarm until she realized he was resting. Asleep? Or maybe unconscious?

Her imagination went wild until Harry sat up and said, "Water. Oh, good." When she handed the bottle to him, he downed it all in one go, the muscles in his throat working. "I needed that."

"You'll have to use me this time," she said, eyeing the poor little tree that now brushed the ground.

"Use *you*?" Harry's response sounded odd.

"To stand," she said impatiently. "Once we get you upright, I'll shove one crutch under your arm. Then we'll add the second one."

When she leaned over and offered her arm to help him, he waved her away. "Give me a minute."

"Ohmigosh, Harry. Quit being such a *dude*. Let's get this over with." She took his arm, settled it across her shoulders and tried to stand. Her back screamed in protest.

With one leg out of commission, Harry was ill-prepared to participate in his own rescue. "Just wait," he said. "We'll have to use the crutch to lever me up, or you're going to throw out your back."

"My back is fine," she lied.

"Give me the damn crutch."

Hurt and cranky. A lovely combination.

"Whatever you say, Mr. Harrington."

Her sarcasm didn't even register. He was too busy planning his moves. While still on his butt, he tucked the crutch under his right armpit. He waved his left arm at Cate. "I think this will work."

This time, she squatted, let him put his arm across her shoulders and nodded. "I do, too."

Slowly, they rose—two, three inches at a time. They were both huffing and puffing. Harry was like a turtle on his back, and Cate didn't have near the upper body strength she needed for this exercise.

They almost made it upright when Harry instinctively tried

to balance with his right foot. His yelp of pain when he put weight on the injured knee made Cate wince in sympathy.

But that wasn't the worst of it. Almost in slow motion, they both started heading for the ground. Cate was helpless to stop the cascade. They crashed hard, with Cate somehow on the bottom.

Harry's big body knocked the wind out of her. There was no opportunity to save herself. For several seconds her eyes were closed with dots of yellow light dancing on the back of her eyelids.

When she could manage a painful breath, she gazed up at him. "How bad are you hurt? Did you hit the knee again?"

He was braced on his elbows, trying to keep his weight off her. He brushed her nose with his. "Let's just say I'm regretting a few life choices in the last two hours."

"What are we going to do?"

"We're going to try the exact same thing, only this time we'll make it work."

"I don't want you to get hurt again, Harry."

"I'm tough, Catie-girl. The question is, are *you* okay? We crashed pretty hard."

"I'm fine. But we need to get you home."

She knew he hurt himself more just by rolling over to let her get up. They took everything slow. When the crutch was in position, she offered him her shoulder one last time. "I believe in you, Prescott Harrington."

He groaned. "Don't make me laugh. Everything hurts."

"I'm ready when you are."

This time, they executed the plan. Once Harry was upright, Cate quickly got the second crutch under his left arm and steadied him.

"I'm good," he said. But the two words were strained.

Now all they had to do was walk a quarter mile in the dark.

Cate decided she needed to take Harry's mind off their trek. "Well, this settles it," she said, matching her steps to his halting stride.

"Settles what?"

"Now you *have* to let me go meet your mother. You can't drive."

"Hell." She could tell by his disgusted response that he hadn't thought of that.

"I'm a very pleasant person. I'm sure she'll like me."

"My mother and I have a fragile relationship. You don't want to get caught in the middle."

"You want to tell me about it?"

"I absolutely do not."

She could hear the discomfort in his voice, so she let the matter drop. Tomorrow would roll around soon enough.

By the time they made it back to the house, Harry was in enough pain that he let her persuade him to go to the small regional hospital that was less than ten miles from Blossom Branch.

Cate was relieved. She would have done her best nursing, but professional help would be better. "Are you okay with me driving your car?" she asked.

"Don't have much choice."

He was barely finishing his sentences now. After she helped him scoot the passenger seat back and fold his legs into the car, she ran inside for her purse.

She punched the hospital's address into her phone. It wasn't hard to find, but she didn't want to waste valuable minutes.

When they arrived at the small medical center, the A-team took over. Cate was left to collapse into a hard plastic chair in the waiting room and exhale in relief. It was an hour and fifteen minutes before someone came to get her.

In the tiny emergency cubicle, she found Harry looking marginally better.

She smiled at him. "What's the damage?"

"Could have been worse." His beautiful eyes were sleepy. "Six stitches. No permanent damage to the knee. They gave me happy pills."

"Any for me?" she asked. "Kidding, of course."

Harry sobered and held out his hand. An invisible connection drew her across the room and tucked her fingers in his.

"Thank you, Cate," he said. "You're the most unflappable person I've ever seen in an emergency. I owe you."

She didn't feel unflappable. Now that all the adrenaline was gone, she felt limp and wiped out. "Can we go home?"

"The nurse is getting my discharge papers."

Less than an hour later, Cate pulled into the carport and shut off the engine. When they made it into the house, she glanced at the clock and adjusted the AC. "It's late. Let's get you into bed."

"That's what all the women say."

Harry's loopy smile was adorable, though she was positive he would hate that description.

"I'll get you settled on the sofa tonight," she said. "I can sleep in the recliner."

The old, recalcitrant Harry reared his head. "All my things are upstairs in my room. That's where I'm sleeping."

Cate counted to ten. "You could break your neck falling down the steps. Be reasonable, Harry."

"I feel great," he said, the words slurred. "All I need is a shower."

Thinking about Harry in the shower was a bad idea. Cate steeled her resolve. "I don't think that's smart. You should go straight to sleep. I'll wash the sheets in the morning."

"Shower first." Before she could stop him, he had his crutches and was headed for the stairs.

She hovered behind him, not at all sure she could break his fall if things went south.

Fortunately, Harry managed the stiff-legged ascent without problems.

When they made it to the hallway on the second floor, she debated her options. *Somebody* responsible had to dispense pain meds during the night. The doctor said Harry would need them for at least forty-eight hours.

That meant she had to sleep on his end of the hallway in the spare bedroom.

"Harry, why don't you rethink the shower?" she pleaded. "You can't put weight on your foot, and you're taking pain meds. Another fall, especially in the bathtub, could be worse. Aren't you supposed to keep the stitches dry?"

He turned awkwardly and shook his head. "I'm sweaty and gross. Plus, your grandparents have handheld showerheads and grab bars. Quit worrying. The doc put a waterproof bandage on me."

Cate bit her lip hard to keep from yelling at him. "I'll wait in your bedroom, so I can hear you," she said.

"You could always offer to wash my back," he said, giving her a grin that made her catch a breath.

His drugged state had lowered his inhibitions. "I don't think that's necessary," she said, her voice strangled. "After I get you settled in bed, I'll get an ice pack for your knee and maybe a snack so you can sleep."

When Harry moved into his room, she hovered in the hall. It would take him a few minutes to get ready for his shower. She would be able to hear when the water started. This old house had noisy pipes.

When she was sure he wasn't standing naked beside his

bed, she moved into his room and listened at the bathroom door. There were some mumbles and a few salty words. But no loud noises. Thank goodness.

She honestly didn't know how he was managing this effort on his own. The whole bathroom would probably be flooded, though that was the least of her worries.

After about fifteen minutes, the water shut off. Cate scooted back into the hall and closed the bedroom door, her heart racing. Even now, Harry wasn't out of danger.

She heard him enter the bedroom from the bathroom. Too late to remember she should have moved the throw rug beside the bed.

Moments later, the mattress squeaked. After that, at least one crutch fell to the floor.

When silence reigned, she opened the door a crack. "Harry? Are you decent? May I come in?"

His response was muffled, but Cate took that as a yes. She peeked, feeling like a voyeur. Harry was sprawled on his back, mostly on top of the covers. He had drawn one corner of the quilt over his midsection. His eyes were closed.

She approached the bed tentatively. "Are you okay?"

One eyelid lifted. His mouth twisted in pain. "Don't you dare say, 'I told you so.'"

"But you're clean," she said, trying to pacify him. "That will feel nice. Let's see if we can get you under the covers."

The task took far too long. Cate had to coax him to one side, drag the top sheet back, and then get him to roll the other way. He could only move his left leg comfortably, so she had to gently ease the covers out from under him.

Every bit of his body she could see was gloriously naked. His golden skin was damp and beautiful. Sleek muscle and sinew marked his tough, toned form. Her response to all that masculinity rattled her, but she tucked those feelings aside to be studied later.

When at last she had him properly in the bed, only his right leg was exposed. That was by design. She didn't want to risk reaching under the bedding to find his knee with the ice pack. Too much dangerous real estate nearby.

"I'm going to run downstairs for a minute," she said, resisting the urge to stroke his tousled hair away from his forehead. "Will you be okay?"

Her only answer was a grunt that could have meant anything.

In her grandmother's kitchen, Cate searched the freezer. She found two medical ice packs and three packages of frozen peas. She would start with the ice packs and come back later for the veggies if it came to that.

Quickly, she checked all the windows and doors and turned off lights. At the last minute, she remembered to grab a bottle of apple juice and a cereal bar.

When she returned to Harry's room, he appeared to be dozing, though it was hard to tell. She fetched a hand towel from the bathroom and used it to cover the bruised knee before she applied the ice pack.

In the midst of the job, a strong male hand grabbed her wrist. "I can do that," Harry said, sounding disgruntled.

"But why should you have to? Be still and let me get this right." The ice pack had an attached Velcro strap. Cate carefully slid that part underneath Harry's leg and fastened it snugly so the ice pack wouldn't be dislodged if he moved.

"All set," she said, trying for a cross between cheerful and competent. Truthfully, she was neither.

Harry's eyes were open now. He patted the empty side of the bed. "Stay here and talk to me," he said. "I'm not sleepy."

Fourteen

The atmosphere in the room was charged. Cate was far too aware that Harry lay naked beneath the covers. In the process of getting him settled, she had seen one unmistakably bare butt cheek.

"You're not sleepy because you're hurting?" she asked.

Long silence.

"Yes."

"I checked the discharge papers to see when they gave you the first dose of meds," she said. "You can have more in a little while. I've set an alarm on my watch. We want to stay ahead of the pain."

"It's not that big a deal," he said.

"You didn't break anything or tear anything, but your kneecap took a direct hit. It's not nothing."

"I like your voice," he said, the words drowsy. "Even when you're fussing at me, it's soothing."

Cate took a seat on the unoccupied side of the bed and rested her back against the headboard. "I haven't fussed," she said, mildly amused. "I'm only trying to take care of you."

"That's *my* job." He slurred his words now, clearly trying to resist the pull of the narcotics.

"Because you're always the one taking care of other people?"

"Yep."

She studied his face. In repose, his features were less intimidating. His lashes fanned out against his cheeks, beautiful and dark. This vision of him as a vulnerable male gave Cate an odd feeling in the pit of her stomach.

He had done so much for her since the wedding. Was that why she battled an urge to care for him now? Her feelings about Prescott Harrington were not easily understood.

Even though she sat still and quiet so as not to disturb him, eventually Harry stirred and opened his eyes. "Did you bring me a snack?" he asked, his expression hopeful.

"I did. But it's to go with the medicine."

"It will stay in my stomach for a little bit. I'm starving," he complained.

"Don't get too excited. The only thing in the kitchen was apple juice and a cereal bar. I suppose we should go to the grocery store now that you're back with the car."

He looked guilty. "Sorry. I didn't think about the fact that you would be stranded."

"It's no biggie. Everything I've needed to do is in walking distance. And I've eaten a lot of meals in town."

Without warning, Harry tried to scoot up in the bed. Disaster beckoned from several corners. First was the way the covers shifted. Cate tried not to look.

But she winced when he groaned in pain. Clearly, the maneuver was not easy. "What are you doing?" she asked, exasperated.

"I can't eat and drink if I'm flat on my back."

"I've always heard men are terrible patients," she muttered

as she scrambled off the bed and retrieved the snacks. She took the top off the apple juice and handed it to him.

Harry wrinkled his nose. "Haven't had this since I was a kid." But he drank half the bottle.

Cate handed him the cereal bar, already opened. "You're going to get crumbs in your bed."

He shot her a sideways glance. "I'm the only one in here, so what does it matter?"

She didn't want to think about who was or wasn't sharing Harry's bed. He'd had two whole weeks to reconnect with any of his women friends back in Atlanta.

Just as he finished the snack bar, the alarm on Cate's watch beeped. She took the medicine bottle and shook out a single tablet. Harry swallowed it down with the last of the apple juice.

"I'm going to sleep in the bedroom on the other side of the bathroom," she said. The words came out calm and steady, not at all reflective of her jangled nerves. "I'll bring your meds when it's time."

Harry scowled. "You don't have to do that."

"But I'm going to," she said, staring him down.

For once, he was the first to blink. "Fine," he grumbled. "If you want a night of no sleep, that's up to you." He scooted onto his back again.

Cate didn't even try to help with the covers. He was grumpy and hurting. She didn't want to poke the tiger.

She took the snack debris and dropped it into the trash can in the bathroom. "I'll be back to check on you after I take a shower."

"Don't go," he said.

Cate froze. His eyes were closed. She honestly thought he was half-asleep. "I won't be long."

"Sit with me, Cate."

If it had been a command, she might have ignored him. But those four simple words were a plea. Harry needed her.

"Okay," she said, all the while thinking she should run in the opposite direction. Even injured, Harry was a powerful temptation. Did their enforced intimacy create an unexpected connection, or was she searching for a relationship to fill the hole in her life?

What would Jason say? He'd always had a knack for reading people. He also knew how to spot a con or a liar. Cate was far too trusting. *Naive*. That was the word. When was she going to grow up? Harry wasn't interested in her. He'd been kind as a favor to Jason.

Despite her misgivings, she sat down on the bed again. Minutes passed. She played solitaire on her phone and let Harry sleep. But he was fidgety, clearly uncomfortable.

After twenty minutes, he slung an arm over his head and sighed. "Talk to me. I'm bored."

"You're not bored. You're just not used to being less than a hundred percent. Consider this a character-building exercise. Patience is good for the soul."

He opened one eye and gave her a look that might have been intimidating if he wasn't naked and helpless.

On second thought, *helpless* was the wrong word. Even drugged and with a bum knee, Harry was a force not to be underestimated.

"My soul is fine," he said.

"Tell me about your family."

His face shuttered instantly. "No."

She touched his arm, squeezing lightly. "Is your father deceased? Why don't you have a good relationship with your mother?"

One minute passed, then two. "It's a long, ugly story." His

lips twisted. It might have been pain from his knee causing that expression, but she had a hunch it was something worse.

"I have nowhere to go," she said softly.

He moved restlessly, searching for a comfortable position and clearly not finding one. His chest rose and fell in a ragged sigh that seemed dredged up from deep inside him.

"My father is in prison," he said curtly.

"Why?"

"Because he beat the shit out of my mother, broke her arm and her jaw and left her for dead."

Cate gasped. She couldn't help it. "I'm sorry," she said. "This isn't a good time to do this. You need to sleep."

He raised up on both elbows and glared at her. "You wanted to know. Now at least have the guts to listen."

Though she trembled inside, she forced herself to nod. "Okay. But lie back down."

He did as she asked, probably because he was woozy. For a moment she thought he had dozed off again. But then he opened his eyes without warning and stared straight at her, the pain there for her to see. "I've never married because of him."

It didn't take a genius to connect the dots. "Oh, Harry."

"What if I turn into him? I couldn't take that chance. No wife. No kids."

"You're not like that at all," she said firmly.

"I have a temper."

She managed a smile despite the tenor of the conversation. "I can't argue with that. But have you ever even hit anyone in anger?"

Harry nodded bleakly. "I punched a kid in middle school. He was harassing this shy little girl who was scared of him, and he wouldn't stop. So I punched him. He had to go to the hospital. I was suspended for a week."

"That doesn't make you an abuser," Cate said, choosing her words with care. He clearly believed it was possible.

"But it *does* mean I could snap. They say it can be genetic."

Unconsciously, she had been stroking his arm. Now she squeezed it for a second time. "I know you, Harry. And Jason certainly does. He thinks the world of you. You're not a violent person."

"Maybe." He closed his eyes again.

His breathing deepened. The pain meds had kicked in. But Harry was fighting them, perhaps unconsciously.

"It's time to remove the ice pack," she said. "I probably should have already done that."

She had to touch the warm skin of his leg to get the ice pack off. Underneath, his kneecap had already turned half a dozen shades of purple, though the swelling wasn't any worse. Carefully, she slipped the Velcro strap out from under him.

"There," she said. "Let me go put this in the freezer." That way there would always be one ready to go.

When Harry didn't protest, she assumed he was asleep.

Downstairs, she moved carefully in the dark. When she opened the freezer door, the air rushed out, cold on her hot cheeks. Would Harry ever have told her the truth if he hadn't been drugged?

Did Jason know? Surely so.

But how did that explain Harry's feelings about his mother?

Confusion and fatigue were a bad combination. She climbed the stairs slowly, feeling a million years old. After a very quick shower, she dried off and put on a pair of knit shorts and a loose T-shirt.

Then she brushed her teeth, gathered her phone cord and a few other things, and tiptoed down the hall.

After turning back the covers on the unused guest bed,

she slipped through the adjoining bathroom and checked on her patient.

Earlier, she had turned off the overhead light and left only a small lamp burning on the bedside table. Harry appeared to be dead to the world.

Her instinct was to turn off the lamp. But if Harry tried to get up during the night and she didn't hear him, the dark would be dangerous.

She left the small light burning and made sure both bathroom doors were open. Then she fell into bed and was asleep instantly.

The alarm in the middle of the night was an obscene shock. No rays of sunlight peeked through the drapes. For a good twenty seconds, Cate was completely disoriented.

Finally, understanding filtered through her groggy brain. Before checking on Harry, she went downstairs and retrieved an ice pack along with more juice and another cereal bar. The cold therapy was long overdue, but a woman could only handle so much when the patient was cranky, naked and not related to her.

The pain meds must have been doing their work. Harry appeared to be sleeping peacefully. The covers weren't tumbled. One hand rested, palm open, on his chest.

She debated waking him. It seemed cruel. On the other hand, the ice pack would help with swelling, and the pills would stave off further pain.

It was a heck of a choice. Finally, she sat down on his side of the bed and put her hand on his bare shoulder. "Harry," she said quietly.

He never moved, though his chest rose and fell with steady breathing. "Harry." This time she shook him.

Those gorgeous eyelashes fluttered and opened. Even

bleary-eyed, the man was beautiful. "What time is it?" he asked.

"Middle of the night. I have your medicine."

"I need to go to the bathroom."

"Oh," she said, blushing. "I'll step into the hall."

She leaned against the wall and listened. When she was certain he was back in bed, she returned to her mission.

Harry was sitting up, waiting. And he had made sure his injured leg was uncovered. This time, she didn't ask questions. She positioned the ice pack, offered the juice and snack, and gave him the pain pill.

The whole process took less than five minutes.

As she turned to walk away, Harry caught the hem of her sleep shorts in his fingers. "Thank you," he said, his gaze sober.

"You're welcome."

"One more thing..."

She frowned. "Do you need another blanket? I know that ice pack can make you cold."

"It's not that. Please make sure I'm awake by nine. I'm supposed to be at my mother's house at eleven. I suspect it will take me longer than usual to get dressed and ready."

"Are you sure you can't cancel?"

"I'm going." His tone brooked no interference.

"Got it."

"And I'm not taking pain pills during the day tomorrow."

"But the doctor said—"

Harry cut her off with a slice of his hand. "No meds. The knee is already hurting less."

"I seriously doubt that." She hadn't meant to say the words out loud, but they escaped her lips, perhaps because the hour was late, and Cate was confused and tired.

Harry's expression didn't change. "Go back to bed, Cate. You're dead on your feet."

She walked out of the room abruptly. The stupid man was infuriating, but she didn't have the heart to let him fend for himself.

Monday morning Cate woke at eight, twisted her hair up in a sophisticated knot and applied makeup with a light hand. Then she went to the closet and pulled out the same outfit she had worn recently to lunch with her parents and sister.

If Cate was going to meet Harry's mother—in any capacity— she wanted to look her best.

Just before nine, she fetched coffee and cinnamon bread from the kitchen, grabbed the spare ice pack, and went to wake Harry as requested. But when she knocked softly at the door and was invited to enter, she found him dressed, with his computer on his lap.

"Breakfast is served," she said, setting the plate and cup beside him. She took the thawed ice pack from the side of the bed and left him the new one.

He looked up with a distracted smile. "I almost blew it," he said. "After the accident last night, I forgot I promised to get some info to my executive assistant for a meeting this morning."

"Are you going to make it in time?"

"Barely."

Now that he brought it up, Cate did remember him mentioning the task. "What time are we leaving?"

"Ten thirty will work."

"I'll be downstairs," she said. "Put the ice pack on your knee."

While Harry was busy, Cate ate her own light meal and then got out her laptop to start a list. *Things Cate Penland Needs to Accomplish Before the End of July.*

1) Find a place to live in Atlanta.
2) Close on the new store.
3) Order inventory.
4) Interview hourly employees and potential managers.
5) Extricate myself from Harry's orbit.

She stared at that last one for a long time. It was perhaps the most important item on the list. Maybe she should move it to number one. Spending so much time with Prescott Harrington was making her think weird thoughts. Like whether he needed a woman in his life and if that woman should or could be her.

Now that she had processed Jason's actions on that terrible day, June 7, she was finally starting to come out of a fog. Or so it seemed. Jason was not her soul mate. If anything, he had done her a favor.

It was a tough pill to swallow. Admitting Jason was right about their relationship made Cate feel foolish, immature and uncertain.

Not that she had confessed her revelation to *anybody*. For now, she was content to let friends and family think she was the injured party. On those grounds, no one would give her any grief while she stumbled around trying to figure out her life.

Why hadn't she stood up to her parents? Why hadn't she insisted on a small wedding in Blossom Branch? Under those circumstances, it would have been far easier for Jason to have talked to her before it was too late.

With the clarity of time, she saw that she had been a coward. Jason had represented safety. Everyone approved of her choice of groom. To have admitted her mistake early on would have been unthinkable.

She was twelve when she'd been forced to leave Blossom

Branch, and her world had been upended. Since that time, playing the part of the *good* girl had been her safety net, a role she once embraced, but now had come to resent.

So she'd learned a valuable lesson. From now on, she wouldn't be pressured into doing something that didn't feel right. It wasn't that the big wedding was inherently wrong. But it had been wrong for her.

Fifteen

Over the next forty-five minutes, her list grew to a dozen entries. Some of them were exciting. A few were chores she dreaded. Like moving her things out of Jason's apartment. She was afraid of how it would feel to walk back inside those walls where she and her one-time fiancé had shared so much fun.

Would she mourn him all over again?

She hoped not.

She did, in fact, move the Harry item to number one. With every day that passed, something was happening between the two of them. It was probably one-sided. But then again, he *had* kissed her.

It could have been a joke. His way of coping with a smashed-up knee. People made odd choices in the midst of trauma.

As she heard Harry's crutches on the stairs, she quickly shut her laptop. Her face flushed. She hoped he wouldn't notice.

When he made it to the living room, she cocked her head and studied him. He was dressed in casual business attire. The upscale sport coat over a crisp dress shirt and dark khaki pants fit him perfectly.

"On a scale of one to ten, how bad is the knee?" she asked.

Harry looked pale beneath his tan. And there were lines at the corners of his mouth that indicated he might be clenching his jaw.

He shrugged. "Not terrible."

"Liar."

"Don't start with me, Cate."

"You've barely been up for three hours, and you're in pain. Either call your mother and cancel or take a pill. Heck, take half a pill if that will satisfy your stupid macho code."

He exhaled. "I'm not being macho. Dealing with my mother requires all my attention. I need to be sharp."

"That makes no sense at all, but okay. I'm going to be with you. Can't I run interference?"

"I think you should drop me off and pick me up at one."

Cate gaped. "Did you not tell her I was coming with you?"

"I sent her a text. So the lunch count would be correct. But I'm having second thoughts."

"Well, I'm not," Cate said. "Sit down while I go get your medicine."

To her surprise, Harry cooperated. When she came downstairs with the translucent orange bottle, she rattled it in one hand. "Half or whole? Your call."

"Half," he muttered.

"There's a little coffee left in the pot. Or the apple juice."

"Juice is fine."

She wanted to look at his knee, but his pants were not the kind to roll up easily. "How bad is the swelling?"

"Not terrible." His tight grin told her she wasn't going to get more than that.

"Are you ready to go?" she asked, trying to decipher his mood.

"As ready as I'll ever be."

He wouldn't let her help him get into the car. It was painful to watch. Clearly, bending the knee was dreadfully uncomfortable.

When he had his seat belt fastened, she started the engine. "Do you want me to put the address in my phone, or are you going to give me directions?"

"I'll tell you how to get there," he said. "For now, head out of town on the old highway."

Cate wondered if Harry was one of those men who hated not being behind the wheel. Last night it hadn't mattered. He'd been battered and bruised and literally bleeding.

Now he stared out the side window as if he was deeply interested in the fields of corn they passed.

There were peach orchards, too. Plenty of them.

At an intersection, Harry pointed. "Take a left here. In about five miles you'll see the driveway on the right. I'll show you."

It was crazy, but she felt the back of her neck and her shoulders tightening. This visit had nothing at all to do with her, but Harry's mood was rubbing off on her.

At exactly 5.2 miles, Harry directed her onto a narrow, paved road. As they left the state highway, two large stone lions atop matching concrete posts flanked the turn.

Once Cate steered the car and paused, she saw they were on private property—a driveway that led up a series of low rises all the way to a hilltop peak in the distance. The perfectly manicured pavement had to be at least a mile long.

"Wow," she said. "This is your home?"

"This is my *mother's* home," he clarified, his voice stiff. "I haven't lived here since I turned eighteen."

Cate began to understand there was far more to this story than she understood.

At the top, the driveway curved into a circle. The house

was enormous, redbrick with a wide front porch and white columns She parked right at the base of the steps. Twelve or fifteen of them as far as she could tell. "Is there another entrance we could use that would be easier for crutches?"

Harry adjusted his dark sunglasses on the bridge of his nose. "Nope. Company comes in the front. Always."

Curiouser and curiouser. Cate hovered at Harry's elbow, ready to help if needed, but she was aware of his body language. He was determined to do this on his own. If he had been able to drive, Cate wouldn't be here at all.

A woman in a navy and teal uniform answered the door. "Hello, Mr. Harry," she said, beaming. "Oh, my. What did you do to yourself?"

"Hello, Justine. A running mishap. Nothing serious." He gave the older woman a kiss on the cheek. "How's the family?"

"All good," she said. "My oldest grandbaby is off to college at the end of the summer."

Harry's eyes widened. He tucked his sunglasses in his shirt pocket. "That's not possible. I remember when she was born."

Justine chuckled. "Time waits for no man. Or woman." She greeted Cate as well with a warm smile. "Would you like a glass of something cold, ma'am? Iced tea? A mint julep?"

A mint julep? What was this? A scene from a 1950s Southern-set movie? "Um, no thanks. I'm fine for now."

Justine gave Harry an odd glance. The two of them appeared to exchange some unspoken message. "Your mother is waiting in the drawing room," Justine said. "We'll have lunch in thirty minutes."

"Thanks," Harry said. He straightened his shoulders, despite the crutches. "Showtime," he muttered under his breath.

Cate wasn't at all sure he meant for her to hear.

The house was laid out neatly on either side of a wide,

marble-tiled hallway. The *drawing room* on the right was easily twenty-four feet in length. Large windows framed the pastoral view. The elaborate furnishings were over-the-top, reminiscent of the Palace of Versailles, if Versailles happened to be found in Georgia and had fewer mirrors.

Harry's mother held court on a red, velvet-covered settee halfway down the expanse of Oriental carpet. She didn't stand as they approached. At first, she smiled, but then she wrinkled her nose. "*Must* you use those ugly crutches, Prescott?"

"Yes, Mother. For a few days at least." He offered Cate a chair and took the one beside her. "This is Cate Penland. She's a friend of Jason's. Cate has plans to open a gift shop in Blossom Branch. I'm helping her with a few architectural details. Cate, this is my mother, Georgia Harrington."

"Hello, Mrs. Harrington," Cate said, hoping her nerves didn't show. Cate was no stranger to a variety of societal occasions and expectations, but this was whole-other-level stuff.

Harry's mother studied Cate. "Penland. Who are your people?"

"Mother…" Harry's tone held an edge.

"It's okay, Harry." Cate smiled at his mother. "I grew up here in Blossom Branch until I was twelve. That's when we moved to Atlanta. My parents are Gillian and Reggie Penland."

"Ah, yes. Your father came from desperately straightened circumstances as I recall."

"Mother!" There was a definite snap in Harry's voice now.

His parent paid him no mind. "It's fine, son. Cate's father has much to be proud of, especially given the extreme poverty of his birth."

Cate gaped in shock. She had never heard anyone offer such a sly, stinging, backhanded compliment.

Before Harry or Cate could say another word, Georgia tapped her chin. "But wait. That means *you* are the jilted bride. Poor dear. That must have been dreadfully humiliating."

Harry dropped his sunglasses and leaned over to pick them up, his face toward Cate. "I tried to warn you," he said, sotto voce.

Cate managed a strained smile as she reacted to Harry's mother. "It wasn't one of my best days, that's for sure."

"Well, don't see this house and get any ideas about courting my rapscallion of a son. Prescott has made it very clear he won't take a penny from this estate. Of course, when I'm gone, he'll do as he pleases, I'm sure."

Cate couldn't think of a single suitable response, so she kept her mouth shut. This was awful. No, worse than awful. Harry's mother was a Flannery O'Connor character.

Georgia rose to her feet with some difficulty. She was as wide as she was tall. "We'll adjourn to the dining salon," she said, her tone regal.

The next room was as ornate as the first. Three places had been set at one end of a polished mahogany table that could easily seat twenty. Cate recognized the china pattern. One of her college friends owned an antique store in Atlanta. Those plates went for a hundred dollars a pop.

Beneath a baroque crystal chandelier, heavy silver with intricate designs gleamed. The pieces would be a bear to clean.

Moments later, Justine appeared with the soup course. Fortunately, this part of the visit was a home run. The gazpacho must have been made with fresh vegetables from a nearby garden. It tasted like the best of summer.

Next was a salad course, followed by lamb with mashed potatoes. Cate wasn't a huge fan of lamb, but she ate enough not to offend. By the time the dessert came around, Cate was stuffed, and Harry was clearly flagging. She had to get him out of this ridiculous house.

They both ate half of their chocolate ganache cake.

"That was a lovely meal, Mrs. Harrington," Cate said.

Georgia dabbed her lips with a linen napkin. "Thank you, my dear. I would, of course, prefer to have a French-trained chef, but we make do with what we have here in the back-woods. Justine does her best."

Since poor Justine was standing no more than six feet away, Harry's mother had to know her remark was overheard. Maybe Justine was used to the careless insults. Her expression revealed nothing of what she might be thinking. "May I get anyone drink refills?"

Harry smiled, though it didn't reach his eyes. He looked like a man at the end of his rope. "No thanks," he said. "Cate and I need to be going soon."

Georgia pretended to protest. "But you just got here," she said.

Harry's veneer of congeniality iced over. "I know how much you enjoy your afternoon soaps and game shows. We don't want to interrupt your schedule." He looked straight at the housekeeper and not at his mother. "Thank you, Justine. The meal was incredible."

"Thank you, Mr. Harry. I hope you and Ms. Penland will come back for another visit soon."

Clearly, Georgia didn't like her son fraternizing with the hired help. "We won't keep you," she said, rising to her feet. "Cate, I'm pleased to have met you. Hopefully your fortunes will take a turn for the better. A woman with your looks will find someone else soon."

The remark was crass and totally rude. When Harry bristled, Cate put her hand on his arm. "I think we'll be on our way. Harry was just at the hospital last night, so he needs to take it easy. I suggested that he could cancel, and you would understand, but he didn't want to disappointment you."

Cate gave Georgia a stern look to let her know that Harry had someone else on his side. He wasn't alone in fielding his mother's nonsense.

Somehow, they made it out of the house and into the car. Harry was gray-faced, and his forehead was damp.

"We'll be home in no time," Cate said, starting the engine and pointing the air vents in his direction. "Why don't you put your seat back?"

Harry didn't say a word. His eyes were closed, but Cate wasn't sure if he was really sleeping or playing possum.

At her grandparents' house, she unlocked the door. "You need a nap," she said, not dancing around the issue.

She watched as his lips formed an instinctive refusal. He wasn't a man to be *handled*. But clearly, his knee was giving him fits.

"Only if you come upstairs, too," he said, daring her to refuse.

"I'll read in my room, so I won't disturb you."

"I'd like you in bed with me," he said, "platonically, of course."

"You don't have to be sarcastic. If you want company, all you have to do is ask."

"I thought I just did."

She recognized his mood as volatile. He was on edge from visiting his challenging mother, and he was in a considerable amount of pain. Since they *still* hadn't been to the grocery store, she grabbed a water bottle from the fridge, along with an ice pack, and followed him up the stairs.

"I'll change clothes and be there in a minute," she said. "Here's your medicine."

He took the bottle, but he stared at her with moody, masculine discontent. "Aren't you going to dole it out to me, nurse?"

"Why are you being difficult? It's broad daylight. I think you can handle taking one pill."

His shoulders slumped. "God, I hate going over there."

"Then why do it?" Cate genuinely wanted to know.

"It's usually twice a year. Three times at the most. I'm an only child, so I feel guilty if I don't visit. She's dysfunctional on her best days and hard to handle on others. But I was taught to honor my father and my mother. Since I have just one parent left, I'm stuck with her."

Something about that wry explanation twisted Cate's heart in ways she didn't understand. For years, she had seen Harry through a single lens. He had been a mysterious figure in Atlanta. Jason's cousin—a talented, wealthy architect who worked hard, and according to gossip, played hard.

Now, gradually, she was beginning to see the man he really was. Complex. Flawed. Kind on occasion, but with a sharp edge.

She escaped to her room and found a pair of shorts and a T-shirt. The temperature outside was brutal, and the house was warm. After she adjusted the AC downward a few degrees, she tapped on Harry's door.

"Come in," he said.

She found him on top of the covers with his leg outstretched, leaning against the headboard, hands tucked behind his head. Like Cate, he had changed out of his nice clothes. He wore loose-fitting gray shorts and a soft, much-washed concert T-shirt.

"Don't you want to lie down?" she asked. He had put the ice pack on his knee, so she presumed he had taken a pain pill as well.

"I'm not sleepy." His outthrust jaw dared her to argue.

Cate suspected he was spoiling for a fight only because he needed an outlet from the day's difficult emotions. She understood, but she wasn't in the mood for conflict.

Sixteen

Approaching the bed where a large, cranky man resided was the equivalent of invading a lion's den. Cate decided to play it cool. Instead of sitting against the headboard as Harry was, she stretched out beside him and turned on her side, hoping he would follow suit.

"Tell me what you were like as a kid," she said. It was difficult to imagine the man she knew growing up in that ridiculous house.

It was a shame narcotics were habit-forming because they made Harry's guarded personality much more open. He scooted down on the pillows, no longer sitting upright, but not flat on his back either.

His eyelids were heavy. Now he laced his hands over his taut, flat abdomen. "Like any kid back then, I guess. My friends and I ran wild outside, both after school and in the summers—as long as my mom didn't know I had slipped out through my bedroom window."

"Did your family always live in that same house?"

"Since I was a toddler. My father's family came from money

all the way back to the Civil War. I've never spent too much time studying his pedigree because I'm sure some of that wealth came from dubious sources."

"And your mom's family?"

"Comfortable, but not rich. She took quite a step up when she married my dad. But it came with a steep price. Along with the Harrington multigenerational fortune was a deep streak of alcoholism."

"I've never seen you drink a lot."

Harry's eyes were closed now. He wasn't asleep, but clearly the pain meds were zoning him out. "Sometimes I want a second shot of whiskey or a third glass of wine," he said. "But I never let myself have it. I've always been afraid."

Cate pondered those words. Harry was quiet. How terrible to always live in the dark shadow of his father's DNA. At last, she asked the question that had bothered her the most. "Did your father hit *you*?"

Harry shifted again. Now he was all the way down in the bed on his side, his posture mirroring Cate's. He took a strand of her hair and wrapped it around his finger, playing with it absently.

His gray gaze met hers. "Not often. Only when it could be categorized as well-deserved punishment. He enjoyed dishing out retribution when I broke the rules."

"And how did your mother deal with that?"

Harry's gaze shifted beyond Cate's shoulder as if he didn't want to look at her. "She didn't. I don't recall her ever trying to protect me from him. My father was a mean drunk. That's when he wrapped cars around trees and came home raging. All the local law enforcement guys back then knew him well. But my daddy greased so many palms, he never faced the consequences of his actions."

"Why didn't your mother leave and take you with her?"

Now Harry met Cate's questioning gaze head-on. "It's really very simple. She likes living in the lifestyle to which she has grown accustomed. For years I heard her make excuses for my father. He was under a lot of stress at work. Or he didn't sleep well the night before. Maybe I had left my bike in the driveway, or my mother had forgotten to carry out some trivial task."

"Poor Georgia," Cate said. "She must have felt trapped with no way out."

Harry's beautiful, masculine lips twisted. "You're a far nicer person than I am, Cate...giving her the benefit of the doubt."

"What do you mean?"

"The week I turned eighteen, I could finally taste freedom. Even without my father's money, I had earned a prestigious scholarship. I was going away to college at the end of the summer. I quietly and secretively began packing my things. I knew my father wouldn't like me leaving. He would see it as a betrayal, no matter how weird and twisted that was."

Cate sensed the story was nearing a climax. She wasn't sure she wanted to hear what came next. The tug of Harry's fingers on her hair was disturbing. It was intimate and odd at the same time.

They were sharing a bed, but not anything else.

Circumstances had brought them closer than they should have been, and yet now that Harry was with her here in this house, she felt as if she knew him, really knew him.

Which was why she had to understand this last bit of his life, maybe the part that defined him.

"What happened on your birthday?" she asked.

He shrugged, his gaze for a moment filled with warm recollections. "I left before breakfast," he said. "Some buddies and I took a boat out on Lake Lanier and spent the day goofing off. Skiing. Tubing. Swimming."

"But no drinking?"

"Surprisingly, no. My friends knew where I stood on that issue. They had seen the black eyes. Sometimes I think that was the worst. Jason's parents wanted to help, but there was not much they could do. Everybody in the community, everybody at school, *knew* who my daddy was and what he was like. I hated people feeling sorry for me. Still do."

Cate heard the warning and hid a smile. "Sounds like a fun birthday. Did your family celebrate that evening?"

Harry shook his head slowly. "When I came up the driveway, it was dark. There were cars everywhere. For half a second, I thought they were throwing me a surprise party. Then the fireworks started, and I felt dumb as a rock. My parents weren't celebrating their only son turning eighteen. The Fourth of July holiday was an excuse to show off the pool and the giant picnic spread and the well-known country music band from Atlanta."

"Oh, Harry." He had told her outright he didn't like people feeling sorry for him. But thinking of that eighteen-year-old boy broke her heart. "So, you're telling me you were born on the Fourth of July?" she asked with a smile, trying to lighten the mood.

Harry still played with her hair, sending shivers of *something* down her spine. "Yep," he said.

"Then we should celebrate this Saturday."

"No, thanks." He pretended to shudder. "I'm very low-key when it comes to birthdays."

During their conversation, she had inhaled his scent, studied the patterns of gray and silver in his eyes, memorized the mix of colors in his thick inky-black hair. Without warning, she found herself in dangerous territory—in part, because her heart ached for him, and she wanted to offer her sympathy and support.

If that had been all it was, she would have been okay. But the feeling was dangerously more. Cate wanted to kiss him. *She wanted to kiss Harry…good Lord…*

It would be so easy. The physical space between them was negligible. All she had to do was lean forward and let her lips touch his. Even the thought of it made her body buzz with excitement.

She was breathless and scared and everything in between.

In an instant, she suddenly understood why Jason had called a halt to their wedding. They had loved each other, but they hadn't shared this wild, trembling passion.

Regrettably, the feelings that gripped her now—making her heart race and her breath saw in her chest—were almost assuredly one-sided. Harry saw her as a project, a problem to be solved.

But he *had* kissed her, so what about that?

Because she was terrified of facing this incredible self-revelation, she went back to Harry's sad tale. "Was there an end to that Fourth of July story? When you went home, I mean?"

His gaze was bleak. "Yes. I found my mother and asked to speak with her. I'd been waiting until I was officially an adult so she would know I was serious. She didn't really want to leave the festivities, but she agreed. I explained that I had been playing the stock market. I had money from my grandparents, and I had worked several part-time jobs. There was enough in my account for the two of us to move out of my father's house and find an apartment near the university where I had been accepted. It meant I would probably have to take a few extra semesters to get through school, but I wanted to rescue her from my father's wild rages. I told her no one should have to live like that."

"And what did she say?"

Harry rolled onto his back and flung an arm across his eyes.

"She laughed. Told me I was overreacting. That she was fine. She loved my father. The truth was, she couldn't conceive of walking away from the money. It was the only security she wanted."

"What did you do?"

"I was stunned. She had been hurt so many times. Mostly, my father would stop short of inflicting any wounds that would require medical attention. He and my mother were good at *hiding*. But occasionally it was worse. I was afraid that my leaving would tip the balance."

"And did it?"

He turned his head in her direction, his expression bleak. "Ten days after I moved out, he attacked her brutally. She nearly died. Even then, I had to convince her to press charges. But thank God, they put him behind bars. Her injuries were so severe, my father wasn't able to bribe his way out that time. It was second degree attempted murder. It's been almost two decades. He'll be released on parole a few years from now."

"You were a good son," Cate said firmly. "You *are* a good son."

Harry rubbed the bridge of his nose as if his head ached. "You see how she is. She's built this entire fantasy life. Her mental state is fragile. Some days I'm not even sure she knows he's alive or that they're still married. The house and the money give her the security she craves."

"I'm sorry. I don't know what else to say. It sucks."

He nodded slowly. "Especially since I won't be able to get married or have a family. I won't bring a woman into that mess, and I won't risk a child's future."

Cate heard the message loud and clear. The attraction between them didn't matter. Harry was a lone wolf. He might eat out of her hand occasionally, but he was a wild animal who couldn't or wouldn't be tamed.

He was telling her what to expect. Warning her.

As she digested the extraordinarily sad story, Harry finally fell asleep.

She slipped out of bed and went to her room. After finding paper and a pen, she wrote a short note telling him she was headed to the grocery store. Then she tiptoed down the hall and dropped the note on the bed beside him.

A text would have worked, too, but he didn't have his phone close at hand.

At the market, she dithered about what to buy. In the end, she gathered things at random—chicken and beef and a variety of vegetables. She wasn't a great cook, but she could throw together a healthy meal.

When she returned home, she unloaded the groceries quietly. Harry came downstairs at four-thirty looking much better. "Something smells great," he said.

She wiped her hands on her shorts. "Nothing fancy. Chicken and veggie soup with baked sweet potatoes and salad."

"Sounds wonderful. Can I help?"

Cate was flustered. "No. Not on crutches. Besides, the soup will need to simmer."

"I probably won't use them tomorrow. I tried putting weight on the knee a few minutes ago. It hurts, but it holds me up."

"Are you nuts? You might do more damage."

His grin took the starch out of her knees. "I like to live on the edge."

Cate had spent the past couple of hours reminding herself of the many reasons she needed to keep an emotional distance between them. But all he had to do was smile at her, and she was mush.

"Why don't you go watch TV in the living room?" she said. "I think there's a Braves game on."

"I need to be on my feet."

"Well, then, go walk around the backyard. Carefully."

Harry cocked his head, staring at her intently. Serious now. As if he was trying to see inside her head. "Do I make you nervous, Cate?"

"Of course you make me nervous. You're you, and I'm me." She felt her cheeks heating.

"Translation?"

"You think I'm a kid."

He scowled. "I most assuredly do not. I'm not blind."

She blinked. The way he looked at her made her body tighten in secret places. "Um. That's not what I meant exactly. Jason said I had some growing up to do. I assume you think the same."

His gaze softened. "I'm sorry he hurt your feelings. I don't think he meant to criticize."

"And you?" She tensed, waiting for something. Some proof that Harry saw her as more than a nuisance.

Harry limped in her direction, set the crutches aside and moved to face her. Then he put his hands on both sides of her neck, bent his head and slanted his mouth over hers for a kiss. "I think you're *very* grown-up," he said huskily. "In all the best possible ways."

Cate was so shocked she dropped the tongs she was holding. When Harry made it clear this wasn't a quick kiss like the one on the street last night, she curled her arms around his neck and kissed him back.

"Oh," she said breathlessly when they came up for air.

It might have been the lighting in the kitchen, but Harry looked pale. "Oh, what?" he said.

"Just *oh*." Cate couldn't decide if she was embarrassed or exultant. Stoic, mysterious, aggravating Harry Harrington *wanted* her. She wasn't misreading the signals after all.

He ran one hand through her hair, separating the strands with his fingers. "Have I shocked you, Cate?"

The rim of silver in his irises seemed to glow with heat.

"A little," she confessed. "I thought you were only being nice to me because of Jason."

Harry's expression went from predatory to wry. "I care deeply for my cousin, but not enough to kiss random women."

"I'm not random," she said indignantly.

"True." He kissed her nose. "You're adorable."

"Now you're back to making me sound like a kid."

"Not at all. I'm impressed with your maturity in every way."

"Sarcasm?"

"Not even a little. C'mon, Cate. You've survived a very public crisis in your personal life with grace and dignity. You haven't whined *poor me*. You've picked up the pieces and started looking for a new direction. That takes guts."

The look on his face made her feel good in a way she hadn't since her wedding day.

"Thank you," she said. The lump of emotion in her throat made the words come out raspy. "I'm not sure what my life is going to look like from here, but I'm trying."

He kissed her cheek as if he couldn't stop touching her. "And lucky for you, one of Atlanta's premier architects is going to spend the next few days designing you a kick-ass apartment over the new store."

"I'm excited about that," she confessed. "But the building's so old, there's no elevator. I'm not sure your knee can handle multiple trips up and down."

"You let me worry about my leg," he said. "I'm making a mental note to see what we can do about adding an elevator shaft."

"You can do that?"

"A small one, yes."

Behind her, the timer on the oven went off reminding her to tend to the soup. "Go do something," she said. "And let me finish getting dinner together."

"Yes, ma'am." His grin was naughty, but he left the room, giving her some much-needed breathing space.

She had the simple meal on the table in another hour. When she called for Harry, and he joined her, the domesticity of the scene sent alarm bells ringing. What was she doing playing house with a man like Harry? She needed to get him back to Atlanta ASAP and then set about breaking the ties that bound them together.

No more shared living spaces. No more borrowing cars. No more stealing breathless kisses at odd moments.

Harry was dangerous. Cate knew that. And as much as she was tempted to take what he had to give, her intuition told her she might not survive the fallout.

Seventeen

After dinner was consumed and the meal cleaned up, Harry went out to his car and brought in a white plastic tube. "Let's look at the preliminary drawings," he said. He spread a stack of large blueprints on the dining room table.

"Drawings?" Cate was puzzled. "But you've never been inside the place."

"An old classmate of mine works at the courthouse. He pulled the tax records and some appraisals for me. All I needed was the basic outlines. Here. Come look at this and see if it's what you had in mind."

Cate approached the table with trepidation. Not that she thought Harry's work would be subpar, but because standing next to him, hip to hip, seemed risky. "What am I looking at?" she asked, trying not to get too close.

He put small weights on the four corners and pointed. "This is the ground floor. From what you've told me, not much needs to change there."

"No. But I was thinking of adding a few built-in display shelves with some targeted lighting."

"Great idea. Those could fit here or here or both." He flipped the top sheet to one side. "This is the upstairs where you want to have an apartment. It looks like the plumbing will have to be replaced, which is not altogether a bad thing. You can do some upgrades. I've penciled in this wall. That gives you storage on one side and a decent-sized efficiency apartment here. If you think you can get by with less storage, I could always make the bedroom separate, and you could have a tiny kitchen and bath."

"That's a lot to think about."

He straightened. "You've got time."

"And the cost estimates?"

"Won't be bad. My work will be free, of course. And I have a few sources here and there where we can get building materials. Sometimes on a huge project in Atlanta there are leftovers. If I round up what you'll need, your costs will be minimal. Scrounging is fun. It's what I did in the early days."

His genuine enthusiasm made her believe this could really happen. "How did you find the time to do all this?" she asked, waving a hand at the neatly drawn pages.

Harry shrugged. "In the evenings. I enjoyed it."

Cate analyzed his explanation. In the beginning—when he left Blossom Branch—he'd given her the impression he'd be in Atlanta a few days, not two weeks. If he was so darned busy, why did he futz around with *her* stuff?

Had he honestly been avoiding her?

"Thank you, Harry," she said. "I really appreciate your help."

"I haven't done anything yet. Not really. Tomorrow will be the test. Once we do a walkthrough in the morning, I may have to alter a few things."

Suddenly, Cate was scared. Scared of the invisible cord that drew ever tighter, binding her and Harry in an odd partnership. "When do you get your stitches out?" she asked.

"They're the dissolving kind."

"But the guy in the emergency room did mention you should check in with an orthopedist to get your knee examined."

Harry frowned. "What are you trying to say, Cate?"

She managed not to wring her hands. Instead, she shoved them in her pockets and leaned against the wall. "If we went back to Atlanta Wednesday morning, you could see the doctor, and I might go to Jason's and pack up my things. If we spent the night at your place, we could come back here on Thursday for the holiday weekend. We don't want to be driving on Friday. The traffic will be nuts."

Silence reigned after her nervous explanation. "You're saying you want to go to Jason's without me?" Harry said.

The complete lack of inflection in his question rattled her. "It's not that," she said. "I was trying to be efficient."

Actually, it was *exactly* that. The idea of being with Harry inside the apartment where she and Jason had lived together was stomach-tightening. It would be weird and uncomfortable and awful.

He stared at her. "It's going to be hot as hell this week. You'll need me to help load boxes. And besides, that little electric car won't have enough room for all your stuff."

"We can talk about it later," she said.

Harry recognized her discomfort with the topic. His expression softened. "How about we go for a walk? Now that the sun is down, it won't be bad."

Cate shook her head slowly. "Not tonight. You shouldn't overdo it with your hurt knee. And I have some emails to answer. I'll see you at breakfast. We finally have real food now, so you can have more than a cereal bar."

All the while she was explaining, she inched toward the doorway and the certainty of escape.

But Harry wasn't going to tolerate her cowardice. He followed her. "Talk to me, Catie. What's going on?"

"Nothing..." The word came out on an embarrassing squeak.

"Are you upset because I kissed you?"

She swallowed hard. "No. But I'm tired. I thought I'd go to bed early."

"You're a terrible liar," he said. "Everything you think is written on your face."

"That's not true," she whispered.

"Then why are you running away?"

Surely, she was imagining the flicker of vulnerability in his gaze. Harry might hurt *her* in the end. Not intentionally. But a man of his experience couldn't possibly be affected by anything Cate might say or do.

She tried to clear the lump in her throat. Maybe it was time for honesty. "I don't know what you want from me," she said.

He ran his thumb from the top of her shoulder down to her wrist. "I think you do. But if it's not what *you* want, Cate, all you have to do is say so."

"You're talking about sex."

His gaze narrowed. "Maybe. When the time is right. There's no rush."

But that was the problem. Cate wanted him now. She wanted him so much, she had started having dreams about him. Hot, carnal dreams.

Still, how could she jump headfirst into Harry's bed without knowing the rules, the parameters? How could she ask about the future?

Wasn't it obvious? Harry wanted to fool around. It was what guys like him did. Because Harry and Cate had both tacitly acknowledged the attraction between them, it made sense from his point of view to enjoy each other physically.

It was simple for some people. Too simple. Not many folks went into a one-night stand wondering if a sensual, seductive moment would lead to a relationship.

Besides, Cate already had her answer. Harry liked women. Harry liked sex. Harry even liked Cate. But he had been painfully clear about his intentions. He wasn't in the market for anything permanent. And even though Cate's carefully planned dreams for her future had come crashing down, she still *wanted* permanence. She still wanted a love that would last for decades.

Cate had made huge mistakes in her relationship with Jason. Surely, she wasn't going to let herself be so foolish again.

She met Harry's gray-eyed gaze. "I'm thinking about it," she said. That was as honest as she could be. "I need more time."

He exhaled sharply, as if her answer disappointed him. "Fair enough." He kissed her on the forehead. "Go to bed, Catie-girl. We don't have to figure this out tonight. I'll be waiting when you're ready."

Cate barely slept. How could she? Prescott Harrington expected to sleep with her. As soon as she worked up her courage.

Or, on the other hand, a simple *no*, and he would back off. Gentleman's honor.

What she really wanted was to be swept up in the moment. That way, *things* would happen organically, and she wouldn't have to make up her mind.

How spineless was that?

She and Harry didn't cross paths at breakfast. He had obviously been up early and made coffee. By the time Cate was awake and dressed and had used a careful application of concealer to eradicate the dark circles under her eyes, it was almost nine. The kitchen was empty. She made herself eat toast and drink juice, but the small meal rumbled in her stomach.

Harry—using both crutches—was in a curiously sour mood when he appeared. "I'm going to drive us into town," he said.

His tone dared her to argue, but Cate did anyway. "Oh, no you're not. It hasn't even been forty-eight hours. And aren't you taking pain meds?"

"Not anymore."

They walked outside together. "Well, you still can't drive," she said. "Get in the car, and let's go."

His scowl was darker than a summer storm cloud. His hands clenched in fists at his sides. "You can't stop me," he said, the words flat and angry. The truculent tone wasn't like him at all. Maybe his night had been no more restful than Cate's.

This was the kind of tricky situation that required the finesse of a bomb squad. She gnawed her lip, searching for wisdom. "Harry," she said. "I care about you a lot. I want to protect your leg. Please let me drive."

She went to him and rested her cheek against his chest, wrapping her arms around his waist. His heart pounded rapidly. And was that a faint tremor in his big, masculine frame?

The sun shone hot on top of her head. Dogs barked nearby. Harry smelled yummy, like he had just stepped out of the shower. His quiet strength wooed her, even without words.

Did Harry *need* her? Was that what drew Cate to him? She'd always had a tendency to rescue people.

Her relationship with Jason hadn't been like that at all. Jason was outgoing and confident. He hadn't needed Cate in any way, really. Maybe that should have been a clue to her that they were in a relationship for the wrong reasons.

Harry was such an enigma. He'd been angry with her once when she said everything he'd always wanted had dropped into his lap. Now that she knew more about his formative years, she realized how wrong she had been.

At that same moment on her wedding day, she had told him she hated him.

Why had she said it? It wasn't true, not at all.

She had been lashing out in her pain, embarrassed that she needed rescuing.

Suddenly, it seemed very important to correct her mistake.

She pulled back and shielded her eyes with one hand. "I *don't* hate you, Harry. I *never* hated you. I was such a mess that day, and your life seemed perfect. I'm sorry for saying such an awful thing. Will you forgive me?"

The fight went out of him. She felt it in the huge exhale that whooshed out of his chest. He cupped the back of her head and stroked her hair. "No worries, Catie-girl." He kissed her forehead. "I knew it wasn't true. Who could hate a peach of a guy like me?"

The self-mocking smile broke her heart just a little bit. In that moment, he seemed so alone.

"I'll be careful with your car, I swear."

"I know that. Forget what I said. Let's go."

She wanted to explore his bad mood, but maybe it was better not to know. The three-minute trip into town was short and sweet. Without Harry's injury, they could have walked.

Cate parallel parked near the quad and got out. The streets bustled already with tourists arriving for the holiday festivities. A work crew busily erected small white tents that would house the craft and food vendors.

Red-white-and-blue bunting festooned the eight sides of the gazebo. Though the Fourth was still a few days away, a celebratory tone filled the air. Cate turned her back on the park and looked at *her* store. Despite everything she had done inside, it still appeared abandoned and empty. And it was.

Harry must have sensed her ambivalence. "It's going to be great," he said. "Don't worry."

Cate unlocked the front door. Harry looked around with interest. She could almost see the gears turning in his brain.

"Well," she said. "What do you think?"

He pulled a laser measuring device from his pocket. As Cate watched, he pointed, clicked a button and jotted down a number. Since he was doing all that while on crutches, she was even more impressed.

He still hadn't answered her question.

"Harry? Say something."

"Hmm?"

"Do you like it?"

"Sure. It has good bones. And the colors you've used are perfect."

"Thanks." She still had the feeling he was *thinking* a lot. "You ready to go upstairs?"

"Yep."

"You first."

He was a lot faster now. The crutches barely slowed him down. On the second floor there wasn't much to be impressed about. Harry walked from one side to the other. Measuring. Making notes.

"This wall isn't weight-bearing," he said, kicking at the baseboard. "No problem at all to move it." Then he looked at the commode. "Has this thing been flushed in years?"

"I wouldn't know."

"Well," he said. "It seems to me you'd rather have a slightly bigger apartment and less storage, but that's your call."

"I thought the same thing." She hesitated. "Will you be honest with me? I'd really like to hear any negatives."

He wandered over to the large windows and looked out at the street. "I like it, Cate. I really do. I can definitely see you setting up shop here. Selfishly, I hope you won't abandon Atlanta for good, but you've made a solid business decision."

Relief and warmth flooded her midsection. "That makes me feel better. If an architect of your caliber signs off on the idea, I guess I'm moving forward."

His grin was quick and charming. "You can quit buttering me up. I've already said I'll work for free."

"You don't have to," she said. "I'm not a charity case."

He chuckled. "Take the offer while it's on the table."

They ended up spending another hour in the old store. Harry agreed with most of her ideas about preserving the nuances of the original structure. But he burst a few of her bubbles.

"Sorry," he said, poking at some decorative molding alongside a cabinet. "This has to go. Dry rot."

"But I love it."

"We'll find something similar."

Harry insisted on exploring the gloomy basement. Cate had been down only once, creeped out by the vibes. A psychopath could have buried bodies down there for all she knew.

When she said as much, Harry laughed. "I seriously doubt that. Blossom Branch may be atmospheric and picturesque, but I'm sure the town forefathers would have noticed a serial killer in their midst."

"Maybe." Cate's stomach rumbled. "Are we done? I'm starving. And I'm pretty sure I saw a food truck setting up down the street."

"What kind of food?"

"Does it matter?" She smiled at him, teasing.

They locked up the store and made their way along the sidewalk, dodging kids with cotton candy and adults looking down at their phones.

Harry shook his head. "They're missing all the ambience.

Why come to Blossom Branch if you're not going to take in the sights?"

"It's hard for people to break away from work. You know how that is, right?"

He grimaced. "I do. But I'm trying to evolve."

Cate burst out laughing. "Evolve into what? Sounds painful."

"I'm serious," he said. "I've spent almost twenty years chasing a dream. All I wanted to do was design buildings that would last."

"And you have."

"Maybe. But somewhere along the way, I've gotten stale. I lost the buzz. Walking through your building brought it back."

"Glad to be of service," she said. "Anytime you want to renovate a money pit, you know who to call."

Eighteen

The food truck turned out to be homemade barbecue. Cate and Harry bought two plates and two soft drinks and ate on a bench in the shade of an old oak tree. With the sun filtering through the leaves and the touch of a light breeze, the summer heat was not bad at all.

Peace wrapped Cate in a mellow mood, though her feelings for the man at her side were anything but calm. She was intensely aware of him. The way he made a little sound of enjoyment as he bit into his sandwich. The strong line of his jaw. The casual shirt he wore that stretched to contain his broad shoulders.

Could she have a physical relationship with him and walk away?

It wasn't so far-fetched. People did it all the time.

Besides, what she felt for Jason was so different from this explosive thing with Harry. Maybe *she* should try something different, too.

With Jason in her life, she'd never had the experience of

picking up a guy in a bar or going on a blind date with a stranger.

Now, contemplating sex with Harry made her stomach drop like she was at the county fair riding a roller coaster. She knew instinctively that intimacy with him wouldn't be carefree.

Harry was intense. About everything. Even if their liaison was temporary and fun, he would expect Cate to be all in. No holding back.

He would *know* her in every way. Was she ready for that? Some days she wasn't sure she knew herself.

As much as she was drawn to Harry, she was also wary. She understood now that her reactions to him over the years had been prompted by an underlying sexual awareness.

What did she know about pleasing a man like him? A man of strong appetites. A man who would plumb the depths of her sexual desires and give her what she didn't even know she wanted.

She fanned herself with a napkin, her throat dry. Unconsciously, she had pressed her knees together. It was broad daylight with fifty or a hundred people milling around in every direction.

Yet all Cate could think about was frolicking naked on the grass with Prescott Harrington.

He shot her a sideways glance. "You're flushed. If it's too hot, we can head back to the house."

Her cheeks burned. "No, I'm fine. How do you feel about ice cream?"

His smile was quizzical. "In general? Or right now?"

She pointed across the quad. "I could introduce you to Ginny Black. She owns Peaches and Cream."

"Sounds good to me."

As it turned out, the ice cream shop was very busy. Even

from a distance, Ginny looked frazzled. When it was their turn, Cate quickly introduced Harry to her new acquaintance.

Ginny's smile was cheerful. "Gonna be a zoo this weekend, but that's good for business. What will you have?" She pointed at a small placard. "I recommend the holiday special."

The picture showed three scoops—red, white and blue. Strawberry, vanilla and blueberry.

"I'm game," Harry said. "But why don't we share one cone?"

Cate went hot from her scalp to her toes. He might as well have said, *Let's take off our clothes and dance in the rain.* "Um, sure," she croaked.

Ginny looked at her curiously, but as the woman bent her head to scoop out the ice cream, Cate was able to regroup.

It was only ice cream. Not sex.

She had to get a hold of herself.

When they were back out on the street, Harry waved his hand. "You go first. Eat what you want. I'll finish it off."

"No," Cate said. "We should share." She took one long lick. "There. Now it's your turn."

What had gotten into her? Harry looked poleaxed. Red crept from his collar up his neck. Cate's comment had come out sounding like an invitation to something far less mundane than ice cream.

When she handed him the cone, their fingers touched. Electricity arced between them. It was a wonder the ice cream didn't melt instantly.

As she watched, Harry bent his head sideways and rescued the bits that were running down the cone already. "Eat fast," he said. Instead of giving her the ice cream, he kept the cone firmly in his hand. The man was on crutches. His range of motion was limited.

Cate was forced to step closer. She licked both sides of the three flavors until they were smooth and even. Out of the corner of her eye, she could see Harry's lips. They were damp and shiny.

"This is good," she said.

He deliberately put his mouth close to hers. "Better than good."

Their tongues met somewhere between the red, white and blue.

Cate jerked back, startled. Harry's beautiful silvery-gray eyes weren't opaque now. They flamed like molten steel. No wonder the ice cream was melting. "You eat the rest," she said. "I've had enough."

Her comment could have been interpreted in two ways. Maybe she meant *both*. Yes, she was still full after the big lunch, but more importantly, she wasn't ready for this intense flirtation, even though—arguably—she was the one who started it. Harry suggested one cone, but Cate was the one who made a big deal about *licking*.

Though Harry kept up with the melting ice cream and polished it off, he watched Cate the entire time. So much so that she fidgeted.

When he was done, he tossed the messy napkin in the nearest trash receptacle. "Hand sanitizer?" he asked.

Cate pulled the small plastic bottle from her purse and squirted a blob into his palm. "I suppose we should go back to the house," she muttered. "It's getting crowded."

"Whatever you want, Catie-girl."

She read a million interpretations into those simple words. He smiled as he said them. Did he mean *she* had to be the one to say she wanted *him*? If so, he was probably going to be disappointed or at the very least, in for a long wait.

It was true she was reinventing her entire life, but propositioning Harry would require a whole other level of courage.

What if she was wrong? What if she had misinterpreted his casual affection?

Back at her grandparents' house, Catie tried to hide behind domestic chores. "I'll have dinner ready at six," she said.

Harry frowned. "No. We'll fix a meal together. How do you feel about breakfast for dinner?"

"Love it. Grammy has an old waffle iron here somewhere. And she used to make the most amazing blintzes. Her version, anyway. Two superthin layers filled with strawberries and cream cheese." Cate squatted to rummage in the deep corner cabinet. "Here it is." The old stainless-steel appliance probably hadn't been used in years. "I'll google a recipe for something simple."

"Do we have eggs? And bacon?"

"We do."

"Then we're good to go. I'm going to handle a few work things, so text me when you want to get started."

"I thought you were on vacation."

"I am." His grimace was sheepish. "But my life next week will be easier if I don't get too far behind."

Cate went to her room and changed into running clothes. She felt guilty about abandoning Harry, but it couldn't be helped. By the time she did her usual route, came home, showered, and changed into yoga pants and a soft cotton sweater in baby blue, he was still holed up in his room.

At five thirty, with her stomach growling, she picked up her phone and sent a simple text. Ready when you are.

As soon as she hit the button, she winced. Should have been more specific. Her subconscious was causing mischief. Ready for dinner. Not sex. That was still in the *we'll see* column.

When Harry came downstairs ten minutes later, she saw that he had showered as well. He stopped in the kitchen doorway, smiling, his gaze warm and intimate. "You look nice."

"Thank you." The compliment rattled her. The polite response might be to mention how good he looked in old, faded jeans and a navy Henley. But better to say nothing. The man had to know he was gorgeous. Women likely had been throwing themselves at him for years.

Preparing a meal together in the relatively small kitchen should have been awkward. Surprisingly, it wasn't. When Harry reached in the fridge for a carton of eggs, Cate caught her breath. "Where are your crutches?" she asked, only then noticing that he wasn't using them.

Harry straightened slowly and turned. "I'm being careful." He propped his bare foot on a kitchen chair and pulled up his pant leg. "See. The swelling has gone down."

"Maybe so, but that bruise is still nasty."

"Before I go to the doctor tomorrow, I want to see how much weight I can put on the leg."

"Isn't that for a professional to decide? What if you make it worse?"

"I'm fine, Cate. Honestly. You don't have to worry."

"You're right," she said. "I don't. But I do anyway."

He blinked, as if her response had startled him. "I'm not used to having anybody look after me."

She sighed, recognizing his discomfort with the topic. "I know you're a big, strong, I-can-do-it-myself kind of guy, but you've done a lot for me. I feel like it's my turn."

"No," he said. "It's not." His expression shuttered. The pleasant atmosphere in the kitchen turned cold. "I didn't do anything out of the ordinary for you. Having you in my apartment was not an inconvenience. Don't assign noble motives to me, Cate. I'm bound to disappoint you."

His sharp rebuke came out of nowhere. Cate was stunned and embarrassed. Because she didn't know what to say or how to proceed, she busied herself mixing waffle batter while Harry handled the bacon and eggs.

At the last minute, she warmed syrup in a small pan and added a bowl of fresh raspberries to the table.

The first part of the meal unfolded in silence.

Finally, Cate was exasperated. It was feast or famine with Harry. Either the two of them were far *too* cozy, or else he retreated behind a wall of indifference. She finished her iced tea and got up for more.

With her back to the table, she addressed him. "How often do you see your father?" It was a question she had wanted to ask before now but hadn't found the courage.

As she sat back down, Harry scowled. "Never. Not since the day they took him away."

Cate was shocked. "And does your mother have contact?"

"We don't talk about it, but I think she visits him a few times a year, maybe more. I'm not sure why."

"Sometimes love can't be turned off like a switch. Maybe she understands how broken he is, but she can't let him go completely."

"Or maybe she's hedging her bets about the money."

"Do you really believe that?"

"You met her. What do you think?"

Harry's irritated response didn't bother Cate. In his situation, she might have reacted the same. He was an only child who had essentially been emotionally orphaned.

Cate had quarreled with her own parents over the years. She didn't always see eye to eye with them on certain subjects. But she had never questioned their love for her. Cate's childhood had been built on bedrock compared to Harry's volatile upbringing.

His mother was flaky at best, and when the man who was supposed to teach him and mold him and *love* him was a mean drunk who sometimes knocked him around, it was no wonder Harry had trouble with *feelings*.

Cate changed the subject, ready to move on. As they cleaned up the kitchen, she bumped his hip with hers. "You want to watch something on Netflix? There's a new Ryan Reynolds movie I haven't seen."

After a long silence, Harry nodded. "Sure." His rigid posture relaxed visibly. "I'm sorry if I was rude. Talking about my family makes me…"

"Crazy? Sorry," she said quickly. "Bad joke."

But her nonsense coaxed a smile from Harry.

"Very funny," he said, his expression droll.

In the living room, she lowered the lights and started to curl up in one of the comfy armchairs.

Harry claimed the sofa and patted the cushion beside him. "I don't bite," he said, his grin daring her to refuse.

"Okay." She went to sit beside him, ready to pretend this was no big deal.

But it was. She and Harry were acting like a couple. A couple on the verge of taking a step toward something that would be impossible to reverse.

Fortunately, the movie was cute and funny and entertaining. Cate was almost able to ignore Harry's arm resting above her shoulders on the back of the sofa.

The fact that he smelled like bacon and syrup shouldn't have been a turn-on. Unfortunately, she was a foodie, so the scent was as titillating as everything else about him.

When the credits rolled, Cate's nervousness returned. "That was fun," she said. "I love his movies."

"And the fact that he's a hottie doesn't sway you at all…"

"I can't help it if he happens to be handsome and funny and down-to-earth and genuinely nice."

The room fell silent. Cate had just described Jason. She heard it, and she knew Harry did, too, because he moved his arm and put distance between them on the sofa. Now that Cate thought about it, Jason and Ryan Reynolds resembled each other more than a little.

Harry rested his elbows on his knees, not looking at her. "What time do you want to leave in the morning? Nine? Nine thirty?"

"Nine is fine."

Her phone dinged quietly. Earlier, she had set it to "do not disturb" for the length of the movie. She glanced at the screen and froze.

"What's wrong?" Harry asked.

"Nothing," she croaked.

He was sitting close enough to read the sender's name. "Jason?" he said, his tone incredulous. "He's been texting you?"

Cate started to shake. This was why she couldn't have a relationship with Harry. The whole situation was too screwed up. "No," she said. "This is the first time."

From Harry's expression, she wasn't sure he believed her.

"Well, read it," he said. "Maybe there's an emergency."

"Why would you say that?" Now all she could think about were plane crashes and terrorist kidnappings.

"You told me he *hadn't* been texting you. Now he has. Seems odd, doesn't it?"

She hated the note of accusation in Harry's question. And she hated being caught in the middle.

With numb fingers, she gripped the phone and tapped the message. It was a photo, a single, heartbreakingly beautiful image of Machu Picchu...the iconic ruins bathed in morning light. Beneath the picture that bore the unmistakable stamp of Jason's artistry were four simple words. I hope you're okay.

Cate's mouth dried. She wanted to cry. She missed Jason, and because of what happened, she might never have the chance to be his friend again.

Harry stood and ran both hands through his hair. "Aren't you going to answer him?"

Cate stood, also. "I don't know," she said honestly. "I'll have to think about it. But I don't think it's any of your business."

"That's where you'd be wrong."

She gasped and dropped her phone on the sofa as Harry pulled her against his hard chest and kissed her. His lips were warm and sweet. The kiss was hot and deep.

Cate felt her legs turn to spaghetti. Her heartbeat raced dizzyingly.

In an instant, she knew that the flash fire conjured by this kiss was dangerously close to flaring out of control. She didn't want this to happen now. Not with the specter of Jason between them.

Though the kiss was everything she craved, she put two hands on Harry's chest and shoved.

He released her immediately.

"Don't apologize," she said quickly. "I like kissing you, and I think you know that. But we both have a few things to figure out."

Harry stuck out his chin and folded his arms across his chest. "I *know* what I want. You're the one doodling two different names in the margin of your notebook paper."

The careless, insolent remark cut deep. He knew she was sensitive about her age *and* his opinion of her, so he had struck where it would hurt the most.

"That's not fair," she whispered. All she had to do was admit that Jason had done the right thing in calling off the wedding.

That would clear the air. But the lie of omission was the only thing keeping her out of Harry's bed before she was ready.

Harry shook his head slowly, his gaze weary. "I'm going upstairs," he said. "I'll see you in the morning."

Nineteen

The atmosphere in the house Wednesday morning was excruciatingly polite. Again, they dodged each other at breakfast. It was beginning to be a habit.

She assumed she would have to confront Harry about not driving, but when he arrived downstairs, he was using one crutch and carrying a small overnight bag. Cate knew better than to offer her help. After a gruff greeting, he folded himself into the car without complaint.

Cate took a deep breath, tossed her own bag in the trunk, and joined him. Leaving Blossom Branch was easy. The morning rush—what there was of it—had ended. The steady stream of tourists wouldn't get heavy until Friday midday. Once she made it to the interstate, she breathed an inward sigh of relief. The traffic wasn't bad at all.

With the radio on, it was easy to pretend things were fine between her and Harry. The trip passed in silence other than the occasional comment. Her passenger focused all his attention on his phone.

For a man who was supposed to be on vacation, he waded through an awful lot of emails.

At last, they left the suburbs behind and reached the city proper. Once she had carefully parked in the garage at Harry's building, she turned off the engine. "I forgot you can't drive to your appointment. What time do you have to be there?"

He shrugged. "One. I'll get a Lyft."

"No. Let me take you."

His eyes were opaque. "And what about getting your things at Jason's?"

She swallowed. "We can go after."

Neither of them had admitted that Harry wouldn't be too much help. His badly bruised knee wouldn't allow him to carry anything heavy.

"Okay," he said. "That could work. I need to change clothes."

"Me, too."

"What do you want to do about lunch?" he asked.

"Where's your doctor's office?"

When he mentioned a street address, Cate offered a suggestion. "You want to indulge at The Varsity?"

The long-standing burger joint near Georgia Tech's campus had the best onion rings in town. The burgers and frosted orange shakes weren't bad either.

A genuine smile lit up Harry's face. "That sounds perfect." He glanced at his watch. "Can you be ready in half an hour?"

"Of course."

Cate ransacked her suitcase and what she had left behind in the closet. It would be far too hot to linger in the car, even in a parking garage. She would have to go upstairs to the doctor's office and sit in the waiting room. That meant she didn't want to wear shorts and a T-shirt.

In the end, she settled on a simple navy sundress with red trim. At least she would match the holiday theme.

Harry came out wearing dress pants and a crisp, pale yellow shirt.

Cate cocked her head. "Are you going to work or to the doctor?"

"It's a classy building," he said.

She laughed as he'd meant her to…and she was glad she had chosen the sundress.

After their greasy but wonderful lunch, Harry directed her to the beautiful high-rise where the ortho doc had his offices. They found parking and rode the elevator upstairs.

Harry—surprisingly using a crutch—wasn't saying much. Last night loomed large, especially since Jason's apartment was one of their stops today.

"How *is* your knee?" she asked as they stepped out of the second elevator.

"Better every day."

It might have been an overconfident response, but he did seem to be moving more easily.

When Harry approached the reception desk to sign in, Cate found a single chair in an unoccupied corner beside a silk fern and picked up a six-month-old *Architectural Digest*. Jason owned copies of the two issues where Harry was featured. He used to keep them on his coffee table and proudly show them off when guests came over.

Jason loved his cousin, and Harry felt the same about Jason.

While Cate was happy for both men to have that kind of mutual support and admiration, it made her situation awkward at best.

Harry was forced to pick a spot on the other side of the room. Doctor's offices were the worst. The minutes ticked by. Then half an hour. Finally, a nurse called Harry's name.

He gave Cate a long-distance smile and a shrug before disappearing through an official-looking door.

Despite every effort Cate made not to risk eye contact, the older woman seated near her struck up a conversation. "I saw you come in," she said. "Your husband is a fine-looking man."

"We're not married," Cate said. She didn't elaborate because she had no wish to chitchat.

"Engaged?" the woman asked.

"No."

"But you're here with him at a doctor's office?"

Cate counted to ten and managed a smile. "He's a friend. He hurt his knee and can't drive."

"Ah." The little woman's mischievous expression dimmed. "You can't blame me for prying. I may be old, but a man like that grabs a gal's attention, if you know what I mean."

Her husband, who had his head buried in *Popular Mechanics*, gave his spouse a warning glance. "Leave the poor girl alone. And behave yourself, old woman. I'm sitting right here."

The way he rolled his eyes had Cate giggling despite her anxious mood. Fortunately, the couple were the next to be called back.

By the time Harry finally reappeared, Cate had been sitting in her uncomfortable chair for almost two hours.

"Sorry," Harry said after he handed over his co-pay and waited for Cate to stand. "The doc got held up in surgery this morning, and it's thrown everything behind."

"I'm fine," she said.

Once they were in the car, she started the engine and turned the AC on high. "Well...what was the verdict?"

Harry leaned back and sighed. "He poked and prodded, and now the knee hurts like hell. I was fine when I went in there."

His aggrieved expression was humorous, but Cate didn't

laugh. She maintained a serious, sympathetic expression. "And the prognosis?"

"He said I could use crutches or not use them, my choice. Suggested wrapping the knee as much as I can tolerate. But no running for a month. If I'm not completely better by my follow-up appointment, he'll do an MRI, but it probably won't come to that. He said since it's only been three days, I'm healing nicely."

"You always were an overachiever."

"Drive the car, woman. Don't give me any grief. I'm injured and grumpy."

"What else is new?" she muttered. Then she tried one more time. "Why don't I drop you at your apartment? I really don't mind going to Jason's on my own. You could get some work done." She threw that out as a carrot.

But Harry wouldn't be dissuaded. "I'm going with you," he said. "We're wasting time."

"Do you have your key? I gave mine back when I moved home before the wedding."

"I do."

Jason's apartment was in a trendy building near Midtown. The rent was astronomical, which was why he and Cate had decided to buy a house sooner than later.

Unlike Harry's place, Jason's did not have assigned parking. Cate had to find a spot on the street. Luckily, she snagged one close to the entrance. The apartment was on the fourth floor.

When Harry unlocked the front door and stood back for Cate to enter, stale air rushed out to meet them.

"We should run the AC," Cate said. "Don't you think?"

"I'll take care of that. Are there boxes here you're going to use?"

She shrugged. "I decided not to bother with boxes. I've got two dozen ultraheavy trash bags in my tote. They'll take up less room in the car. I'll carry most of them to my parents' house later this evening. It's a long time until cold weather. Who knows where I'll be living by then?"

Harry's brow furrowed. "I told you to stay as long as you needed."

"Sure. And I appreciate it. But I'm not a permanent resident. I'll have to find housing of my own."

She could tell from his expression that her response displeased him. Didn't matter. She couldn't live with Prescott Harrington indefinitely. Especially if they indulged in a frothy affair.

Inwardly, she snickered. *Frothy* was the last word she should ever use to describe Harry. If they *did* sleep together—and that was still a big if—there would be nothing frothy about it. Sex with Harry would be intense. At least that was how she imagined it.

Thinking about it made her nervous. She shoved the possibility to the back of her mind and got to business.

Her winter stuff was in the spare bedroom closet. She started there. Unfortunately, cold-weather gear—mostly used for skiing out west and in the North Carolina mountains—was bulky. Like the proverbial nursery rhyme, it took her three bags full to clean out that closet.

Harry made himself scarce, thank goodness, perhaps giving her privacy. Maybe he was in Jason's small office. Cate put the first three bags in the foyer and sucked in a deep breath.

The dining room and kitchen were perplexing. There was glassware and cookware she had picked out, placemats, decorative Italian tiles she and Jason used for hot pads. Cate's influence was everywhere, but all the items were *shared* pieces. She had no wish to take them, even if Jason wanted them gone. All of it reminded her of a woman who didn't exist anymore.

It occurred to her in one stunning, odd revelation, that

among all the happy times she remembered in this apartment, the ones that stood out most were the large gatherings of friends. There had been many times when she and Jason were alone. Of course, there were.

But had she been in love with the idea of being a couple more than she loved Jason? How had she not seen that before now?

There was one room left.

She couldn't put it off any longer. When Jason finally returned home, there should be no trace of Cate in his apartment.

He had severed their ties. It was up to her to honor his wishes.

Despite the fact that she had come to terms with knowing she and Jason were marrying for the wrong reasons, walking into the bedroom they'd once shared hurt.

On the bedside tables, she saw the porcelain giraffe lamps they had picked out together. Jason had been excited about taking her on an African safari. It had been their Christmas present to each other four years ago. The inexpensive lamps were a whimsical remembrance of an amazing trip.

The rug on the floor, the color of the walls, the bedding ensemble…all those were Cate's choice. Jason had been happy to let her decorate. Though he had an eye for detail and a creative vision for his photography, he wasn't interested in picking out home decor.

Cate had happily built their nest, never once imagining that her world would take a dark turn.

It didn't make sense to take furnishings with her. Jason could donate what he didn't want. Cate needed to start fresh, wherever she ended up.

There were only a few things to gather from the bedroom and bathroom, mostly workout clothes, toiletries and an outfit or two. Soon, she had erased the last personal traces of Cate Penland from her ex-fiancé's life.

She paused beside the bed and picked up the framed, five-by-seven picture of herself. Technically, the photograph belonged to Jason. She had given it to him on some birthday or anniversary several years ago.

The woman smiling at the camera looked painfully young and happy. Cate felt ancient compared to her.

A sound at the door had her whirling around. "Harry," she said, one hand at her throat. "You scared me."

"Sorry." His face was expressionless. He scanned the room briefly. "You almost done?"

"Yes." She returned the picture to its original location.

Harry winced. "I'm sorry, Cate. So sorry. About this whole damn mess. If it were up to me, I would have made sure you had your happily-ever-after."

"But you can't. And for what it's worth, why would I want to marry someone who doesn't want to marry me?" The king-size bed stood between Cate and Harry. It was too big for the room. She and Jason had argued about it. Now she wondered if Harry was seeing his cousin and Cate in that bed.

For some reason, she found herself wanting to comfort him. "It's okay, Harry. I'm okay. Really, I am. Let's get out of here."

It wasn't her imagination. Harry's gaze remained glued to the bed for several long moments. Then he seemed to shake off whatever unpleasant thoughts occupied him. "Right," he said. "Let's go."

Between the two of them, they were able to carry what turned out to be only five bags of *stuff*. The contents fit easily into the trunk and back seat.

When Cate was behind the wheel, she gave a sideways look at her passenger. "Any more stops?"

"Lord, no. Let's go home."

"I agree." She was happy to oblige. It had been a hard day, and it was barely five o'clock.

Once they were back at Harry's place, he got out and raised an eyebrow. "Are we taking this upstairs?"

"No. While you were in with the doctor, I texted my mom and sister. They're expecting to see me after dinner. I told them I was going to dump these bags in my old room. You're welcome to ride over there with me. I'm sure my dad would like to thank you again for the financial assist."

Harry shuddered theatrically. "No thanks. It will be nice to have a quiet evening at home."

He didn't add the words *by myself*, but Cate wondered if that's how he meant them. After the days in Blossom Branch and then his accident, maybe he was ready for some downtime alone. After all, this week was supposed to be a vacation for him.

They ended up ordering in for dinner. Cate chose a Caesar salad topped with grilled chicken. Harry wanted beef and broccoli stir-fry. When the food arrived, they ate at the table in the living room beside the windows.

Cate was pensive and quiet. She had a feeling her time with Harry was inevitably coming to an end. Even if she eventually slept with him, she needed to get out of this apartment and get herself established somewhere that was hers and hers alone.

She poked at her lettuce. "You don't have to go back with me tomorrow," she said. "Especially if you don't mind me borrowing the little red car for a few days."

His paused his fork in midair as he frowned. "You're un-inviting me?"

"Well, the crowds will be crazy. Your knee is hurt. It's going to be hot."

"Don't ever apply for a job at the chamber of commerce," he said, his smile returning. "I want to be there in Blossom

Branch with you, Cate. I haven't done a small-town Fourth of July in ages. It sounds like fun. Unless you've changed your plans."

"No. I still want to go back for the weekend. Besides, I'll need to clean the house Friday and Saturday. Wash sheets. You know. Get things ready for Grammy and Grandpa."

"Then it's settled," Harry said.

When they were done eating, Cate was suddenly anxious to get away. Every time she was alone with Harry, she felt herself yielding to temptation. She'd never been the kind of person to make reckless decisions. Now was surely a bad time to start.

Harry wanted her. She wanted him. But neither of those realities justified jumping into a sexual relationship that might make her life an even bigger mess than it already was.

"I don't know how long I'll be at my folks' house," she said. "But I'll try not to disturb you when I come in."

Harry's gunmetal eyes glittered with strong emotion. "You always disturb me, Cate." He trapped her wrist in a loose grip.

She could have pulled away easily. Instead, she looked at him, her stance wary. "Why do you say things like that? I never know if you're teasing."

He rubbed his thumb where her pulse beat rapidly. "Nothing to tease about when it comes to me and you wanting each other."

The way his words echoed what she had been thinking about startled her. "Don't you ever worry about making mistakes?"

"I'm an architect," he said. "Mistakes on paper can be erased easily enough. Or with the delete key on the computer. But I don't get a shot at the truly exciting projects if I'm not willing to take a chance and push myself."

"Maybe I'm more risk-averse than you are," she said, searching his face for reassurance.

Harry released her and stepped back, leaning a hip against the kitchen counter. "All you need to do is say the word, and I won't mention any of this ever again. Is that what you want, Catie-girl?" His smile was gentle. "You can tell me. I'm a big boy. I can handle disappointment."

Twenty

Cate's tongue was thick. Her throat constricted. "You have to understand," she said, the words barely a whisper. "I screwed up my life majorly. In front of more than a thousand people. I'm having a hard time dealing with the fact that I want you."

Harry paled. "You want me?"

"You know I do. But you said there was no rush."

His lips twisted in a self-derisive grin. "My mistake."

Cate rubbed her temples where a headache brewed. "I know this is different. We're not talking about spending a lifetime together. I get that. But what if you and I are intimate and Jason hears about it? What if that upsets him and strains his relationship with you? I would never forgive myself. He considers you more a brother than a cousin."

Harry's gaze was stormy, and his pallor deepened. "Be honest, Cate. Are you worried about *me* and Jason? Or *you* and Jason?"

The questions were razor-sharp. She gasped, hurt and angry. "I've told you. There *is no* Jason and me. Period. It's over."

"Maybe it is and maybe it isn't."

Harry looked as coldly furious and miserable as she felt.

The atmosphere in the kitchen was rife with memories and confusion. From Harry's point of view, maybe his skepticism made sense. He'd witnessed the tense interaction when Jason stopped by on the night of the wedding. Harry had seen her collapse in those early days. He had held her as she cried.

When he remained silent, Cate inhaled sharply and wrapped her arms around her waist, trying not to give in to the wave of hurt and despair. She could never be intimate with Harry if he thought she was still in love with Jason.

The only real way to convince him was to admit that Jason had done the right thing. That she and Jason had let runaway wedding plans drag them to the brink of disaster. Because they *loved* each other, but they weren't *in love*.

Cate was grateful to Jason even though she was still angry on a visceral level. But if she opened herself up enough to tell Harry that, she would be incredibly vulnerable. Too vulnerable.

Harry would inevitably hurt her, too. Because he was not ever going to give his heart to a woman.

He'd made that perfectly clear.

"I have to go," she said.

"I won't wait up."

The cynical response was almost more than she could bear. She fled down the hall and out the door and all the way to the parking garage. It was at least fifteen minutes before she could leave. She was crying too hard. Quietly. Wretchedly.

Wasn't it time for karma to give her a break? Or was there no going back from this?

When she was calm enough to drive, she dried her face, repaired her makeup and headed for her parents' house. Oddly, she never referred to it as home anymore. Even before her wedding day, she had made the shift to being an official adult.

Or so she had thought.

When she pulled up in the driveway, it looked as if every light in the house was shining. Becca came out to meet her.

Cate hugged her sister. "What's going on?" She was gratified when Becca hugged her back…with surprising affection.

Becca wrinkled her nose. "It always creeps me out to stay here alone. All those doors and windows."

"But where are Mom and Dad?"

"They forgot their dinner group was meeting tonight. She asked me to tell you she was sorry."

"Oh." A little bit more of the sand shifted beneath Cate's feet. Had she burned all her bridges without realizing it had happened? Was even her own mother frustrated with her?

Becca must have picked up on Cate's unease. "Come on in," she said. "I'm actually glad it's just the two of us. I need to talk to you about something. How's Harry doing?"

"He's fine." Cate was glad she hadn't convinced him to come along.

After they dumped the trash bags full of Cate's personal items in her old bedroom, Becca waved her down the hall. "Let's hang out in the kitchen," she said. "I made snickerdoodles."

Something was up. Becca had made her sister's favorite cookie and was *smiling* at Cate. Was the whole world off-kilter?

They settled in the cozy alcove with the bay window that looked out over her father's neatly manicured lawn. Nothing to see in the dark, but Cate remembered it well enough.

When they first moved here from Blossom Branch, Cate had wanted to plant daisies from Grammy's house. Her father's flat refusal had led to the hiring of a professional landscaper.

Now there was nothing cozy or sentimental about the foliage. But it was one of the most immaculate yards in the neighborhood.

Becca brought a pitcher of iced tea and a plate of cookies. "You want something stronger?" she asked.

"No. I'm driving. What's up, Bex?"

Her younger sister gnawed her bottom lip and sat down with one leg tucked beneath her. "You know how I've been trying to convince Mom and Dad to let me take a gap year?"

"Of course. Last time I checked you hadn't made much headway."

"True," Becca said, her expression gloomy. "They want me to sign on the dotted line at the university of my choice and be there in six weeks or eight or whatever. It doesn't matter," she wailed. "I have no clue why I would even want to *go* to college. I need *time*," she said. "Is that so much to ask?"

Cate weighed her answer. "I get it," she said. "Being eighteen is scary. Heck, I'm barely twenty-five, and look how well I've done. Crafting a life's plan is a lot to ask at your age."

"So, you agree with me?" Becca had the hopeful expression of a puppy begging for a treat.

"I don't *disagree*," Cate said carefully, "but my opinion doesn't carry much weight, especially not now. I'm your sister, not your parent. Huge difference. If they say you have to go to college, well…"

Becca leaned forward. The smudge of cinnamon on her chin made her look more like a kid than a legal adult. "I have an idea, Cate. A really good idea. Mom's been telling me all about the store you're buying in Blossom Branch and how you want to open this cute boutique-y place."

"Wow, I'm surprised. I've barely mentioned it to her."

"I get the feeling she and Daddy are thrilled you have something to take your mind off Jason and the failed wedding."

"Ah. Okay."

"You and I haven't hung out together much in the last four or five years. I was busy being an annoying little twerp, and you had this fabulous life. I was jealous, and I made you miserable when I could."

Cate smiled. "You're not that bad, Becca. Don't be so hard on yourself."

"Well, here's the thing. I did great in high school, really great. I'm a whiz at math. I'm super organized, and marketing was one of my favorite subjects. I'm also extremely trustworthy. I know it may not seem that way to you, but it's true. You can ask any of my teachers."

"What are you trying to say, Becca?"

Her sister straightened, a look of determination on her face. "Hire me to be your manager. It will keep Mom and Dad off my case for this first year. If I'm not good for your shop, you can fire me. But I *will* be. I love stuff like that. I can live with Grammy and Grandpa in Blossom Branch. You can come and go knowing someone is on the ground steering the ship."

"That's a mixed metaphor, isn't it?" Cate couldn't help smiling at Becca's enthusiasm.

"I'm dead serious. And I can start anytime. Heck, if I stay with the grandparents, you could pay me minimum wage until I prove myself. *Please*, Cate. I'm begging you. This could change my life."

Cate was taken aback by Becca's idea, but the more she thought about it, the more she realized it might work. Cate didn't want to move permanently to Blossom Branch. If Becca helped get everything up and running, then Bex would know everything she needed to know. And once the store opened, Cate would have flexibility.

"I think it could work," she said. "But give me a few days to think about it. I'm moving out of Grammy and Grandpa's Saturday afternoon and coming back to Atlanta until I go back for the closing. Can we talk about this again Monday or Tuesday?"

Becca's face fell. Clearly, she had been hoping for an unequivocal yes. "I suppose," she said. "And of course we can talk about it again. If you have any questions, text me. I'm not going anywhere."

"Do you have plans for the Fourth?"

"Several of my friends and I are spending the day at Lake Lanier. You know… Jet Skis, waterskiing. Soaking up the sun."

"You'll be careful?" Cate was suddenly anxious. Because of the span of years between them, it was hard not to think of Becca as a little kid.

Becca grinned. "Always."

Cate left soon after, her brain analyzing the pros and cons of working with her sister. She had always wanted a closer relationship with her sibling. Now might be their chance.

Becca didn't come outside this time. She waved from the door and presumably locked herself in.

For the past two hours, Cate had distracted herself with Becca's unusual welcome and her interesting proposal. Now reality intruded.

Thinking about returning to Harry's apartment tightened her stomach in a knot. In an instant, she knew she couldn't do it. Before she could change her mind, she composed a text…

I've decided to drive on to Blossom Branch tonight. As far as Saturday goes, you can come or not come. It's up to you. I need time to regroup and do some thinking…

She held the phone and stared at the curt words she had written. Would Harry hear the hurt she carried? The uncertainty about him? And her? And them together?

Quickly, she hit send before she could change her mind.

She had nothing with her. Not even a toothbrush. When

she got to Blossom Branch, she would have to visit the twenty-four-hour pharmacy in town and buy a few necessities.

Her chest felt hollow. Not as bad as after the wedding, but still bad. Life was supposed to be moving forward, getting easier.

Why had she let herself fall under Harry's spell?

As she started the car, her phone dinged.

Don't leave. No more fighting. Come home. I need to know you're safe.

The urgency in the text took her by surprise. Honestly, she thought he wouldn't care one way or another. If she wasn't ready to sleep with him, her presence in his home was an inconvenience. Right?

She weighed the strain of a late drive versus stepping back into the dragon's lair. That was a whimsical way to think of Harry. He was dangerous and beautiful, and he breathed fire on occasion. But when she was with him, she always felt warm and secure.

Her finger hovered over the screen. She didn't know how to answer.

Before she could respond, a second text arrived...

Come home, Catie-girl. I won't hassle you. I won't make you cry. I won't even look at you if that will help. But that last one will be hard because you dazzle me. Come home...please...

The tight knot inside her chest loosened. She smiled despite her wildly vacillating mood. Harry might frustrate her and confound her, but she was drawn to him in ways she couldn't explain.

When it came to men, she was zero for two so far. Jason

apparently loved her platonically. Harry cared about her and had cared *for* her in some awful moments, but honestly, he was mostly interested in sex, no matter how charmingly he approached the subject.

Cate was tired of trying to keep her head above water. Maybe it was time to indulge herself. How much worse could things get?

When she unlocked the door to Harry's apartment and stepped inside, he swept her up in his arms. "Thank God. I thought you weren't coming back." His embrace was so hard, she winced.

He didn't even kiss her. All he did was hold her tightly as if he had been scared.

"Oh, Harry," she said. "I didn't answer your texts, did I?"

He pulled back, his gaze roving over her face with intensity. "No. You didn't."

"Sorry. I didn't mean to *not* answer. I was sitting in the car for so long, trying to decide what to do, I didn't realize I never said anything one way or the other." She frowned. "You look dreadful." His hair was standing on end, and although he had changed out of his nice clothes, his casual shirt was buttoned wrong.

"What changed your mind?" he asked, the words quiet.

She shrugged. "I want to have sex with you. I want to feel normal again. I want to know that you and I are friends and not enemies."

Harry closed his eyes for a long moment. When he looked at her again, she could have sworn his eyes were damp. "We're friends, Cate. With or without the sex."

"But here's the thing," she said. "I think I finally figured something out. If I have sex with you, I want to *choose* intimacy. I want to choose you. Does that make sense?"

"At the risk of starting another argument, not really." His smile was strained. "But I'm listening."

"You and I could have a few drinks and start fooling around and lose control. That's one scenario."

"And?"

"And then things would get complicated. But if I tell you I want you, and we make a mature, rational decision to sleep together, everything will be neater, less emotional."

Harry's jaw dropped a split second before he snapped it shut and stared at her. "You want to have unemotional sex?"

"I want to have sex with clear expectations. You've already told me you don't do serious relationships. And I respect your honesty. I think I need to be honest in return."

"Oh, hell. I'm not sure I like where this is headed."

"You're trying to make a joke, but I'm serious. I can't have sex with you if you believe I'm still in love with Jason."

His face went blank. She'd seen it happen a million times. "And you're not?" he asked, the words flat.

"No," she said simply. "As hard as it is for me to admit, Jason did the right thing. We loved each other, but we weren't *in* love."

"Why is that so hard to admit?" Harry asked, his big frame braced.

"Because it makes me look silly and foolish and blind. I've been trying to impress you, but this one for sure goes in the negative column. I was prepared to get married for all the wrong reasons."

Harry exhaled. "That's a lot of self-revelation for one day. Where do we go from here?"

"Well," Cate said. "I think I'd like to take a shower, change into something nice and join you in your bedroom."

Dark color stained his cheekbones. Gray eyes glittered. His breath rasped in and out as his chest rose and fell. "What happens if I get emotional?" he said. There wasn't a trace of humor on his face.

"Don't tease me. I'm already self-conscious."

"Self-conscious about what?" He frowned.

"I don't have experience with a partner other than Jason."

"We aren't comparing score cards. Period."

"Okay." Cate didn't want to know about his other women.

"To be clear, though," he said. "I shouldn't kiss you right now? Because I might lose control and take you here on the floor?"

Cate glanced down at the sleekly modern foyer rug, then back at Harry. Her eyes widened. "You're kidding, right?" The idea of him being so spontaneous and crazy and carried away by passion rattled her.

"Not even a little bit." He shook his head slowly. "But if you want to do this step by step, I agree to your terms. No emotional throwing of caution to the wind. No communal showers. Meet in my room in half an hour."

Oh, gosh. This was going to happen.

Her knees went weak. She could have sworn that only happened in books.

She swallowed. "Are you sure about this?"

"Dead sure."

"Then I guess I'll see you shortly."

Harry stepped back for Cate to pass him. But he pressed a kiss to the top of her shoulder as she moved. "I'll be waiting."

Twenty-One

Cate stared in the bathroom mirror, dazed. She had to wipe condensation from the glass. But that really didn't help. The source of her hazy vision was inward.

She had showered and shaved her legs already. Selecting what to wear had been tricky. Everything fancy in her suitcase was supposed to have been worn on her honeymoon. She decided the lingerie with the tags still attached had nothing to do with Jason.

Truthfully, all Cate could think about was Harry. What did he like? Virginal white? Probably not. Sin red? Not her style. Baby blue seemed too innocent for what they were about to do.

Cate chose black. Naughty black. A lacy cami with matching thong. She didn't have the confidence to stroll down the hall like that. Fortunately, the thigh-length black satin robe gave her a layer of defensive armor.

Her big speech about mature, unemotional choices yielded to flat-out panic. The woman in the mirror was no help at all.

Cate was neither vain, nor self-conscious about her body. Her

blond hair, blue eyes and pale skin didn't seem exceptional—
though she knew many men responded to her *type*. She didn't
want to be a *type*. All she cared about in this moment was pleasing Harry and pleasing herself.

She had used up twenty-two of her thirty minutes. Perhaps
she should arrive early. Throw Harry off his game. That was
laughable. The man had no weaknesses at all.

When she opened the door into the hall, she gasped. Harry
stood there, leaning against the wall.

His gaze widened appreciatively. "Wow."

"Wow, yourself." Harry was mostly naked except for a pair
of snug black boxer-briefs and a navy terry robe. His olive
skin was tanned all over, lightly dusted with dark hair. His
chest was a thing of beauty. "What are you doing?" she asked.

He smiled. "I thought you might get nervous about the
walk down the hall. So here I am."

"Harry..." She squeaked as he scooped her up into his arms.
"Your knee!"

"It's fine," he said. But he limped as he carried her from
the guest room to his suite.

Though his strong arms held her comfortably, she suspected
the romantic gesture pained him more than he was letting on.
"Put me down," she insisted as they stopped in the doorway.

Finally, he gave in and lowered her gently to her feet. His
wince was involuntary, but impossible to miss.

Cate propped her hands on her hips. "Do I need to get an
ice pack?"

"Nah. I like to be naked in bed." He leaned down and unwrapped the bandage supporting his sprained knee.

"Very funny." Harry said those things to make her blush.
She knew it, but she blushed anyway.

He waved an arm. "Welcome to my bedroom, Cate."

"I've seen it before," she admitted.

"Oh." That raised eyebrow made her feel guilty.

"One of the first days I was here, you went to the office downtown, so I explored. But to be honest, I only came as far as the doorway. I didn't snoop, I swear."

He cocked his head, amusement tilting his lips in a mocking smile. "And what did you learn from the doorway?"

"Not much. Your room is a lot like you…iceberg-ish."

"Excuse me?"

"You're an enigma, Harry. No one ever knows what you're thinking. A guy like you is 90 percent below the surface."

He sobered. "You've seen more of that 90 percent than most people, Cate."

She stared at him. "I have?"

"You have," he insisted. "I don't want you to think of me like that. Especially not when we're being intimate with each other. I won't hold anything back."

"Oh." She felt dizzy. Was she ready for a version of Harry who was a hundred percent open and available to her? It boggled the mind. "Should we get under the covers?" she said. "My feet are getting cold."

Harry chuckled. "Well, we can't have that. Which side of the mattress do you like?"

"Does it matter? For sex, I mean?"

"I want you to be comfortable." He caught her wrist and tugged her toward the bed. Then he placed her hand flat on his chest over his heart. The steady, rapid *ka-thud, ka-thud* told Cate he was more revved than he was letting on.

His gaze clashed with hers. The silvery gray gleamed, mesmerizing her. Her fingernails dug into his warm skin. "We're going to have fun, aren't we?" she whispered.

"You can bet on it, sweet Cate."

With gravity and ceremony, he folded back the sheet and blanket and comforter and waited for her to scoot in.

"Thank you," she said, feeling breathless when they hadn't even started. If this was what it was like to make a mature, rational decision, why did it feel so wicked and dangerous?

Without warning, Harry tossed his robe aside and casually ditched his briefs. One glimpse of his erect sex stopped Cate in her tracks. She knew he wanted her, but he *really* wanted her.

That knowledge gave her the oddest feeling.

She touched his thigh when he settled beside her. "I'm glad we're doing this," she said. "Really, I am."

He traced her lips with a fingertip. "Who are you trying to convince? Me or you?"

Bravely, she slid out her tongue and tasted his finger. "Both of us?"

Her simple action made him shudder. "Slow down, Cate."

She laughed at him. "Seriously?"

He was reclining on his side leaning on his elbow. His eyelids were at half-mast. "I could devour you," he said, the words low and raspy. "I'm exercising more control than you can imagine at this very moment."

"Oooh, I'm scared," she said.

"Are you mocking me, brat?"

"Maybe a little." She felt her heart turn over in her chest. A wave of something warm and sweet and yet wildly passionate roared through her veins and kindled a blaze of longing deep in the core of her femininity. "I adore your funny side, Harry. I've never met anyone like you. Grumpy and sweet. Masculine and yet so gentle when you need to be. I want you so much it scares me."

"Ditto," he growled. He stripped her camisole over her head and moved half on top of her, capturing her mouth in a hungry kiss. When he cupped one breast in his hand and plucked at the nipple, her hips came off the bed.

They had barely done anything yet, and she was so close to an orgasm, it was embarrassing.

Her arms went around his neck. She kissed him back frantically, as if they were the last two people on the planet and the world was in danger of exploding. *Her body* exploded with *feelings*, so many feelings.

Harry put a hand between her thighs and found her damp and ready. He used the center strip of her undies to tease her. "Don't regret this, Cate."

It was an odd thing to say, but she barely processed his words. She was far more interested in the way he stroked her. "Wait," she said, trying to claim control of a situation that was rapidly igniting and spreading a wildfire of insanity.

But Harry was diabolical. He knew exactly what she wanted, and he gave it to her. When she hit the peak and cried out, he held her close, stroking her hair as she trembled and slid down the other side.

Embarrassment found a chink in her mellow afterglow and set up housekeeping. Cate stiffened in his arms. "I don't like leaving you behind," she said, feeling exposed and awkward.

"Relax, Cate. We're just getting started. We have all night." He nuzzled her nose with his. "You're sexy when you come."

"I don't want to *talk* about it," she said, burying her face in his shoulder. His body radiated heat. His size and solid presence were reassuring and arousing at the same time.

"You're a prude, aren't you?"

"I am *not*," she insisted. "But you didn't even turn out the lights."

Harry laughed, his body shaking. "And I don't intend to." He ran his hand from her shoulder down between her breasts to her navel. Then he palmed the slight curve of her belly. His face was close to hers, his eyes gray pools that beckoned her into the deep end. "I want to see every inch of you, Cate," he said huskily. "I want to wallow in your soft, sexy body and lose myself in your screams."

Cate literally went limp. She shuddered. His words conjured imagery that was all too real. If he was going to demand that of her, she would torment him in return. She wrapped her fingers around his erection. "Help yourself, big guy. But don't be surprised if I do some wallowing of my own."

Her first climax turned into three…in quick succession. Every time she tried to return the favor, Harry let her touch him for a few moments and then dragged her hand to his mouth. The way he sucked on her pinky finger was probably illegal in the state of Georgia.

Cate didn't care. She had fallen down a rabbit hole of hidden desires stripped bare and yearning need coaxed to the surface and set on fire.

When she tried once again to pleasure him with her hand, he shook his head. "It's been months for me, Cate. I want to come inside you this first time."

"First time?" she said, the words breathless.

"We'll lose count, I swear. Are you on the pill?"

"Yes."

He was looking at her as if she was the culmination of all his wicked fantasies.

He removed her undies and settled between her thighs. "I haven't had risky sex."

She had known that, but his reassurance was sweet. Harry had a streak of honor a mile wide. He hid it beneath a veneer of faux self-indulgence.

Maybe she did see more of the ninety percent than she realized.

When he positioned the head of his sex at her entrance, he hesitated. She had instinctively closed her eyes, but now they shot open as she wondered what was going on inside his head.

"What is it, Harry?" she asked softly. She could almost feel his ambivalence. Or maybe it was something else.

He rested his forehead against hers for a moment. "Will you look at me," he said, "when I take you?"

For the first time since she entered his bedroom, his eyes did that opaque thing she knew so well.

"Of course I will," she promised.

It wasn't easy. He was demanding a kind of trust and openness that frightened her, especially knowing that for him this was going to be a physical relationship, while for her, it was already far too personal.

Despite the lack of expression in his eyes, his voice told a different story. "I've wanted this for a long time," he said hoarsely. "Wanted *you*."

She felt the press of his erection—the blunt head and then the sensation of fullness as he entered her carefully. The whole time, they held eye contact. It was emotionally raw and terrifying.

"I won't break, Harry," she said. "Take me like you want to…"

The skin was stretched tight across his cheekbones. His jaw was rigid. "I can't, Catie-girl."

She cupped his face in her hands and pulled his head down so she could kiss him long and slow. "Yes, Harry. Yes, you can. It's okay." She lifted her hips into his thrusts, feeling the tight hold he had on his physicality.

"Oh, damn," he groaned. He was shaking now, his brow damp.

Suddenly, she saw more of the 90 percent. What he craved. What he feared.

She set her fingernails into his shoulders and raked his hot flesh. "Do it, Harry. Take me hard. Make me scream."

As if her words had unleashed a kind of ancient sorcery,

Harry jerked and moaned. She felt his control snap. Heard his muttered words of praise and pleading.

He hammered into her, shaking the bed, shaking her body as he took what he wanted. It was scary and exhilarating and everything in between. Cate was satiated before this, but he coaxed her need to the surface, making her gasp and arch blindly, reaching for the bliss he had shown her time and again.

Harry found the end before she did. He roared out his pleasure along with her name, thrusting and thrusting until he slumped on top of her.

Cate didn't mind. Her body hummed with banked need, but it would keep. For now, she found herself in an unknown space. With a man who had rescued her heart and now might take it forever.

She knew the risk. Many people were like that. It was a curse. Oh, to be able to separate physical bliss from emotion.

Stroking his hair was another forbidden pleasure. For a man so self-contained, this level of vulnerability was rare.

When he roused at last, his expression was impossible to read, though it was perhaps shell-shocked for a quick second. "I'm sorry," he said, the tone ridiculously formal for the current situation. "You didn't finish."

She traced his eyebrows with her fingertips. "Don't be an ass. If you're going to give me multiple orgasms, you have to be okay with me sitting one out now and then." She paused, painfully unsure of herself. "You were amazing," she said softly.

He sat up, yawned and ran his hands through his hair. She sensed he shared her unease. The cataclysm they had birthed was more than either of them had expected.

"Did I hurt you?"

She heard it then. A tiny, unexpected need for reassurance. "No," she said firmly. "It was incredible. *You* were incredible." She laughed softly. "Or maybe we were incredible together."

"Damn straight." The smug satisfaction in his voice was more like the Harry she knew. "What do you want to do now?" he asked.

Because his most impressive body part was once again at attention, she had no doubt about his agenda. But if he was going to ask...

"Eat," she said. "Food," in case there was any confusion. "If we're going to keep this up for a while, I need sustenance."

Harry blinked. *"Keep this up?"*

She felt her face go hot. "Oh, gosh, you know that's not what I meant. Keep up our sexual extravaganza."

"Fine," he said, pretending to grumble.

She got an eyeful when he climbed out of bed. His ass was almost as impressive as his other attributes. Because she wanted to prove she wasn't a prude, she slapped the nearest cheek, grinning when her handprint appeared on one firm masculine buttock.

"Eye candy," she said. "That's what you are."

He disappeared into the bathroom, calling out over his shoulder. "Don't start something if you want to raid the refrigerator."

Because she was feeling shy, she used her own bathroom, freshening up quickly in case he came to find her. Once she was wearing her cami and panties and robe again, she knotted the belt tightly, brushed her hair and went in search of her lover.

She found him in the kitchen wearing briefs but no robe. The sight of Prescott Harrington, mostly nude, standing in front of an open refrigerator, was like staring directly at the sun. After a moment, she had to look away, pretending it took all her attention to walk around the counter and settle into a seat.

"What sounds good?" he asked, perfectly serious.

Dinner was a long time ago. And they had each expended

a fair amount of energy. Cate's stomach growled. "Ice cream sundaes? Do you have the ingredients?"

"I do." His grin was so lighthearted, it took her breath away. She had never seen that expression on his face. He looked young and happy. Was Cate responsible for the change, or was this version simply *vacation* Harry? He handled a huge amount of responsibility in his business. Maybe he had needed time away more than he knew.

Cate was content to sit and watch Harry do his thing. She could have offered to help, but this was more fun.

The man had not a single iota of self-consciousness about his nudity. He heated sauce, fetched bowls and scooped ice cream like he was the expert on a TV cooking show.

At last, he set the treat in front of her. "Eat up," he said. "I need you to have energy."

This time she didn't blush. Progress. She looked at her bowl. "You forgot the whipped cream."

"Oops. I guess my mind was on other things."

Was he kidding or serious? She could never tell.

When he squatted to retrieve the red can from the back of a bottom shelf, Cate needed to fan herself. His body radiated power. His masculinity was a palpable force. In another era, he would have been a knight in chain mail setting out to protect the kingdom.

In the twenty-first century, he had to channel all that testosterone into rescuing fleeing brides and creating buildings from scratch.

She watched as Harry checked the expiration date on the bottom of the can. "We're okay," he said. "Still a month away."

"I'm surprised you care. You strike me as a guy who likes to live dangerously."

He took her teasing seriously. "Maybe in some situations. Not when it comes to food poisoning."

"Hurry," she said. "The hot fudge is melting my ice cream."

Harry's eyes gleamed with mischief. He sprayed a generous amount on her sundae. Then, before she could react, he leaned over the counter, squirted whipped cream on her mouth and kissed her.

The hard male lips and sticky sweet topping were a staggering combination. His tongue probed hers, offering naughty pleasure. Cate returned the favor by biting his lip and licking up as much of the cream as she could manage.

Harry moaned. Or maybe it was Cate. Why had she ever put the bar between them?

"Cate…" Harry panted. His face was flushed. "How badly do you want that sundae?"

She glanced down at her bowl blankly. At least two-thirds of the ice cream had melted into soup.

Then she looked at Harry. His expression was not hard to read right now. She could see every bit of his hunger and desperation.

"Snacks can wait," she said.

"Hallelujah." He dragged her out into the hall and toward his room. "I'll feed you later, I swear."

He didn't pick her up this time. Instead, he stopped in the center of the room—a few feet shy of the bed with the rumpled covers—and undressed her. His big hands removed her lingerie one piece at a time. And after each one, he lingered, touching…stroking.

The room was comfortable, but gooseflesh broke out on Cate's skin. Harry was breathing hard. His sex was rigid. Still, he gave her his utmost attention and care. As if she were incredibly precious.

Her eyes stung with tears. She didn't let them fall. Sharing Harry's bed was her reward for not giving up when life knocked her down. She had no notion of being with him beyond a few days or a few weeks at most.

When you didn't expect much, you couldn't be disappointed.

For once, he didn't pick up on her mood. When she was naked, he pulled her body close to his, running his hands over her back. His hard sex pushed against her abdomen.

Cate reached up to wrap her arms around his neck. "I like having sex with you more than quarreling with you."

"Amen." A rumble of laughter accompanied the single, wry word.

She wanted to ask if he'd really had a crush on her once upon a time.

So many things she wanted to ask. But icebergs were dangerous. Best not to get too close or go too deep. "You seemed in a hurry when we were in the kitchen," she teased.

He pinched her butt, hard enough to sting. "I'm practicing patience. And foreplay."

Cate laughed softly. "I'm ready. So ready. You've turned me into a puddle of goo."

"I thought that was the ice cream." He stepped back and cupped her breasts, his gaze reverent.

"That, too." She shivered when her nipple received a butterfly caress. "Oh, Harry…"

He kissed her lazily but with great effect. "Did you hear that?" he whispered, using the tip of his tongue to trace the shell of her ear.

"Hear what?"

"My patience shattering in a million damn pieces."

"Thank goodness." She didn't wait for him this time. She scrambled into the bed and patted the mattress. "I saved your spot."

Harry shucked his briefs and joined her. When she launched

herself into his arms, they both sighed. "I may be addicted to your body," he said, his tone conversational as he played with her butt.

"The feeling is mutual." Cate measured the width of his shoulders with her hands, felt the fascinating interplay of muscle and skin and bone.

"It's a shame we have to go back to Blossom Branch in the morning," he said. "I'd like to keep you in this bed for a week straight."

Cate closed her eyes as a wave of longing spread from where her heart thumped in her chest all the way to her belly and beyond. "You wouldn't want to miss all the excitement," she mumbled, hardly able to speak.

Harry took her hair in one big hand and used it to pull her head to one side. Then he sank his teeth into the tender flesh of her neck. "We'll make our own excitement, Catie-girl. I promise."

This time was very different. Not different bad or even different good. Just different. Harry seemed more relaxed, though no less focused on the end game. He gave her that orgasm she had missed and one more besides.

Then—when she was still trying to catch her breath—he entered her slowly. The aftershocks from her climax were magnified.

He rolled to his back, taking her with him. "This is a nice view," he said, his eyes gleaming.

"Um..." Cate wasn't comfortable enough with him yet for this level of intimacy, but he wasn't giving her much choice.

He captured her wrists in a firm grip and held them behind her back. "Have I told you how beautiful you are?"

"No..." This was embarrassing...having Harry study her nude body so intently.

"I used to think you looked like an angel. We had one at the top of our Christmas tree."

"But?"

"But that was before I saw you as a living, breathing woman. You're stubborn and brave and kind. And you have a temper, I think, though maybe you hide it well."

"Pot. Kettle." She pouted.

When she tried to free her arms, his hold tightened. "Not so fast."

He was buried deep inside her. Cate's body hummed with the feeling of helplessness. She knew he would release her if she asked.

For now, she enjoyed the kick of trepidation.

Harry sat up, cradling her in his arms. In this position, he claimed her, he owned her. She was a vulnerable woman yielding to a man. Yet this was her choice.

She would make the choice again and again for as long as this odd and unexpected relationship held together. It might take glue and tape and twine, but Harry was hers. For now.

He tried to draw out the pleasure, but they were both ravenous. He rolled again and set her beneath him, claiming her swiftly and thoroughly until they both cried out.

When they could breathe again, his face was smashed into her wildly tangled hair. "Do you still want food?" he asked, the words barely audible.

"Too late," she said, curling into his side. "Let's sleep."

Thursday morning dawned clear and sunny and hot as the first level of hell. Since Cate was ensconced in Harry's comfy bed, none of that really mattered. Except that her lover had disappeared.

When she opened her eyes, yawning and stretching, his studly body was nowhere in sight.

It was hard to squelch the feeling of disappointment. She had imagined an early morning of lazy lovemaking.

Instead, she tiptoed back to her own bedroom, showered, and changed into a tiny khaki skirt and a teal camisole with a built-in bra. She put her hair up in a ponytail and finished packing her suitcase.

When she was all set, she went to the kitchen to scrounge for breakfast. The bowls of uneaten ice cream still sat in the sink. She frowned. That didn't sound like her host. He had removed them from the counter but not rinsed them out? She took care of that and put them in the dishwasher.

The coffeepot was still warm with half a cup at the bottom. So he had definitely been here at some point.

After she drank her juice and ate a banana, she tiptoed halfway up the stairs toward his office. She heard the low rumble of his voice. Who was he talking to? Not that it was any of her business.

She had hoped to be on the road by ten, but Harry probably wasn't even packed. He didn't need much for three nights.

While she hovered halfway up and halfway down, the office door opened suddenly, and Harry strode out, still wearing nothing but his gray robe and a different pair of underwear. His hair was damp.

His face lit up when he saw her. "Sorry," he said. "I tried not to disturb you. I showered early, and then I had a text from the office. Since we're leading up to the long holiday weekend, they needed me to sign off on a couple of things." He came down to stand on the step below hers, so they were eye to eye.

"Is it always this hard for you to take a break?" she asked.

He shrugged. "I've never minded the extra hours. It's my company. Other guys might coach Little League or take their wives to Paris. I don't have those distractions."

Something about that explanation bothered her. "And you don't regret missing baseball and the Champs-Élysées?"

"Nobody can have it all, Cate. If they tell you they can, they're lying."

"I see."

He tipped up her chin with his finger and kissed her. It was probably supposed to be a good morning kiss, quick and sweet. Instead, the kiss went deep. He backed Cate up against the wall of the stairwell and ravaged her mouth until they were both panting.

Cate knew she was on dangerous ground. She unwrapped her arms from around his waist. "Good morning, indeed." The flirty tone was supposed to show Harry she could handle sex without feelings. She touched her lips, surprised to feel they weren't puffy and swollen.

He didn't look as happy now, nor as openly glad to see her. In fact, he had trouble looking her in the eye. Fine with Cate. She didn't know how to handle this *morning after* situation.

Harry glanced at his watch. "I know you must be itching to get on the road. I can be ready in twenty minutes."

"No big rush. Take your time."

In the end, it was closer to forty-five minutes before they exited the apartment. A second work call slowed Harry down.

As she waited for him in the living room, Cate wondered if there really was a crisis, or if last night had spooked the commitment-phobic Harry. Maybe his big speech this morning about work was a not-so-subtle warning.

It wasn't at all necessary. Cate was very clear where she stood.

Despite the rocky start to the day, things improved as they traveled. Harry professed himself fully able to drive, so Cate didn't argue.

When they entered the outskirts of Blossom Branch, it was

clear that the weekend was gearing up. One out of every ten historic houses in town was a B and B. Cate saw license tags from all over the eastern US.

They stopped at Peach Crumble for lunch and then went on to her grandparents' house. Cate carried her suitcase upstairs. Harry followed right behind her. When they met back in the hall, he lifted an eyebrow. "What's the schedule?"

"Well, tomorrow has to be work. I want to clean the house from top to bottom."

"Okay. And today?"

"We can enjoy ourselves."

He took her wrist and reeled her in. "Define *enjoy*."

Her heartbeat sped up. "I assumed we would do *that* tonight."

He chuckled. "Ordinary people have daytime sex. It's not breaking the rules."

When he nuzzled her neck, she inhaled sharply, realizing that if he tried, Harry could talk her into almost anything. "I'm not opposed to daytime sex in general...and I'm not a prude. But..."

He pressed a kiss below her ear. "But what?"

She laid her hand on his collarbone, petting him. "This connection between you and me is *new*. I suppose I'm saying I want to take things slowly."

Harry released her. He laughed and laughed and laughed some more until his eyes were wet and he could barely catch his breath.

Cate folded her arms and scowled. "I don't see what's so funny."

He stared at her, grinning. "Were you *there* last night? In my bed? With me? We'd have to back up about a thousand steps if you want to take things slowly. The cat's out of the bag. The horse has left the barn. Pandora's box is open—"

She held up her hand to cut him off. "Okay. Okay. That's enough. I take your point. Let me say what I really mean. Harry, I would be much more *comfortable* picking up where we left off if we wait until the end of the day."

Her face was hot, but she couldn't blame it on the weather.

His smile gentled. "To be clear, anything you want to do or *not do* is okay by me. You have my word."

"Thank you."

"So if we're not going to fool around, what do you have planned for our afternoon entertainment?"

"I thought we could go for a walk. Around town. It's especially fun right now because there's a lot of people and energy." She bit her lip. "Unless you think your knee won't be up to that much exercise."

He rolled his eyes. "I think I can handle a gentle stroll without passing out on the sidewalk."

"Excellent," Cate said. "And then tonight, I'll do all the work."

Twenty-Two

Sometimes, getting the last word in was really, really fun. Harry's mouth opened and shut like a dying fish.

She smiled at him. "Problem?"

"No, ma'am. Not a single one."

When he still didn't move, she leaned in and kissed him boldly, letting her tongue trace his lips and slide inside to duel with his. "Don't people say anticipation is half the fun?"

"Stupid people do." His disgruntled retort was perfection.

She hugged him. Pressing her cheek over the spot where his heart thumped was becoming a habit. "I like you, Prescott Harrington. I don't care if you *are* a workaholic and a terrible patient, I like you."

Harry returned the hug and stroked her hair. "Ditto, Catie-girl. But if we're going to take things slow, you'd better get me out of this house."

She assumed he was kidding until she glanced up and saw the expression in his eyes. The man was burning up from the inside out. For her.

Her legs wobbled, especially when he pressed even closer, and she felt the evidence of his desire.

"Oh…"

"C'mon, woman. Let's get going."

His mood mellowed once they were outside and headed toward the park and the gazebo. Though town had been busy on Monday and Tuesday, the crowds were markedly larger today.

They made one circuit all the way around the quad, stopping now and again to look in a shop window. Cate's store—that's the way she thought of it now—looked forlorn, as if it was sad to be missing all the excitement.

Harry stood beside her as she pressed her face to the glass. "Do you want to go inside?" he asked.

"No. I left the key at home. But it's okay. Nothing has changed since we were here last."

"Have you decided when you'll want to have a grand opening?"

"I was hoping for Labor Day weekend. What do you think? There's a lot still to be done."

"It's doable," he said, "barring any surprises when we start ripping things out. These old buildings can break your heart."

"Thanks for the pep talk."

He kissed her square on the mouth, totally ignoring the people milling around them. "Your store will be wonderful, Cate. Just like you."

When he said things like that, her heart squeezed. But she wouldn't let herself go there. Harry could be affectionate without meaning anything by it. Cate was his temporary project. That's all…

"Let's go see the school," she said.

The original Blossom Branch Elementary was two streets over behind the ice cream shop. Though a fancy new consolidated school had been built on the edge of the county closer to the interstate, this building was still used for board offices and other related departments.

Cate stood close to the shiny chain-link fence. It hadn't been there when she was young. The single-story white brick building with the green tin roof was long and squat. A center corridor with classrooms, one deep on either side, meandered from one side of the property to the other.

Pine trees, lots of them, offered shade and a surface of needles where kids used to swing and slide and play kickball.

Cate sighed. "I spent six years of my life here, seven if you count kindergarten."

"Is that why you and Leah and Gabby are such good friends?"

"No. We knew each other, played together at recess, but our families weren't close. It was only when we arrived at UGA as freshmen that we met up again. I think we were all feeling a little shaky about being away from home. Picking up the Blossom Branch connection bonded us. And then I dragged both of them into sorority life. I like to think they enjoyed it."

"But you and Jason go way back."

She searched his tone for hidden meanings but found none. "Yes. We were in elementary school together. My dad moved us to Atlanta after that. Jason's family made the same choice, but it was two years later, right before he started high school. He and I reconnected and started dating in college."

"I remember that his parents wanted him to go to a prestigious prep school."

"Exactly." Cate knew she would never get a more organic opportunity. "So how did you and Jason get so close?"

Harry pushed on a gate. "This padlock isn't locked," he said. "You want to go sit on that bench in the shade?"

"Sure."

There might be people working inside the building, but

Cate doubted anyone would care enough to run them off. The respite from the July sun was welcome. She sat down and dabbed her forehead with the back of her arm. "Harry?" she said, prompting him to answer her question.

He leaned back and extended his legs, crossing them at the ankle. His expression was relaxed. "Jason and I aren't first cousins. I knew *of* him, of course, but I didn't really meet him until a family reunion when he was six years old. I was sixteen and pissed because my parents made me go. Jason was either oblivious to my bad mood or was savvy enough to charm me. He followed me around the whole day."

"That's sweet."

"It didn't feel that way in the moment. I was already worried that one of my parents was going to cause a scene."

"And did they?"

"Not that time. But they had before. Anyway, after the meal, Jason and I went out in the backyard. He got his glove out of his parents' car and wanted me to teach him how to throw a baseball."

"You must have been a great teacher. Jason has always been good at baseball."

"Yeah, well, who knows. Anyway, there were two other reunions that summer. A Southern thing. You know."

Cate laughed ruefully. "I do know. That usually meant going to a strange house and meeting strange people. Only the grown-ups thought it was fun."

"So true. By the end of the third reunion, Jason's parents caught on to the fact that their kid had bonded with me. They were getting ready to go to Aruba for a week and hadn't been able to find anyone to keep Jason. They offered to pay me a thousand bucks to come stay at their house with him."

"Whoa…that's a lot of money for a sixteen-year-old kid."

"Didn't matter. I never took their money. Wouldn't have

been right. But I couldn't say no to Jason. He looked at me with big eyes, and I caved. Those seven days we spent together were one of the best weeks of my life. He and I had a blast."

"I've never heard that part of the story. I just knew that you two were related somehow."

"The connection is complicated. Something about his great-grandfather and my great uncle's wife."

Cate closed her eyes and listened to the rustle of the wind in the trees. This town held so many threads of a tapestry that included her family, Jason's, Harry's. And then there were Leah and Gabby and their clans.

Blossom Branch had given them all a start in life. Small towns weren't inherently wonderful. As sentimental as Cate was about this spot on the globe, she wasn't blind. Small towns could be good or bad. Gossip thrived. There were the haves and the have-nots. Prejudice. Poverty.

But there was a sweetness here. A simplicity of purpose. Something about the acres of peach orchards marked this place with the changing seasons and the ripening fruit. You couldn't get more elemental than that.

After a grief-filled beginning, she had grown to love Atlanta. Now it felt as much like home as Blossom Branch. But knowing she was going to start a business here made her very happy.

Harry had dozed off, his head resting on the wooden back of the bench. Cate watched him sleep and wished she believed in happy endings.

Her fairy-tale wedding had turned into disaster.

Though Harry had rescued her afterward, she didn't believe in knights on white horses. It wasn't fair to the knights to put them on those big chargers.

In the twenty-first century, females had learned the value and satisfaction in pursuing their own dreams and destinies.

It was confusing, though. Cate was as independent as the next woman, but she didn't want to go through life alone. Even after the Jason debacle and then realizing she wanted to open a business in Blossom Branch, she still yearned for passionate love. When she looked at her grandparents' marriage, she knew she wanted someone who would be a companion, a friend and a warm bed partner, whether the warmth came from crazy sex or from a decades-old promise to love and to cherish.

Or maybe both.

When her phone dinged suddenly, she pulled it out of her pocket and read the text. "Oh, yikes," she said.

Harry opened one eye. "Problem?"

"No." Cate read the text a second time. "You know how my degree is in art history?"

"I recall."

"Well, I met the director of the High Museum at a party a few months ago. She was dabbling with a plan to bring low-income kids into the museum and give them a chance to interact with art in a way most of them likely never would."

"What does that have to do with you?"

"She asked me if I would be willing to facilitate the first few sessions. If all goes well, I might do it twice a month as a volunteer."

He sat up and scrubbed his hands over his face. "Are you up for that? With all this store stuff?"

Cate flushed. "You're saying I've overcommitted?"

"I'm not saying any such thing." Harry frowned. "I only wondered if you're still interested now that you have this big project facing you."

"I think I am. In fact, I know I am. The art museum job will be giving back to the community. As a kid, I had op-

portunities that enriched my life enormously. I feel the need
to pay it forward."

"I think that's admirable."

"Seriously?"

"Seriously." He linked his fingers with hers. "Just think,
Cate. If Jason hadn't called off the wedding, your store in Blossom Branch would never have happened."

"That's true. I hope I've made the right choice."

"I know you have."

His vote of confidence gave her a boost. "At the risk of
feeding your ego, I think you're a pretty smart man."

He pressed his thumb to the back of her wrist where her
pulse beat steadily. If Harry was paying attention, he might feel
the increase in her heart rate now that he was touching her.

"So what next?" he asked.

"You mean right now or with my grand life plan?"

"Either."

"Well, I have thoughts about both."

"Fair enough. Start with the here and now."

"Are you one of those men who likes to grill?" she asked.

He smiled. "I've been known to char meat on occasion."

"You want to have a cookout for dinner? My grandparents
are old-school. Their grill is charcoal, not gas."

"I can handle that. But first, I want to hear more about
your grand life plan."

Cate had been dreading this moment, but it had to be
done. "I appreciate you giving me a roof over my head when
I needed it so badly. But this week I'm going to start looking
for my own place. It's time."

Harry released her and sat back, folding his arms over his
chest. "Have I made you feel unwelcome?"

"Oh, stop. It's not that, and you know it."

"Then why move out?"

"Are we really going to have this conversation?"

He scowled. "Apparently we are."

She sucked in a breath and said a quick prayer for courage, although asking the Almighty for advice about how to handle a volatile sexual relationship might be a tad sacrilegious.

"You and I have started something," she said. "Something fun and exciting. But we both know it's not permanent. You've made no bones about the fact that you aren't going to get married or have children."

"So?" His expression was mutinous. In some ways like a disgruntled boy who knows he's not getting his own way.

"So, I need to keep this casual. I can't let myself develop feelings for you. Living together is too cozy. When our sexual relationship reaches an end, it would be far less awkward if I had my own place."

"You've already told me you like me," he pointed out.

"That's not what I meant. I'm talking about romantic feelings."

"You don't have much faith in our longevity," he said. He searched her face as if looking for deeper clues in her explanation.

The truth was, she *already* felt too much for him. It was dangerous. Even having sex with him was dangerous, but she couldn't walk away from that. She didn't want to.

"We may be together two days or two weeks or two months. The time doesn't matter. I need my own place, Harry. I'm doing you the courtesy of giving you notice. So you won't be taken by surprise when I leave."

He was quiet for long seconds. Then he rolled to his feet and stretched. His shirt rode up, exposing a narrow slice of flat abdomen. She couldn't tell if she had made him angry or not.

Finally, he gave her a wry look. "I can't stop you moving out. But it seems dumb to waste your money. Not to mention the fact that the real estate market is tight right now. You do what you have to do, Cate. Just know that you are welcome to stay."

"And if we stop having sex? If there's a huge blowup? A terrible argument? Or we simply scratch the itch and decide it's over?"

"Why do women overthink everything?" he asked, his tone exasperated.

"Maybe because stupid men jack up our lives, and we always have to be prepared."

Harry's open mood shut down abruptly. "I get it," he said. "Men are pigs."

"That's not what I said."

"But it's what you think." He paused. "Is this the kind of argument you had in mind?"

"Something like that." She had to smile, despite her heartache. "It's no big deal, Harry. Time moves on. People change. I want to be ready. I've had enough uncomfortable surprises this year."

"And the sex?"

She stood and curled her arms around his neck. "I'm not giving that up anytime soon."

The rigid set to his jaw relaxed. "Thank God. I'd hate to have to tie you to my bed."

"You wouldn't," she said.

He kissed her nose. "Maybe for fun."

She told herself not to blush. "Fun for whom?"

Harry cupped her face in his hands and traced her cheekbones with his thumbs. "You have the most beautiful skin. But it's turning pink, so we'd better get you out of the sun."

She chose to let him think it was the sun turning her face hot and not an image of Harry holding her captive for his manly pleasures. All he had to do was *talk* about naughty sex, and Cate melted.

Tonight, once the sun went down, things would happen. Fun things. Sensual, arousing, exciting things.

Cate couldn't wait...

Twenty-Three

Cate and Harry danced around each other like sparring partners. Too close, and someone could steal a kiss. Too far away, and the sizzling need pulled them back together.

For Cate, the late afternoon and early evening crawled by. After visiting the school, she and Harry went to the grocery store before they went home. He spent an inordinate amount of time picking out two perfect T-bones. Cate gathered salad ingredients and selected potatoes to bake. Harry hefted a bag of charcoal and grabbed some lighter fluid.

By the time they checked out, paid and drove home, the sun was sinking lower in the sky. While Harry fired up the grill, Cate microwaved the potatoes for a few minutes and then put them in the oven to finish baking. Then she made the salad and set the table.

At the sink, she had a clear view of the chef. Watching him work gave her an odd feeling. If all they wanted from each other was sex, why were they playing house?

If she were smart, she would run away and not look back. She and Leah had texted a lot in the last couple of weeks.

Though they hadn't been able to get another lunch date on the calendar, they'd talked on the phone a few times. But since Cate was withholding information, there wasn't a lot she could say other than to assure Leah that she was doing fine.

Leah and Gabby were her best friends in the entire world. She should be able to tell them the truth about Harry. But every time she thought about spitting it out, she panicked.

How could she tell them she was sleeping with Jason's cousin?

Friends were supposed to accept you, warts and all, but what if they judged her without meaning to? What if she saw confusion and disapproval on their faces? That would be dreadful. She knew they were worried about her. Honestly, Cate was worried about herself. She wasn't ready for somebody else to tell her that a relationship with Harry was a bad idea.

And then there was the other thing. Cate still had the impression that Gabby was upset about something. Cate had suggested getting together for a meal several times, but Gabby was always busy at work. It hurt to think Gabby was keeping her at a distance.

Even if Cate was doing essentially the same thing...

Cate had been more than willing to rent a car and drive back from Blossom Branch if either or both of her friends had wanted to get together for lunch. But it never seemed to work out.

Her own secrets weighed heavily. Perhaps Leah and Gabby had picked up on Cate's evasions. Maybe she had hurt their feelings by not staying with them instead of Harry.

No matter how Cate explained that choice, the other two women were suspicious of Harry and his motives. To hear that Cate and Harry were sleeping together might shock them and really make them upset.

Cate had her own questions. Why was Harry attracted to

her? He'd told her his long-ago crush was nothing. He'd been very convincing about it.

Was he covering up his emotions?

She hated feeling uncertain. Of all the things Jason's betrayal had set in motion—humiliation, embarrassment, strained relationships with her family and friends—destroying her trust was the worst.

How would she ever be able to depend on a man's words, or even his actions? The spectacular irony was that her rebound relationship had turned out to be with the absolute last guy she should trust. Harry didn't lie and cheat with other women. In a way, his unsuitability was worse.

He'd told her from the beginning that he didn't want anything permanent. With *any* woman. But permanent was what Cate wanted most.

Then why was she recklessly indulging in adult playtime?

In her entire twenty-five years, she had never done one-night stands or short-term hookups. Before Harry, Jason was her one and only. She'd never slept with a stranger. She had been a *good* girl yet look where that had landed her.

Dumped in front of society's elite.

Left alone with her life derailed.

Forced to accept help from her nemesis.

When Harry opened the back door and walked into the kitchen, Cate jumped. She'd been lost in her thoughts, trying to unravel the Gordian knot that kept her from going forward.

"Hey," she said. The word came out squeaky.

Harry glanced at her curiously. "You okay?"

She swallowed hard, wiping her damp palms on her jeans. "Sure. Just waiting for the potatoes to finish."

"How long do they have? Don't want the steaks to get cold."

"Um…" She had forgotten to set a timer, either on her phone or on the stove. The potatoes could have been baking for ten minutes or half an hour. Who knew? She had been lost in her thoughts, content to watch Harry unobserved. "I'll poke them with a fork," she said brightly. "Why don't you pour the wine?"

He saw too much. If she didn't get herself together, Harry would begin to ask questions.

He filled the wineglasses with a beautiful Aussie Shiraz. "I haven't had this one before, but one of my buddies loves it."

Cate pulled the potatoes out of the oven, relieved they were done. "It smells good," she said, lifting one glass and swirling the contents.

By the time they sat down to eat, she thought she had covered her tracks. But Harry was not dumb. He cut his steak, tried a bite, then sat back in his chair. "Something's wrong," he said. "I haven't seen you this jumpy in a long time. Maybe ever." His gray eyes studied her face, trying to discover her secrets. Cate didn't like that.

"You're imagining things." She stared down at her plate, carefully slicing into her steak.

"No." Harry said.

"Let it go, Harry," she said. "All I want to do is have a nice evening."

He didn't press her further, but the meal was uncomfortable. They ate mostly in silence.

Finally, at the soonest possible moment she could get up from the table without triggering another round of questions, Cate stood. "Leave the dishes," she said. "I'll take care of them later."

He frowned. "Where are you going?"

"To my room. I'm not feeling well."

She knew she was acting crazy. Why was she suddenly on the verge of tears? Harry was the perfect antidote to her old life. He was exciting and fun, and he made her ache with wanting him.

Maybe that was the problem. She didn't want to want him. But she didn't know how to stop.

Upstairs, she looked for comfort and found none.

Sitting in the dark on the bed seemed overly dramatic but she couldn't help herself. She didn't want to turn on the lights. She was hoping Harry would think her stomach was upset and he would leave her alone. Maybe he would assume she was having her period. Either way, she hoped he would take the hint.

She was honestly terrified. There was no way she could continue an affair with Harry and not get in over her head.

Now, with the luxury of time and space, she finally understood that she and Jason had been friends with benefits. Her longtime relationship with him had eliminated any possibility that Cate might find a man who turned her good-girl persona on its head. Until the relationship ended...

After the non-wedding, in her moments of grief and despair, Harry had somehow slipped past her defenses and made a place for himself in her heart.

It was a crush. She swore to herself that was all it was. After the wedding, she had been vulnerable. Harry's attention had soothed her hurt feelings. His obvious physical attraction to her had been a balm to her pride.

So what now?

She had to get through this weekend. She knew the danger. Rebound sex was one thing, but letting her emotions get involved was a huge no-no.

When they returned to Atlanta, it wouldn't take long to find her own place and move out.

In the meantime, she had to shore up her emotional resolve.

No more thinking that Harry needed her. That was a fiction she had invented to justify her affair with him.

She couldn't repair the damage his parents had inflicted. Harry was not her pet project. He was a grown man, and his problems were his own.

And no more imagining that he might have feelings for her. He liked her. Maybe he even cared about her in a general way. But it wasn't enough. She had learned that much this summer, if nothing else. She deserved to be with someone who adored her.

Love wasn't too much to ask.

An hour passed. Cate wasn't keeping track, but she heard the bells on one of Blossom Branch's picturesque churches chime the hour and then chime again. A knock sounded at her door.

Harry's voice, low and quiet spoke. "May I come in, Cate?"

She sucked in a breath. "Sure."

If he was surprised to find her in the dark, he didn't let on.

Cate turned on the small lamp beside the bed. She sat against the headboard, knees to her chest, arms wrapped around her legs. Her hands were cold, even though the house was warm.

Harry perched on the foot of the mattress. "Do you want to talk about it?"

Maybe going on the offensive was the only way to deal with a big, gorgeous hunk of temptation. "I don't think I can have sex with you in my grandparents' house. It feels weird and disrespectful."

She *lied* to Harry without a twinge of remorse. *Wow.*

He studied her face. Concern radiated from his careful gaze. "I understand. But you could have told me that earlier. It's nothing to get upset about."

"If you want to go back to Atlanta, I understand." *Please go, please go, please go.*

His jaw tightened. "I'm here for the weekend. I want to

spend it with you. With or without sharing a bed. Do you believe me?"

She stared into his steely eyes, trying not to be mesmerized by that odd but perfect ring of silver. "I want to." It was perhaps the most honest thing she had ever said to him.

The twist of his lips was part grimace, part amusement. "But something is stopping you?"

"Yes. Men say anything to get sex."

His temper flared, turning the steel molten. "I don't think that's fair. Have I ever made you feel like that?"

She winced. "I guess not." Truthfully, he had cherished her, cosseted her, indulged her.

But was he *acting* to get what he wanted?

Cate had known Jason her entire life, yet she had misjudged his feelings and emotions. Why would she think she understood Harry?

He exhaled and stood, his expression inscrutable. "I'll leave you alone. Get some sleep. I hear we have a big to-do list tomorrow."

"You don't have to help," she muttered.

Harry didn't even kiss her goodnight. But he paused in the doorway and stared at her so intently a shiver worked its way from her scalp to her toes. "We're good together, Cate. But I won't be accused of pressuring you. You're not a victim. Not anymore. The jilted bride thing has run its course. Decide what you want from me and let me know."

Cate slept poorly. She was up at dawn and out on the quiet streets, trying to elude her problems.

She was running from guilt, too. Not only had she lied to Harry, but she had insulted him to his face. She had accused him of playing games for his own sexual gratification. And not the good kind of games.

Was that disappointment she had seen in his eyes? Had she let her own insecurities destroy her confidence? Harry didn't want an immature young woman in his bed. He wanted a partner, an equal.

By the time she got back to the house and showered, she had steadied her nerves and convinced herself she could handle Harry.

But when she found him in the kitchen wearing nothing but khaki shorts while he scrambled eggs and fried bacon, her mouth went dry. His chest was sleekly muscled and utterly masculine. No one would ever mistake *him* for an immature kid.

"Good morning," he said, his smile guarded but cordial.

Cate snitched a warm, crunchy piece of pork fat. "Did you forget to pack any clothes?" she asked, pretending that his state of undress was unremarkable.

His smile broadened. "I worked outside in the yard while you were gone. It's hot."

"What needed doing outside?" The teenage boy down the street had been mowing regularly.

Harry scooped the perfectly cooked eggs onto a warm plate. "If you must know, I was tending to the trellis and the roses. I'm guessing you didn't want your grandparents to hear about your breaking and entering skills."

"Oh, gosh. How bad is the damage? I'd forgotten all about it." That first night when she landed on top of Harry in the upstairs hallway seemed like a million years ago.

He motioned to the table. "Sit." He offered her a plate. "No biscuits today. Sorry." Then he joined her. "I trimmed off all the broken blossoms and buds. And I found some white paint in the shed to touch up the spots where you scraped the wood. All in all, I think it will be fine so long as nobody looks too closely."

"Thanks," she said, drinking her hot tea. He had fixed it for her without asking. No cream, two sugars. And a side of orange juice.

"You're welcome."

When his smile reached inside her chest and warmed all the cold, alone places, she knew her armor was going to have to grow a lot thicker.

Friday passed in a haze of activity. They vacuumed and mopped, and Harry even washed windows. For lunch, they finished up leftovers. While Cate dusted the living room and cleaned the bathrooms, Harry wiped out the refrigerator.

For dinner, they went back to Peach Crumble. Shirley worked mostly morning shifts, so she wasn't around. But Cate had begun to recognize other servers. And even some of the regulars.

Afterward, they took a turn around the park. The vendors had already been set up and selling their wares while Cate and Harry were busy all day. Now it was late enough that exhibitors were closing tent flaps and securing valuable items.

Harry stopped to watch a woodcarver wrangle a six-foot bear into the back of his pickup. "What time do you want to see everything tomorrow?" he asked Cate.

"Honestly, I'm beat. What if we sleep in?"

"I'm assuming that means in our chaste, separate beds?"

"Don't make fun of me," she protested.

He kissed her forehead, tucking a few stray tendrils of hair behind her ears. "I'm not. Teasing is different. It's kinder. Gentler."

"Not from where I'm standing," Cate grumbled. "I told you to go back to Atlanta. It's fine."

"And *I* told *you* I want to stay. Celibacy never killed anyone."

She pondered his wiseass remark. As far as she could tell, her arrival in Harry's home must have constrained his sex life. There had been no visible girlfriend to be offended when he rescued Cate and let her stay.

But then again, Harry didn't do girlfriends. Right? He was probably a love 'em and leave 'em kind of guy. So he must mean *celibate* in the context of their newly discovered sexual compatibility.

What she needed was for Harry to reveal himself as a man with indiscriminate tastes in women. That way she would be forced to see his true colors. She could break free of his spell.

Unfortunately, he seemed determined to stick close.

"We might as well walk tomorrow," she said. "There won't be any parking for miles. What if we head down here to the park at noon?" she said. "One of the local bands is putting on a bluegrass concert. We can get food from a street vendor. And then after that, shopping, of course."

His lips twitched. "Shopping. Right."

"I can come on my own."

"Oh, no. You might buy a huge carved bear, and you'll need me to carry it all the way to my car."

Cate laughed. "Maybe I'll stick to jewelry and candles."

"And after the shopping?"

"We'll go back to the house, pack up our odds and ends, and chill for a little bit."

"Any dinner ideas? I'm assuming we're not going to dirty up the kitchen."

"I've reserved a table for two at The Peach Pit."

Harry raised an eyebrow. "The bar takes reservations?"

"Only during festival weekends. They're offering red and blue beer and appetizer sampler platters. All you can eat."

"Count me in. So we'll watch fireworks here on the quad?"

"No. I have a surprise location. Strictly need to know. But we'll have to go get the car around eight thirty."

"Sounds like you have everything all planned."

She winced. "I know. It's boring, right? I kind of like control."

He leaned against one of the huge oak trees and folded his arms. The breeze ruffled his thick hair. "That's partly why the wedding fiasco was so hard on you. It messed up your whole life plan. You felt adrift."

Cate felt her face heat. "How do you know that?"

He smiled. "I've spent a fair amount of time with you, Cate. Enough to see that you don't appreciate your own gifts and strengths as much as you should. And that you're too hard on yourself. I'm all in favor of having plans. My whole career is centered around plans. They get me where I need to go."

She searched his face, wishing his plans included her. But he was talking about business, not pleasure. When it came to things like sex, Harry was far more spontaneous.

Twenty-Four

Back at the house, Cate nearly caved. She wanted nothing more than to climb the stairs with Harry and end up in his bed or hers. The strength of that need made her shaky and weak.

Like a diet that had only lasted twenty-four hours, she wanted to give in and devour him. In the same way someone would consume jelly doughnuts or cheesy pizza or even an entire bag of chips. Comparing Harry to food in her imagination was not smart. Now she was hungry *and* horny.

Before she could break her own rules, she murmured a hasty goodnight and hid out in her room. Later, she could hear him climbing the stairs. And she heard his shower running.

Fortunately, because she hadn't slept well the night before, she was able to crash hard after her own shower.

When she awoke on Saturday morning, the weather was postcard perfect. Blue skies and white fluffy clouds. She checked her weather app. The temps were already in the upper seventies and climbing.

She chose a white tank top and paired it with a gauzy skirt

of navy and pink, then added navy espadrilles that would be comfy enough to wear all day.

It was only when her stomach growled that she realized one flaw in her plan for the Fourth of July. At almost the same moment, her phone dinged.

Apparently, we both forgot we'd need breakfast. I dropped a little treat outside your room. H

Cate listened at the door and then stuck out her arm to grab the brown paper sack and the tall paper cup with a lid. Harry had been to the coffee shop in town! Her portion of the bounty was a slice of cinnamon coffee cake and fresh-squeezed orange juice.

She ate the yummy meal a little at a time as she emptied drawers and filled her bags. Though her grandparents were still gone, the house had provided the same warmth and peace Cate remembered as a child.

Healing had come to her slowly. The future seemed brighter now, and happiness more attainable.

It was impossible to separate Harry from the mix. His hand was on almost everything that had happened in the last weeks. Except for the store. That had been Cate's decision, her dream. And she was proud of it. Even then, she had welcomed Harry's input after the fact.

One at a time, she put her various pieces of luggage in the hall. On the dresser, she laid out the few things she would need for tomorrow morning.

It felt odd to be leaving. Even though she would return to Blossom Branch for the real estate closing and to visit her grandparents, today marked one chapter of her life ending and another beginning.

She had survived. Now it was time to grow.

When she went downstairs just before noon, her luggage had disappeared. Harry had clearly been loading the car.

As she peeked into the carport, he saw her immediately and slammed the trunk. "It's going to be a tight squeeze tomorrow, but you can hold the carved bear on your lap."

"No carved bear," she said with a laugh. "I promise."

Harry rounded the car, pulled her into his arms and kissed her. "I missed you last night," he said, nibbling a sensitive spot beneath her ear.

She resisted the urge to say, *ditto.* "Thank you for my breakfast. I guess I'm not such a great planner after all."

He tugged on her earlobe with sharp teeth. "You were distracted by my animal magnetism," he said.

She could smell his warm skin and the soap he had used shaving. "You are so full of it." Her heart racketed in her chest. It was hard to feign nonchalance when everything he said and did tantalized her senses. "It's almost noon," she pointed out. "Are you ready?"

"If you mean ready to take you without mercy in the playhouse, the answer is yes. That wouldn't technically count as your grandparents' home—right?"

"It's a thousand degrees out there. And I know you're kidding."

The hungry expression on his face said otherwise, but Cate had to steer them onto safer ground. "We don't want to miss the concert," she said, kissing him lightly because she couldn't bear not to kiss him at all.

"Lead on," he said.

Was it her imagination, or did the man radiate sexual hunger? He was like a barely domesticated tiger, ready to snap and bite if she let down her guard.

Was she going to spend the day balanced on a knife-edge of danger and need?

By the time they strolled the three blocks into the center of town, Harry's mood was less edgy. He found them a seat on the grass and leaned back against a tree, pulling Cate against his chest.

It was the most comfortable spot on the whole quad. And the most perfect. She would steal these last innocent moments with Harry because she knew the end was coming.

Unlike on her wedding day, she recognized the heartbreak ahead. This time she was prepared. Besides, she wasn't in love with Harry. She had a deep, sexually exciting crush. He was her rebound guy. The one who had saved her and nursed her back to emotional health.

Though he didn't want to hear it, she would always be grateful for his caring and kindness. Beneath his gruff, no-nonsense exterior, she had caught a glimpse of that teenage boy standing in his parents' driveway, for one happy, surprised moment, expecting a birthday party.

Cate wondered if he thought she had forgotten today was his birthday. July 4. She hadn't forgotten.

When the music started, she closed her eyes and let the day seep into her soul. The warmth of Blossom Branch. Harry's strong embrace. The sounds of laughter and chatter. The smell of funnel cakes.

The band played for an hour. Halfway through, Harry stepped away for a few minutes and brought back chicken pitas and frosted lemonades.

Cate gobbled hers down and licked her fingers.

Harry laughed at her, but his food disappeared nearly as rapidly.

When the concert was over, he took her hand and pulled her to her feet. "Shopping now?" he asked, with a morose expression.

She knew he was teasing her, but she smiled. "Definitely."

The vendors ran the gamut. But there was nothing cheap or tacky. Handmade stained glass. Polished wooden boxes. Sterling silver jewelry with semiprecious stones. Small oil paintings and pastels.

And of course, the wood carvings.

Several of the offerings impressed her so much, she asked for business cards with a thought to stocking her store later.

While she was chatting with a woman who made traditional caning for wooden footstools, Harry disappeared.

When he returned, she traced his jaw with her fingertip. "I thought I'd lost you."

His eyes darkened. "Not a chance." He dangled a small lavender bag in front of her. "I bought you a present."

"Whatever for?"

"Because this reminded me of you."

She opened the gift that was wrapped in white tissue. Inside she found a delicate gold chain probably eighteen inches long, with a single tiny charm—a stylized peach blossom, made of pink Swarovski crystals with tiny clear accents.

"Harry..." Her eyes stung with tears.

"It even matches your outfit." He took the chain from her. While Cate lifted her hair, he fastened it at the nape of her neck. Then he kissed that same spot, his lips lingering.

"Thank you," she whispered.

When he faced her again, his smile was warm and intimate. "I figured the woman who holds the unbroken record of being Miss Georgia Peach Blossom four years running ought to have something as beautiful as she is."

"I don't know what to say."

Harry touched the small flower. "Tell me you'll reconsider moving out. I like having you around. You're better than a puppy or a cat. And I'm not allergic to you."

She chuckled. "You're awful. I'll still see you occasionally. We're friends, Harry. Nothing will change that."

He pulled her close, wrapping his arms around her waist and steering her through the crowd. "Good friends," he said. "Very good friends…"

By the time they finally made their way to The Peach Pit, Cate's feet ached, but her heart was full. A petite server with purple hair and a steel stud in her tongue showed them to their table in the corner. "Stella will grab your order in a sec. Enjoy yourselves."

The atmosphere was loud and raucous, and the food amazing. Cate was too full too fast, but Harry polished off what she didn't eat.

When the band cranked up, one of the guitarists coaxed diners out onto the dance floor.

Harry smiled. "You game?"

Cate gaped at him. "Prescott Harrington can dance?"

"Miss Letitia Madison's Ballroom Salon. Sixth and seventh grade. Every Thursday afternoon from four till six. Worst experience of my life. But I promise not to step on your toes." His grin deepened. "Don't look so shocked."

Cate had expected line dancing, but although the band cycled through traditional country favorites during dinner, they tossed in the occasional make-out number. When Cate and Harry took the floor, the lead singer segued into an Anne Murray song.

Cate's heart sank. She wasn't a huge country music fan, but she knew this song. It was an old one…maybe even from her grandparents' teenage years. And it had been played at a million wedding receptions.

When Harry pulled her close to his chest and wrapped his arms around her, Cate rested her cheek on his shoulder. The band's vocalist had a mournful voice that matched the lyrics perfectly.

Cate tried to ignore the words, but every verse was a snapshot of her life in this moment. Nothing about losing Jason. But everything about falling for Harry. It *did* feel right to be with him, even though she knew the relationship was all wrong. Harry hummed the melody, his lips in her hair.

He held her confidently. Their feet never stumbled once. It was as if they had been dancing together for a lifetime.

Cate steeled herself. She wouldn't be swayed by the low lights and the romantic mood. Or the large man whose stance was protective.

She shouldn't be surprised by his grace. It was the way he made love, too. As if he was moving to some unseen choreography.

How was a woman supposed to protect herself?

When the song ended, Cate headed for the table. The next tune was loud and fast. No scary romance.

Harry joined her. "You didn't think I could keep up?"

"No, it's me. My feet are tired."

"Chicken."

"I might *look* like a chicken if I tried that," she said, shaking her head ruefully. "Check out the crowd on the dance floor. They're all under twenty or over seventy."

Harry turned his head. "Well, you might be right."

They stayed for a few more songs. Then Cate reluctantly put an end to the fun interlude. "We should give up our table. They told me all reservations were only for two hours. So they can get more people in and out."

"Seems fair." Harry paid the check.

After the press of people in the bar, even the summer night felt pleasant when they made it outside.

Cate glanced at her watch. "We'd better hurry."

Harry matched pace. "*Now* will you tell me where we're going?"

"Not yet."

At the house they went inside to freshen up and grab water bottles. When they were back in the car, Cate muttered under her breath.

"What's wrong?" Harry asked.

"I forgot we'll need something to sit on."

"Folding chairs?"

"No. We'll be on the ground."

"I have a canvas tarp in the trunk. It's fairly clean."

"That will do."

Harry pulled out of the driveway. Cate directed him down a series of back roads. He pointed at the clock on the dash. "It's getting late. You don't want to miss the highlight of the day."

"Almost there."

Finally, she spotted the turnoff. "Go up that road," she said.

"This looks like private property."

"It is. But my grandparents have known the owner for decades. We turn here."

When Harry stopped the car at Cate's direction, she got out. "Grab the tarp, please. We have to walk this last bit."

Cate took the water bottles, and they set out on foot, moving quickly.

Harry inhaled. "Ah, the scent of peaches. I should have guessed."

"The orchard's rows are lined up in such a way that this hilltop has a perfect view of town and the fireworks. I thought it would be fun to watch from here."

Harry flipped out the tarp. They smoothed it before sitting down. "Should we expect company?" he asked.

"No. All the owner's family are grown and gone. I think it will be just you and me."

"You're forgiven for keeping secrets," he said. "This is a nice surprise. All the beauty and none of the crowds."

"I thought you would like it."

Harry cupped her face in his hands and kissed her. "The whole day has been great. I should take a vacation more often."

She put her hands on his wrists. Was she going to stop him, or simply hang on? When Harry deepened the kiss, she knew the answer.

His tongue dueled with hers. Harry eased her onto her back. "I want you, Cate."

She nodded. "Yes." At some level, she had known this would be the outcome of seeking out privacy. Yet still she had brought him here.

Harry moved on top of her, settling one large thigh between her legs. They were both fully dressed. His breathing was ragged. She could feel his heart pound against her chest.

"I wish things were different," he said, leaning on one hand and sliding the other beneath her top to cup her breast.

"Different how?"

"Me. My life. You deserve someone uncomplicated, Cate. Someone who will worship you and make babies with you."

"I don't need to be worshipped. And not everyone has children."

He stared down at her. It was too dark to read the expression in his eyes. But she felt the war inside him. "Enough of that," he said, the words barely audible. "I haven't been inside you in months."

His exaggeration made her smile until he tugged at her nipple and sent liquid fire coursing all the way to her belly and beyond.

"Harry..." She said his name, hearing the yearning, the need in her own voice. In the sky above them, the fireworks started with one perfect starburst of white and crimson. Cate felt compelled to point it out to her partner. "You're missing it," she said.

"I'm not missing a damn thing." He gave one quick look over his shoulder at the whirls of color and immediately went back to his focus on *her*. "Tell me what you want, Catie-girl."

I want you.

But she didn't say that. "I want to see the fireworks. Please."

He flopped to his back and groaned. "I could *give* you fireworks," he said.

She reached for his hand and linked their fingers. "Relax, Harry. We have time for everything."

Twenty-Five

Cate had witnessed a lot of fireworks displays in her life. But she would always remember this one. She wanted Harry every bit as much as he wanted her. Drawing out the pleasure was her aim.

She wouldn't change her mind this time.

Sometimes rain or low-hanging clouds might dampen celebrations on the Fourth. Not tonight. The sky was clear and cloudless. Whoever was putting on the display hadn't skimped on the pyrotechnics.

The colorful explosions lit up the sky, each one brighter and more extravagant than the last. Though Cate and Harry were some distance away, even the muted booms reached them. When she sneaked a surreptitious glance at her companion, she caught him smiling. Not at her. But at the sky, as if he was enjoying the display.

Maybe this would make up for a few of the disappointing birthdays he had experienced over the years. With her thumb, she monitored the pulse in his wrist, feeling his life force. Strong. Dominant.

Harry was unique. Fascinating. She hated that his parents hadn't nurtured his ambitions and his talents. Everything he had accomplished in life he had done on his own.

Maybe that was all he knew. Being alone.

She snuggled into his side, her hand landing on his thigh. She felt his chest move when he chuckled. "Oh, no," he said. "Not yet. We're watching till the bitter end. Never let it be said that I kept a woman from her fireworks."

"They're almost over," Cate said, sliding her hand under his shirt and unfastening the one button at his waist. His flat abdomen fascinated her. Firm as a rock, but warm and smooth.

"Cate…"

She teased his navel. "I've seen enough."

At that very moment, the grand finale popped and boomed and sizzled in the sky. All the reds and blues and golds and greens cartwheeled together in unrestrained excess.

Cate raised up on one elbow, seeing the rainbow of color reflected on Harry's face. When she kissed him, a shudder ran through his body. Strong arms wrapped around her pulling her tight against his chest.

"About damn time," he groaned.

After the first five seconds, there was no question who was in charge of the kiss. His lips and teeth and tongue ravaged her mouth. Cate had the oddest feeling she had been tossed up amidst the colors in the sky.

Little pops of sensation fizzed in her veins.

"More," she begged.

He yanked at her top, managing to get it off over her head. Her bare breasts felt cool against the hot, muggy night air. Harry buried his face between them, nibbling the slopes, licking the tips.

Once, he even paused to play with the flower he had given her. Cate squirmed, wanting his hands elsewhere.

"I like it," he said. "Looks even better when you're naked like this."

She grabbed handfuls of his shirt. "Take this thing off. Please."

He sat up to unbutton the soft cotton garment and shrug out of it. When he tossed it aside, Cate wrapped her arms around him, stroking his back, biting his neck, driving them both crazy.

Only seventy-two hours had passed since they first explored each other's bodies. It might as well have been a lifetime. Yet the feel of Harry's skin and the contours of his broad shoulders felt familiar beneath her fingertips.

He unfastened his shorts and released his erection. Then he pulled her across his lap. "I love skirts," he groaned. He nudged her panties aside and joined their bodies with a sharp upward thrust. His sex filled her.

Cate moaned, the sound echoing on the night breeze. "Harry," she breathed. Her words were lost. All she could do was rest her forehead on his shoulder.

He palmed her butt. "I love your ass," he said. "Talk about a ripe peach..."

Even amidst sexual insanity, he made her laugh. "Why did you stop?" she asked, her tone unwittingly petulant.

"I'm savoring the moment." The gasped explanation didn't satisfy either of them.

They shuddered there on a canvas tarp, sitting skin to skin, chest to chest, clasped together as if the very forces of nature might pull them apart.

Cate didn't let herself think about the future. It hurt too much.

"I'm sorry I made us wait," she whispered. "I was afraid."

He pulled back. "Afraid?"

She was glad he couldn't see her face in the dark. "I didn't want to feel this way. I didn't want to care about you, Harry."

Gently, he rearranged their bodies, still connected, until Cate was beneath him. "Don't be afraid, Catie-girl." He kissed her lips gently, as if the storm had passed. But this was only the eye of the hurricane.

Slowly, he moved in her. Claiming. Possessing. All the while he murmured to her. Soft, nonsensical words crooned in his low, sexy voice.

Her body climbed slowly now. As if fearful of the fall on the other side. She didn't want to feel. She didn't want to yearn. She didn't want to love.

Love hurt. She knew that well.

But Harry wouldn't allow her to keep even a piece of herself. He took her as if she was his to take. He made her cry out his name again and again as she wrapped her legs around his waist.

Then his control snapped, and he thrust like a madman. Hard and fast and wild. Stealing her heart, her body, her will.

Gasping for breath, Cate clung to him in the end, unwilling to admit what she knew deep in her gut.

If she didn't say the words, even to herself, she might survive.

When it was over, neither of them stirred. The scent of ripe peaches hung in the air. That distinct aroma would forever remind her of this moment, whether she coveted the memory or ran from it.

She stroked Harry's shoulders and slid her fingers through his hair. He hadn't said a word since he…finished. What was he thinking?

The night was dark, the shadows deep. While they stayed in this orchard, everything was okay. Just the two of them. Alone together.

His body on hers was a welcome weight. It told her this moment was real. No matter what happened in the days and weeks ahead, this experience, this connection was real.

But nothing lasts forever, whether good or bad.

Harry rolled to one side and wiped his hands over his face. "What did you do to me, Catie-girl? When I get within ten feet of you, I feel as desperate as I did when I was eighteen."

Cate didn't know how to answer that. So she didn't. Besides, the question was rhetorical. It was meant as a compliment… probably.

She reached for her top and pulled it over her head. As she did, her fingers brushed the chain with the flower. Once she and Harry were no longer together, she wouldn't be able to wear it again.

To remember this day—this night—would be too painful.

Harry located his shirt and her shoes. Cate didn't even re-member kicking them off, but she must have.

She was glad of the dark. She felt raw and uncertain.

These moments with Harry had rocked her world. What a silly cliché. But now she understood what it meant.

Whether he felt anything more than physical release was a moot point.

Prescott Harrington didn't want a woman in his life.

By the light of the flashlight on his phone, they made their way back to the car. When Cate's stomach growled audibly, Harry chuckled. "You want drive-through Peach-aria on the way home?"

"Yes, please." Though it felt like the middle of the night, her watch said it was not even eleven. The pizza place stayed open until midnight on the weekends. They always had sin-gle servings of cheese or pepperoni available at the window. Cate asked for two slices of plain. Harry ordered three of the other along with a couple of Cokes.

They sat in the parking lot to eat the greasy food. A security light provided enough illumination that it might as well have been daytime.

When he finished his meal—second dinner as he called it—Harry sighed. "We're sleeping apart tonight, aren't we?"

Clearly, he was referring to her fib. About not wanting to have sex in her grandparents' house.

Cate could have set the record straight and spent the night in his arms. But she felt the need to retreat and regroup.

"Yes," she said. "But the evening is not over quite yet."

Harry frowned. "What do you mean?"

She reached in the pocket of her skirt and pulled out a crumpled piece of paper. "Happy birthday, Harry."

He stared at her. "What's this?"

"Just open it." Cate had produced the form on her Grammy's printer. "It's not legal. Yet."

As she watched, Harry unfolded the faux document and read the words. He looked up, stunned. "You're giving me 5 percent of your store?"

Cate nodded. "You saved my life, Harry. In a way no one else could. You gave me space and time to grieve after the wedding ended. You shored up my confidence."

"You would have done just as well without me," he said gruffly.

"I don't think that's true. I wanted a special gift for you, but what does a man like you need? I decided to do this. It won't mean much. Not for a few years at least. But even after you and I go our separate ways, you'll still have a connection to me and to Blossom Branch." Something about his expression bothered her. "But you don't have to accept if you think it's weird."

"Cate." His voice was husky. "Come here, woman." He pulled her toward him, with the console awkwardly between them. "Thank you. So damn much. This is the most perfect birthday gift I've ever received."

His kiss was gentle and sweet. But it still generated a buzz.

When they separated, she gave him a wry smile. "I'm sorry you have to share your birthday with the United States of America."

He grinned. "I always get the day off, and fireworks to boot. Not a bad deal."

"Let's go home," she said.

Inside the house, Harry took her in his arms. "Good night, sweet Cate. This was a perfect birthday, top to bottom. I'm glad I spent it with you."

"Me, too," she said, kissing him and trying to make it seem casual.

After they climbed the stairs and went their separate ways, Cate lay awake in her bed, counting all the reasons a relationship with Harry was impossible.

Even if none of *his* deal breakers existed, there was always the reality of Cate's wedding fiasco. What would people think if they knew she went from Jason's bed to Harry's?

For that matter, what would Jason think? Would he assume she was trying to hurt him? Maybe that's what it would look like from the outside.

How could Cate explain the progression of her relationship with Harry when she barely understood it herself?

The next morning the two of them made sure everything was in order and then closed up and locked the house.

Cate replaced the key in its hiding spot.

Harry put the last of their personal items in the car.

"You ready?" he asked. His mood was subdued, as if he had wrestled with the same impossibilities Cate had.

"Let's go," she said.

Despite knowing this wasn't a final goodbye to Blossom

Branch, she felt a rush of wistful emotion as they drove away. She and Harry had experienced so much closeness here. Even with his two-week hiatus, she had met his mother. Harry had shared some dark secrets. Cate worked through her feelings about her wedding day.

All in all, Blossom Branch had served as a watershed moment for Cate's relationship with the inscrutable Prescott Harrington.

Or maybe not so inscrutable after all.

He had laid it out there. No wife. No kids.

She couldn't accuse him of deceiving her.

Cate would either accept the truth or be bitterly disappointed for a second time in her life.

They were almost back to Harry's apartment building when he shot her a sideways glance. "I know tomorrow is still the holiday. But I really need to get some work done. Because I was on vacation this week, I'll be behind come Tuesday."

She lifted her chin. "No worries. I have half a dozen errands I need to run. Don't worry about me. In fact, this whole week will be busy for me, too."

He entered the parking garage and slid into the numbered space. When he shut off the engine, he half turned in his seat and faced her. "And the nights?" His expression was guarded, even though a faint smile tipped up his lips.

Cate saw the choice clearly, but it was really no choice at all. She reached for his hand, lifting it to her lips and kissing his knuckles. "We'll share your bed until I move out."

His jaw tightened. "And after that?"

"After that, we'll see…"

Twenty-Six

Cate found herself in deep water. It was much harder than she anticipated to pretend she was with Harry for sex and convenience.

On Monday, when she met with a listing agent to tour condos and apartments and traditional homes, not a single place looked appealing.

The prospect of living alone when Harry was so clearly happy to have her stay with him was dismal. She second-guessed her decision time and again. The thing that kept her going from building to building was the absolute certainty that when her relationship with Harry reached its inevitable end, Cate would be less wounded if she already had a place of her own.

Even so, she didn't mention house-hunting to her lover.

Tuesday, she looked at more real estate and afterward met with the art museum director.

Wednesday, she entertained her first class of young visitors.

The children were intimidating. Ranging in age from ten to fourteen, they came bounding into the museum classroom with varying degrees of interest. They eyed Cate with suspicion.

Their backgrounds ran the gamut. Multiple ethnicities. Atlanta was, after all, a city of many languages and skin colors. These students were part of a summer day care program.

"Well," Cate said. "I'm glad you all are here."

Twenty pairs of eyes surveyed her, unblinking.

"My name is Ms. Cate," she said. "I love art, and I'm going to spend the next hour showing you why."

A boy raised his hand. "Can I go to the bathroom?"

Cate shot a glance at one of the chaperones. The woman shook her head in a firm negative. Cate looked back at the boy. "Not yet. But we'll take a break after half an hour."

One of the older students raised a hand. "Do you have real rockets and stuff here? Space is cool," he said.

"No." Cate realized she was fast losing control. She picked up two marble animals—a rabbit and a turtle—that had been purchased by a wealthy donor and given to the museum for this exact purpose. "These are original sculptures. The artist takes a hunk of rock and then uses a chisel and other tools to reveal the shape inside."

A small girl with golden skin and a Hispanic accent frowned. "How does the artist know what's inside the rock?"

Cate wanted to laugh, but she kept her expression neutral. Kids were so literal, even at this age. "That's where an artist needs imagination. Raise your hands if *you* have an imagination."

Every arm shot into the air. Cate smiled. "Exactly. That means any one of you has the potential to be an artist. Over the summer we're going to talk about paper and paint and metal and string. Basically, *anything* can be part of an artist's vision."

A tall thin Asian boy wearing a BTS T-shirt was next to quiz her. "Are you an artist, Ms. Cate?"

His question had an edge, as if he might be calling her on perceived bullshit. Cate paused half a second. "Well," she said, "I guess I am. My major in college was art history, which means I studied all the different centuries—the artists who were active at that time and what they were doing—where and when. Along the way, I fell in love with watercolors. When I have the time, I try my hand at that."

He still stood. "Music is art," he said, his tone defiant.

"You're right. But here in this museum, the collection is about things you can see and touch. The other senses—taste and smell and hearing—are equally important, but not so easily assembled and displayed."

The teenage girl beside the boy waved a hand. When Cate called on her, the young woman blushed. "Our phones are like little museums for photography and music, don't you think? And they're all different depending upon where we live and the age of the person who is doing the collecting."

Cate stared, taken aback at the girl's ability to synthesize ideas. "You are spot-on," Cate said. "Very perceptive."

Bathroom Boy raised his hand again. Cate smiled. "I'm going to pass these sculptures around while we take an informal break. Study them up close. And think about what animal you might have chosen to create. We'll meet back here in ten minutes."

Fortunately, the rest of the class period passed without incident. The adult chaperones were complimentary as they eventually shuffled their crew outside and onto the school bus.

Cate shielded her eyes from the sun and watched them drive away. She felt oddly energized, though the afternoon had been physically draining.

In one startling moment of clarity, she realized why she was still staying at Harry's place. She was collecting artifacts of their time together, artifacts both literal and mental. The peach blossom necklace. The way he smiled when he saw her walk into a room. The blue shirt he gave her to wear on her wedding day. The sound of his voice singing in the shower.

Museums were important. They preserved art and beauty and so much else. Cate wouldn't always have Harry, but she had unconsciously been assembling memories that would carry her through the days ahead.

After saying her goodbyes to the museum director and other staff, Cate rushed out to meet Becca and Leah at a nearby bistro. She was the last to arrive. Her sister and her best friend had already snagged a table. Both women got up and hugged her.

"Sorry I'm late," Cate said. "The first museum class was today."

"How was it?" Leah asked.

"Honestly, I was petrified at first. I'm not a teacher. But I jumped in and tried to let them see how diverse art can be… and how fun."

"I think it's awesome you're doing that," Becca said.

Cate smiled. "Thanks. I'm just trying to keep up with Leah." She looked at her friend. "How are things going with getting the non-profit and the camp started?"

"It looks like we'll be ready to have our first campers in early summer of next year. I may need some of your museum contacts to identify the kids who need our services."

"Of course. Just let me know."

They ordered an appetizer to share and drinks, then settled in. Cate put Becca out of her misery right away. "I've thought it over. If Mom and Dad are okay with it, I'd love to have you come manage the store with me."

Becca squealed.

Leah beamed. "I can't wait to see it. It's such a great idea, Cate. I knew you would bounce back."

Cate winced. "I don't know about bouncing back, but at

least I'm moving forward." She *was* moving forward. To a murky future perhaps, but forward was better than backward.

Leah and Becca exchanged a glance.

"What?" Cate looked from one to the other.

Leah sighed. "Jason is back in town. We didn't know if you'd heard."

A heartbeat of silence passed awkwardly. "Well, I assumed he would be…based on our previous plans." Cate did her best to hide her unease. "It doesn't matter, though. I'm fine."

She wasn't sure her companions believed her. Fortunately, they changed the subject.

Her sister started the inquisition. "So, how is *Harry?*"

"He's great. But you both should know—I'll be moving out of his place soon. I've already been looking at property, rental and otherwise."

Leah's expression morphed to guilt. "I wish my apartment wasn't so tiny. I hate for you to rush into something."

Becca smirked. "You can have my room when I move to Blossom Branch."

"Very funny." Cate sighed. "I'll admit, it feels strange. Jason and I were supposed to be house hunting right about now. But that's in the past. I'm learning how to pivot. Honestly, I'm okay. Maybe not a hundred percent yet, but I'm getting there. You don't have to worry about me anymore."

Leah squeezed her hand. "I'm glad, hon. That was a terrible, awful, no good very bad day. None of us want to remember it."

Becca nodded. "She's right. But the thing we've been afraid to ask you is…"

Both Cate's sister and her friend looked uncomfortable. "Go ahead," she said. "Ask me anything."

"Are you still in love with Jason?" Leah's face was sober, her gaze concerned.

This was tricky. Cate had been struggling with similar questions since June 7. "I've spent a lot of time pondering that. I feel stupid and clueless when I say this, but I think Jason was right to do what he did. Not the timing. That was agonizing. Still, I've come to realize that our relationship was having a few bumps I had been ignoring."

"Oh." Leah frowned. "Meaning what?"

"I love Jason. I think I always will. But we weren't *in* love. I was so caught up in planning the wedding that I didn't see the truth. There were signs...now that I look back. I wish I had been more tuned in to Jason's feelings. And my own, for that matter."

Becca scrunched up her face. "I've seen you two together for years. If you didn't have the kind of love it takes to sustain a marriage, how will any of us ever find that?"

"Good question," Leah said glumly. "Men say we're complicated, but I think it's the other way around."

Cate almost blurted out the truth about Harry. But was there any point? She and Harry were sleeping together. That was an intimate detail she didn't feel comfortable sharing. Not when the relationship wasn't going anywhere long term.

There was one last thing Cate had wrestled with...and still had no answer. She looked at Leah. "Do you know why Gabby is acting weird?"

"You asked me that before." Leah shrugged. "I've talked to her several times. And we had dinner one night recently. She seemed fine."

"So, it's just me?"

Becca drained her water glass and set it down with a thump. "Maybe she doesn't know how to help you. That can make people act odd. Especially when their friends and family members are grieving. No point obsessing about it."

"I suppose."

Leah nodded. "She's probably hurting for you and doesn't know how to express it."

By the time Cate made it back to Harry's place, it was almost six o'clock. She had texted him to let him know when she would be home.

Harry had offered to cook. Spaghetti again.

When she walked in the front door, she smiled. "Something smells wonderful."

He came out of the kitchen and kissed her, his lips lingering until her knees wobbled. When he finally released her, he grinned as if he knew exactly what he did to her.

"It's just about ready," he said. "I've poured you some wine."

While they ate, she told him about the museum class and seeing Leah and Becca afterward. "I've officially offered my baby sister a job. I hope that's not a mistake."

"Why would it be?" he asked. "People usually thrive when they're motivated. I predict Becca will turn out to be invaluable."

They chatted a few minutes about Harry's work, and then he poured more wine for each of them. "This is nice," she said, relaxing as some of her stress melted away.

Harry stared at her intently. "I feel like I've hardly seen you this week."

"It's only Wednesday," she pointed out. But she knew what he meant. They had shared a bed Monday night, but Tuesday had been nonstop for both of them. In fact, Harry hadn't made it home from the office until 1 a.m. last night. Cate had gone to sleep in her own bed. Harry had scooped her up and carried her to *his* room when he found her missing.

Though they hadn't indulged in sex, they had slept in a

tangle of arms and legs with Cate's head on Harry's chest. It had been warm and wonderful.

Now he was looking at her as if it had been weeks of deprivation instead of forty-eight hours. "You never told me what you did Monday and Tuesday," he said.

"Well, I met with the museum director for an hour..."

"And?"

She stared him down. "I looked at apartments and houses."

His face darkened. "I see."

"Oh, come on, Harry. We've talked about this. I can't stay here. I need my independence."

"Have I tried to clip your wings, Catie-girl?" His tone was snarky.

"Of course not. Let's not argue. Please. What would you like to do tonight? Do you have more work to finish, or can we watch a movie?"

He reached for her hand and ran his thumb over her pulse. "I thought we might go to bed early."

Her heart pounded. Eight simple words. She was ready to melt at his feet. "Um...okay."

They cleaned up the kitchen with almost no conversation at all. Harry pointed out that his housekeeping lady would arrive Thursday afternoon, but Cate couldn't bear to leave such a mess all night.

When everything was spotless, she dithered. "I guess I should go take a shower."

Harry lifted her chin with one finger and kissed her lazily. "You haven't seen *my* shower yet."

It was true. Cate had used her own bathroom every time. She had only gotten as far as Harry's bed.

He chuckled. "Was my hint too obscure? Or are you feeling shy?"

"You want us to shower together?"

"Couples do," he said.

Were they a couple? Surely not. She cleared her throat. "Okay. Just let me know when you're ready."

"Now," he said bluntly. "I'm ready now."

Her mouth dried. "Oh. Sure. I'll get my things."

"Don't make me wait."

That sounded like more teasing until she studied his face and his posture. His cheekbones were flushed, and his shoulders were rigid. He had his hands stuffed in his pockets. In that stance, she could see the outline of his erection.

Because she couldn't think of anything to say, light and funny or otherwise, she escaped to her bedroom. Quickly, she put her hair up in a messy bun, shaved her legs and removed her mascara. There were certain things a woman didn't want to do during a sexy shower.

She had worn the peach blossom necklace to the museum today. She removed it now and laid it on the dresser along with her watch and earrings.

Wearing the same black satin robe Harry had already seen, she walked down the hall, pretending she wasn't afraid of the big bad wolf.

When she opened the door to Harry's suite, she caught him buck naked in the middle of the room. He was beautiful. That was the only way she could think to describe him. If she had *been* a sculptor, she could have immortalized him in stone or metal. Any artist in the world would concede that Prescott Harrington was a striking man.

"I didn't expect you so soon," he said.

"Should I leave?"

"What do you think?" His eyes glittered.

While her toes curled into the carpet, Harry took three strides in her direction and scooped her up into his arms.

"How's your knee?" she asked. It was hard to talk.

He nuzzled her nose with his. "My knee is great. Why do you look like a petrified fawn?"

She laughed softly. "You read minds now? I was just imagining you as the big bad wolf."

"Ready to gobble you up?"

"Something like that."

In the bathroom, he set her on her feet. "Don't move," he said. He turned on the water, adjusting the temperature until he was satisfied. The walls and floor were done in travertine tile complemented with brushed brass fixtures. Large, fluffy amber towels—soft and luxurious—hung nearby.

"All that tile looks awfully slippery," Cate said. "I hope you aren't considering anything too acrobatic."

Harry's quick grin warmed her to her toes. "No Cirque du Soleil, I promise." He held out his hand. "Join me."

Her hands were ice-cold. Her veins pulsed with a combination of eagerness and anxiety. Harry continued to ask for more trust, more intimacy. She wouldn't have minded if he hadn't made his stance on permanence so painfully clear. He was adamantly opposed to bringing a woman into his family, giving her the Harrington name. Was there any hope of changing his mind?

She lifted her chin and unfastened the knot at her waist. Then she let the robe slide to the floor in a pool of inky silk.

Harry sucked in an audible breath.

They had been intimate multiple times. She knew so much about his body and so little about the secrets hidden inside him.

Carefully, she stepped over the small ledge and into the shower enclosure. There was no door. The shower was large. The water simply drained to the center and disappeared, not impacting the bathroom at all except for the cloud of steam.

Cate winced when the water hit her shoulder.

"Too hot?" Harry asked.

"Maybe a little."

He adjusted the faucet one more time and pulled her close. "Wet is a good look on you," he said, the words hoarse.

When she felt his hands settle on her ass, she nestled closer, resting her cheek on his chest. "How many women have you entertained here?" she asked. As soon as the words left her mouth, she stiffened, mortified. "Sorry. I didn't mean to ask that."

He tipped up her chin and stared into her eyes. Drops of water lingered on his dark lashes. Gray eyes blazed with emotion. "But you want to know?"

"Yes."

"You're the first." His self-mocking smile confused her. "And you're the first person I've invited to move in with me."

What was he saying? "No other runaway brides?"

"Only you, Cate."

Twenty-Seven

The oddest mix of feelings clogged Cate's chest. Could she believe him? And did it really matter?

Because she didn't know if it mattered or not, she shoved away the confusion and concentrated on the way he felt in her arms. Harry was a rock, a port in a storm, an anchor. All those clichés.

When she fled the church on the day of the wedding, Harry was the only person who showed up outside to help her. At least in that moment. And he had kept showing up... mostly. She couldn't forget about those two weeks when he disappeared.

Had he fled because the two of them had *almost* kissed in the upstairs hallway? Or because he had admitted to being jealous once upon a time?

Why did the man have to be so mysterious?

Harry pinched her butt. Hard.

"Hello in there," he said. "Where did you go, Cate?"

Apparently, her troubling thoughts had lasted long enough

to be notable. *Dumb mistake.* Why was she *thinking* at all right now when the man she wanted was naked and available?

"I didn't go anywhere," she said. "I'm enjoying the moment." She proved her point by leaning backward to cup his face in her hands and rub her thumbs over his cheekbones. "I'm right where I want to be."

Harry's gaze, for once, was unguarded. Deep in his gray eyes she saw hunger and determination but also tenderness.

The tenderness scared her most. She could walk away from carnal pleasure. But if Harry cared about her at all, it was going to break her heart to leave him alone in this huge apartment.

He isolated himself. By his own admission. His life was all work and no play. And as for the sex, well, she suspected he wasn't the indiscriminate man his reputation indicated.

"Kiss me," she whispered.

Their lips met and clung. Harry held her in a crushing grip, nearly lifting her off the floor. Tenderness presided for ten seconds, maybe fifteen. Then desperation rushed in, shoving aside finer emotions and seizing the moment.

Harry muttered against her cheek. "Don't distract me, Cate. I'm supposed to be getting you clean." The water sluiced over them in a steady stream.

She cupped him intimately. "Only if I get to do the same."

His breath hissed between his teeth. His eyes closed. When he moaned, the hair on her arms quivered.

Blindly, he reached for a squirt of shower gel and used both hands to smooth it over her breasts.

She wiped the water from his eyes. "I'm not that dirty."

"I don't really care." His sensual, cocky smile weakened her legs. Especially when his fingers massaged every inch of her aching curves.

"Enough," she gasped.

It was her turn to pleasure him. The gel had a light pleasant scent, like summer sunshine and pine trees. She cradled his sex between her palms and slicked his flesh with a firm pressure.

Harry went rigid, his hands clenched on her shoulders. "Cate..."

He said her name like a prayer.

When he cursed, she knew he had reached the limits of his control.

Even so, she gasped when he picked her up.

"Put your legs around my waist," he said.

The dominant strength in his body, his stance, his hold, made her weak with longing. When he entered her, she cried out. This angle was new, the pleasure deeper, rawer.

She clung to his shoulders and buried her face in the side of his neck. Harry was in control. He used every bit of his power to drive them to the brink. At the last moment, he turned and pressed her into the shower wall. The cold stone was a shock.

But when Harry hammered into her and found his release, everything else faded away.

She relished every second of his pleasure, knowing he would soon give her what she needed.

And he did. After drying off, they stumbled into the bedroom and fell into Harry's bed. Before she could protest, he was between her legs, sprawled on his belly, his intimate kiss teasing her sex.

She was so primed, she came quickly. The pleasure was like those recent fireworks. Bright and hot, lighting up the dark.

When it was over, they dozed, though the hour wasn't late.

Sometime later, Harry took her again, this time face-to-face with her leg draped over his hip. She watched him watching her and felt undone. Could he see inside her soul?

It was a heck of a time to discover she was falling in love with him. To be fair, she had never fallen in love before. Not the real thing. So it had taken her all these weeks to understand what was happening.

Instead of being fun and lighthearted and entertaining, this was a scary, terrifying ride into the unknown.

Harry kissed her roughly. "Come with me, Cate." He touched the spot where their bodies were joined. It was like pouring alcohol on an open flame. She shuddered and gave him everything. Her trust, her orgasm, his own climax and—though she dared not tell him—her heart.

Harry slept like the dead through the night.

Cate dozed in restless catnaps until sheer exhaustion claimed her before dawn. When she finally awoke, Harry was gone.

He had left a note...

Had to be in early. Sorry. See you later...

It wasn't exactly a lover's sonnet. Cate battled disappointment and fear. Was she screwed? Was there even a shred of hope that Harry wanted more than her body? What would happen if she were honest with him?

Could she beg him to change his mind about what was possible?

All day she moved in two dimensions. The practical, goal-oriented Cate searched for a place to live. Finally, one small house caught her attention. It was the definition of a *fixer-upper*. On the fringes of a nice neighborhood, it seemed alone and abandoned.

If Cate ended up alone and abandoned, maybe she and this little bungalow could grow old together. The fantasy kept her going, even as she ran a few more errands.

It was late when she made time for lunch. She grabbed a sub from her favorite sandwich shop and took it to a nearby park. The sky was overcast. Rain was on the way. But for now, the air was pleasant.

As she made her way along a crushed gravel path, a voice from behind her called out.

"Cate. Cate. Is that you?"

She turned around and felt her stomach fall to her knees. "Jason?"

He stopped, leaving eight feet between them. "Yeah."

Maybe she should have prepared a speech for this moment. It was bound to happen sooner or later. As it was, she found herself completely unprepared.

Her first instinct was to hug him. But that initial jolt of pleasure combined with the reality of what stood between them.

"Hello, Jason."

She saw his throat ripple as he swallowed. "I wondered if I would see you again," he said.

"We both live here." She frowned. "You look good." It was true. His fair skin was deeply tanned. His blue-eyed gaze was clear. His tall, rangy body appeared healthy and fit. "Peru must have agreed with you."

He shoved his hands in his pockets. "It was amazing. You would have loved it." He smiled ruefully. "Though I did take a few extra jungle excursions you'd have skipped."

She raised an eyebrow. "Because?"

"Snakes. Tarantulas. Poisonous frogs."

"Gross." She shuddered. "And I suppose you got pictures."

His smile broadened. "You better believe it."

"I'm glad it was a good trip." She took a step backward. "I should go."

"Wait, Cate." The words were urgent. "You can't begin to understand how sorry I am for what I did to you."

"Your timing sucked," she said, unable to entirely forget that awful day. Seeing Jason brought it all back.

"Yes, it did," he said. "I was a coward."

"Maybe. You did the right thing, though, as much as I hate to admit it. But you and I should have seen the problems earlier. Or at least I should have. Clearly, you knew something was wrong."

"I loved you, Cate. How was I supposed to destroy what we had built?"

"Well, you found a way, didn't you?" The sharp rebuke didn't make her feel any better at all.

He winced. "I hope one day you can forgive me. You've been part of my life forever. I don't want to lose you as a friend."

"That's asking a lot."

"I know." He rolled his shoulders and sighed. "I'm glad Harry was there for you when I couldn't be."

Cate had no control over the hot blush that rolled up from her chest and quickly covered her face. There was no way Jason didn't notice.

His gaze narrowed. "Cate?"

"What?" She stuck out her chin.

"Harry was good to you, right? I would trust him with my life."

"He treated me very well. *Very* well."

Jason cursed under his breath. "I know you probably want to hurt me, but that isn't funny. Harry wouldn't take advantage of a woman in your situation."

She eyed her ex-fiancé coolly. "Maybe I took advantage of him."

"Oh, God, Cate." Jason scrubbed his hands over his face, his expression distraught. "He'll never settle down. There are too many skeletons and demons in his closet. Tell me you haven't slept with him."

Cate relented when she saw how miserably guilty Jason looked. "Relax," she said. "I've gotten close to Harry because of all he helped me through, but he's been more than clear about his *rules*."

"Thank God. For a minute there, I thought I had handed you over to the big bad wolf."

Cate flinched inwardly. Hearing that expression twice in two days sent a cold, eerie trickle down her spine. "Don't be silly. Harry has been nothing but a gentleman."

"Could we sit and talk for a minute?"

It was hard to ignore Jason's plea. Besides, she had missed him…in spite of everything. "Only if I can eat my sandwich. I'm starving." There was a picnic table a few steps away. Cate sat at one corner. Jason went to the other side and picked the farthest spot.

For two people who had been on the verge of getting married, this awkward reunion was poignantly sad.

Cate unwrapped her sandwich and took a bite. "So talk."

His jaw firmed and his eyes flashed. Cate rarely saw that side of him. "These next few months are not going to be easy."

She took a sip from her water bottle. "Why?"

"Because we move in the same circles. People are going to be watching us all the time."

"I hadn't thought of that. Maybe I'll just lay low for a while."

"So your solution is for both of us to disappear?"

The irritation in his voice told her he was taking this more seriously than she was. Maybe because Harry had been the focus of her attention.

"I don't know what you want from me," she said. "You're

the one who aired our dirty laundry in front of a who's who of Atlanta society."

"I know what I did." He rested his elbows on the table and put his head in his hands. Then he looked up at her. "Do you even have a place to live? I feel bad that you gave up your apartment."

"I've been looking," she said. "All this week in fact."

"Are you at your parents' house?"

For a moment, she yielded to pettiness. "No," she said. "I'm staying with Harry."

Jason stared at her. "Still? He never mentioned that when we've talked."

"You told him to keep an eye on me, right?"

He paled. "Harry was supposed to be casual about that."

"Well, I figured it out eventually. Did you really think I was going to go off the deep end?"

"I didn't know what to think." Jason sighed. "I felt like hell, and I assumed it would be worse for you, as the bride."

"You can quit worrying. I'm reinventing myself. In fact, I'm buying a building in Blossom Branch and opening a trendy gift shop."

"That was fast." His scowl was equal parts suspicion and surprise.

"I spent some time at my grandparents' house. It helped me take a step back and work through things. Blossom Branch has always been a special place to me. You know that."

"I do." Jason's gaze settled on her face, as if he was trying to see inside her head. "Are you *really* okay, Cate? You must hate me."

She ate one more bite and stuffed the unfinished sandwich in the paper bag, all the while trying to figure out what to say. "I don't hate you, Jason," she said slowly, weighing her words. "Maybe I should. I was mad at you. I was hurt. Embarrassed.

Lost. But hate you? No. How could I? You've been a part of my life since we were kids. In fact—"

"In fact what?"

"Oh, gosh, this is humiliating. My mother said she always thought you and I acted more like brother and sister. Is that true? Was I so blind?"

He stood and rounded the table, sitting down beside her and taking her hand. "If you were blind, then I was, too. We let ourselves slide into a comfortable relationship that brought us both pleasure. It wasn't a grand passion, but I got the feeling you didn't want that."

"Honestly," she said, "I didn't. With you, I was safe. Until I wasn't."

He released her fingers and sighed. "If we'd had this conversation in Key West when we were so stressed about planning the wedding, we could have avoided so much heartache."

"Maybe we were both cowards."

"Maybe so." He exhaled. "Thank you for talking to me. I was half-afraid you would call the police."

Cate laughed because she thought that was impossible. "No, you weren't. A nice girl like me?"

He turned sideways on the bench seat and faced her. "You *are* a nice girl," he said. "And you're an incredible woman. I think you'll find that grand passion one day, whether you want to or not."

Her heart wobbled in her chest. *Harry...*

She concentrated on Jason's dear familiar face. "And what about you?" she said. "What's next?"

His shook his head slowly. "Despite my parents' vehement objections, I'm going to pursue photography as a full-time career. I know it's a long shot, but what the hell. I won't know until I give it a try."

"So lots of travel?"

"Yes. Eventually. I'm making connections already. And with nothing to tie me down, I can go where the wind takes me." He stopped short. "Damn, that sounded cold. You weren't holding me back, Cate. It's not what I meant."

She patted his shoulder. "I know. I forgive you, Jason. Don't carry that weight around. I hope you'll forgive *me* for not seeing you were unhappy. I hate that more than anything."

He kissed her cheek. "Thank you, Cate. Your generosity of spirit means a lot."

"Does this mean we can text each other?"

His grin was not much of a grin, but it was enough. "I think it does."

"You saved us," she said soberly. "From a disaster."

"It wouldn't have been a disaster."

"Maybe not now. But in five or ten years when the kids had the flu and we were sick of each other..."

His smile this time was more genuine. "We're not going to worry about what might have been. Keep your eyes on the road ahead, right?"

"Right. I should go," she said, standing up and looking at the sky for half a second. Still no rain.

Jason stood as well. "Me, too. Will you give me your new address when you have one?"

"Of course." She went up on her tiptoes and kissed him on the mouth, just to see if she was wrong about Harry. Nope. She wasn't. "Goodbye, Jason."

When he turned and walked away, she watched him. They had avoided disaster. They were doing the right thing.

Now, all she had to worry about was Harry...

Twenty-Eight

Cate finished her errands. As the afternoon wound to a close, she realized that she felt lighter, happier. The burden of failure she had carried all summer was gone. Jason was going to be okay, and so was she.

Even without Harry, she knew she was strong enough to face the future. There would be someone else for her. Someone more her type, someone who wanted the same things she wanted.

All she needed was patience and time…

At Harry's building, she stood on the street for a moment and decided that her time was up. She needed to make a choice. Either a bland condo or a frumpy little house. Either one would do.

Nothing was permanent.

In the meantime, she was determined that these last days with Harry would be pleasant and laid-back and at night—sex, pure and simple.

He had been texting her for the last half hour. Getting her dinner order for Chinese delivery. When she opened the door and let herself in, the wonderful smells led her to the dining room.

Harry was leaning over the table setting out plates and silverware and opening containers. "Right on time," he said.

She hugged him from behind. "Thanks for feeding me."

He turned around and pulled her in for a lazy kiss. "Who else would I feed?" Suddenly, he cocked his head. "You're in a good mood. I might go so far as to say you're glowing."

"It was a good day," she said. "I ran into Jason."

Harry went still. He released her casually as if nothing was amiss, but the air in the room was different. Stilted. Charged.

"I see. How did that happen?"

"In the park. I had a sandwich. He saw me and asked if we could talk."

"And?"

"We talked. It was nice. I'd been dreading it. Running into him, I mean. But it turned out okay. I think we cleared the air. I told him I forgave him. Which is why I feel better now."

Harry rounded the table and took a seat, pouring wine into two glasses, sliding one in her direction, and then focusing his gaze on his food. "You forgave him?"

Cate heard the note of incredulity. "I know. I should still be mad. But holding a grudge requires too much energy."

"I see."

She changed the subject awkwardly, unable to read Harry's mood other than to know *he* thought her easy forgiveness was bogus.

There was no choice but to bring up another sore subject. "I think I found a place to live. I've narrowed it down to two. I'll be out of your hair in no time."

Finally, he lifted his head. His eyes were carefully blank. She hadn't seen that look in days or weeks. She hated it just as much now as she had before.

"I've told you you're welcome here," he said quietly. "But I have some good news." He pulled a business card from his shirt pocket. "A friend of mine has renovated an industrial space into artsy condos—exposed brick, that kind of thing. She'd like to have a few tenants in place before she begins advertising. I suggested you, and she jumped at it. It's a fabulous spot. You won't do any better. She's even offering a cut rate for the first six months, if you want to rent instead of buy until you make up your mind."

Cate blinked, her ears roaring. *She?* "This must be a very *good* friend," she said, her voice tight.

Harry shrugged. "We go way back. She's expecting to show you around tomorrow morning at ten."

"And if I don't want to go?"

"It's time, Cate. You said so yourself. Besides, if you don't show up, it will make me look bad."

"Well, we wouldn't want that." She tried to swallow the lump in her throat. It was one thing for Cate to *choose* moving out. It was another thing entirely for Harry to foist her off on his smarmy girlfriend. "Are you kicking me to the curb?" she asked quietly.

For some reason, he didn't meet her gaze. "I'm catching a flight to LA early tomorrow morning for an architectural conference. I can arrange movers as soon as you let me know a firm date."

"And how long will you be gone?"

"Hard to say." Finally, he lifted his head. Despite his patented opaque expression, she could swear she saw pain. "It's been fun, Cate. I'm glad I could help out during a hard time."

Inside her body, every cell and drop of blood crystallized and shattered. "And what about tonight?" she whispered, unable to believe the change in him. What had she said? What had she done? This couldn't be about Jason…could it? Surely Harry knew how she felt.

He grimaced. "I have several hours of work to do before I fly out in the morning." He came around the table. She had the impression he was forcing himself to do so. He kissed the top of her head and stepped back quickly. "Good night, Cate. And goodbye."

Cate spent the next hours and days walking around Atlanta in a shroud of heartbreak and confusion. What was it about her that invited the careless cruelty of men who were supposed to care about her? First Jason. Now Harry.

As required, she met with Harry's sophisticated lady friend and discovered that the condo was indeed perfect. Signing on the dotted line gave her no pleasure at all.

Because Leah was willing to help, Cate didn't contact Harry about movers. What was the point? All she had was clothes and suitcases. While Cate waited for furniture deliveries—a bed and a sofa, a TV, and a washer and dryer, she stayed a few nights in Leah's apartment.

It was awful. *Pretending* to be happy and upbeat was almost impossible.

Especially because Leah knew her so well. At dinner the first night, Leah's big brown eyes studied her with concern. "The last time we were together, I had the feeling you were doing much better. But now you look so sad. Talk to me, Cate. Tell me what's going on."

"I saw Jason. We ran into each other in the park. Cleared the air. It was good."

"Does that mean you might get back together?"

"No. Oh, no. That part of my life is over. Jason was right. We love each other, but we're not in love."

"And that makes you sad?"

"Well, of course it does, but that's not why I'm—" Cate stopped short. She desperately needed to talk to someone. Leah was the perfect sounding board. But the end of Cate's relationship with Harry was so terrifyingly raw.

"Cate?" Leah's troubled gaze held both compassion and doubt. "You're hurting so badly. I can see it."

Cate swallowed hard and manufactured a smile. "Some things take time. I'll be okay, I swear."

"I hope so. But don't hold it all inside. You've always been there for Gabby and me. I'm here whenever you're ready."

Finally, Cate made it to her first night alone. Her new place was lovely. Cozy, homey. Even without a full complement of furnishings, it was clearly where she was meant to be.

Unfortunately, the aching void in her life meant walking the floors at night, unable to sleep because her heart was crushed.

A million times she asked herself if Harry had been upset that she had seen Jason. He had to know it was going to happen sooner or later. Why would he react so vehemently?

All along he had let her know their relationship was based on physical compatibility and affection. He'd been almost insultingly clear on that point. A man who decided never to marry or father children wasn't going to get into a situation where the woman wanted more.

The calendar mocked her—all the squares empty until she invented ways to fill them. Becca went with her to close on the property in Blossom Branch. Their grandparents were delighted to spend time with Cate and Becca both.

One day, a set of architectural drawings showed up on Cate's doorstep. She hired a man Ginny Black knew to carry out the changes on the second floor of her shop and to construct her built-in display shelves.

The museum gig was more successful every week, so much

so that Cate committed to two classes instead of one. The students charmed and touched her. They made a little of the ice around her heart melt when she was with them.

Being with Becca was therapeutic, too. The two of them had a great time ordering stock and planning all the ways they were going to create eye-catching displays when the remodeling work was done.

It felt good to be friends with her sister for the first time ever, really. In the past, their rivalries had defined their sibling relationship. The new shop had served as a neutral environment where they could cautiously learn how to trust each other. They had both changed. In positive ways.

One month passed, then another. Cate missed her Labor Day deadline, but she decided late October would be soon enough. That would be a popular tourist time, too. Apples and fall leaves. A home run. And if the shop wasn't finished until November, she would deal with it.

When she looked in the mirror at night, she could see she was losing weight. Food wasn't appealing at all. Added to that was the strain of pretending to all her family and friends that she was delighted and content with the new direction her life was taking.

The lie grew heavy.

She and Jason texted occasionally. Nothing of significance. Mostly just cautiously maintaining a connection.

It was a shock to open her door near the end of September and see her former fiancé standing on her doorstep.

He didn't wait to be invited in. Instead, he pushed past her and took a seat in the living room. The comfy seating area was still missing a few key pieces, but she couldn't summon up the energy to care.

"We have a problem," he said. "Something's wrong with Harry."

Her heart stopped. "What do you mean?"

"I stopped by his place to return a book he loaned me. He looked like death warmed over. Sunken eyes. Crazy hair. I've never seen him like that. He wouldn't let me in. Said he had a bad cold."

"So he's sick? Is that all?"

Jason leaped to his feet and paced. "More than that. I'm telling you, Cate. It's bad. I've never seen him like this."

"Did something happen with his father?"

Jason gaped. "You know about him?"

"Yes. But it's too soon for parole...right?"

"That's my understanding."

"Do you think his mother is harassing him? That woman is one big bowl of trouble."

Now Jason's gaze narrowed. "You've met her?"

"Yes. When Harry hurt his knee and couldn't drive, I had to take him there."

"When did Harry hurt his knee?"

"While you were in Peru. He fell."

"Here in Atlanta?"

"No. He and I were staying in Blossom Branch. We were out running one night, and Harry tripped on a piece of broken sidewalk. I had to take him to the hospital, but it wasn't as bad as we first thought."

Jason held up his hands. "Whoa, whoa, whoa. Why am I just now hearing about all this?"

Cate glared. "You dumped me. What I did was none of your business." She had needed an impartial sounding board for weeks now. But how could she tell Jason the truth about Harry when she hadn't been able to tell anyone else? All her rapidly changing feelings had been bottled up inside for so long now, they strangled her.

His expression gentled. "Come here, Cate. Sit down. Tell me what's going on."

And just like that, her heart cracked wide open.

Jason was the one person who might understand.

"I fell in love with him."

She burst into tears. Keeping her secret all these weeks with no one to talk to had been agonizing. Jason held her as she sobbed. He produced a handkerchief from his pocket so she could wipe her face.

"I don't know what to do," she wailed.

"Tell me, Cate. Tell me everything."

So she did. She started with the day of the wedding and read Jason every verse and chapter of her relationship with Harry. Well, not the sex stuff. She glossed over that. But Jason wasn't stupid. He could understand what she wasn't saying. She ended with the day she and Jason first saw each other in the park.

Jason stood and paced. "So Harry freaked out after you told him you had forgiven me?"

She sniffed. "Yes."

"And he flew to LA."

"That's what he said."

"He's never been to an architectural conference in his life. The man's a loner. Good Lord, Cate. I think he's in love with you."

"No." Her heart stopped, jerked and pounded. "No. He said he had a crush on me years ago, but when you and I started dating seriously, he got over it."

"For a smart woman, you're not great at recognizing lies."

"He doesn't want to get married because of his unbalanced parents."

"Then change his mind. Or offer to live in sin." Jason grinned. "I get credit for this one if you make it down the aisle."

"Oh, shut up. My track record with that particular *walk* isn't great."

Jason hugged her. "I am so damn glad I didn't ruin your life. Go to him, Cate. Make the big romantic gesture."

"I'm scared." More like petrified. She was shaking all over.

"You can do this."

"It's too late. I'll go tomorrow."

Jason put his hands on her shoulders. "Nothing ventured, nothing gained. You deserve happiness, Cate. More than anybody I know. You've spent your whole life caring about other people and giving them what they want and need. Meeting their expectations. Do this for you."

"Are you sure, Jason? What if it's just a head cold? What if he's really sick? I'll die of humiliation."

His grin was mischievous. "If you didn't die when I balked at the altar, this will be a piece of cake. I believe in you, Ms. Georgia Peach Blossom. Now go. Go get your man."

Twenty-Nine

Cate had left her key to Harry's apartment with the concierge when she moved out. Now—because she knew all the staff—taking the elevator up to Harry's floor was no biggie.

But what if Harry closed the door in her face?

She stood there for at least three minutes before she worked up the courage to ring the bell.

When the door swung backward, Harry stood framed in the opening. Jason was right. He looked terrible. But the sight of him was like water in a desert. She wanted to throw herself in his arms and never let go.

Since that wasn't really a choice, she debated her options. She had thought catching him by surprise might make a difference—that she could possibly determine if he was glad to see her.

But his expression was blank. "What do *you* want?" His mood was surly.

"Jason said you were sick."

Harry raised an eyebrow. "Unless you've brought chicken

soup, I'm not interested." He was wearing navy sweatpants and the gray Emory T-shirt she had come to love.

She decided to take a page from Jason's playbook. Instead of waiting for an invitation, she pushed her way in. Immediately, she was swamped with a million memories. Her eyes dampened, and her throat constricted.

But this was no time for a sentimental walk down memory lane.

"Why are you hibernating?" she said. "It's not winter yet."

"Jason told you. I'm sick."

She put her hand to his forehead. "No fever. You're not coughing. And your voice is fine. I think you lied to him."

"Then if I lied to him, feel free to leave." He practically snarled the words.

The place was a wreck. Prescott Harrington, the neat freak, was living in squalor, relatively speaking.

"Why hasn't your cleaning lady been here?"

"She's sick."

Cate sighed. "Lot of that going around."

Harry rubbed a hand across his face. Suddenly, he looked exhausted. "What do you want, Cate?"

"When was the last time you went into the office?"

"I work at home—remember?"

She touched his face, testing the stubble on his chin. "And when was the last time you shaved?" She sniffed his shirt. "I think you stink."

Harry's eyes narrowed. "If this is some kind of cosmic tit for tat because you think I was mean to you back in June, I get it. We're even now."

"Not by a long shot. Is there any food in your kitchen? Let me fix you a meal."

"I'm not hungry." He paced, running his hands through his

hair, making his dishevelment worse. "Please go. Shouldn't you be neck-deep in running your new store?"

Cate took a seat on the sofa, folded her arms and stared at him. "We weren't able to make the Labor Day opening date. My contractor flaked out on me. I had to find a new one."

Dull color flooded his face. "Things got busy at work."

"Right." She didn't believe that for a minute. "How's the design going for the atrium building?"

"I finished the drawings. The client was pleased." He sat down, too, as though his legs wouldn't hold him up. If he wasn't eating, it was no wonder. He had chosen the love seat, which was as far away from the sofa as possible.

Cate didn't know her next move. Or if she even had a next move.

While she waited for inspiration, Harry leaned forward and rested his elbows on his knees. "Please go, Cate. I don't know why you're here."

"Because Jason was worried."

"So why send you? I've seen him half a dozen times in the last month. He never mentioned your name."

"Makes sense. The last time *I* was with him was that day in the park after he got home from Peru. The only reason he came by my place tonight was to let me know you were having a crisis."

Harry scowled. "That's absurd. I'm not having a crisis." Then he stopped. "You haven't been with Jason?" His jaw was granite, his gaze opaque.

"No," she said softly. "Jason and I are not a couple anymore. I told you that a long time ago…back in Blossom Branch. He and I are not getting back together."

After a long silence, he shook his head slowly. "Well, it has nothing to do with me."

"I think it does," she said softly. "I think you threw me out of your apartment because you were upset I had forgiven him. You freaked because you thought Jason and I were picking up where we left off."

Harry rolled his eyes. "I don't *freak*. And besides, I never threw you out. You were looking at housing. I found a great place for you. End of story."

On wobbly legs, she stood and crossed the room to sit beside him. It hurt when Harry shifted to put distance between them. Was this the same man who had made love to her so beautifully?

She sucked in a deep breath. If she had thought standing at an altar in front of twelve hundred people was scary, that occasion was nothing compared to this moment. "Harry," she said. "Are you in love with me?"

"No." The man didn't even flinch. Nor did he pause to think about it.

Tears sprang to her eyes, but she didn't let them fall. He was lying. She had to believe that. Or else she would be forced to concede that all the feelings and emotions between them were coming only from her and not him.

She scooted closer and took one of his hands in hers. His skin was warm against her icy fingers. "I fell in love with you, Harry," she said. "It was so slow. I hardly even realized it was happening. One minute I wanted to smack you, and the next I knew I couldn't live without you—or I didn't want to," she said, trying to be as honest as she knew how. "I'd never been in love before...not the real thing. So it took me a long time to understand."

"You don't love me." The words were curt. "It's Stockholm syndrome, if anything." His eyes burned hot with emotion, but the emotion was negative.

She sighed. "You didn't *kidnap* me. This is a totally different situation. You helped me out in the middle of a terrible personal tragedy. You fed me and gave me a place to stay, and you kept me safe."

"I felt sorry for you. Don't confuse compassion with love."

"Harry…" She was rapidly losing hope. Maybe Jason was completely wrong.

There was only one way to find out. She scooted closer to her obstinate, closed-off, stoic lover. Harry was trapped by the arm of the sofa. His body language was rigid.

Looking him in the eyes, she gave him everything in her heart. "I *love* you, Prescott Harrington. I love your prickly exterior and the deep vein of caring you hide. I love your brilliance and your creativity. I love the way you're willing to set your work aside to help me. I love the fact that you have an uncomfortably unpleasant mother, but you still honor her. And most of all, I adore the way you make love to me. It's incredibly wild and tenderly sweet at the same time. Passion and peace. I love you, Harry. So very much."

Raw pain radiated from his beautiful eyes. He cupped her face in hands that trembled. "I think I fell in love with you when you were seventeen. I saw you sitting on the back of that red convertible wearing a princess sash, and I was struck dumb with longing. You were luminous. I was a peasant, groveling from afar. But it doesn't matter, Catie. You're the kind of woman who needs marriage and permanence. I can't give you that. I won't screw up your life. I'm a loner because it's safer that way."

Tears wet her face. "We don't have to get married. But I want to be with you. We need each other."

He scowled. "You're suggesting we live together without a permanent commitment? Come on, be realistic. You've said that's not what you want."

"Maybe I was wrong," she said. "I survived my ill-fated

wedding, and I learned a lot about myself. What I can't survive is losing you."

She curled her arms around his neck and kissed him feverishly. For interminable moments, he was like a dead man in her embrace, his lips cold, his body frozen. "Harry, please," she sobbed. "Don't make me go through life without you. I can't bear it. Please let me come home."

Just as she was ready to give up, a huge groan worked its way from deep in his chest. "Cate. God, Cate. I've missed you desperately. Like losing a limb. But it won't work, my precious sweetheart. It can't."

She jerked a lock of his hair, hard. "It *will* work, Harry. You're nothing like your father, nothing at all. And as for your mother, we'll deal with her the best we can."

"And when my dad is up for parole?"

The thought curled her stomach, only because she didn't want Harry to be forced to confront his abusive father. "We'll deal with him, too."

Harry clenched his hand in the hair at the back of her head. He dragged her even closer until they were nose to nose. "You don't understand, Cate. If we start this, I won't *ever* let you go again. You'll be mine. *Always.*" He kissed her roughly, possessively.

Thank God. "I'm good with that," she said softly. "We're in this together, Harry. There's no one else." She nestled against his chest, determined to let him see that he was the only man in her life.

At last, Harry pulled back and stared at her, his gaze filled with baffled wonder and cautious happiness. "I'm serious about *always*, Cate. I've thought about marrying you. So many times. And I want to, but..."

"But what?"

"You've been hurt so badly. I couldn't bear to be the man

who causes you more pain. I don't *think* I would fall into my family's patterns, but who knows?"

"Harry, I fixated on getting married before. I thought that's what everyone expected of me. I wanted to make my parents happy, make Jason happy. And I fooled myself into believing all that would make me happy, too. But it didn't. You're the only person who has made me believe I deserve to be happy in my own way."

"Because I love you." He grimaced. "But marriage feels selfish on my part. I'm not there yet."

"Then we'll make it happen sometime. There's no rush. One wedding a year is probably all I can handle."

He winced. "Too soon, Cate. Too soon."

"Fair enough." She kissed him softly, letting her lips cling to his, savoring the hitch in his breath, the pounding of his heart beneath her palm. "I'm glad you waited for me, Harry."

He shrugged, his eyes brilliant with pleasure. "And I'm glad you're even more stubborn than I am."

She slugged his arm. "You take that back."

He grinned. "Nope. I think we're a perfect pair."

"Or at least perfectly imperfect."

"Does this mean our life is going to be *just peachy*?" he asked, making a face.

"I doubt it. It's going to be messy and sometimes hard, and always wonderful. I love you, Prescott Harrington."

He kissed her nose. "And I love you, Miss Georgia Peach Blossom." A huge sigh lifted his chest. "Does this mean we get to have make-up sex now?"

"I thought you'd never ask…"

Epilogue

Cate stood on the sidewalk outside her newly opened shop and greeted people as they entered the store. The numbers had been more than she could have asked for or expected. It seemed everyone in town had shown up.

Even better, Leah and Gabby were walking down the sidewalk in her direction. They each hugged her when they arrived, laughing and smiling.

Gabby, for once, seemed like her old self. "This is amazing, Cate. And so perfectly you. If you ever need me to look over the books or make tax suggestions, I'd be honored."

Cate took her friend's face in her hands, trying to communicate how much she had missed her. "*I'm* honored that you're *here* today, Gabby. I think I must have hurt you somehow— earlier in the summer—I don't know what it was, but I am so very sorry. I hope you'll forgive me."

Gabby looked stricken. "Oh, no," she said. "You didn't do anything wrong. It was all me. I let my own stuff get in the way of our friendship."

Leah snorted, her brown eyes gleaming with humor. "Would you two cut it out? You're blocking the door."

Cate and Gabby stepped apart, their expressions equally chagrinned. Cate didn't know if the odd breach was successfully healed, but she hoped so.

Becca popped her head out of the door. "Good news! We're so popular the fire department sent someone over for crowd control. They'll be kicking people out any minute now."

Cate raised an eyebrow. "We're celebrating that?"

"You bet." Becca waved at Leah and Gabby. "So glad you came. In the spirit of full disclosure, you've missed some of the best items. Our shelves are getting bare. I'll chat with you later."

Leah smiled. "It's cool to see you and Becca on such good terms."

"It really is." Cate nodded. "There have been a lot of good things to come out of my wedding failure. My relationship to my baby sister is one of those."

Gabby studied Cate's face, her expression a mixture of hope and concern. "And you're really happy with Harry?"

Cate had finally told both her friends the whole story days ago. "So much more than happy," Cate said. "I had no idea what love really was. Until now. Harry makes my world complete."

Leah sighed. "That's what I want. What I've always wanted. But I don't know if it's in the cards for me. Most men seem to prefer tall skinny blondes. You know. Peach Blossom Queens like you, Cate." She grinned teasingly.

Gabby shook her head. "You're perfect the way you are, Leah. Any guy would be lucky to have you." She glanced at her watch. "Shouldn't we go in and buy something? We want Cate's first day to be a success."

Cate stood between them, wrapping an arm around each

of their waists. "I have all I need. Thank you for always being there for me. I couldn't ask for two better friends."

Leah nodded. "From Blossom Branch to UGA to Atlanta and back, our friendship has survived. Men may come and go, but our bond is forever. Now, come on, ladies. Let the shopping begin."

* * * * *

Look for Leah and Gabby's stories, coming soon!
Only from Canary Street Press

ACT LIKE YOU LOVE ME

One

Laney Marshall, like many people, enjoyed a guilty addiction...
to Amazon. To be fair, living in Blossom Branch, Georgia,
was partly to blame. Atlanta's glamorous stores were an hour
and a half away. When a woman needed a new set of earbuds
or a hard-to-find book for a coworker's birthday, one-click
ordering was a lifesaver.

Whether it was UPS, FedEx, or even the postal service,
Laney knew most of the delivery people on sight. So when her
doorbell rang after dinner on a Friday evening, she swished
the curtain aside and checked the porch.

The meal she had consumed while sitting in front of the
TV rumbled in her stomach. Her heart stopped for a full ten
seconds. Even at eight o'clock, there was plenty of light outside, thanks to the recent time change.

The man on Laney's porch was not a courier of any kind.
He was Blossom Branch's most famous citizen, Brit Sheffield.
The kid who'd made it big. Star of stage and screen. Border-
ing recently on *superstar* if the tabloids were to be believed.

And Laney had seen him naked.

To be fair, the naked thing was a million years ago when she still believed in fairy tales, but that image was hard to forget.

She opened the door a crack. "What are you doing here?" she whispered. He looked both the same and different—tall and brooding, with his broad shoulders hunched into a leather jacket that evoked Chris Evans, at least when Chris wasn't wearing his Captain America uniform.

They hadn't seen each other in a very long time. Four years, to be exact.

The fact that the two of them texted each other several times a week was a fluke of their long-standing friendship, nothing more. They certainly weren't friends with benefits. Not now.

She had too much self-respect to be *available* anytime Brit showed up.

"Let me in, Laney," he said, his words laced with irritation or impatience, or both. The male, gravelly baritone had the power to make her legs wobble even now.

Any one of a dozen houses nearby might have nosy neighbors on the lookout. Gossip was the life's blood of a semirural town. Reluctantly, Laney stepped aside to let her unexpected guest enter. In the process, she inhaled the faint but tantalizing scent of expensive aftershave.

As she shut the door and locked it, she noticed the black SUV in her driveway. Its tinted windows gave it a Secret Service vibe. "A rental?" she asked, more for something to say than out of any real curiosity.

When he nodded, the overhead light caught gold highlights in his chestnut waves. His cut was shorter now. Back in high school, he'd been the stereotypical bad boy with hair that brushed his shoulders. Laney remembered the way it felt to sift her fingers through the thick waves.

She cleared her throat. "Have you eaten?" She wasn't entirely surprised to see him. Maybe her subconscious had tried to warn her this moment was a possibility. But his presence in her small house was still a shock to the system. Being close to Brit Sheffield again caused stress fractures in her hard-won peace. *Look*, but *don't touch*.

He shook his head. "No. As soon as the plane landed in Atlanta, I grabbed a car and hit the road. You don't have to feed me, though."

That last was a pitiful attempt to be polite. For an actor, he was painfully transparent. "It's homemade chicken pot pie," she said.

For the first time, his expression lightened. "Have I died and gone to heaven?"

"Bathroom's down the hall on the left. You wash up. I'll have it ready when you come back."

In the kitchen, she put her hands to her hot cheeks. *Focus, Laney.*

She pulled the casserole dish out of the fridge and scooped out a man-sized portion. Because the microwave wouldn't do justice to the flaky top crust, she put the plate in the oven and set a timer. The leftovers hadn't been chilled long enough to need much.

When Brit reappeared, the sexy leather jacket was gone. His turned-up sleeves revealed manly forearms dusted with golden hair. The watch on his left wrist probably cost more than her car. But the sleek timepiece suited him.

His gaze was wary, as if he was expecting her to kick him out.

She had thought about it. Just like she had thought about not letting him inside in the first place. Resisting his potent appeal was too damn hard.

"Sorry," she said. "I don't have any alcohol. Not even a beer."

He shrugged. "Not a problem. Tea sounds good if you've got that."

She cocked her head and stared at him. "You've traveled the world, Brit. Eaten in five-star hotels. I'm sure your tastes have changed."

He leaned his chair back on two legs and grinned. "A guy never forgets his first sweet tea."

Brit's insinuation made her jittery. The two of them had both been virgins when they became boyfriend and girlfriend their senior year in high school. That sexual status hadn't lasted long. For the entire summer after graduation, they made love with all the abandon of reckless teenagers who thought the world was theirs for the taking.

In Brit's case, it had been true.

Laney did an abrupt about-face to conceal her agitation. The jug of freshly brewed tea in her refrigerator was a staple, though she had cut back on the amount of sugar she added a long time ago.

Instead of handing the glass to Brit, she set it on the table, not wanting to chance a possible finger brush. Books always mentioned that. The little zing of attraction when two people were very aware of each other. She had no idea about Brit's emotions, but her own were all over the map.

"Why are you here?" she asked, wiping her damp hands on a dish towel and leaning against the sink.

"You know why."

"Because of Mr. Tom?"

"Yeah."

They stared at each other, misty-eyed. Mr. Tom was the longtime drama teacher at the high school. He had presided over more productions of *Oklahoma!*, *The Music Man* and *Romeo and Juliet* than anyone could count.

Mr. Tom had recognized Brit's talent and mentored him.

A week ago, after a lifelong habit of two packs a day, he had succumbed to lung cancer.

Laney gazed at Brit wistfully, remembering happier times. "They've named the new auditorium and stage at the high school after him."

"Did he get to see it before he died?"

"Just barely. His daughter took him in a wheelchair three days before the end. I think he was holding on to see the finished project before he let go."

Brit's gaze was bleak. "I wish I had gotten here sooner. We were filming in Singapore. The final scenes of the movie. I couldn't leave."

"I'm sure he understood."

"I texted him. Almost every week."

Laney smiled at last. "He loved that, you know. It tickled him that he had your personal cell number. He guarded it like the Holy Grail."

Brit's shoulders slumped. "Damn, Laney, why does life have to be so hard?"

"It keeps moving on whether we want it to or not."

The timer on the oven dinged, putting an end to their downer of a conversation.

She grabbed a place mat, silverware and a napkin and set the meal in front of him. "Be careful. The plate's hot."

"Thank you," he said, sounding genuinely grateful.

She knew why Brit hadn't expected any alcohol in her house. Laney's father had wrapped his car around a tree in a drunken, fatal accident when she was sixteen. That loss had taken her and her mother from barely getting by to living on the edge of poverty.

As if Brit had read her mind, he swallowed a bite and wiped his mouth. "How's your mom doing these days?"

"Really well. She remarried last year and moved to Chattanooga. Edward came down to Blossom Branch to do some duck hunting. Mom was waitressing at the diner. They met there, and boom. Next thing I knew, I was at the courthouse with them signing my name as a witness. I'm happy for her."

Brit studied Laney's face as if trying to see inside her head. "So what keeps you here, Laney?"

The question made her uncomfortable. Many times, she had shared with him her desire to travel the world. She shrugged. "What keeps anybody anywhere?" she said. "Eat your dinner before it gets cold." Now was not the time to talk about the stash of glossy cruise and expedition brochures tucked away in her desk…or the online articles she had printed out detailing Brit's career.

Was she ashamed of still living in Blossom Branch? Did comparing her mundane life to Brit's far more glamorous one make her feel like a failure? Laney had spent the last decade burying her own bucket list—out of an obligation to her mother.

The thought of being with Brit in a committed relationship was too fantastical an idea to even include on the list.

Now her mother no longer needed Laney, but those long-deferred goals seemed beyond reach. Money was always an issue. Or maybe Laney was a coward. Maybe choosing safety and security was her default. At eighteen, she had been more ready to take risks. Now, not so much. Unlike Brit, she wasn't prepared to give up everything to chase an impossible dream. Was she?

Spending time with him four years ago, however briefly, had added an element of painful, adult yearning to her feelings. Unfortunately, like expensive world travel, he had always been out of reach.

Brit frowned slightly. "Come sit with me, Laney."

She had tried not to…she really wanted to keep a healthy

distance. But there was no polite reason to refuse him. She grabbed a Coke from the fridge and took the chair opposite her guest.

After taking a sip, she reiterated her question. "When I asked why you were here, I meant why are you *here*…at my house."

His entire body went still. Carefully, he set down the fork he was holding and eyed her with an unreadable gaze. "I was hoping you might let me stay a couple of nights. The motel out at the interstate is decent enough, but it has zero privacy."

She felt herself blush from her hairline to her toes. Brit. In her house. "Um…"

"I won't be a bother," he said.

"Why wouldn't you stay at your parents' place?"

"You haven't heard?"

"Heard what?" Her heart pumped.

"I bought my daddy a big fishing boat. He and Mama have moved to a cute little town down on the Florida panhandle. The house here is mostly empty now. It'll go on the market in a week or so."

"I see." What did it mean that of all the residents in Blossom Branch, Brit Sheffield showed up at *her* door seeking asylum? She wanted to believe that their tenuous text connection was as important to him as it was to her, but it was a dangerous fantasy. The man had a million plus Instagram followers. More likely, Laney and her house were convenient. "Aren't you sad your childhood home is being sold?"

"Maybe a little. But I was never going to live there."

Ouch. It was true. Brit had moved on from Blossom Branch while they were both still teenagers. Leaving Laney behind.

While Brit finished his meal, Laney studied him unobtrusively. He had aged well. At twenty-eight, almost twenty-nine, he was even more handsome and appealing than he had been as a cocky, self-confident kid. Now he was a man with all the rugged masculinity a woman could hope for.

But Brit's allure was more than physical. He had that mysterious *something* that made him stand out in a crowd. His most recent film franchise had taken his career to the next level. Now people around the world knew his name.

Yet here he sat in Laney's kitchen.

She firmed her resolve. "The bed in the guest room is an old-fashioned full-size, not even a queen. And my bathroom is tiny. I love this old house, but it has its drawbacks."

"Are you trying to get rid of me, Laney?"

"I should," she muttered. "I don't trust us."

His face went blank, and his cheeks reddened. Four years ago, when his grandmother died, Brit had come home then as well. Before he left to go back to Hollywood, he and Laney had spent an entire night talking and reminiscing. They started out in a dimly lit corner booth down at the Peach Pit—the local watering hole—and then when the bar shut down, they had parked out on a dark, secluded road and waited for sunrise.

In those hours when defenses were down and Laney's good sense wavered, they had indulged in some old-fashioned necking. His nimble fingers unfastening her bra. Her hands exploring under his shirt.

They had both been heavily aroused, and yet somehow, they managed not to go the distance. Laney hadn't wanted to be a notch on a movie star's belt. And Brit...well, who knows why he hadn't tried harder to get her out of her clothes.

For weeks afterward, she regretted not encouraging him to make love to her. She was a single woman living in a small town with an even smaller pool of eligible men. She was lonely. But even in the midst of heady passion, she had known instinctively that sex with Brit would make things worse.

Years before, she had survived his leaving her behind. She wasn't sure she could handle it a second time.

The more recent experience had marked her midtwenties. It left her with questions. And regrets. Now here he was again.

He cleared his throat. "You can trust me, Laney. I would never force you to do something that makes you uncomfortable."

"That's not the problem," she said bluntly. "I want you. I've always wanted you. But I won't be some pitiful groupie grabbing a quick lay so I can have bragging rights."

His scowl was dark. "Don't do that. Don't minimize what we have."

She muttered a rude word and stood with her arms wrapped around her waist. "What *do* we have, Brit? A string of mostly impersonal emails and texts? A teenage love affair that's a decade in the past? Two separate lives that only intersect once in a blue moon?"

Was she trying to stoke an argument?

If so, Brit didn't rise to the bait. He rolled to his feet and confronted her, his face expressionless. "I've been awake for almost twenty-four hours. If you don't mind me staying the night, I'd like to get some sleep."

Well, heck, that was blunt enough. She swallowed her hurt pride and nodded. "Get your bags out of the car. I'll make sure your room is ready."

The guest room was completely clean and neat. Even so, she smoothed covers and grabbed a set of towels from the hall linen closet. The towels found a home on the ladder-back chair beside the window. She pushed aside enough hangers in the closet to make a spot for Brit's things. There wasn't much she could do about the Christmas decorations on the floor underneath. She had *zilch* storage space.

After rearranging and stacking boxes, she straightened, holding a metal reindeer that she normally put on the porch for the holidays.

When Brit walked into the room, she clutched the chunky piece of decor to her chest. He raised an eyebrow. "It's March, Laney. Did I miss something?"

She rolled her lips inward, trying to look stern, pretending with all her might that she hadn't found a minute to fantasize about climbing into that small bed with the man in front of her. "I was making room for your things, that's all."

"I didn't bring much."

For the first time, she saw sheer exhaustion on his face. He must have been flying for hours. "Make yourself at home," she said. "You can have first shift in the bathroom. I'll try not to bother you in the morning."

Something flashed in his eyes. A look she couldn't decipher.

"Are you still at the bank?" he asked.

"Yes." She wouldn't apologize for her unimaginative career. It was a solid job with health insurance and good benefits. Compared to how she had grown up, she was practically living in luxury now.

He rubbed a hand over his tanned face, then stared at her with a laser gaze. His irises were dark green, an unusual color speckled with hints of amber. "Is there any way you could take the day off tomorrow? I'll be here in Blossom Branch until Sunday evening. After that, I've got a room booked near the airport, because I fly out of Atlanta very early Monday morning. I'd like to spend time with you, Laney."

Wow. He wasn't dancing around the issue.

What did Brit want from her?

"You could have asked ahead of time, instead of springing it on me," she muttered.

"Maybe I was afraid you'd say no." His bleak honesty revealed a hint of vulnerability.

She wanted so badly to believe that she was special to him. How pathetic was that?

"It's not my Saturday to work," she said slowly, weighing the personal risks of playing with kryptonite. "By the way, what did your mom get?"

"Excuse, me?"

She gave him a teasing look. "Well, you gave your dad a fishing boat, so I was just wondering…"

"Ah…" Even exhausted, his smile held a kick. "I'm flying her and my dad to England and Scotland in September…for the whole month. She's giddy with excitement."

Laney felt a twinge of envy. "Well, I guess so. That's an incredible gift."

Most people who were acquainted with Brit's mother knew she was a longtime anglophile. She had even named her son *Britain* Sheffield. He used the full moniker for his screen name, but here at home, he would always be Brit.

He yawned hugely, apparently catching himself by surprise. "Sorry," he said. "I don't want to be rude." He ran both hands through his hair. "I promise I'll be better company tomorrow."

It was a prosaic statement. He didn't mean anything by it. But heat coiled in the pit of Laney's stomach. "No worries. It's getting late anyway." She backed toward the door, still holding the dumb reindeer. "It's good to see you," she said quietly. She hadn't intended to say that, but the words slipped out. She wouldn't take them back, even if she could. Because they were true. "Good night, Brit."

His stubbled jaw made him look rakish and dangerous. Just the thing for a movie hero, but not at all what a small-town woman needed.

He gave her a sweet smile that took the starch out of her knees. "Good night, Laney. Sweet dreams."

Sweet dreams. Ha. Fat chance. Laney tossed and turned for an hour. Mid-March was that awkward season when it was warm enough not to need heat, but it felt too early to use the A/C. Consequently, the bedroom was stuffy.

Ordinarily, she never slept with her windows open because her bedroom was at street level. Blossom Branch was a safe town in general, but bad things still happened. Tonight, though, she had a big strong man to keep her from harm.

At 1:00 a.m., she gave up and raised the heavy sash. Crisp, cool air filtered in immediately, scented with hyacinths. When she climbed back into bed, she fell asleep almost instantly.

Sometime later—it was hard to say how much time had passed—she jerked awake, roused from deep sleep by a noise she couldn't place. Adrenaline raced through her veins, making her weak and shaky. And then she recalled. Brit was here.

Surely, what she heard was not an intruder. Likely, her guest had gotten up for a drink of water or to use the facilities.

It felt decidedly odd to know that a man might be wandering around her small house. Not just any man, but an all-grown-up version of the boy she had loved as a girl. And if she were brutally honest, the one guy she still wanted.

She lay quiet and still for long minutes, listening. And then it came again. The loud creak of a floorboard. The sound of human movement.

Though she didn't really think she had anything to worry about when it came to sinister activity in the middle of the night, she couldn't go back to sleep without checking on Brit. Never mind that he was a grown man who had traveled the world and knew how to handle himself in all sorts of situations.

She had to know for sure.

Her sheer-white cotton nighty reached a respectable length above her knees. If she tossed a pink satin robe over it, her modesty would be assured.

Knotting the belt tightly, she eased open her door and peeked into the hall. Brit's door was closed, but from the direction of the living room, she saw a light. She found him sprawled on her sofa, remote in hand, channel surfing with the sound on mute.

She nearly had a fit of the vapors when she saw he was nude from the waist up. Heather-gray sleep pants clung to his body in interesting ways. If she were smart, she would tiptoe backward into the hall and keep her distance. But she was tired of making boring choices.

Brit grimaced when he saw her. "Sorry, Laney. I slept for three hours and then was wide awake. It's midafternoon in Singapore right now. With the long flight, I'm all jacked up. I was hoping I wouldn't wake you."

"It's okay," she said. "I'm just glad you're not a burglar." She smiled when she said it, to let him know she was joking.

Brit frowned instead. He sat up, making his abs ripple in mesmerizing fashion. "You don't have a security system?" His tone was incredulous.

Laney counted to ten. "Security systems are very expensive."

To his credit, he backed down. "Sorry," he muttered.

She sat in the chair closest to the sofa, unable to resist the urge to be near him. "What can I do to help you sleep?"

Two

Brit sucked in a breath before realizing that Laney wasn't flirting. Good lord. Had he become so accustomed to women throwing themselves at him that he had forgotten the real world? He cleared his throat, hoping his boner was disguised.

"I don't know that anything will help at this point. It usually takes me a few days to adjust. I'll be fine."

He took her in with a hungry gaze, feeling the best he had in months. Laney's tousled hair was a silky, streaky blond mess around her shoulders. The layers of caramel and gold were natural. He knew, because the color had been that way since she was a kid.

They had known each other on and off since first or second grade, though he hadn't *noticed* her in a sexual way until they were juniors in high school. His dad had kept him involved in multiple sports, probably to sublimate the urges of a hormonal adolescent boy. But Brit had noticed plenty.

Laney was tall, though not skinny. Her curves matched the sensual gleam in her gray eyes. He used to think he could read her mood by those eyes. Stormy when she was pissed with him. Cloudy and serene when she melted into his arms.

No matter where he went in the world, the memory of Laney's eyes stayed with him.

She had matured into a beautiful woman with a kick-ass body. Right now, her long legs were on display, no matter how much she tugged at the hem of her sexy robe.

When she pursed her lips, she looked like an erotic school-marm. "Shouldn't you at least *try* to get some more sleep?"

He shrugged. "Never works. I'd rather watch TV."

"Oh. Okay then." She stood, perhaps preparing to leave him alone.

"Or we could play cards."

Laney blinked. "Cards?"

"You know…rummy. Strip poker?"

Hot pink stained her cheeks. "Very funny."

"I'm not laughing."

Now she scowled at him. "Do you flirt with all women, or do they fall into your lap on their own?"

He dared not tell her how close she was to the truth. By the time he became *Britain Sheffield*—leading man—and not a supporting actor anymore, his whole world had changed, including the availability of female companionship. That surfeit of attention had gone to his head for a couple of months. He had even been propositioned by a leading lady who was far more famous than he was…and older.

He'd turned down the award-winning actress diplomatically. But a couple of other women had become one-night stands. The way he felt afterward made him reevaluate his priorities.

As a young man, he'd heard people say Hollywood was constructed of smoke and mirrors. Already, he had found it to be true. People were invisible until they achieved that elusive thing called fame. Then *friends* came out of the woodwork. Everybody wanting something, even if it was only a chance to rub shoulders with a celebrity.

"I'm not flirting with you, Laney," he said firmly. "Flirting implies lighthearted fun. There's never been anything lighthearted about what I think of you." Though she had taken a seat, he still feared she might bolt. Her posture was edgy, and she must have been tired, too.

"I'm afraid to ask," she muttered. Her porcelain skin was still rosy with embarrassment. "Never mind," she said quickly. "Let's talk about something else. You've never told me how exactly you supported yourself when you first went to California."

He winced, remembering those frustrating days. The few auditions he'd wrangled had been hell on his ego. "I worked construction," he said. "I decided if it was good enough for Harrison Ford, it was good enough for me."

Laney chuckled. "Did you even know anything about construction?"

"Not really. But I was a fast learner, and I put on a good act." He had played a part, and it had worked long enough for him to gain real skills.

"It's a long leap from hammering and sawing to the silver screen," Laney said.

He nodded, remembering those surreal days. "I'm getting to that. If nothing else, I've learned that part of life is luck and being in the right place at the right time."

"What does that mean?"

"My boss bid on a job to build a pool cabana at a well-known director's house. All of us young guys were thrilled. We thought we might see famous models in bikinis. But it was nothing like that. The director lived alone. He put in long hours at the studio. At some point, he fell into the habit of bringing his morning coffee out to the pool and watching us work. The crew always started early. Most of the guys were afraid to talk to him, but I decided he might be able to give me some advice, so we struck up a friendship."

"That's where the luck comes in? Sounds like you created luck for yourself."

"Not really. Without the job, it never would have happened. Anyway, this director was famous, really famous. So much so that a kid like me from Georgia had even heard his name. He was in the middle of filming a movie. They were using a sound stage in Burbank. One day, he quit showing up. I was so disappointed, and then I felt stupid. My life wasn't a cinematic romp. Everything wasn't going to magically go my way."

"But?"

He shook his head slowly. "It was the damnedest thing. About a week after he went missing—so to speak—he came out to the pool again. But this time, he asked my boss for permission to speak to me in private."

"Whoa. That's um…"

"Scary? Weird? Uncomfortable? Yeah, all those things. I was covered in sawdust and sweat. We went inside this amazing house, and he offered me coffee. We sat at his kitchen table. I can still remember the pieces of fruit in a melamine bowl on his counter and the loud tick of a clock on the wall."

"What happened?"

"He offered me a walk-on part. One line. A total of ninety seconds on screen."

"What kind of character?"

Even now, Brit had to laugh. "I played a construction worker."

Laney's eyes widened. "You're kidding."

"Nope. He was dead serious. Told me I was a good kid who deserved a chance."

"And the rest is history."

Brit shook his head. "Not quite that easy. But things did start rolling after that. There were a couple of national commercials, a bit part on an afternoon soap. Finally, a real movie with a supporting role. And I landed an agent."

Laney shook her head slowly, her gaze wry.

"What?" he said.

"I appreciate hearing about how you got your big break, but other than that, I knew the rest of it. My gosh, Brit. Everyone in town has seen everything you've ever done, bit part or not."

"Oh." He honestly hadn't thought of that. California seemed like the other side of the moon. His career had taken him farther and farther from home. Though his memories of Blossom Branch were fond ones, they mostly centered around Laney. The idea that his hometown had been watching his acting endeavors from the beginning surprised him. "That's nice, I guess." Laney yawned hugely making him feel guilty. "You should go back to bed," he said. "Don't worry about me."

Her heavy-lidded gaze made him itchy.

When she didn't move, and she didn't say anything, he patted the sofa beside him. "Or you could stretch out here and doze while I watch TV."

It was a calculated gamble. He got the feeling Laney didn't want to go back to bed. On the other hand, he wasn't sure she wanted to stay in the living room either. Brit was happy to help her make up her mind.

She yawned again. "Okay," she said. "If it won't bother you."

It *would* bother him. A lot. But in the best possible way.

Laney grabbed a small blanket off another chair. Brit scooted to the far end of the sofa. Though the house was old, this piece of furniture was modern and cozy. He was glad of that, especially when Laney stretched out and laid her head in his lap. She had to curl her legs, but she seemed comfortable as she got settled. "This is nice," she said.

He didn't know whether to be pleased or insulted when she was asleep in minutes.

An odd feeling came over him. A combination of relief and contentment and yet at the same time fear. He was not even thirty years old—and already at a crossroads.

His parents often visited him in California, because they knew how hard it was for him to get away from filming commitments. Neither his mom nor his dad tried to make him feel guilty about turning his back on Blossom Branch.

He frequently bought them first-class plane tickets and made sure they knew they were welcome on his doorstep anytime of the day or night. He might have left Blossom Branch, but he had never abandoned his family.

The only person he had forsaken was Laney. That searing regret haunted him to this day. To stay would have meant never realizing his dreams. Laney had known that. Not once had she ever tried to stand in his way.

But his decision had cost both of them deeply.

Nothing on the TV screen held his attention. Not when Laney was so close. It was impossible not to think about the time he had come home for his grandmother's funeral four years ago. It was his one and only pilgrimage to his hometown since he left at the age of eighteen. Grief and nostalgia had affected him strongly, and after the service, he had jumped at the chance to spend time with Laney. A drink at the local bar and a late-evening drive had turned into an all-nighter.

He had almost slept with her. Laney had been ready and willing. No question at all about her state of mind. Still, knowing that he was getting on a plane the following day had made Brit cautious. He didn't want to be a jerk. He didn't want to disrespect Laney.

So in the end, they had kissed and done a few other things that even now made him sweat. Oddly, Laney hadn't asked him a single question about his career that night. They had mostly talked about old times...friends...school.

She was deeply asleep now, her soft pink lips parted. He stroked her hair gently, careful not to wake her. How had no one else snapped her up? Were the men in this town clueless? Laney was one in a million.

Her neck was tilted at an awkward angle. As much as he wanted her to stay, he knew she would be more comfortable in her own bed.

Carefully, he eased out from under her and got to his feet. Then he scooped her into his arms and carried her down the hall. In her room, a single small bedside lamp burned. The covers were tossed back from when she had climbed out of bed.

As he bent to lay her on the mattress, her eyelids lifted, revealing warm gray eyes. "Stay," she whispered, her gaze sleepy and sweet.

His erection twitched and turned to iron. "I shouldn't..."

Laney caught his wrist. "It's okay. Really. I'm glad you showed up on my doorstep. I don't expect anything from you, Brit. Nothing but pleasure."

His scruples crumbled. That, he could give her.

His sleep pants hit the floor, but he froze. "Protection?"

She wrinkled her nose. "In the nightstand. They probably expired a long time ago."

It bothered him that Laney had condoms beside her bed. And it *really* bothered him that he was bothered.

While she stripped off her gown and robe and scooted over to make room for him, he grabbed what he needed and ripped open a packet. Her rapt gaze as he sheathed himself sent his hunger spiraling higher.

He was shaking all over, his heart pounding, his arousal white hot. Though he was absolutely sure he remembered every detail of her body, he was wrong. His teenage memories were shadowy, pastel recollections in the face of a living, breathing woman.

He explored her reverently, from her brow and her nose to her throat and the valley between her breasts. Laney watched him all the while, but she was frozen.

"Touch me, Laney," he groaned.

When he skated his thumb over her raspberry nipple, it tightened. A tiny gasp marked her response. Her arms wrapped around his neck.

He gave her honesty. "I've thought about this moment for the last four years."

Her eyes searched his face. A tiny smile tilted her lips. "You're not the only one."

She couldn't have been any clearer about what she wanted. But was he being fair? To drop into town and let her think this was a booty call? He knew it was more than that. She couldn't, wouldn't understand what he was feeling unless he bared his soul.

That prospect was scary as hell.

When Laney curled warm fingers around his erection, he was lost. Carefully, he maneuvered between her legs. Then, feeling as if he was drowning, he surged into her until they were joined as closely as two people could be.

Though they had been lovers a decade ago, this felt brand-new.

His parents had taken him to Sunday school as a kid. He had learned the difference between right and wrong. What he didn't understand was how a guy who had made as many dumb mistakes as Brit had could possibly end up in Laney's bed.

Only moments before, he'd been on the edge, sure he

wouldn't last long. Now he found patience mixed in with the wanting. An urge to give Laney everything she deserved. He moved in her slowly, taunting both of them. In. Out.

The feel of her body clasping his was indescribable. "God, Laney," he whispered raggedly. "Was it always like this?"

Her teeth were sunk deep in her bottom lip, as if she was trying not to cry out. To hell with that. He withdrew and stroked her hard, exulting when he felt her respond.

"Yes," he crooned. "Come for me, Laney. Come for me."

When she shattered in his embrace, he found his own release and collapsed, burying his face in her shampoo-scented hair.

Three

When Laney woke up the morning after Brit's unexpected arrival, he was gone. Well, not gone completely, but gone from her bed. She could hear the shower running. The two rooms shared a wall.

Soon after, she heard a door open and shut across the hall.

Inexplicably, her eyes stung with emotion. What had she expected? That Brit would whisper in her ear as the dawn broke, ready to make love to her again?

Foolish fantasies were for women less grounded than Laney.

With her jaw tight and her heart bruised, she climbed out of bed and took her turn in the bathroom. Mr. Tom's service was at one. No point in dressing twice. It was already almost ten. The disturbed night had caused her to sleep far later than normal.

In the back of her closet, she found the simple black dress she kept on hand for funerals. It was nothing fancy. Knee-length. Short sleeves. Scoop neck. It was also six or seven years old, but since she seldom wore it, there was no reason to get something new.

She dried her hair in the bedroom sitting at her antique vanity. The furnishings in her rental house were a mishmash of styles. Some had come from her mother. Other pieces from neighbors. It was Laney's dream to one day have a small house that was all her own from the ground up. But new construction cost money, and her meager savings account had a long way to go before she could realistically begin.

Her reflection in the mirror as she twisted her hair in a loose knot at the back of her neck showed a woman with a wary gaze and a bent toward practicality. Though Brit had spent the night in her bed, Laney had to remind herself what *really* happened. She had *invited* him. It was her own fault if she now regretted that rash decision. Unfortunately, the all-grown-up Brit was an even better lover than her onetime boyfriend.

When she could postpone the confrontation no longer, she opened her bedroom door. She found Brit standing in the kitchen drinking a cup of coffee. "I hope you don't mind," he said. "I made enough for two."

"Sounds good to me." Her heart was knocking against her ribs so hard she thought he might actually be able to hear it.

Looking at him was a mistake. In a dark hand-tailored suit and expensive tie, he was gorgeous. She far preferred the rumpled traveler. This man, this impeccably dressed gentleman, made her feel inadequate and unsophisticated.

"I have leftover roast beef," she said. "Would you like a sandwich before we leave?"

He shook his head. "You go ahead. I don't feel like eating," he muttered.

"Me either." She couldn't tell if he was grieving about Mr. Tom or regretting what had happened the night before. And she was too insecure to ask.

They drank their coffee in silence as the awkward tension in the room mounted. Brit leaned against the sink, looking like a model in an ad for expensive cars. Laney sat at the kitchen table with her eyes focused on her coffee cup.

Finally, Brit spoke. "I've been rethinking the funeral," he said gruffly. "I'll go to the church, but I'm going to sit outside in my car and watch the livestream."

She lifted her head. "Why?"

His cheeks flushed. "This day is about honoring Mr. Tom and his life of service to the community. If I go inside..." He trailed off, visibly uncomfortable.

"Oh, right," she said. "I understand." She should have thought about that earlier. Brit's evaluation of the situation was both candid and admirable. "Do you mind if I sit in the car with you?" she asked.

His expression lightened. "I'd like that very much."

"If you want to," she said, "we can drive out to the cemetery afterward. I know a place where we can park at a distance and still see the burial."

"Sounds like a plan."

They ended up leaving the house around noon. It wasn't far, but parking on the street would be an issue if they waited too late.

The day was warm with a light breeze. Laney had picked simple black sandals that were dressy enough to be appropriate for the occasion.

"I'm going to take the long way," Brit said. "Do you mind?"

"Not at all." As he drove, Laney tried to eye the town of Blossom Branch through the gaze of a favorite son who now made his home on the opposite coast. What did this place look like to him? Incredibly rustic? Boring? Provincial?

The town had been built by people who had an eye for future development. In the middle of everything, a beautiful green space occupied two full blocks, creating an inviting rectangular park similar to a university quad. In the very center, an octagonal gazebo held the place of honor.

Surrounding the park, Blossom Branch's businesses thrived, most of them with a peach theme. The nearby counties were filled with vibrant orchards. From May until August, tourists came in droves to buy fresh peaches and to indulge in parades and artisan showcases and, of course, the Peach Festival in early June.

For Laney, this town and its people were home. She couldn't imagine living anywhere else. But then again, she'd never really had a chance to try. People who said any dream was possible had clearly never survived with less than ten bucks in their checking account and bills that regularly went unpaid.

At one time, when Laney's mom had been hospitalized for a complicated surgery, they had been forced to exist on church donations and food stamps afterward. Laney had been too young to work, and there was no nest egg to fall back on.

As a child, she had never felt deprived, but once her father was gone, she had gradually come to understand all her mother's struggles. One thing that had attracted Laney to Brit in the beginning was that he didn't judge her for her circumstances. His family hadn't been quite as poor as Laney and her mother, but close.

Brit drove aimlessly through town until it was time to grab a parking spot. He found one on a side street near the church. Laney watched as people she recognized flocked toward the modest brick building with the single stained-glass window over the double oak doors. "It's going to be packed," she said.

"That's good. Mr. Tom deserves a big sendoff." Brit opened his laptop, set it on the dashboard, and used his phone for a hotspot. When they were connected, the visual of the sanctuary was clear, and the sound good.

An organist played a medley of old-time hymns. "I'll Fly

Away." "When the Roll is Called Up Yonder." "Precious Memories."

At the top of the hour, the young pastor stood behind the lectern and began to speak with a calm presence and gentle reassurance.

"I don't remember him," Brit said.

"He's new. I met him once when he and his wife opened an account at the bank. They have two elementary-aged kids. Moved here from Kansas."

Brit chuckled. "That must have been culture shock."

Now the choir sang a number. Mr. Tom's son said a few words. There was a prayer. Then the pastor stood up a second time and read a letter.

It was Brit's letter. A tribute to how Mr. Tom had changed his life.

Laney listened in shock, touched by the words. When she glanced sideways at Brit, his eyes were damp. Without over thinking it, she reached out and grabbed his hand. His fingers squeezed hers painfully. "That was beautiful," she said softly. "What a lovely thing for you to do."

"It's not much," he muttered. "How do you thank someone for believing in you? He changed my life."

The service ended. Folks began spilling out of the church, many of whom would head over to the cemetery.

"Let's go," Laney said. Brit knew the way, of course. But Laney directed him to a small side road that wound around the far side of the property and up onto a shallow rise. Below them, they could see the small green tent for the family and the open grave. "Do you want to get out?" she asked. The sky was blue, and the day was pleasantly warm.

"Yeah." Brit donned sunglasses.

She wondered if he meant them to be a disguise.

The pastor's words at the graveside were shorter than the

funeral. Laney and Brit couldn't hear what was being said, but at least the two of them were present to witness Mr. Tom's final goodbye. Clearly, the pastor was reading some scripture. Then a bagpiper played a mournful rendition of "Amazing Grace" as the casket was lowered, and the family tossed flowers into the gaping hole.

Laney hated funerals. For the most part, they were depressing as hell. Unless, of course, the deceased was in his or her nineties and had lived a full life. Otherwise, Laney always felt weighted down by the inescapable reality of lost hopes and dreams.

"Let's go," she muttered. "If you let me drive, you can scrunch down in your seat and put a ball cap over your face while I order lunch at the drive-through. You up for burgers and shakes?"

"Yep." Brit handed her the keys and used his thumb to wipe a tear from her cheek. "Thanks for coming with me today." His gaze was whimsical and searching as he kissed her full on the mouth. But it was a tender, grateful gesture, not anything sexual.

Or so it seemed. Laney tried not to reveal how susceptible she was, or how her legs trembled, and her breasts ached. After last night, her body was attuned to his.

They made it through the fast-food line without incident. Perhaps they should have gone home to change, but her house was in the opposite direction.

She found a quiet spot outside of town and pulled off the road so they could eat their meal in peace. Brit took off his jacket and rolled up the sleeves of his crisp white dress shirt. It was warmer now. She inhaled the scent of peach blossoms combined with his familiar aftershave. He smelled like a man should smell. Masculine and appealing, and good enough to give a woman naughty ideas.

When they were done, Brit stuffed his garbage in the paper bag and sighed. "That was great."

She eyed his muscular forearms. "I guess you have to stay away from junk food to keep in shape."

He shrugged. "I work out with a trainer for an hour and a half every morning at five thirty. What I eat is my business."

"Five thirty?" Her voice squeaked. "Now I feel like a slacker."

His grin curled her toes. "You always did like to sleep in. And I've known you to be up at 1:00 a.m. balancing your checkbook."

The gentle teasing made her blush. "I guess that's why we weren't compatible in the long run," she said.

Now he scowled. "Are you nuts? We were *always* compatible."

"If you say so…"

Perhaps Brit was right. They had been a perfect couple. To a point. But Brit wanted to get out of town, and Laney hadn't been able to see herself tagging across the country with him. Not that he had ever asked. He had hinted. A couple of times.

For better or worse, she had ignored those hints, despite the temptation. Laney had felt an obligation to her single mother, a woman who struggled to raise her only child, and one who had never lived alone. Not only that, but Laney had been mature enough to know that Brit's dreams of becoming an actor would have been hindered by a wife. Two mouths to feed instead of one.

Suddenly, Brit climbed out of the passenger seat and came around to her side. "I'm going to drive now. I want to see a few places before I have to go home."

Did he mean "home" as in California, or was that a reference to Laney's small house? She wasn't sure, so she didn't question his remark.

The big, fancy rental had a bench seat. She was able to slide over and let him in without getting out. He checked his mirrors and pulled onto the two-lane highway. At first, she thought he was driving at random, but soon his route seemed oddly specific.

They turned off onto a gravel and dirt road that accessed one of Blossom Branch's older farms. The couple who owned this spread had both died of old age during the winter. Now the heirs were squabbling over who got to keep the valuable piece of land.

The farmhouse was quaint, but rundown. The *real* pièce de résistance was the sprawling peach orchard. The soil was fertile, the trees mature and the harvest one of the best around. The owners had even cultivated their own variety called Sunshine Bliss.

At the moment, pink and white blossoms covered every branch of every tree, their scent unmistakable. In a few months, the flowers would yield to heavy, sweet fruit covered in velvety skins.

Brit passed the clearly deserted house and headed into the hills on the back side of the property. By the time he made it to the highest point, the view spread for miles.

Laney felt uneasy. "Aren't we trespassing?"

Brit opened his door and got out. "We're not hurting anything. No one's around."

"I'm not wearing the right shoes for tramping in the woods," she pointed out.

He came to her door and leaned his elbows in the open window, grinning. "I'll piggyback you, Laney. I haven't lost my touch."

"And where are we going?" she asked, trying to pretend she was calm when she was anything but.

"While you were getting ready this morning, I grabbed our old quilt out of the guest closet. I could use a nap. Let's enjoy the afternoon."

She managed not to gape at him. *Their* quilt? When she peeked into the back seat to see what he was talking about, he was right. It was an old quilt her grandmother had made decades ago. She and Brit had spent many a lazy summer afternoon on that quilt. By the creek. In the woods. Even at the drive-in theater in the back of his truck.

Although Laney had two of her granny's heirloom quilts tucked away in her cedar chest, this was the one she treasured for entirely different reasons.

"Okay then," she said, trying to seem blasé about spending the afternoon with a renowned heartthrob. Not that she really cared about Brit's fame. She was uncertain about the situation for a whole different reason. Why had he sought her out?

Riding piggyback in a dress meant that Brit's big warm hands ended up supporting her bare thighs. Fortunately, there was no one to see when a blush covered every inch of her face. She clutched the quilt in one arm and held on with the other. Brit's easy strength was on display as he strode through the woods. Laney was no lightweight, but he carried her easily.

When he found the spot he wanted, he let her slide off his back.

"This will do," he said. He flipped out the large quilt and smoothed it over the leaf-strewn ground. "Take off your shoes," he said. "Get comfortable."

Laney hesitated, not because she was opposed to the idea, but because this whole thing was getting far too cozy. She should have felt awkward around Brit. He was practically a stranger, wasn't he?

Yet as she kicked off her sandals and stretched out beside him, something about the moment echoed a hundred other times they had done this exact thing. The guy she had known in high school didn't dress as well. And he'd been a tad skinnier, his limbs as pale as hers. But Brit hadn't changed at heart.

Or so she hoped.

She didn't want to think that fame and fortune had gone to his head.

When they were both on their backs, staring up through the sun-dappled treetops, Brit linked his hand with hers. "Will you be insulted if I take a nap?" he asked. His voice was rough with fatigue.

"Not at all." She suspected that today's emotional wringer had been as taxing for Brit as the jet lag. Maybe more so.

"Thanks, Laney…"

When he sighed and shifted moments later, she knew he was still awake. "Are you happy?" she asked. "In Hollywood, I mean."

His silence was so long, she wondered if she had offended him.

Finally, he sighed. "Yes. Mostly, I guess."

"What does that mean?"

"I miss Blossom Branch sometimes, and I didn't think I would. All I ever wanted was to get out of this one-horse town. But once I lived somewhere else, I began to see what I had sacrificed. I wanted to be an actor. I wanted to be successful. I wanted to be comfortable enough not to have to worry about paying the bills every month."

"But?"

He turned his head to face her. His green eyes picked up the color in the foliage overhead. His lips twisted in a self-derisive smile. "I thought when I landed this most recent role, it would change my life."

"And it did. You're an international star now."

"Then why do I feel like the same guy inside? And why do I feel like I left the most important part of me here in Blossom Branch?"

Four

When Brit opened his eyes, he wasn't sure how long he had been asleep. But his head was clear, and fatigue no longer stalked him.

Laney was curled on her side, facing him with one hand tucked beneath her cheek. Her eyelashes fanned her soft cheeks. His sex stirred. That was all it took. Just looking at her. Some things *never* changed. She was as beautiful and appealing as she had been at eighteen, maybe more so.

It shamed him at times to know he could have taken her with him back then. Maybe deep in his heart, he had known that an unexpected pregnancy or a sexy wife would have derailed his dream. He had finally made it to the big leagues, but at what cost?

When she eventually stirred, he touched her cheek with a fingertip. "You're cute when you sleep."

Her eyes widened as her cheeks turned pink. "I hope I didn't drool or snore."

"Not much," he teased.

"You're mean." Laney sat up and sifted her fingers through

her hair. She'd had it up in a knot for the funeral, but most of it had come loose while they slept. She found the pins and tucked them in the pocket of her dress.

"So, what's the big news in Blossom Branch these days?" he asked.

Laney scrunched up her nose. "Nothing much," she said. "Well, I take that back. Do you remember Cate Penland?"

"Vaguely. Unless, wait. Wasn't she the girl who won Miss Georgia Peach Blossom four years running? My mother sent me news clippings after the last time. The local press had a field day with it."

"You got it. Her family moved to Atlanta a long time ago, but her grandparents and other relatives still live in Blossom Branch. Cate is marrying Jason Brightman in June. They sent out save-the-date cards a few weeks ago, and that's all anybody can talk about these days. Receiving an invitation to that wedding will be like buying a winning lottery ticket."

"Did you get one of the cards?"

"What do you think? No. Not only am I older than she is, we didn't exactly run in the same social circles."

"I've never seen the point in splashy weddings," Brit said.

"Her family can certainly afford it."

"That's not the point."

Laney stared at him with a narrowed gaze. "I'm surprised you've ever pondered the subject at all. *'Britain Sheffield won't be pinned down.'* I read that in the checkout line," she said, her tone tart.

"You can't believe everything you read."

"So you *do* want to get married?"

"Don't try to pick a fight with me, Laney. Not today."

An awkward silence fell. "I suppose we should get back," she said.

Brit noticed she never once looked him right in the eye.

He reached for her wrist and wrapped his fingers around it in a gentle grasp. "What's your rush?"

They couldn't have asked for a nicer afternoon. Not too hot. Not too cold.

Laney chewed her bottom lip. "Why would we stay?"

"Is that a real question?" he asked quietly. "Or are you having second thoughts?"

Her eyes widened. "About what?"

"About giving me asylum. Am I in your way, Laney? Do you want me to go?"

His thumb monitored her pulse. He knew full well when the tempo sped up.

"Is this about sex?"

"I hope so." He laid it out there, plain and simple. He wanted her with a raw, powerful ache. But what he was feeling was so much more.

When she tugged at his hold, he let her go immediately. "Did you bring protection?" Her gaze remained wary, yet he also saw need, the same need that clawed in his belly.

"As a matter of fact, I did."

Later, he could never quite remember how they undressed each other. It was a slow dance, a familiar ritual. But somehow, new. And in the sheer wonder of the moment, he found himself playing the what-if game.

This time, Laney moved on top of him. He liked her confidence.

She sucked in a sharp breath when he surged upward, joining their bodies to the limit. "You've learned a thing or two," she said.

Somehow, it didn't sound like a compliment.

He found himself feeling guilty for no good reason. "I've been with a few women, Laney. But not as many as you might think. I've worked damn hard. Not much time for playing the field."

She leaned forward and rested her hands, palms flat, on his collarbone. "This is probably a bad time to compare notes, *Britain*."

He frowned, even as his body urged him to go for the finish. "Don't call me that, damn it. I'm Brit. I've always been Brit to you."

When she rotated her hips gently, he saw spots dance in front of his eyes. "Easy, woman. We have to pace ourselves. Unless you're close."

"You sure are bossy for a man on the bottom."

He couldn't decide whether to groan in pain or laugh at her impudence. Taking her by surprise, he rolled her beneath him and set a new rhythm. Now the flush on her cheekbones darkened, and her gaze went hazy.

Nuzzling her throat, he set his teeth against her pulse and sucked gently. "I used to give you hickeys," he said. "Do you remember?"

Laney used her inner muscles to squeeze him.

Sweat beaded his forehead.

Her smile was a combination of sweet and seductive. "I had more neck scarves than any girl at Blossom Branch High School. But I don't think we fooled anybody."

He bowed his head and rested his forehead against hers. "I hope you didn't have regrets," he said raggedly. "About us. I've thought about it a lot."

Some of the animation left her face, and he saw a flicker of pain in her eyes. "There were plenty of regrets, Brit. But I was happy for you. I still am."

That was all the talking he could manage. His libido wrested control and sent them rushing toward a finish that was powerful and sweet and ultimately frustrating.

Because as soon as they could breathe, he wanted her again. Laney was walking the line between heaven and hell. Years ago, she had convinced herself to give up the dream where she and Brit made a life together. If they had married, there was a good chance poverty and lost chances might have driven them to divorce. Was anything different now, or was she fooling herself about Brit's current advent into her life?

He had come home to pay his respects at a funeral, not reclaim their lost past. She'd be naive to think otherwise.

Sharing this time with him hurt. A lot. Because it showed her everything she had missed. Being his *pen pal* these last four years had brought a quiet joy to her life, a meaningful connection. At least *something* had been salvaged from their past.

A more courageous woman might have asked for what she wanted, but though it was a cliché, Laney couldn't risk losing Brit's friendship. It was better to keep what they had than for her to ruin everything.

As she gently caressed his warm shoulder, she felt emotions well up inside her. Bright and warm and joyful. Those feelings were dangerous. They made a woman believe in precious *maybes*.

She told herself she had to be strong. This reunion wouldn't last long. Brit was leaving tomorrow night to drive to the airport...and flying out before dawn Monday morning. How would she manage to survive the hours between now and then?

They had dozed again after making love. Naked. Wrapped in each other's arms on the same quilt where this man had taken her virginity a million years ago.

To be fair, Brit hadn't *taken* anything from her. She had been so in love with him, she would have pressed the issue if he hadn't.

And she certainly couldn't accuse him of keeping her in the

dark. He had told her about his plans to move to LA from the beginning. Mr. Tom had given him five hundred dollars as a graduation present and had connected him with a reliable friend and a rent-free room over a garage.

How could Laney stand in the way of that? How could she compete?

Like many towns, small or large, Blossom Branch had encompassed the haves and the have-nots. Some kids in Laney and Brit's high school had graduated and set out for college— eager to test themselves with academic opportunities or high-profile sports careers, and for many, Greek life. Cate Penland had been one of those golden girls.

Laney and Brit had recognized and accepted that their circumstances were far different, Laney's even more so than his.

As a young woman on the cusp of adulthood, Laney had understood Brit's need to strike out on his own. To leave the chafing restrictions of a small town, even one as elegant as Blossom Branch. Everything he felt, she felt, but unlike Brit, she hadn't had a way out. And she hadn't fought for any dreams of her own. That was on her, not him.

As the sun dropped toward the horizon, the air cooled. Without speaking, she and Brit found their rumpled clothes and got dressed. Once again, he piggybacked her to the car. They made the trip to her house in silence.

Laney wasn't sulking. That wasn't her personality at all. But what was there to say?

Because it began to rain just as they got back, she suggested ordering a pizza for dinner, rather than trying to go out. Brit agreed. They took turns showering. She went first and then dithered in front of her closet, looking for something to wear that was comfortable and warm and mildly flattering.

In the end, she chose navy sweatpants and a lemon-yellow

cotton knit top that clung to her breasts. She didn't put on a bra. What was the point?

Her thick wooly socks matched the sweats. A front must have come through. Her not-so-well-insulated house was freezing.

She ordered the pizza and turned on gas logs in the living room. For a moment, she stood in the doorway, trying to imagine what Brit saw. He was a man of the world now. Wealthy. Well traveled.

Laney had eventually finished a four-year community college degree with the help of scholarships and part-time jobs. Any studies beyond high school hadn't been a real option for Brit under the circumstances, but he had acquired the polish and sophistication that came from *experiences*. She envied him that.

Laney wondered suddenly if he saw her as incredibly unsophisticated. Instead of traveling the world, Laney had chosen to be the good daughter, the ordinary girl, the woman with a steady job and a predictable future.

None of those choices had chafed overmuch until four years ago. Why was she letting Brit make her want things? Her life had been perfectly acceptable before he showed up again.

But had it? Or had she been lying to herself for a very long time?

The pizza arrived before Brit did. The little mom-and-pop Italian restaurant was only two blocks away. Peach-aria had the best deep-dish anywhere in the county.

She grabbed paper plates, napkins and soft drinks from the kitchen and took them to the living room just as Brit appeared from down the hall. He was drying his hair with a towel, and unfortunately, his body was appropriately clothed. Only his feet were bare.

"Something smells amazing," he said, smiling at her in a

way that nearly torched all the resolutions she had made in the last hour.

"I ordered two mediums." Laney avoided the sofa and took the armchair. "There's plenty. You want to watch a movie?"

Brit shook his head. "I'd rather talk."

"I'd rather eat."

Her joke fell flat when he looked at her strangely.

Laney knew she was acting weird. How could she not? She needed to protect herself ASAP. Brit was *leaving* tomorrow. This little slumber party was about to be over. Deep in her heart, she knew she couldn't sleep with him again.

The decision brought her no joy. Being sensible sucked.

The meal and the rain pounding on the roof cocooned the two of them in cozy comfort. Everything might have been perfect if Brit had been a plumber or an actual carpenter, or even a banker like Laney. He'd always been good at math.

But there was nothing ordinary about Britain Sheffield. And he didn't belong to Laney.

At ten o'clock she managed a convincing yawn. "I think I'll call it a night," she said, not looking at him. "Feel free to stay up as late as you want. You won't bother me."

There was one flaw in her plan. She couldn't escape the living room without passing the sofa on her way out. Brit simply reached for her arm and stopped her.

"What's wrong, Laney?" he asked.

"Nothing," she said brightly. "It was a great day." Then she winced, not looking at him. "Well, not the funeral, but you know what I mean."

He tugged her wrist until she sat down beside him. "Talk to me. Don't run away."

Brit might be the professional actor, but Laney knew a thing or two. She managed to meet his gaze without flinching. "I'm not running away." She laughed lightly. "It's *my* house. I'm tired, that's all."

"And may I sleep with you?" he asked. "Emphasis on *sleep*?"

Laney swallowed, trying not to burst into tears. "The bed is tiny. You'll be more comfortable in yours." She paused, placing her hand on his cheek to prove she wasn't afraid of him. "I hope you rest well. Good night, Brit."

This time, Brit let her go. Mostly because he couldn't bear to see that look on her face. Laney was fooling no one. If she'd had her way, she would have kicked him out of her house. He knew this beyond a doubt, but he didn't know why. Not exactly.

As the hours crept by, he couldn't blame his insomnia on jet lag entirely. His whole existence had been distilled into this one odd weekend. Saying a final goodbye to an old mentor. Reconnecting with the one woman who had ever tempted him with hearth and home.

He couldn't just walk away from his livelihood. It was his profession. His only source of income. And besides, he had recently signed a lucrative contract that tied him up for a trio of films that might take him even further into the stratosphere.

Still, those dizzying heights were dangerous. Ephemeral. Being back in Blossom Branch held a mirror to who he had become. He was proud of most of it. And satisfied with the choices he had made.

Yet something was missing. He had known it for a very long time though he had ignored the jagged hole in the puzzle. Seeing Laney four years ago had triggered something in him, a need to bring his relationship with her full circle.

At eighteen, he had made the decision to follow his dream. Now he pondered the far reaches of that exercise.

When he couldn't stay awake any longer, he crashed in

his lonely bed in the guest room. The next time he surfaced, sunlight poured through the window. He hadn't closed the curtains the night before. Truthfully, something else had awakened him. The smell of bacon cooking. His stomach growled audibly.

After a quick trip to the bathroom where he used a splash of water to slick his hair into submission and then brushed his teeth, he made his way to the kitchen.

Laney looked up when he entered. Her expression was natural this time. Welcoming. Not skittish like last night.

"What can I do?" he asked gruffly.

"Help yourself to coffee. I'll scramble the eggs. Biscuits are in the oven."

"You didn't have to do all this, Laney." He felt guilty. He didn't want her waiting on him. He liked doing things for her, not the other way around.

She shrugged. "I've always enjoyed cooking. At least on the weekends when I have time. Do you want cheese in your eggs?"

"Sure..."

He poured himself a cup of coffee and sat down at the small kitchen table, nursing the mug and watching Laney. She was a graceful woman. Serene. And so irresistibly feminine and sexy.

Five minutes later, she set a plate in front of him. "Don't let it get cold," she said.

Brit was starving suddenly. But he did wait for Laney to join him after she refreshed her own drink.

They ate in silence at first. The food was amazing. He wolfed his down and sheepishly asked for seconds of bacon and biscuits. Laney had cooked plenty, so he was able to indulge. Tomorrow morning, there would be nothing but airport food.

The silence threatened to become awkward, but when

Laney finished eating, she sat back and gave him a gentle smile. "So where are you filming next?"

He relaxed. "Italy. Rome and Florence and then a rural location in Tuscany."

Her eyes widened. "That sounds incredible. What's the story about?"

"I play a private investigator working with Interpol to track down the perpetrator of a jewel heist. Everyone thinks the thief is a man, so the actual burglar is walking around free. She's a beautiful woman who seduces me to keep from getting caught."

Laney had been sipping her coffee, but she stopped with her cup in midair. "And then what happens?"

He felt his face get hot, which was dumb. It was just a story. "We fall in love. She doesn't confess, but I finally connect the dots and realize the truth. I struggle with whether or not to turn her in. Before I can decide, she runs away. I find her, handcuff her and turn her over to the authorities. After a heart-wrenching goodbye scene, of course."

"That's the worst thing I've ever heard." Laney made a face. "Ten to one a guy wrote that script."

"What do you mean?"

"Oh, come on, Brit. Men write those blockbusters where no one lives happily-ever-after."

"So?" He sounded defensive even to his own ears.

Laney shook her head slowly, looking at him as if he just didn't get it. "Did you know that in one of the early James Bond movies he gets married?"

"No. But to be fair, I'm more of a sci-fi nerd when it comes to movies. What's your point?"

"In the movie I'm talking about, Bond meets a girl, falls in love during the course of the movie, and then with the poor woman still in her wedding dress, Bond witnesses her shot to death by the bad guys."

He raised an eyebrow. "If that's your movie review, I think I'll pass."

"Written by a man. So nobody is happy."

Brit chuckled. "Are you saying I shouldn't be doing this movie?"

She made a face. "I was hoping one day to see you in a Hugh Grant rom-com kind of picture."

"It could still happen."

"No." Her expression was glum. "You're too much of a bad boy for that. I'll have to settle for watching you get your heart broken again and again."

"My heart is just fine at the moment, Laney." As the words left his mouth, he realized this was probably his last chance. "Although that brings up something I want to talk to you about. Real life. Not movies."

Five

Real life? Laney eyed Brit with suspicion. Breakfast was going fine. If she could hang on until later this afternoon, he would be gone in no time. Then she could nurse *her* broken heart in privacy.

"I need to clean up the kitchen," she said. "We can talk in a little while. Why don't you check your email? Or pack your suitcase."

His scowl made mincemeat of her paltry attempts to sidetrack him. "I'll help you with the dishes later. This is important, Laney." He pulled out her chair and waited for her to stand. "Come on. Let's get comfortable in the living room."

When Laney heard the words *get comfortable,* her brain immediately translated them as *get naked.* Last night, she had been restless in her lonely bed. The decision not to sleep with Brit had been the right one, but it hadn't been fun.

Reluctantly, she preceded him into the living room. Quickly, she chose a chair before he could suggest she sit on the sofa.

Brit frowned but didn't comment. His posture wasn't exactly relaxed. Instead of sprawling backward against the comfortable cushions, he sat up straight, his hands loosely fisted on his thighs. One of his knees jumped nervously.

What did Britain Sheffield have to be nervous about?

Sixty seconds passed. Then another thirty. She shifted in her chair. "What do you want to say, Brit?"

He inhaled and exhaled, his expression impossible to read. "Have you ever wondered why neither of us has been in any kind of long-term relationship?"

Her jaw dropped for a second before she snapped it shut. She hadn't expected a question like that. "Well," she said slowly, choosing her words, "you've been chasing your dreams, and I suppose I'm picky."

Brit chuckled. "Fair enough. But don't you think it might be more than that?"

Her heart pounded, and her palms grew damp. "What do you mean?"

Brit was silent for the longest time. His laser stare seemed to dig into her darkest secrets. "Maybe neither of us has found anything close to what you and I had."

His words shocked her. Surely, he wasn't saying what she thought he was saying. "We were kids, Brit. Immature. Horny. Selfish."

He laughed. "Sure. I can't argue with your list, Laney. But despite all that, we fell in love. You and I both knew it was something special. Yet I was too dumb to realize feelings like that were rare. I left without you."

She swallowed. The lump of uncertainty in her throat didn't budge. "You didn't really have a choice. You wouldn't be where you are today if you'd always second-guessed your priorities. I would have complicated your life."

"And yet, here we are. Knowing that we missed out on something."

Inside, she was shaking, torn between foolish hope and a dogged determination not to be stupid. Where was this going? "I don't think it's healthy to look back."

"It is if it means not repeating mistakes."

"I don't understand what you're talking about, Brit. You're confusing me."

His expression had been stoic, almost stern. But now he smiled, that same grin with the power to make her do just about anything. How could it be both comforting and arousing in equal measure?

"Come with me to Italy, Laney. Please. I went online last night and bought you an open-ended ticket."

"Are you insane?" She blurted it out without finesse, terrified by how much she wanted to say yes without a thought for the consequences.

Brit winced. "You're hell on a man's ego. I want to spend time with you. I can't stay in Blossom Branch right now, but I don't want us to be separated for another year or two or four. Time is precious."

"I can't argue with that," she said. "But I have a job."

"Turn in your notice," he said quietly. "It's a fine job, but you always wanted to travel, Laney. This is your chance. No," he said abruptly. "This is *our* chance. I'm not proposing marriage. We both realize that would be premature. But I know this is right. You and I were meant to be together."

She felt faint. "Marriage?"

For the first time, she realized he was not as confident as he seemed.

He grimaced. "It's a scary word, I know. Believe me. But there's another one even more terrifying."

She held her breath. "Oh?"

He looked at her with such intensity her heart wobbled in her chest. "Love, Laney. This might be love."

Because she couldn't sit still another second, she jumped to her feet and paced. "What would I do in Italy?"

"Anything you want. Learn Italian. Explore photography. Help me run my lines. Make friends with the cast and crew."

What he was describing sounded like the most delightful movie plot ever. But this was reality. This was life, her life. "That makes me sound like a kept woman. What do you get out of this deal—and don't say sex," she muttered quickly. "Because I know you can get that anywhere."

"It's not sex, Laney. It's the whole package." His focused stare penetrated her defenses.

"I've never known you to be so impulsive," she said. "And you know I analyze everything to death. Why don't we think about this for a month or so?"

In which case, it will never happen.

His smile was wry now. "It isn't as impulsive as it seems. I've been having a form of this conversation in my head for the past four years."

"Ever since you came home for your grandmother's funeral?"

"Exactly. That night we spent talking until dawn was one of the best moments of my life. It was as if everything that had been fuzzy and uncertain snapped into sharp focus."

"I'm supposed to believe you've thought about me all this time?"

"Yes," he said simply. "Why do you think I've been texting you like a lovesick teenager?" He sighed. "But I know you may need a little time to catch up."

"Ya think?" she said, the sarcasm a mask for her emotions. She was in way over her head. "Be honest, Brit. You'll fly out to LA and then to Italy, and in no time, Blossom Branch will be nothing but a pleasant memory."

His jaw clenched. He paled beneath his tan. "You have such a wonderful opinion of me, Laney."

She sensed she had hurt his feelings. "I'm not being critical. But your life is a heck of a long way from this sleepy town."

"That's where you're wrong," he said.

The four flatly voiced words confused her. "How can I be wrong? Your parents' house is on the market. You haven't lived here in ten years."

"When I made love to you yesterday on a quilt in the woods, I was staking a claim. Laying the first brick. Making a new start. Six weeks ago, I bought the peach orchard, Laney, the whole farm. I was hoping that one day you and I could design and build our dream house on top of that very same hill."

She gaped at him. This was worse than riding the Tilt-A-Whirl at the county fair. She couldn't decide if she was having the time of her life or if she was going to puke. "You're scaring me," she whispered.

He joined her in front of the fireplace, scooped her into his arms, and went back to the sofa, settling her in his lap. He nuzzled her temple. She rested her cheek over his heart, feeling the steady thump.

When he sighed deeply, she felt the rise and fall of his hard, muscular abdomen. "Well, we can't have that. Don't be scared, sweetheart. The only scary thing to me is that I might be making assumptions about you and your feelings. If I'm not what you're looking for in a man, you can say so."

She punched his arm. Hard. "Don't be ridiculous." What she couldn't get past was the idea that Brit might think he was *rescuing* her. "I've been happy here, Brit. Blossom Branch is home, and I love it. Still, the thought of traveling the world with you is exciting."

"But?"

"But I hate the idea that you feel sorry for me."

He moved her over beside him so they could communicate eye to eye. "That's absurd. If anything, you're the one who has saved me. You've kept me grounded, even though you may not have realized it."

"That doesn't even make sense," she said, searching his face for reassurance.

He cupped her cheeks in his hands for a moment and gave her a quick kiss. "I nearly lost myself, Laney...when my career began in earnest. It's easy to do. Suddenly, people are throwing money at you and telling you how wonderful you are. There were days when I looked at myself in the mirror and barely recognized the man I was becoming. But remembering *us* helped."

"So what changed?"

"When I came home for my grandmother's funeral and spent the night with you, I finally felt like me again. Brit Sheffield, country boy. Not Britain Sheffield, the actor. When I'm with you, the world makes sense. I don't know how else to say it."

There was no doubting the sincerity in his voice and in his gaze.

"You really mean it, don't you?" It was hard to wrap her head around this kind of sea change in her life.

His smile was gentle but tinged with sexy intent. "You supported your mother, Laney, for years. You've been an integral part of this community. But now it's time for someone to spoil *you*. Let me be that person. It's a two-way street, except that you'll be giving me far more than I can ever return."

She tried to look at him like a stranger would. The broad shoulders, the beautiful hair, the emerald eyes that melted a woman's resolve. "What happens if I come to Italy and we find out we hate living together, that we irritate each other?"

Brit laughed, his eyes dancing with humor. "I'm willing

to take the chance. And I'm betting on the fact that Italy is too darned romantic. You won't be able to resist either of us."

"And the L word we're afraid to talk about?"

He reached for her and pulled her into his arms, holding her tightly, stroking her hair. "Love is love whether we name it or not. If we try this and it's not what you want, I'll trust you to tell me the truth."

She pulled back, teary-eyed, and smiled at him. "The truth is, you've always been my fantasy, Brit. I guess we'll just have to see if reality is as good."

His eyes flared in shock as he processed her words. "Thank God," he muttered. He kissed her hard. Laney exulted in his warmth, his passion.

Eventually, they had to come up for air. Brit's cheekbones were flushed. Laney felt rumpled and flustered.

She ran her hand over his stubbly chin. "I won't be able to leave immediately. I'll have to turn in my two-week's notice."

He grumbled under his breath and then kissed her again. "I won't let you change your mind."

"Fair enough." She pressed her lips to his softly, letting her kiss express all she was feeling. "I'm sorry about Mr. Tom, but I'm glad he brought you back to me."

Brit shook his head. "I was coming anyway, Laney. Very soon. Coming to steal you away. At least that's what I was hoping."

She laid her head on his shoulder and felt the future unfurl in brilliant, amazing color. "You're an actor, Brit. You should know better than anyone that timing is everything. I won't regret our past, and I don't want you to, either."

"You swear you'll come to Italy?"

"I swear." She curled her fingers with his. "I can't wait to see how this movie turns out…"

He laughed ruefully. "Well, you're writing the plot, not me. 'Cause I want that happy ending you promised."

"That's a lot of pressure," she complained, feeling so happy and lighthearted she might float up to the ceiling.

"You can handle it, my sweet Laney. I have faith in you."

Now it was her turn to feel the world shift into sharp focus. "Correction," she said. "I have faith in *us*."

★ ★ ★ ★ ★